Warriors of Ethandun

N.M.BROWNE

BLOOMSBURY

LONDON BERLIN NEW YORK

Bloomsbury Publishing, London, Berlin and New York

First published in Great Britain in 2009 by Bloomsbury Publishing Plc
36 Soho Square, London, W1D 3QY

A CIP catalogue record of this book is available from the British Library

ISBN 978 0 7475 9418 5

The paper this book is printed on is certified independently in
accordance with the rules of the FSC. It is ancient-forest friendly.
The printer holds chain of custody.

FSC
Mixed Sources
Product group from well-managed
forests and other controlled sources
Cert no. SGS - COC - 2061
www.fsc.org
© 1996 Forest Stewardship Council

Typeset by Dorchester Typesetting Group Ltd
Printed in Great Britain by Clays Ltd, St Ives Plc

1 3 5 7 9 10 8 6 4 2

www.bloomsbury.com

*For Owen and for all the fans of Dan and Ursula
who have written to me anxious to know more of
Ursula's fate*

~ Chapter One ~

Dan stepped out of the Veil of mist. He had to let go of Braveheart's collar to readjust his grip on Ursula's inert body.

'I can't hold her like this, Taliesin. I think I'll have to carry her over my shoulder.'

Taliesin looked bleak. 'This place . . .'

Dan tasted exhaust fumes. He heard the distant roar of traffic and saw the column of giant skeletal pylons stretching into the far distance. He no longer heard the insistent jabber of voices in his head. He was home.

'Take Braveheart and the sword and find somewhere to hide. Get away from here or they'll blame you for Ursula . . .'

Dan could not tell if Ursula was breathing. He could barely think of anything else.

Why was Taliesin still with him? 'Go, Taliesin! They'll lock you and Braveheart up. Get away from here, go home, but look after my dog!' Taliesin didn't argue, but Dan thought he looked scared. It didn't matter. Taliesin could look after himself; Ursula couldn't.

Dan was distantly aware of the bard grabbing the war dog by his collar and dragging him away towards distant trees. He sensed rather than saw Braveheart's reproachful look. He would miss Braveheart, but this was no place for a war hound that tore out men's throats at Dan's command. Braveheart could not survive the twenty-first century. Dan was not sure that he could either – not without Ursula.

He hefted her over his shoulder awkwardly. She was heavy, six foot plus of muscled warrior now pale and bloodstained and almost dead . . . His face brushed her cheek and he saw how her fine, fair hair was streaked with gore. She stank of sweat, offal and excrement – the stench of battle. He fought back tears and stumbled forward. He was strong – he'd spent the last who knew how long training and fighting. He had to get her to safety. He could not let her down. It was his fault she was in this mess. It was down to him to make it all right.

He found the car park where he and Ursula had left the school coach some immeasurable span of time ago. He didn't not know how long had elapsed. He was impressed that Taliesin had brought them back so close to their point of origin. He did not know if there was a hospital near. All he knew was that Ursula did not have much time. He tried to send her some of his strength but in this world he was neither Gawain nor the Bear Sark. He had no special power; he was simply Dan again. He felt that loss in the small part of himself that was not wholly taken up with Ursula.

'Dan!' A small older woman ran towards him. It took

2

him a moment to recognise Miss Smith, the teacher in charge of the history trip. 'Where have you been? I said everyone had to be back at the coach by . . . Oh my God! What has happened to you? What have you done?'

Dan glared at Miss Smith. Was she stupid?

'Get an ambulance. Ursula's dying.' Miss Smith responded quickly. Her face was ashen and she kept glancing at Dan as if she did not know him. His former friends stood apart from him, huddled in a group, staring and pointing. He was grateful that he didn't have to hear their thoughts – that gift, or curse, had left him as he passed through the Veil. It was good to be alone in his own head again, free. His friends looked shocked, as if he were a stranger to them. He felt as if he were. They seemed so innocent-looking, so young. He hadn't felt innocent, not since he'd crossed through the Veil. He felt tainted with experience, stained, exhausted. He could not look at them. Instead he watched over Ursula, stroking her hair, willing time to slow and her heart to keep on beating until the ambulance came.

He had not noticed that he too was drenched in blood, drying dark and brown. It was lucky none of it was his, but then he had barely taken part in the battle. He'd left the heroics to Ursula.

The tourniquet he had fashioned to stop her bleeding was soaked. He pressed his hand against it to try to keep her lifeblood in. They had left behind Ursula's helm and facemask, but she still wore the light armour of the Sarmatians. She did not look like a sixteen-year-old school kid. She looked like some kind of warrior goddess – so beautiful, so cold. He leaned over her to lend her some of his warmth and wrapped his woollen monk's cloak round her. He could not guess what the medics might make of that. It wouldn't matter if only they would get there quickly. She was fading, he could tell. Suddenly there were lights and sirens. Too much ugly noise – he wasn't used to it: it jarred his nerves. Uniformed bodies crowded round him. He could hear the buzz and static from their radios. None were armed with more than a baton, but he wished he still had his sword. He did not like being surrounded. His heart was racing. He saw the wariness in the officers' eyes and knew that they were afraid of him. That made him feel a little better.

A man with quiet authority spoke to him, asked him about what had happened, where Ursula was hurt. Dan's throat was dry. He cleared it. How could he explain?

'She's lost a lot of blood from her thigh – a stab wound, I think . . .' There were other injuries, he knew; she'd led a cavalry charge into the thick of battle, but he thought the blood loss the worst. He had seen men die from blood loss. His memory was so full of pictures of the dead and dying that he had to shake his head. That must have looked odd. He didn't want the emergency services to think him odd. They did, he could tell. Firm hands detached his grip from her arm. He almost fought them, but he made himself let Ursula go. It was something he knew he had to do. He let them guide him away. He could not help. He had to pray that the calm man in the incongruous green jumpsuit could do what he could not, that he could save her.

The emergency crew strapped Ursula on to a stretcher and hoisted her into the ambulance. She looked already dead. Dan tried to follow her, to scramble into the back of the van, to keep her safe from other danger whatever that might be. He dived after her, but they held him back. The men in uniform were not so big or so strong that he couldn't have fought them had he wanted to. He was not so lost that he didn't know it wouldn't help. He let his body sag, did not reveal his strength. He might need it later and it did not do to let a potential enemy know what you could do. He no longer trusted uniforms. He no longer trusted anyone.

Doors banged and suddenly she was gone. He listened to the wailing siren change pitch and fade away. Miss Smith was sobbing, on the brink of hysteria. Dan and Ursula had been lost for about an hour and when they returned she did not know what had happened. She'd been teaching thirty years and nothing remotely like this had ever occurred before. It was not her fault.

Dan had no sympathy to spare for Miss Smith, though she looked fraught and old. His legs felt cold and light without Ursula's weight. Without her there he felt anchorless in every way. He was home, but there was no joy in that. He'd been a coward; he'd known how it must end and still he'd let her fight without him. He allowed the police officer to bundle him into a patrol car, allowed some man to push his head down so that he didn't bang it against the roof. His hair was flecked with battle spatter. The officer stared at his stained hand in horror. Dan felt only contempt for the man's shock. What did the officer know of death and killing? Dan knew himself to be an expert.

'Is this Ursula's blood?' The big policeman was wiping his hand on a tissue and putting the tissue away in a bag. Dan considered his response. It might have been Ursula's blood, but then he'd killed a couple of men on his way to rescue her. Blood and gore travelled in unpredictable ways and he had ridden into the centre of a tightly packed melee. He could not say for sure. He could not explain that so he merely shrugged. That probably looked bad, but he did not much care what these men thought. If Ursula lived, he'd pay whatever price they liked.

~ Chapter Two ~

Dan sat awkwardly between his father and the youth liaison officer. His father was in his only suit. He smelled of beer and fear. It made Dan queasy. Everything was wrong: this room that stank of vomit and disinfectant; his own skin, scrubbed raw to rid himself of the stench of battle; the plastic table and the moulded chairs. Everything felt alien, fake. The scent of shampoo and aftershave made him sneeze. It wasn't right. Nothing was right since he'd come back through the Veil.

'You understand, don't you, Daniel, that the charge will be attempted murder? The girl you stabbed, er – a Miss Ursula Dorrington – is stable, but her injuries are so severe that it won't do you much good. No one can believe she has survived . . .'

Thank God! Something in Dan relaxed a little then. If she lived, it was all right. Ursula would live! He tried not to show his relief, his sudden joy; they would misunderstand that as they had misunderstood everything else. He allowed himself the slightest of sighs. His father shifted in his seat and laid shaking fingers on Dan's arm to reassure him. Dan tried not to flinch away.

It was difficult to concentrate on the police officer – on any of it. He was shocked to find that it wasn't good to be home.

They had kept him in a cell overnight. It was warm enough and, though spartan, a good deal more comfortable than a Celtic barracks in the winter. They'd fed him too and after the monotonous diet of a sixth-century army on campaign, even institutional battered fish and chips had tasted good. What had bothered him most was that he hadn't yet seen Lizzie, his sister. He'd missed her while he'd been away and he'd worried about her through all the days of his absence. Fortunately, as far as she was concerned, he had never been away. He wanted to tell her that he hadn't meant to do wrong. Maybe if she believed him it would be all right. How could he explain that he'd been further away than she could imagine? So far away that perhaps there was no real coming back.

He kept having flashbacks. He'd had terrible nightmares in which he had fought and fought to save Ursula. The rotting corpses of the dead he'd killed were piled high all round him and he still couldn't save her. He'd woken in a muck sweat crying out into the emptiness of his cell. They were only dreams, but dreams born of experience. He couldn't remember how many men he'd killed. They haunted him, the dead men, but he made no attempt to count them. He was too busy trying to forget them and the smell of them in his hair and on his skin, so pungent that all he could taste was blood and death. He missed his sword. Things never felt so bad when he had it, the sword Bright Killer, in his grip. He hoped Taliesin kept it safe.

Dan knew that he was good at killing people – really good at it. He was better than people who'd trained for it all their lives. It was his special talent and he was the best. He was ashamed of that talent here. He was, after all, some kind of psychopath and when the police found that out he would never be free. He could probably kill this police officer – if he wanted to. But he didn't because killing was wrong. He knew it was wrong and back in his own world his skill did not make him a hero: it made him a murderer. He had not hurt Ursula; of that at least he was innocent. But it didn't matter. They could do what they wanted with him because he *was* guilty.

He was glad when the night had ended and they'd brought him in for questioning. Not that he could answer any of their questions. He could not account for his strange clothing nor for Ursula's changed appearance. He could not account for Ursula's mortal wound or his own bloodstained state. He wasn't so stupid as to tell them that he and Ursula had magically gone to other worlds and fought with Celtic warriors to repel the Roman invasion and had fought with the High King Arturus against the invading Saxons. He'd mumbled general stuff about Ursula being attacked by someone he didn't know. It was impossible to answer the police honestly and he was a terrible liar.

The officers left him alone with his father for a few minutes. Dan would rather have preferred to have been locked back in the cells. His father could not sit still. He never had been able to – not for years. He got up and began pacing the room, as if he could walk away his tension. His father's hands shook badly as he pulled a packet of cigarettes from his pocket, remembered where he was and put it back again.

'Dan,' he began, and Dan knew by his tone that he was going to try to have a fatherly talk. It was too late for that. 'Look,' he began hesitantly and coughed. 'I know how it is.' He coughed again. Dan wanted to tell him to get it over with, whatever this embarrassing thing was that he wanted to say. 'I know I've not done much of a job as a dad since your mum . . .' He let his words die away. He had never been able to talk about her. 'What I want to say is, I'm sorry. I mean, I know I've spent too long at the Pig and Whistle but I didn't expect all this . . . What's going on?'

Dan shrank into his seat and pushed his hands into the pockets of his jeans. He shrugged in an exaggerated way, like the boy he'd once been. He didn't want to meet his father's eyes. He felt immediately ashamed. He wasn't that boy any more. He'd spent too long with men, and if his dad was no warrior like Kai and Macsen, no wise man like Brother Frontalis, no loyal friend like Bryn, he was no villain either. Dan had seen villainy and it was uglier than anything his father could ever have contemplated. The worst his father had done was to lose himself in grief and beer, and Dan had seen braver men than his dad do that. Dan made himself speak.

'This is not your fault, Dad. I didn't try to kill Ursula, whatever they say. I've not gone bad because you're too fond of a pint.'

Anger flashed in his father's eyes then, and his arm came up quickly to slap Dan, but Dan's hand was there before he'd even thought about it, catching his father's arm so that he couldn't strike, holding it firm.

'Not here, Dad,' Dan said evenly. His father's face was flushed, but he knew he lacked his son's strength and he pulled his arm away.

'You're not too big to be taught who's boss,' his father said.

'Yes, I am,' said Dan. His dad seemed surprised; perhaps he hadn't noticed before, but Dan was taller than him by a good three inches and now that they were both on their feet he could see where his father's curly black hair was beginning to thin on top.

'It's not too late to be a proper dad to Lizzie,' Dan said, softly. He hadn't meant to say it, but in all the time he'd been away that had been his hope – that somehow his dad had managed to step up to the mark for Lizzie.

'I don't know who you think you are, but it's not for you to tell me what to do. I'm your father and I'll have some respect.'

Their conversation was cut short by the reappearance of the police officer. He brought with him a tall, cadaverous man in an expensive-looking suit.

'This is Professor Merlin, an expert on youth trauma. He has been brought in by the boss to interview you, Dan. This is an unusual case – not the kind of thing we see round here too often. I hope you have no objection, Mr Jones.'

Dan was about to object as strenuously as possible until he looked into the grave face of Professor Merlin. Taliesin? It couldn't be. It was.

The tall man gave no sign of having recognised Dan. He waited until everyone was seated. Dan's father crossed and recrossed his legs under the table, as ill at ease as if he were the one accused of attempted murder. Dan, on the other hand, did his best to appear as calm as possible, mainly because he didn't want Taliesin to think he was like his father. Taliesin knew him as a warrior and a wielder of magic, a hero and a man. He could not act like a frightened boy or a sulky child in front of him.

The police officer reiterated the charges against Dan and reminded him that he was entitled to the presence of the duty solicitor or another lawyer if they had one of their own. Dan was not listening; he was watching Taliesin. He had trimmed his white beard and cropped his equally white hair so that he most resembled some kind of Hollywood version of an elder statesman – hawkish and wise. What was he doing there? How had he acquired his disguise? Had Taliesin got real magic in this world? Magic varied from world to world. Neither Dan nor Ursula had magic in their own world, but Dan had no idea what Taliesin might be able to do. Anything was possible. Dan tried not to stare too much at his friend and one-time betrayer. He tried to stay in control and to reveal neither his curiosity nor his excitement.

'Well, thank you, officer,' Taliesin said when the

policeman had finished talking. 'That is very helpful – a fine set-up you have here. Now, Dan, tell me.' He paused and his eyes glittered. 'Isn't it time we got you out of this stinking hellhole?'

~ Chapter Three ~

Ursula opened her eyes and then shut them again. She could not make sense of what she saw. There was a lot of blue that wasn't sky, and pinks, different shades of pink, and other colours too. There was a lot of electronic noise. Something was beeping and somewhere above her head a strip light flickered and buzzed. There was a powerful smell of disinfectant overlaid with the sweet, floral fragrance that she associated with her mother.

'Sula, darling?' It sounded like her mother's voice. Only her parents called her 'Sula'. She knew that her mother hadn't been at the battle. She did not want her mother to know about the battles. She opened her eyes again. The blue colour resolved itself into the form of a curtain and the pinks into her mother's face, red-eyed and exhausted. Somehow she was home.

Ursula tried to smile. Everything hurt and her mind felt slow as if some nutter had padded her skull with cotton wool. She was very thirsty.

'Mum?' It took an age to form the word and longer still to make her dry throat and numb lips work. Her voice when it finally emerged was little better than a croak, but it made her mother happy.

'Sula? You're OK. Oh, thank God! Thank God!'

It was good to be hugged by her mother. It was good to be alive. From what she remembered, there had been a long period of time when living had seemed unlikely. Dan had saved her, rescued her from the Battle of Camlann, where so many had died, where she'd killed so many. She didn't want to think about that. She pulled herself away from those memories, though the general pain through-out her body suggested it wasn't that long ago. She'd been caught badly by a spear that had sliced through the top of her leg. She'd all but passed out from the pain, but the Sarmatians she'd led had fought to protect her. There were gaps in her memory but she remembered that Dan had used his magic and lent her enough of his strength to get her through. They must have gone through the Veil, but who had directed it? She knew that Dan would not have had that skill.

Someone – Dan? – had brought her to what she now recognised as a hospital. So where was he now?

She didn't ask then. She felt weak, and when she tried to hug her mother back she seemed to be tied to the bed by wires and tubes and it was hard to move. A nurse came in and did something and then she went away and Ursula found it impossible to resist sleep.

She woke briefly and slept for some time. There was a lot of pain and then there wasn't. Someone filled her brain with cotton wool and she didn't mind the cotton-wool feeling so much because it made the pain go away. People came and went. Her dad came and the new baby cried and would not be shushed and her mother told him off for bringing the child. She had been glad to let herself drift away from that row. The bad pain went away and then she merely felt uncomfortable: stiff and achy and weak, as if her muscles had melted away to water. She knew that time was passing, the days marked by her mother's conversations and the changing of dressings and tubes, and then one day she woke up and felt OK. Not great, not normal, but OK.

It was only then that she was able to ask the question that had been bothering her for so long: 'Where's Dan?'

Her mother paused in her bed-straightening.

'How are you feeling, darling? The doctors are amazed at how well you're doing. They say you might be able to come home in a day or two and they are going to take the last of the tubes out today. I'm afraid the police are going to want to talk to you now . . .'

Ursula waited for her mother to finish, but she just let her sentence die away.

'Where's Dan?' Ursula repeated. She was surprised he'd not been to see her. Surely all that had happened between them would still matter? Surely he wouldn't abandon her just because they were back home and he was with his friends again? Dan was not that shallow, she knew that, and yet she couldn't help feeling a little hurt and disappointed that she'd not seen him.

'Dan? Is that the boy who was with you? The one who did this to you?'

'Dan didn't do this to me. He saved me.'

Her mother shook her head. 'The police have taken him into custody. They're saying that no one else was involved. Why are you protecting him?'

Ursula took a moment to make sense of this. Dan was in custody?

She tried to imagine what he might have said to explain her wounds – the state she was in. Would he have tried to tell the truth? She thought not. He wouldn't want to be locked up as a madman any more than he'd want to be locked up as a criminal: there had to be another way.

'Mum, I want to talk to the police now. They've got to let Dan go.'

Her mother plumped up her pillows.

'I don't know. You've been so ill. You've gone so thin. I can barely recognise you. I think you should leave it a bit longer. Even your father agrees that you shouldn't talk to them until you've recovered. The police are being very understanding. They know you've been traumatised, that you nearly died, that you've been pumped full of painkillers and I don't know what drugs . . .' Her mother sounded tearful.

'Dan is my friend. He didn't hurt me. Tell the police I'm ready to talk to them.' Her mother gave her a look of surprise. 'Please, Mummy,' Ursula added, suddenly aware that the old Ursula was never so forceful at home. She had grown used to command. It was going to be hard to be a child again. She washed her face and tied back her hair to face the police. Her mother did not seem to have noticed that her hair had grown five or six inches or that she had lost far more weight than could be possible in the brief period of her convalescence. Her sleeveless nightdress revealed arms that any athlete would have been proud of. How had her mother not noticed? When Ursula checked her face in the mirror, she barely recognised her own reflection. Her face was a completely different shape, sculpted where it had been chubby. Her eyes looked enormous in this new thinner face and there was a hardness, a toughness in them that hadn't been there before. She didn't look like a young girl any more. She had killed, had seen sights no one else alive but Dan could even imagine. How could her mother not see all that she had lived through etched on her face, in the new muscularity of her body and in the darkness in her eyes? Perhaps people did not see what they did not expect to see.

She was unimpressed by the two policemen who arrived to question her. She would not have had the younger of the two in any troop of hers, nor would she have fought willingly at his side. The older man was all right, but he didn't really look at her. He treated her like a little girl.

'Dan did not hurt me,' she said without preamble. 'He saved me. Why have you got him in custody?'

'There are a number of very confusing aspects to this case, Miss Dorrington. No explanation has been given for the curious costumes that both you and Mr Jones were wearing. Your injuries were very severe, consistent with being violently hacked by a sharp implement – a long-bladed knife or some such. Whoever did it to you would have been covered in blood. The only other person present at the scene was Mr Dan Jones and both he and his costume were drenched in it. I believe that you are lucky to be alive, Miss Dorrington, and our only plausible suspect is Mr Jones.'

Ursula controlled her temper with difficulty. 'I was there, remember, and I'm telling you Dan was covered in blood because he rescued me. My attacker was gone by then and I didn't know him.' That was true enough. In all the confusion of battle she could not be absolutely certain who had hurt her where, and many of the enemy had worn helmets . . . Was that near-fatal blow from the hand of Medraut, Count of the Saxon Shore in sixth-century Britain? She could not remember.

The policeman did not appear to believe her. 'And what did he look like, this stranger who attacked you?'

'He was older – middle-aged. I couldn't see his face. He was wearing a helmet.'

'A motorcycle helmet?'

'I don't know what to call it.' That was true – she only knew its Celtic or Roman name; she did not know what the word was in English.

'Dan wasn't there when he attacked me. He ran to get me when he realised what was going on.'

'And what happened to this middle-aged men with a helmet?'

Ursula thought she might have killed him, but she couldn't be sure. It was hard to keep track of events when in a battle and she had been struggling to stay conscious at the time. She'd killed Medraut, but she was not certain that it was Medraut who had nearly killed her. She cleared her throat. 'I don't know. I think I passed out. Dan will tell you.'

The two policemen exchanged a look and Ursula found herself wondering what exactly Dan had told them. She had to trust that it wasn't the truth.

~ Chapter Four ~

Dan looked at Taliesin in horror – he could not say that kind of thing in a police station. Dan glanced at his father, still jiggling his crossed leg, and the officer – his name was Inspector Frith – still staring at him with a look of bored indifference. They didn't appear to have heard.

'It's OK, Dan – they can't hear us. I've worked a simple charm.' Taliesin grinned, showing newly even white teeth. 'I thought I'd rescue you. This is no place for a hero.' Taliesin – bard, wizard and former adviser to kings – waved a bony arm and Dan and he were suddenly else-where. It took a moment for Dan to recognise that they were standing back in the field near Hastings from where they'd come. The sky was grey with unshed rain and a bitter wind ruffled Dan's hair and he shivered in his thin T-shirt; it was good to be out of that stinking room.

'So?' Taliesin said.

'So? Very clever, Taliesin. Thanks. I'm happy for you that you've got your magic back, but I can't just disappear – I'll be in even more trouble and I'm in enough already.

This is my world, Taliesin – it doesn't work like that.' Dan softened his words by forcing a smile. He doubted that it would fool his old friend.

'Magic isn't the answer,' he added and folded his arms, which were now covered in goose pimples.

'It is true that magic has been well buried here.' Taliesin sighed. He was no more suitably dressed than Dan and his nose was already beginning to redden with the cold. Dan put his hand on Taliesin's shoulder and squeezed it. 'It's not that I'm not grateful, Taliesin, and I didn't mean to sound so graceless, it's just –'

'How can you live here, Dan? All the earth is covered in concrete and the bits that aren't are fenced off and hedged around. The air stinks and the water is fouled and the magic is so locked away. This is no place for a man and especially not a man like you. They can't imprison you.'

Dan took a deep breath of the tainted air. It smelled better than the police station but Taliesin was used to the air of an unpolluted past. 'I understand what you're saying, Taliesin, but this is my home. My family is here. The police will have to let me go. Ursula is alive and she'll tell them I didn't attack her. There is no real case against me. It might take a few days, but then I'll go back to school.'

Taliesin snorted in derision. He thought literacy weakened a man. It was a Celtic thing. Taliesin had learned all the lore he knew by heart, for a man's memory was his secret stronghold and the written word was only for the weak and the foolish, for men who could not keep their mysteries. 'And what will you learn in school, Dan? You know about war and power and the hidden secrets of men's hearts. What more have you to learn?'

Dan refrained from explaining about GCSEs: he did not think it would help.

'Taliesin, I am grateful for what you are trying to do, I really am, but I have to face this . . . misunderstanding and then get on with my real life. This is where I belong.'

Taliesin shrugged thin shoulders: 'What if Ursula wanted to go back to Macsen's world. Would you go then?'

Dan thought about his life with the Celts, about how he had been welcomed among the warriors as a brother, as a son, as one of their own, and he felt a poignant sense of loss. 'Ursula won't want to go back – she belongs here too.'

'You think that Ursula will not miss magic? You've only known a little of it, Dan. What she had back then, in Macsen's world – that wild power in her veins . . .' He shook his head. 'I don't think you appreciate how much Ursula will miss it – the way magic sings in your blood . . .'

Taliesin was wrong. Dan did know about that, had felt it for himself when he'd touched Ursula's mind. But none of that mattered. They belonged to their own century, their own world, and that was all there was to it. Taliesin's expression told Dan that he'd understood.

'All right. I'm not a fool. I know obduracy when I see it. I have two things for you. Here is your sword.' Taliesin held out his hand and suddenly Bright Killer was in his fist, as if he were some kind of common or garden conjuror. Dan's hand ached to hold it – the sword that made him complete – but he wouldn't let himself stretch out his hand to take it too eagerly. Taliesin would see that as evidence that he longed to be a warrior again and that wasn't true. He kept his sword arm down by his side until Taliesin held it out to him hilt first. When he slipped his right hand round the hilt, Combrogi fashion, the sword fitted him like a glove – it had moulded to the shape of his hand when Ursula, worrying about his safety, had lent him her magical strength and overdone it. He smiled at the memory. So? He still liked to hold a sword. That meant nothing. 'I thought that you might have need of this one day.' Taliesin opened his left hand to reveal a crystal ball. It was the kind of thing Dan thought you might see in a fairground tarot-reader's tent. 'If you want to go back to Macsen's world, rub it and the Veil will open.'

'Where did you get that?' Dan thought Taliesin had to be joking.

'Your yesterday happened three years ago for me. A lot has happened to me since I stumbled through the Veil with you and Ursula. There are places where movement through worlds is more routine. They have learned not to depend too much on their own power. It can be used many times. Oh, and don't worry about Braveheart. He is still safe and if you want to see him again you will find him through the Veil.'

Dan nodded. The Veil allowed a person to skip forward and backwards through time in ways that made his head spin. He still found it hard to understand but he no longer found it unbelievable. The wind was making his eyes water.

'It is good to see you again whether it is after a day or after three years,' Dan said, speaking in the formal language of Arturus's court. It was Taliesin's turn to smile.

'Oh Dan, you are too good for this world – a warrior and a courtier! What will you do shut up in a school without the wind in your hair, without Braveheart at your side, Bright Killer in your hand and an army at your back?'

'I'll just have to cope, Taliesin, and it will be the harder without you. Where will you go next?'

'I will go to visit Ursula. I do not think it will take much to make her seek out magic again.'

'That's cruel, Taliesin. Her place is here. You shouldn't try to take her away. She nearly died in Camlann. She is sixteen and she nearly died. Let her be.'

Dan could not bear the thought of Ursula entering the Veil without him – if she left he'd leave too and Taliesin knew it.

'You cannot fight her nature for her, Dan. Ursula is "addicted" to magic. Is that not what your world would call it?'

She had managed without it in Arturus's world when only her warrior's strength had been magical, but Dan said nothing. Taliesin was right.

'It's time I went, Dan. I believe you will see me again, but whether I will see you is another matter.'

They embraced like brothers, like warriors, and Dan found that his eyes were streaming and it was not just from the rawness of the wind.

'I need to go back to the station, Taliesin, and I cannot take these gifts with me.'

Taliesin waved his arm and the sword and ball disappeared. 'You will find them again when you need them,' he said cryptically. 'Dan, what if I send you back and they find you guilty? What then? Promise me you will raise the Veil if that happens – that you will not rot away in a jail somewhere because you think you should.'

'They won't find me guilty,' Dan said with more confidence than he felt. 'Give Ursula my . . . my best wishes.'

'Oh Dan! What has happened to you? Has this world leached away all your passion? You send Ursula best wishes? You send Boar Skull, the Lady Ursa, the woman you would die for, best wishes? I do not understand this place you call home. It has no soul and it robs true men of theirs. I have to go now, but please, I beg you as an old man with a measure of wisdom, do not turn your back on your true nature. Goodbye, Dan.'

Taliesin stepped away and waved his hand in farewell, and Dan found himself back beside his father and his hyperactive legs, as if he had never been away. There was still some expert sitting beside Inspector Frith, but it was no longer the charismatic Professor Merlin, just a plump woman with a bad haircut and an apologetic smile. It was all very well for Taliesin to talk about Dan's true nature, but his true nature was that of a killer – a ruthless, blood-crazed, merciless killer – and he had to turn his back on that; he had no choice.

~ Chapter Five ~

Ursula was startled awake by a man's voice calling her name. At first she thought it was Dan's voice, then King Macsen's, but when she opened her eyes she saw it was Taliesin.

He was looking exceptionally neat in a white coat, with a stethoscope draped artistically round his neck. He looked quite different from the last time she'd seen him, but she would have recognised him anywhere.

'Lady Ursa! Living and breathing and more lovely than ever!'

Ursula knew that she was blushing. Taliesin had always had the measure of her.

'Taliesin! I didn't expect to see you. How did I get here?' It was good to see him – if a little confusing.

'Dan saved you and I brought you back to this world – with a little help from Rhonwen. Perhaps you also do not remember that? In the end she acknowledged you as brave enough even for the Combrogi. She called you a hero. For her you were the better part of King Arturus, and our Princess Rhonwen of the lineage of druids and kings is not easily impressed. She is right, Ursula. I will never forget the way you led that cavalry charge – your courage! You made my Combrogi heart sing with pride, girl, and Rhonwen's too. She stayed behind to tell your story.'

Ursula could not hide her surprise. It was Rhonwen, the Celtic princess, sorceress, then Aenglisc priestess, who had first brought them through the Veil and who had been Ursula's enemy from the moment she had first laid eyes on her. Ursula considered this news for a moment. Her last meeting with Rhonwen had not been such a happy one.

'Camlann changed her, I think,' Ursula said softly, 'and the magic – the magic changes everything.' She tried not to sound too wistful. 'So. Here I am, home at last!' she said brightly. 'What do you think of it, Taliesin? What do you think of the wonders of the twenty-first century?'

Taliesin wrinkled his prominent nose and waved an expressive hand. 'I could not stay here for all the gold of the gods. It is a terrible place, but I am leaving soon. The question is, what do *you* think of it now that you're home at last?'

Ursula manufactured a smile. 'I am very happy to be back,' she said with more firmness than she had intended.

Taliesin grinned. 'I am glad, though I cannot with all the wit in me understand why you would stay here, hemmed in like this, when you could be a princess, if not a goddess, in Macsen's land – and indeed in other lands that I have seen in which your gifts and your beauty would be received with joy and gratitude. I do not understand why you would stay here in a world without magic.'

At least where there was no magic there could be no terrible sense of loss. Ursula almost said as much, but then the truth struck her.

'But you have magic here,' she said, and she knew he had. It was not the greatest kind, but it was strong enough to call the Veil and to do other things – quite a lot of other things. She could smell the magic on him and it made her heart beat faster and her palms sweat as if she were having some kind of panic attack. She had never known that there was real magic on her own earth before. She had never felt the slightest hint of it before she went through the Veil. The realisation that magic existed even in her own technological, modern world stunned her into silence.

'Come with me, Ursula. You are well now and I can fix the bits of you that aren't. Come with me to a place more worthy of you. Why don't you come back and see King Macsen? I know you would find the warmest of receptions.'

Thinking of Macsen did nothing to calm her. Long ago he had offered to marry her. She had known herself a child then, but now?

'Taliesin, please stop.'

'I am doing nothing.' Taliesin's expression was all outraged innocence.

'You are using magic and you are doing it on purpose to sway me.' She could feel it crackle in the air, feel it raise the hairs on her arms and neck, taste it on the tip of her tongue, and yet she could not wield it, she could not get inside it, let it possess her, let it fill her with its intoxicating power.

'What magic am I doing?' Taliesin asked, affronted.

Ursula shut her eyes and saw the golden threads of power working in her, healing her, strengthening her broken bones, repairing damage more swiftly than nature intended, giving her back the incredible strength that had all but ebbed away.

'Please, Taliesin. Stop. You know exactly how it makes me feel.' He did too. She saw that in the hint of cruelty in his smile – that look in his eyes. He was her friend, but he had something of the druid in him and his motivations were not always the purest. He had been locked out of magic in the past and Ursula knew that he was aware of exactly what he was doing to her. It made her obstinate. She did not like to be manipulated.

'Come with me, Ursula. I know how much you want to.'

She shook her head savagely, fighting to keep control. 'Go away!' She was shaking and she wanted to cry. He was torturing her.

Taliesin got to his feet and the leather of his soles squeaked against the lino as he turned to leave. 'Dan sends his – you know . . .'

She tried to smile. She did know. At least Dan was in this world too; she was not sure she would be able to survive here without him. She found her self-possession. 'Thank you, Taliesin, for bringing me home. You saved me – you and Dan and Rhonwen. My mum would thank you too, if she understood.' It was as well that she didn't.

Ursula's teeth had started to chatter quite against her will. She could not stop it. It was as if her rebellious body craved the magic as much as she did.

'Dan can help you when – I mean, if – you change your mind. He has the means to raise the Veil.'

'Dan has magic?' Ursula was startled.

Taliesin shook his head. 'He'll explain. He has an artefact that should take you back to Macsen.' He leaned forward and kissed her on the forehead. The magic on his lips burned her skin, as he had known it would.

'Go, Taliesin! I can't stand it!'

He waved his hand in a casual gesture of farewell and disappeared. The scent of power lingered in the air like gunpowder, stronger than longing. His voice echoed in the empty cubicle: 'Your magic is through the Veil.' And his words rang in her ears and through her mind like a kind of madness. It was hard to breathe. She reached for the tepid drinking water on the nightstand, but her hands trembled too much and she dropped it, so that water pooled under the high bed. She waved her hand to clear it away with power and for a moment the residual magic in the air almost responded. She felt that part of herself that had once wielded magic strain, try to move again like a muscle wasted from lack of use, or more like a ghost memory from an amputated limb. Nothing happened; the water remained on the floor. There was no magic any more. Not for her. She rolled over and buried her face in her pillow. She did not want her mother to find her crying.

By the time her mother had returned with a toasted

sandwich and a bunch of grapes, Ursula had pulled herself together.

'Mum – I feel fine . . . Do you think I could go home now?'

'It's not been long, love. What if you were to relapse? How would I get you back here on my own?'

'It's fine, Mum. I've healed. There won't be a relapse. Could you ask the doctors, please?'

'You do look better . . .' Her mother stared at her face intently.

Ursula had tied her hair back so it more nearly resembled the cropped hairstyle she'd had before entering the Veil. She knew that her face was flushed and her eyes over-bright after her meeting with Taliesin, but again her mother saw nothing amiss.

'I don't want you to wear yourself out. You're not strong, Ursula.'

Ursula smothered a smile. Her mum had no idea. Now that Taliesin had restored her to health she was stronger than most men and, she knew, some way tougher. She stretched. It was good to be fit again. 'Hey, Mum. Have you seen this? I think I might have to go shopping!' She jumped out from under the covers to reveal that she had already dressed herself in her old jeans, which were now several sizes too big and had to be pinned with a safety pin to stop them falling down. She'd also put on her favourite men's extra-large navy sweatshirt that effectively disguised her newly fit and toned body as well as it had her unfit one.

'Well, you have certainly lost weight. Are those really

your jeans? I might have brought the wrong pair. I'm worried, though. Darling, you mustn't lose any more weight. You need to build yourself back up, Ursula, you've been so very ill.' Her mother's eyes filled with tears.

'Mum. I'm fine. Never better.' Ursula put her arm round her mother's shoulders. Her mother felt slight, delicate, like a porcelain doll. Ursula got her size from her rugby-playing father. She held her mother's small hand in her own strong one. Her mother was as emotionally fragile as she was physically frail. Ursula could not hurt her by telling the truth. In all the pain and worry of battle and its aftermath, Ursula had forgotten how terrible it was to crave something she could never have. She had forgotten how exhausting it was to desire something so strongly. Physically she felt fine, bursting with energy, free of any twinge of pain. Even a few old injuries from earlier encounters were fully restored and free of scar tissue. But still the void within her ached like the empty socket of a lost tooth. Being home was not enough. She wanted the magic back. She had to battle to ignore it. Her mother patted her hand.

'Oh, I almost forgot. Silly me! Your father's going to give us what I asked for – more money every month, and he's backdated it. It was a pity it took nearly losing you to make him see sense. But it means we have a bit of a windfall. We can afford to go shopping and get you some new, prettier things!' She looked at the navy sweatshirt with disdain. 'I never did like that top!'

Shopping was a bit of a nightmare. Ursula had forgotten

how much her mother complained about her father, about what he spent on his new wife and how his new baby, who was quite plain and not a bit like Ursula as a child, was dressed in designer clothes – she'd seen the labels for herself. How her dad had started dying his hair and lost at least a stone trying to keep up with that young floozy he'd taken up with.

It was hard for Ursula to keep quiet. She had seen more of life than her mother now and she understood that things could be complicated. She had guilt of her own. Once, in Arturus's world, she and Dan had abandoned an eight-year-old boy who was devoted to them, who'd risked his life for them and who was entirely their responsibility. They had taken their chances to try to escape from a place they did not want to be and had run. Ursula finally understood how her father could have made that same choice, though if his marriage to her mother had been a battlefield it was much cleaner and less bloody than the one she and Dan had fled: probably not much quieter, though. Bryn, the boy they had so grievously betrayed, had turned out well in spite of their dereliction of duty and care. He was brave and honourable, loyal and honest. He had not blamed them but had learned to forgive. She could turn out well too; it was up to her.

Of course she did not tell her mother all that. Her mother had no doubts at all; Ursula's father had betrayed them and he would forever be in the wrong. His sin seemed trivial compared to Ursula's own. She had looked into the face of a corpse and known herself responsible for someone's death, for many deaths. She wanted to tell her mother that in any hierarchy of evil in the world her father's was not the worst. She didn't, of course. She couldn't; it wouldn't have been fair. Instead she tried to be the girl that she'd been before. Somehow that worked.

'Oh Ursula, isn't this sweet? I love young girls in pink. You will look so cute in this. We must have it.'

Ursula opened her mouth and then shut it again. Did it matter that she would rather not wear a pink miniskirt with glitter detail? Her mother was as excited as she had ever seen her.

'Does it come in a different colour?'

'No, no, no. I always think blondes look good in pink, and look at this scarf with the hearts on it. It would look so nice with that and a pretty top. Oh, and look – it's in the sale! Ursula, it's perfect!'

The shop assistant, a nice-looking man in his early twenties, smiled at Ursula. He at least did not think she was twelve. She did not smile back. She had seen that look he wore before – on the faces of too many men who'd followed her to their deaths. She ignored his smile, gritted strong teeth and agreed to the pink skirt. There were worse things than being inappropriately dressed.

~ Chapter Six ~

Dan was relieved to find that he'd been right about the charges – they had to be dropped once Ursula denied that he'd hurt her. He had wanted to go and see her but the lawyer his father had engaged had strongly advised him to stay away. The police did not believe Ursula's story. They were still obsessing about their clothes. They appeared to believe that Dan and Ursula had been having some secret relationship, that he'd attacked her in a jealous rage. It made no particular sense, but then the truth made no sense at all.

Ursula came back to school surprisingly quickly. She looked stunning and one glance in her direction told Dan that she'd lost none of her strength. He didn't know how he knew, but he knew. His schoolmates clustered round her like wasps round a jam jar and Ursula did nothing to discourage them. The one exchange he'd had with her had not been very satisfactory. He sought her out the first day that she was back. She was briefly alone by the lockers.

'Are you all right?' He spoke to her in the language of

the Combrogi, the language that had become theirs. She smiled at him and he wanted to fall at her feet, but that wouldn't do at all.

'I'm good. Taliesin came and finished the job of the doctors. I'm good as new. Thanks for saving me, Dan. I owe you my life.'

He shrugged as if it were nothing, as if it had cost him nothing. He would have paid even more to have kept her safe. He did not want to say that, though. He didn't want to burden her with that. He kept his voice non-committal. He spoke to her casually, as if she wasn't . . . everything.

'What did Taliesin say?'

'Oh, what you might expect – that I should go with him back to Macsen's world, that I would be appreciated there.'

Dan knew that was true enough. King Macsen had been more than a little in love with her and would have liked her magical bloodline running through his descendants.

'Did you want to go?'

Ursula tidied a stray hair and stuck it behind her ear. She pulled a face. 'This is home. Right?'

He wanted to touch her – just to hold her hand – but things were different for her now. She had a certain glamour that came with her newly uncovered beauty and the fact that she had nearly died in mysterious circumstances. Everyone wanted to be her friend. He didn't want to feel she had to be with him because he'd saved her. Taliesin was right. He knew too much about how people worked. The time he'd spent being able to read minds had changed the way he looked at people, had made him cynical, uncharitable. By and large he'd prefer to avoid them. He wanted Ursula to be free – of him and of the guilt and horrors of their shared past.

'Yeah. No one even had time to miss us,' he said easily.

'Dan, I . . .'

He did not want to hear her tell him that things couldn't be the same between them now that they were home. He didn't think he'd be able to bear it. He'd prefer to stay out of her way and leave everything unsaid. He could hear someone coming and then the bell went. 'Got to go! See you later!' he said and hurried away.

It was a big school and he made sure that he was always busy at the few times their paths might have crossed. He stopped hanging out with the smokers and with his other mates. He could not care about the things they talked about and, of course, they all fancied Ursula now and wanted to know what had happened to the two of them in that lost hour after they left the re-enactment. His friends seemed hurt by his withdrawal but left him alone. He took to going running and to using the gym every lunchtime, as if by wearing out his body he could somehow control his mind. It did not work.

He was in the library one wet lunchtime when for some reason the gym was closed and he could not face running in the cold. He sensed Ursula's arrival before he saw her. He always knew where she was – it was the one hangover from the magical bond between them that had saved them so often in the past. He watched her from behind the bookcases. She was with a group of Year Elevens, mucking about and being a little too loud. Dan's mate Josh was shouting – showing off. 'So what happened with Dan, then? He must have done something because he's turned into a right weirdo since that day.'

Ursula shrugged and sent a pointed look in Dan's direction. So she knew where he was too. Some vestige of that old link still existed for her too. He busied himself with finding the book he needed for his homework and then he heard raised voices again. 'Look. Leave it alone, will you. I have said that Dan never touched me. He would never hurt me!' They all picked on that remark and started teasing Ursula that she had some kind of thing for Dan, and Dan just knew that Ursula was getting angry. They really did not want to make Ursula angry.

One of the girls, Lucy – she'd been queen bee until Ursula had started causing a buzz – suddenly said, 'Yeah, Ursula, why don't you go out with Dan and leave all our boyfriends alone? You've turned into a real slag since you came back from hospital.'

Dan found that he was holding his breath. Ursula had gone very white and her blue eyes seemed to flash Lucy ample warning, but Lucy didn't know what she was dealing with.

'What did you say?' Ursula said dangerously.

'You should get with Dan – he's more your type. You're both weird.'

'Dan is not weird,' Ursula said emphatically. Lucy did not seem to know when to stop.

'Look, you might have got all thin and interesting since your "accident", but we all know that he did it and you

39

pushed him to it. You were weird two weeks ago and you're weird now.'

Dan saw Ursula get to her feet. Even if he'd been unable to feel her fury, her body language must have told Lucy it was time to shut up.

'Do you want a fight, Lucy?' Ursula said softly.

Lucy laughed. 'I'm not afraid of you. Josh wouldn't let you hurt me anyway. Would you, Josh?'

Josh was not an idiot and he recognised something in Ursula that Lucy did not. 'Stop it, Lucy.'

'You're not afraid of Ursula, are you, Josh?' Lucy had an instinct for trouble and because Josh was actually afraid of Ursula, because he had instincts of his own – good ones – he had to deny it.

'Of course not. Anyway, I don't hit girls.'

'Oh go on, Josh. She's asking for it!'

It was impossible to read Ursula's expression. She was impassive as stone. Dan had to stop this now.

He stepped out from behind the bookshelves.

'Hey!' he said.

'I think Josh just challenged me,' Ursula said flatly, without looking at Dan.

'Don't be silly, Ursula. Josh wouldn't fight you,' Dan said.

'He's too scared,' Lucy chipped in.

Josh coloured. 'Of course I'm not.'

'Go on then, hit her. I dare you.'

'Don't, Josh!'

'Or what, Dan? Will you stop me?' Josh was squaring up to Dan now and the last thing Dan ever wanted to do

40

was fight another human being. He had seen where it led.

'I don't have to stop you, Josh. Ursula can look after herself.' As soon as he'd said those words he knew he'd made a mistake. Couldn't they see what Ursula was? She was six foot one or more, lean and muscled, and her eyes were two hard blue stones, bright as sapphires. There was no mercy in her eyes – no fear and no mercy. She could have killed every one of them and not broken into a sweat.

'Are you saying Ursula would beat me in a fight?'

Dan didn't know what to say. He could sense Ursula listening with keen interest. He should lie and say that Josh would win – maybe that would defuse the situation. What did Ursula want him to say? He shrugged. Let them make of that what they wanted. He thought it was over. He knew Josh didn't want to take on Ursula; he'd seen it in his eyes.

The library as a body seemed to let out a quiet sigh of relief. Ursula sat down and Dan turned away to get his backpack. Then, without warning, Lucy launched herself at Ursula like some kind of demented wildcat.

In one fluid moment Ursula was on her feet and had lifted Lucy off hers. Ursula's strong right hand had Lucy's throat and Lucy's eyes were beginning to bulge. Her legs dangled helplessly in mid-air. Ursula remained expressionless.

Josh, seeing Lucy's danger, tried to punch Ursula, which was a mistake. She deflected the blow easily and with a casual backhand sent him reeling across the floor, where he collided with the bookshelves. The girls Lucy was with started screaming and one of the librarians was shouting. Ursula still didn't say anything, but Lucy was turning blue.

'Stop it, Ursula! She's a kid! Put her down!' Ursula relaxed her hand and Lucy fell to the floor, gasping for air and sobbing. Before anyone else could move, Dan grabbed Ursula's arm and dragged her out of the library.

'For God's sake, Ursula, what are you doing? You could have killed her! You nearly killed a young girl. She's not a bloody warrior. Are you out of your mind?'

'Maybe, Dan. I can't stand this any more. Please get me out of here.'

How could he not respond?

~ Chapter Seven ~

'Run to the end of the playing fields and I'll meet you there in a minute. The librarian may call an ambulance – maybe even the police! Stay out of sight. I won't be long.' As Dan sprinted away Ursula started to run. She could not believe how easy it would have been to kill Lucy – it took barely any strength and worse, at that moment, as she had grabbed Lucy by her thin neck, she had not even thought about what she was doing. Instinct alone had directed her – instinct and experience and her terrible strength – a strength that she had not fully appreciated until back in her own world. She did not see how she could stay in a place where she posed such a risk. She knew that Dan was a killer – if a reluctant one when not overwhelmed by his berserker madness – but she had always felt that she was in control. She had only ever fought men, warriors, people who wanted to kill her. The idea that she was herself a killer – a danger to ordinary people – was a new one. It shook her. It had not occurred to her before.

She reached the cluster of trees and rested her back

against one of them. What were the limits of her strength? She stood up and wrapped her arms around the trunk of a horse chestnut tree. Her arms did not quite encircle it. She started to squeeze, to hug it as hard as she could – and she felt the trunk weaken, threaten to collapse. She tightened her grip and there was a terrible cracking sound; the wood shattered, the trunk split and the topmost branches leaned towards the neighbouring tree. It would fall if she continued. She stopped. She was panting with her effort and tears were running down her face. She had hoped that now, when she looked more like everyone else, things might be easier, but she was more of a freak than ever.

'Ursula? What are you doing?' Dan was suddenly beside her; in her distress she had not heard him coming.

'I had to see how strong I was. I didn't know. I think Taliesin must have made it worse.' She was still crying, though she herself didn't know if it was because of what she had so nearly done to Lucy or what she had actually done to the tree.

'Dan, I don't want to be a freak – not here. How can I fit in when I can do this?'

Dan looked at the damaged tree impassively. The upper part of the trunk was leaning at an improbable angle against the oak tree next to it. The stresses Ursula had placed it under had fractured it and caused a fissure in the trunk that would probably kill it. She watched his face for a reaction, but he kept it very still. He remained calm, as he often did in a crisis. He did not answer her directly.

'Taliesin gave me this,' he said. He opened his backpack and Ursula saw that he had Bright Killer with him, wrapped in oiled linen. The unmistakable shape of the sword's hilt stuck out of the partially zipped bag. Ursula felt her stomach grow cold at the sight of it. She knew all too well that such a sword had not been made for peace. They had both wielded it and killing invariably followed. Did she really want to go back to a world where killing was ordinary, normal? Did she want to go to a world which her parents would never see, a place where she would be without family, without any prospect but endless battles, endless grim encounters, endless death? She hesitated. But she knew that there would also be magic.

Dan had dumped his rucksack by the damaged tree and was holding a round clear ball of some semi-translucent material It looked like a paperweight or an object from the school's prop department.

'What's that – a crystal ball?' She almost laughed. Taliesin was having them on. 'What are we supposed to do – call to him through it? As if he hasn't caused us enough trouble already.'

'Taliesin has his faults, Ursula, but it's thanks to him that I could bring you home.'

'It was thanks to him we were involved in the battle that nearly killed me in the first place,' she answered shortly. She knew that the object in Dan's hands had power. It had set her tongue tingling and she could feel the buzz of it all the way up her spine. The base of her skull itched, as if the magic held some irritant. It certainly took hold of her mind. Its presence made it very hard for her to think, let alone speak. She felt dizzy with the need to touch the object that was so full of it, but she used all her willpower and held back. Magic waited for her beyond the Veil.

'What are you going to do with that thing?' Her voice trembled a little although she tried to sound normal. Dan probably thought she was still shaken because of Lucy and the tree, which she was, but the thought of the magic shook her more.

'What do you think? Should I just rub it?' Dan said. There was the distant sound of an ambulance arriving. 'I hope Lucy is OK.'

'Of course she is. I didn't snap anything and she was still breathing.' Ursula's reply, she knew, could have been more sympathetic. She couldn't think of anything but the smell and taste of magic thrumming in the air. She tried to sound casual, as if Dan's answer was not the most important thing in the world. 'So, what are you going to do about the Veil?'

'You really want me to raise it? Even after all we've been through?'

'For God's sake, Dan, just *do* it. Yes. I want you to raise the Veil – how clear do I have to be? I nearly killed someone, probably would have done if you hadn't stopped me. What do you want? Us to be joined at the hip for the rest of our lives so you can keep me out of trouble?'

The truth was she didn't think she could live without magic. Since Taliesin had shown her that it still lurked in her own world she kept detecting its elusive scent, carried in the wind, rustling through the grass – fragments only, stray filaments of power. It set her whole body on edge, made her desperate for more.

Dan looked hurt. 'You want to go back to Macsen's land? To King Macsen?'

Yes, yes, she wanted to scream but she managed to hold herself back. Dan was being unusually slow – she had said so, hadn't she? Did he want her to spell it out?

He paused. 'Do you want to do the honours?'

She shook her head. Of course she did! But Taliesin might have given the crystal ball to Dan for a reason. Perhaps it would only work for him.

'OK then.' Dan did not look happy. He was risking a lot, she knew; in Arturus's land his magical gift for empathy, for mind-reading, had almost driven him mad. In Macsen's land he'd been mad too, when he'd been a berserker. He must have been worried about what another trip through the Veil would do to him. But he was all right; they'd got through. They'd manage. She knew that he would not deny her what she wanted. She saw it in his face, briefly unguarded. He'd take any risk to give her what she wanted, and what she wanted was magic.

He held the orb in his left hand and rubbed it with his right. Nothing happened. Distantly Ursula heard more sirens and she could see that a panda car had arrived in the car park.

'Hurry up, Dan! They'll be looking for me. I don't want to be done for assault or, worse still, attempted murder . . .'

'I can't concentrate if you talk. What do you have to think about to raise the Veil?'

'Wanting it. Wanting it desperately,' Ursula said, but it was more than that. She thought back. Raising the Veil was a kind of prayer. It was difficult to explain, maddened as she was by the presence of the orb, by her own craving. She tried to calm herself down and to remember how to do it. She spoke more slowly. 'You have to be still – inside. You have to want it but you also have to ask permission – from, you know, from God, I suppose . . .' Her voice tailed away, embarrassed. Opening the Veil wasn't like opening a door. It was hard to explain, impossible to share. It was almost too private. Thinking about it made her ashamed; she doubted her motives for opening it this time. This time her motives were wholly selfish. Would such a request be granted? She wanted power again, that was all. But she wasn't opening the Veil, Dan was, and he wanted to raise it for her; his motives were utterly selfless.

Dan wasn't listening. He'd understood. He could do still. His eyes had taken on a slightly unfocused look as he continued to rub the orb. Ursula felt the magic catch, latch on to something bigger, call to it, and suddenly the first faint tendrils of yellow smoke began to form and thicken and grow, swirling in front of Dan like the birth of a tornado. It was not quite the way it had formed for her or for Rhonwen, but then neither of them had ever raised the Veil using a theatre-prop orb.

'I think that sometimes it needs blood – the druids thought so,' Ursula said. Her heart was beating wildly as she felt the power grow.

'Don't worry about that,' Dan said with a grimace, and she could see that his left hand seeped blood as if the smooth round surface of the crystal ball had somehow cut it.

'Ursula, this feels wrong. I don't think we should go.' He did not look at her. She knew he was holding on to the Veil, that he was still not entirely with her. Even with the magic of the orb, he still had to exert his own control over the now billowing mist.

'I have to, Dan. I need to.' She couldn't look at him, but ran straight towards the swirling mist. Magic was calling to her and she had no power to resist.

~ Chapter Eight ~

Dan had no choice but to follow Ursula, and quickly, through the Veil. He had been here before – that first time they'd encountered the seething yellow mist. He grabbed the package that was Bright Killer and, still clutching the orb against his chest, launched himself through the mist before it dispersed. He shut his eyes and held his breath. He hated the Veil – the way the oily droplets that made it clung to him, the way it tasted – but he could not leave Ursula. She was not herself. He had seen her fight before, but what she'd done to Lucy was out of character. Something was wrong with her and he did not know what; he was frightened for her.

He knew enough about the workings of the Veil to be unsurprised when he emerged from its greasy clutches alone.

There was no sign of Ursula. He had emerged from the magical yellow mist into an ordinary grey damp and stifling fog, a fog that blanketed everything in an ominous silence. He shook his head as if to unstop his ears and shivered. His school sweatshirt wasn't warm and within one pace he found himself knee-deep in slimy mud. He lifted Bright Killer above his head to keep it dry but his left hand was slick with blood and the orb slipped from his hand to land with a decisive plop in the bog beside him. Shit. In panic he rooted around for it with his foot. That was a stupid move. All that happened was that his foot caught in some reeds. He might have called out for help, but he did not know where he was and in his experience it was not a good idea to advertise your vulnerability to strangers. His sword was valuable in any world and he had no idea if he could fight with one foot buried in a bog. There was solid ground within a stretched arm's reach and he carefully laid Bright Killer on that. There was nothing else for it but to take a deep breath and plunge under the icy water to attempt to release his foot.

It was hard to see anything in the murky darkness. His eyes stung. He found his foot and the roots that held it trapped. He pulled and wriggled and worked it free but his lungs were screaming by the time he surfaced. He spluttered and gagged. The water was foul. It was pointless to search for the orb – it would have sunk into the mud, but he knew he had to try. He put his face into the water again and opened his eyes. He could see nothing. He surfaced again and shook the slime from his hair. Within seconds of arriving in this unknown place he had lost any hope he had of getting home. He swore savagely under his breath, soldier's oaths in Latin that would have made his Latin teacher turn pale if he'd known what they meant. He hauled himself up to rest under his sword.

Fan-bloody-tastic. There was still no sign of Ursula. He hugged his knees in an effort to get warm and then did what he had wanted to do for a long time.

He hadn't opened the wrapped sword since he'd found it in his locker. He had been shocked to see it there that first day he'd been allowed back at school once the charges against him had been dropped. It made a kind of crazy sense, he supposed. He would not have wanted his sister or his father to come across it at home, and at least his locker had a combination lock. Now he finally unwrapped the sword, his sword. He was surprised to see that it had a new belt and scabbard – fine work too, though neither Celtic nor Roman. He fastened it over his hip where it fitted easily. He would have been lying to himself if he didn't admit that it felt good to have it there again.

He perched on the almost-dry ground and listened hard, sniffing the air for clues. It was very quiet. The wind was cold and it rustled through the reeds. Overhead a bird called. The air smelled of mud and stagnant water, of wet grasses and distant woodsmoke. That was it then. There was no smoke without fire and he needed a fire before he developed hypothermia. He was shivering very badly and his teeth were chattering. His trainers were sodden, so he took them off and wrapped them round his neck by their laces. His socks were horrible too, so he stuffed them in his pocket. Then he began to pick his way carefully across the marshland, through the thick mist, following the elusive smell of woodsmoke and baking; he was almost sure he could smell baking.

In the poor light he fell into further bogs and twisted his ankle so that he had to rest and catch his breath. He had no great instinct for magic, unlike Ursula, who had known at once that she had no magic in Arturus's land. He could not sense any human thoughts, which was a great relief to him. He knew himself to be tough – tougher than most boys his age – but he couldn't stand to experience that again. He didn't *feel* magical in this world; all he felt was cold and wet. He didn't want anything to do with magic – it brought only trouble – but, on the other hand, it would be good to know if that magical bond he had with Ursula still persisted. He shut his eyes and tried to think of her. It wasn't difficult. His memory was full of her: the time she conjured an eagle, the time she turned herself into a man, the time she wore the mask of Arturus, and all the many times when she was just herself. They had been so close in those other worlds, and in their own they had become like strangers again. He tried to search her out with his mind; he willed it, but it didn't work . . . He had no idea where she might be.

He was worried about her but he knew he was being stupid. If one thing had been proved time and again, it was that Ursula could take care of herself. The landscape gave him no clues as to his location. He was in marshland, that was all. He could be back in the land of the Celtic leader, Macsen, when most of Britain was wild and untamed – but a bit of him hoped that he wasn't. Much though he admired Macsen for his skill in battle and his courage and decisiveness in fighting the Ravens, he was altogether too handsome and perfect a specimen of manhood for Dan to be happy for Ursula to see him again. He wasn't surprised that she was so keen to come back through the Veil, and it wasn't just about the magic. Ursula had always had a bit of a thing for Macsen. He knew he was being stupid and that concerns about Ursula falling in love with a Celtic king ought not to be top of his priority list at that moment, but he couldn't help but hope that Ursula had not found herself at the court of a king while he struggled through a mire. He smiled grimly to himself. It struck him that in his adventures through the Veil he had grown so used to discomfort that he did not even waste energy worrying about his own unpromising circumstances. He waited until the pain from his ankle began to pass before he struggled to his feet. The light was fading quickly and he forced himself to limp forward further and faster. It would not be clever to be lost in a marsh when darkness came.

He followed his nose and the homely scent of smoke and baking until he stumbled on a small house, set on a sizeable piece of solid-seeming land, a small island surrounded by streams and bogs.

It was not much bigger than a large shed, but he was very glad to see it. It was a long single-storey affair thatched with rushes and plastered with mud. Now that he was closer he could detect the stink of the midden, of ordure, of dung and damp dirt mingled with the pungent smoke from the fire, which glowed a welcoming orange in the murky half-light through the homestead's open door. He saw a few pot-bellied pigs and three or four chickens scratched at hard-packed reed-strewn ground. It was clear enough from all this that he wasn't in his own century, but he'd guessed that already.

What he didn't know was whether this was a land at peace or war. Should he take off his sword belt? He was about to call out a warning and a greeting, a request for a place at the sparking fire, but he had another problem: he did not know what to shout out. What language did they speak here? Thanks to his experiences through the Veil and, no doubt, a little bit of magic, he had mastered the languages of the Combrogi tribes and the Latin of the first and fifth centuries. He knew a few words of Aenglisc too, but only curses and the like. In the main he had fought the Aenglisc, not conversed with them.

Dan hesitated for a moment outside the dwelling and gently eased Bright Killer out of its scabbard. It moved as smoothly as ever. Taliesin had looked after it well.

'Hey!' he shouted. It was a kind of multi-purpose greeting. He peered through the open door into the fire of the single room; the smoke made his eyes water and the brightness of the fire blinded him to whatever lay in the shadowed gloom away from it. Gradually he made sense of what he saw.

A man was sitting by the fire, facing the doorway. He had a knife in his hand and, as Dan approached, he got rapidly to his feet. Dan did not take in too much of the detail of his appearance other than the knife and the fact that he held it like he knew how to use it. He was an older man, well muscled but not tall. The hairs of his sparse beard looked auburn in the fire's glow.

Dan, crouching in the low doorway, moved his own hand away from his sword hilt and showed him his empty palms. The man spoke to him in a rush of guttural nonsense, a tirade of harsh syllables. Dan didn't understand a word. He needed the warmth of the fire though, and the man made no effort to attack him, just looked ready to stab him if he did anything untoward. Dan was not much of an actor but he did what he had to do and put on a dumb show, moving deliberately so that his innocent intentions would be clear. He shivered melodramatically and rubbed his arms as if to warm them, then pointed first at the fire and then at himself.

The man neither nodded nor shook his head. Dan took a gamble and, stooping, walked inside. The knife man watched him. Through the smoke Dan could see that he had very intense blue eyes in a weathered face. He didn't look like a man who missed much. Dan was suddenly conscious that he was still dressed in his sweatshirt and school trousers, with his trainers hanging round his neck. It wasn't a costume designed to make him blend in. Knowing what was to come he'd left his watch, phone and iPod in his locker at school, but there had been little he could do about his clothes.

Dan moved very carefully and deliberately towards the fire. He kept his hands visible at all times and smiled maniacally to show his goodwill. The man did not loosen his grip on the blade, which Dan was sure was a scrama-seax, an Aenglisc weapon, something longer than a belt knife but shorter than a sword. That was not good news. He racked his brains for any Aenglisc words, but his wits seemed to have deserted him. He did not think the Aenglisc spoke Latin but he tried using it anyway. The man appeared shocked and said something in reply. It was horribly mangled, but when the man repeated it for the third time Dan thought he caught the word that Arturus used to describe his priest and confessor. The man thought Dan was a priest. It might have been wiser to play along with that, to pretend that he was a cleric of some kind, but Dan preferred honesty – or at least what honesty he could manage without speaking a word of the other man's language. He shook his head and shrugged elaborately in the hope that the man might accept that he regretted that he could not describe himself so easily. He mimed opening a book and reading – to tell the man that he was some kind of student. The chances were that no such occupation existed in whatever world he had come to, but he did not want to suggest that he was a warrior. He was done with fighting. The man became very animated then and laid his knife ostentatiously beside him on the ground – close enough to grab should Dan prove troublesome, but still relinquishing the weapon and putting Dan a little further out of danger. Dan felt more confident.

The man was obviously not stupid and quickly realised that Dan did not understand him; he simply held out his hand to warm it by the fire, indicating that Dan should do the same. Dan inched closer to the blaze and allowed some of the tension to leave his shoulders. Warmth was good. Dryness was good. He did not know anything about this place but he knew how to take advantage of brief moments of pleasure. He was warming up. There was the possibility of food and of shelter, and no one had tried to kill him yet. Dan was all too aware that there were worse ways to enter a new world.

~ Chapter Nine ~

Ursula felt the power of the Veil enfold her. It engulfed her, burned against her skin. She breathed it in and breathed it out again . . . It was terrible to know that there was so much power there, locked in the yellow droplets of mist. It was a kind of torture to perceive all that power there for the controlling and to have no means to direct or to access it.

Ursula knew she should have waited for Dan. She knew that once separated they would not emerge together on the other side. But she had seen the look on his face when he saw what she'd done to the tree. She had seen his expression change, seen his familiar mask of bland indifference cover his horror and his confusion. The very blankness of his face was a criticism, and she didn't need Dan to criticise her. She knew that she'd behaved badly with Lucy, but she didn't know how to stop. Dan would forgive her if he understood how the need for magic drove her – how it was an ache in her heart, a terrible gnawing hunger that had to be fed, an itch in her very soul that could not be scratched. She felt sick with it, weak with need. Needing it had made her careless, absent-minded, so that she'd nearly done more harm to Lucy than she had intended. But the girl had had it coming in a way. She was stupid not to know that Ursula was at the end of her tether, on the very edge of a kind of madness, teetering on the brink and likely to fall in if she didn't get away. If only Dan and she still shared their old link. If he could know her thoughts for even a millisecond, she knew he'd understand. He'd know that she only did what she had to do, that there was no real choice. He would not expect her to endure that terrible exile. He would not expect her to stay in school when she could sense the hidden magic of a whole world locked away and out of her reach.

She ran through the Veil, fighting its gluey oiliness that clung to her clothes and her hair, desperate to be free of it, to get to Macsen's world, where her magic waited. She burst out of the Veil screaming, only to find herself in a forest clearing on a warm sunlit afternoon.

She stopped screaming. It was so peaceful. Magic no longer buzzed like a mosquito in her ear, insistent, demanding and outside her. The air was clean, and high overhead, where a latticework of dark branches made patterns against a pale blue sky, the first buds of spring were appearing. Birds sang. Ursula took a deep breath that quickly became a sigh. It was OK. She had magic here. It was inside her again. Her heart beat to its rhythm, her blood pumped to its pulse. She felt the power coursing through her veins, through her nerves, through her every cell, making her whole self tingle, making her whole self alive again at last. It was like water to a desiccated plant, air to a drowning man. It was a kind of ecstasy. But there was too much of it. It made her dizzy. She fell to her knees, unable to balance the weight of her head upon shoulders that were pulsating with power. She tried to crawl on all fours towards the great trunk of an ash tree. As the bare skin of her knees touched the soft earth she felt the magic rising through her with even greater force. It was hard to remember who she was or where she was. She leaned heavily against the tree, feeling the sap rise through it as the magic rose through her.

It was magnificent, overwhelming, more than she had dreamed of. She closed her eyes and felt the roots growing beneath the ground. She called to them and more grew. Like snakes slithering through the earth they twined around her, keeping her anchored, keeping her close to the earth from which the power came. It was barely spring but she willed the tree to bear leaves to shelter her and low branches to shield her from the rain. It was so easy. It needed no effort on her part to request these things and then all that she asked for suddenly was there. There was no gap between thought and action: it was as straightforward as tucking her own hair behind her ears.

She could sense all the small creatures going about their business, saw the wood briefly through their eyes, smelled and heard all they did, and still her awareness had found no limits. She found an eagle flying high above the forest and borrowed its eyes to see in sharp focus her own body lying, still as a corpse, beneath the tree – such a small tree viewed from this distance. She sent her will back to the tree root and the solid tree trunk and urged both to grow bigger and stronger so that they would mark more clearly the spot where she, the vessel of such magic, lay resting, testing out the limits of her power.

It was intoxicating, but wearying. She sent her awareness more deeply into the earth, through the lines of power that bisected it. She let herself flow through streams and riverbeds, under homesteads and halls, into the dreams and thoughts of men and then away again to share the hunger of the hunting wolves. And all of it meant nothing and everything; all of it was the same. She could see whatever she wanted to see and there was no sound that she could not hear if only she listened. Her body burned with the power in her and in the heated ground where she lay the bulbs blossomed as if spring had already come.

She did not know who she was and she did not care. She experienced the fear of the prey and the triumph of the predator, felt flesh tear and was torn. She felt the baby's first eager breath in the cool of the place beyond the womb, felt the death rattle of an old man's last desperate gasp. She was lost and did not know it, barely Ursula and she did not care. Night came and she was not hungry or thirsty but stared up at the starlit skies, seeing nothing but the visions her magic brought to her, feeling nothing but the steady pulse of power.

~ Chapter Ten ~

The man indicated that Dan should unbuckle his sword, which he did reluctantly. He set it next to his feet, then he sat in a strangely companionable silence with the knife-bearing Aenglisc man by the fire.

Once the Aenglisc man had established to his own satisfaction that Dan posed no danger, he seemed to lose himself in his own thoughts, for he did not try to speak again, but stroked his light beard with a calloused hand. He was a fighter this man, that much was evident from his build and the state of his hands, but even that did not frighten Dan. The heat made him drowsy and, though his warrior's instincts and plain common sense told him it would be foolish to sleep in a place of such obvious danger, he struggled to stay awake. This was not Macsen's world – it was nowhere that he knew. He needed to stay sharp and ready to defend himself, and yet his body, usually so tireless under stress, betrayed him. He had not slept well in his own world – had not, in fact, slept well for weeks. His bed at home lacked stability; he seemed to be perched on something too high and too soft to support the weight of his bones, and he was ridiculously fearful of falling off. The air in his centrally heated room had stifled him, and then each night he had fought for Ursula and failed her, burying them both under a mound of carcasses and suffocating them. He felt more at ease by a strange hearth next to an unknown man with a seax than in his own bed at home.

Something about the crackle of the warming fire and the silence of the cottage lulled him into a light but restful sleep.

It was barely a moment later that he started awake at the sound of voices. A woman was complaining bitterly about spoiled cakes. It was not his sister's voice nor his dead mother's nor even Ursula's. He opened his eyes and saw a stout woman in what he thought of as peasant dress, shouting at the friendly knife man. That was not too weird; what was strange was that he understood her perfectly. The knife man was apologising, and the tumble of undifferentiated sound had suddenly resolved itself into comprehensible words and phrases.

'I have no excuses to offer, good wife. I was lost in my own thoughts and I forgot my duty. Please forgive my inattention.'

The woman was unimpressed and berated him for some time. The small homestead stank so badly of burning that Dan wondered why fear of being burned alive had not woken him up. It was not long before she turned on him, and though he wasn't surprised he had not prepared a defence. Luckily he didn't need one.

'I hope I haven't presumed too much in asking this fellow traveller to rest by your fire. He has fallen into the marsh and I feared he might catch fever from the chill.'

The woman turned to Dan then and looked him up and down. She wasn't old but had hidden her hair under a stiff veil so that all he could see was her lined, round face and the irritation in her shrewd eyes.

'Well, I haven't much in the way of food to share with you now that the cakes are burned, but you are welcome enough if you are peaceful. You would do better to take off your clothes and dry them properly – I have a blanket to keep your naked shame covered.' She laughed at that, a full-throated cackle, and Dan doubted that she was too much older than he was. She pulled out a blanket from a storage space beneath his bench. It had been hidden by a screen of rushes – it was a neat arrangement.

'It's warm yet so I haven't needed it on my bed.'

Dan was a bit embarrassed to get undressed in front of strangers and began to do the behind-the-towel contortion that people do on beaches, but the woman laughed so much that he simply stepped away into the shadows to preserve his modesty. He kept the sword by his side. Her eye settled on it for a moment and Dan saw her stiffen, but she said nothing. If she had weapons hidden in the space under the bench, they were not easily grabbed. He was unsurprised that she did not challenge him.

The blanket was of thick, soft wool and he guessed it to be a treasure in what seemed otherwise to be a simple house. He thanked her carefully in the same language that she had used with him. Somehow the words were there as he needed them, at the tip of his tongue, at the back of his throat, and it was obvious that he had not entirely lost all his magical gift. He was pleased that it made life easier but concerned about what other changes might have afflicted him. Unlike Ursula, he wasn't a great fan of magical power. The knife man looked at him suspiciously.

'You have found your tongue, I see,' he said. Dan felt uncomfortable.

'Yes. Thank you for supporting me – before . . . I am sorry. I . . . um . . .' Dan's mind went blank. 'I – I didn't understand your accent.'

'Odd as you speak with the same one – you are a Wessex man? I would like to know who you serve with that fine blade of yours. It is strange that I have not seen you in the muster of the King's fyrd.'

Dan opened his mouth without the slightest idea of what he was going to say. The man's former calm had been replaced by an acute curiosity that might turn any moment into aggression. The woman came unwittingly to his rescue.

'We'll have no talk of kings and that here. I owe allegiance to no king but God and I ask for no protection from any either. If any man gets through the demons of the marsh and lands at my door, then I reckon God has tested him and found him honest. If by the wit of the dark one a dishonest scoundrel should wash up here, then my husband's long seax will make sure they get a final reckoning.'

She gave them both a quelling look and Dan was glad to take refuge in silence. He had gained knowledge of the language but nothing else. He now knew that there was a king and that a man with a sword might be expected to serve in his army. Somehow he had to avoid getting caught up in the affairs of this world. He wanted to find Ursula and hoped that she had enough magic to raise the Veil and get them back home. That was the limit of his ambition. He should not have allowed himself to be persuaded to raise the Veil. Damn Taliesin. It was his fault.

The woman handed him a pottery beaker of ale and he drank it gladly. It was not strong and he was familiar with the taste – barley, malt and herbs, a hearty combination that he preferred to the sweetness of mead and the bitterness of wine. He smiled his thanks and raised his pot to his hostess, who had bought him time. He obviously needed some story to account for his presence in the middle of the marsh, but his brain resolutely refused to provide one. Why was the other man here? He was not the woman's husband, that had become clear when she'd complained about the cakes. Perhaps he was an outsider like himself. If the woman was to be believed and it was not easy to cross the marsh, was he some criminal escaping justice? Dan looked at the man more closely. He was dressed plainly, though his tunic was fastened with a finely worked brooch which might have been gold. He wore boots of soft leather, and though his hands were calloused his fingernails were clean and Dan thought he could detect a paler area of skin at the base of several of his fingers, as if he was accustomed to wearing rings. A rich man, perhaps, fallen on hard times, or a renegade warrior who'd had to bribe his way out of some mess? Dan did not know and speculation was fruitless. So long as the man did not hinder him in his search for Ursula, their paths need not cross again. Dan sipped his ale slowly. He didn't want the woman to feel she had to give him more. Hospitality seemed to be an obligation here and he'd rather not abuse it. It would be better to look for Ursula with food in his belly and it would be safer by far if he could stay in this woman's homestead until dawn.

The woman's husband arrived a little while later, stinking of sweat and swine. He was not pleased to find his hearth crowded by two strange men.

'They can stay. I'll not have a man's death on my conscience, but I'll take their blades for safe keeping. I don't want us murdered in our beds. They could be Danes for all we know. They could feed us both to their demon gods and no one would be the wiser.'

He made no effort to keep his voice low, so that neither Dan nor his companion had any doubt that they were not entirely welcome. The husband was a big man and Dan found himself automatically evaluating his likely ability in a fight. He was probably in his late thirties and he moved a little stiffly, as if already suffering with arthritis. Dan was confident that he could take him if necessary, with or without his sword. The magic of this world worked slowly, but just as he found himself able to speak the language of this land, he found himself certain that should he need to fight, he would. His earlier lethargy and exhaustion had disappeared, which was as well because he could see no easy way of finding Ursula or of finding out what he needed to know to escape the business end of a seax.

~ Chapter Eleven ~

Ursula did not sleep, but in the dark night explored the country with the eyes of a fox, a badger and a tawny owl. She could not contemplate sleep. There was too much power burning through her; she could not rest. She experienced the dawn through the senses of a thousand eyes and ears, felt the damp earth through paw and claw and talon and was intoxicated by the rich and ever-changing scents and stinks that were carried by the wind. She heard the tread of the hunter's boots and sensed his hunger for the kill long before he arrived. She knew the fear of the deer as she ran leaping over Ursula's own inert form and heard the hiss of the arrow as it struck home. The pain too she knew, only she pulled away quickly to share in the exultation of the hunter. He forgot the hind and fell to his knees when he saw her and bowed his head in supplication.

She saw herself through his eyes and he was stunned by what he saw. She lay encased in a latticework of roots, at the base of a huge ash tree. Her eyes were closed like one asleep and in repose her strong-featured face had the kind of beauty she had always admired. Her hair was so pale a blonde that it shone as if it were somehow lit from within. Her unearthly appearance took Ursula by surprise, although it no longer mattered to her in any real way. She could change her face should she wish to as easily as she once changed her clothes. She saw that to the hunter she seemed larger than life, taller than any real woman and unblemished – like a goddess. He named her to himself as Freya, Goddess of Love and Fertility, one gifted in witchcraft and beloved of warriors, the Goddess who takes half of the warriors dead in battle to her own hall. Ursula found this identification briefly amusing. Once, she'd had much to do with battles and with the reaping of death. She was amused too by the man's terror and awe – both seemed ridiculous to her . . . Then she was distracted by the sudden flight of a flock of birds and joined them with her mind.

She was only distantly aware of the man calling to his companions and making preparations to carry her body away from its bower of roots. It was not quietly or easily done. The roots had to be carefully cut with an axe and the hunter was sweating before he was finished – with exertion and with the fear of accidentally hitting her and incurring the wrath of an important divinity. Ursula was not so lost to common sense that she did not surround herself with a barrier of power to protect herself should the axe slip.

The hunter's companions were equally overwhelmed by Ursula's presence and helped him haul the deer's carcass away. They butchered it nearby. Ursula was not interested in watching that; she was not much interested in butchery of men or animals – it was all too familiar to her.

After a while the hunter returned with yet more men – young, proud men, armed with axes and dressed in war gear. Some of it was very fine – mail shirts and iron helms, thick woven cloaks fastened by gold brooches, and round, painted shields. These were important men, warriors, predators. It showed in the way that they moved. She was surprised that they too bowed to her where she lay, surrounded by unseasonal flowers and dressed in her blue polyester school sweatshirt. These new important men had brought servants or slaves to help bear her away. They had a wooden cart and horses. The horses were good specimens but weary and thirsty. She lost herself in them for a moment. She felt the burden of the cart for an instant before she pulled away. The cart was decorated with leaves and berry-bearing branches, with gold belts and silver chains, with chalices and church plate, jewelled boxes and decorated crucifixes – with all the wealth that could be found at short notice to carry the Goddess home. It was all plundered treasure; Ursula knew that and did not care. What had she to do with such things?

The men spoke a language that was new to her, but it was easy enough for her to learn it. It was, in any case, clear that they took delight in the riches in the cart and that they thought they had come by it legitimately by the killing power of their weapons and the honest greed of their hearts. They honoured her. She found herself unmoved by their care for her inert body. No one dared touch her with their bare hands and those that accidentally brushed their naked skin against hers jumped away, burned. They sang as they lifted her reverently to the cart and carried on singing as the cart bore her through the woods. Their songs had an unfamiliar rhythm, which held her attention for a while because they were quite unlike the songs she had heard in Arturus's court. She hadn't much of an ear for music, but when the hunter added his voice to the song even she could tell that his singing was very bad, off-key and discordant. She turned her attention away, glad to explore further afield. For all her power she could only listen to one thing at once. She wondered what it would be like to split her consciousness. It was probably possible, but she was a little afraid to make it happen. There was time enough for all that later. She let herself drift away from all that anchored her to her body, becoming lost in the thoughts of a wild hare, and then eventually, exhausted by so much experience, she fell into a kind of a doze. Waking up was disorienting. She forgot about the magic for a moment and opened her eyes to find herself looking straight up into the grey gaze of a warrior. Fear flashed across his face and he called out:

'She has woken!'

Ursula was aware of a crush of people all around her, while a bonfire burned not far away. The stars were briefly lost in the smoke from the flames and the pungency of woodsmoke was everywhere. Her eyes watered.

She could not easily turn her head, as it was wedged in place by a number of hard-edged objects. It was as well that magic heated her from within because the night was a cold one and she could see her breath in the crisp air. For the briefest of moments Ursula was panicked by the sudden press of men staring at her, their faces curious, frightened, awestruck. She started to pay attention to them. They were all of them alert to any danger she might pose but not one of them backed away. They were ready for whatever she or anyone else might throw at them and that caught her interest. She wondered where she was and when. They were strangers to her, she knew that, and yet they were familiar; their readiness was familiar as was their suppressed violence. She had fought with men like these once, or maybe she had fought against them. It didn't much matter.

The crowd parted to let one of the richly dressed warriors she had seen before make his way to her side. He was young, not much older than she was, and he had a fierce, hawk's face – not handsome but arresting. When he spoke, it was without humility. He was a warrior and feared nothing. She liked that.

'Goddess.' He bowed a quick bob of the head, nothing more – an acknowledgement that she was important and powerful. 'We are honoured by your presence among us. How can we welcome you to our camp? We are merely a hunting party and our riches are elsewhere, but whatever we have is yours.'

Ursula wondered what response she could give. It was hard to collect her thoughts, which kept flitting round the camp like some hyperactive demon. She was in the fire, dancing in the flames, then flying overhead, hooting with an owl and then back lying on a fur-lined cloak, staring at a man with a proud face. Then her stomach rumbled in a most ungoddess-like way and she realised that she was very hungry – and thirsty too. Her body felt weak, worn out, leached of all its natural health.

Everyone was staring at her. There was little sound but the clink of belt knives and coin pouches as men jostled one another to get a closer look. She licked her lips and used magic to give her voice a little extra resonance. There was no reason to sound as feeble as she felt.

'I am hungry. I would have you bring food and drink.' She kept it short and demanding. She wasn't sure what a goddess might say and she didn't feel inclined to explain her true nature, whatever that was . . . She was an Ursula not a Freya, she knew that, and she had not always been in full possession of this power. There was more that she knew: she had not always been in this place; there were people she had left behind. She wasn't very good at concentrating on anything for very long. The magic coursed through her with all the force and relentlessness of waves crashing on a shore. Magic swept her away and she was powerless to resist its endless distractions. She closed her eyes and lost herself in the mysterious life of worms. Food was brought, roasted venison and a hare, bread and berries and a golden chalice of ale. It smelled enticing but she forgot that she was hungry. She got lost again, following wherever the wild, restless impulses of magic took her – away from her body, away from herself.

~ Chapter Twelve ~

The light from the fire had all but died out when Dan woke. He had always been the kind of person who moved from sleep to full wakefulness in the space of a heartbeat. He knew at once something was wrong. He listened. Someone was moving around. He reached for Bright Killer and then remembered: the householder had taken it. The glowing embers of the dying fire reflected in the dull gleam of a blade, the glint of steel in the darkness. Dan could just make out the bulky form of a man leaning over his sleeping companion. Dan did not pause to think but was on his feet and pulling the man away as soon as he realised what was happening. The man was big, strong. He grunted his surprise at Dan's sudden arrival and turned towards him, his teeth bared like an animal's, a patch of lesser darkness in the shadows.

'What are you doing?' Dan hissed, but the man's intentions became very clear when he raised his seax to strike Dan. The man did not speak but lurched forward. Dan saw the knife and launched himself at the bigger man in the same instant, using his weight to drive him backwards so that he overbalanced. He hit the ground hard and groaned and cursed, making it easier for Dan to find the man's sword arm and to stamp hard on his wrist so that the man released the seax. In one swift motion Dan had it in his own hand. He felt better for holding a blade, however unfamiliar. His heart was beating too fast and his blood was up. He was on the brink of entering the dark place he found when he had fought as the Bear Sark, a berserker. He was not there yet, but even so it would have been very easy to stab the man with his own knife, it was difficult not to. He had been well schooled in the art of warfare and mercy was not a part of that training. He had to force himself to lower his arm to let the seax rest by his side. The encounter had taken less than a minute. Dan was breathing heavily: he was fit and strong but a fight was something different and he was out of practice. He had hoped to have remained that way.

Dan was suddenly aware that the woman who had offered them her hospitality had lit a tallow candle. The householder lay on the ground groaning. Dan suspected that he might have broken his wrist. The packed earth of the floor was hard and he had not been gentle.

'What are you doing? You abuse my hospitality?' The woman's fury was tempered by the sight of her husband's seax in Dan's hand.

'Your husband was about to stab . . .' Dan hesitated.

'Aelfred,' his companion supplied, getting to his feet. 'Aelfred, King of Wessex, in your debt.'

The woman gave a little cry and swayed as if she might faint, but she was made of stronger stuff than that. Instead of fainting, she took two bold steps towards Aelfred and kneeled at his feet.

'Begging your pardon, Sire. My husband is a good God-fearing man, but worried for our safety in such dangerous times. He mistook you for a bandit.'

Aelfred shook his head. 'You offered me hospitality, for which I am grateful, but attempted murder at your hearth? That I cannot easily forgive.'

'I wasn't going to kill you!' the householder protested, supporting his right wrist with his left hand, 'You have a gold brooch on your tunic. I would have taken it to sell at Aller – there's things we need. Any man can claim to be King – how can we know you tell the truth?' He struggled to his feet, levering himself up on his elbows and wincing as this movement jarred his wrist. 'By the Cross, how am I going to work now?'

Dan could not quite bring himself to feel sorry for a man who had just tried to kill him. He raised his sword arm so that neither the householder nor his wife could fail to see that he still had the weapon and was prepared to use it. He felt his heart sink at the realisation that in saving a king he had once more put himself at the heart of important events. He did not want to get involved with this King Aelfred. He wanted to find Ursula and slip quietly away, home. If he stayed in this world, he knew it would not be long before he killed again. His berserker madness was still in him, a great venomous viper of violence coiled in his brain and ready to strike: that frightened him more than anything else.

The King paused before answering the man, then

reached inside his tunic and pulled out a fine leather pouch from which he produced a seal ring. 'This is the ring of the King of Wessex.'

He held it out to show the woman, who still kneeled before him. She brought the candle up closer to her face so that she could view the object more clearly. Dan could see only that it was a very large gold ring, shaped like a bishop's mitre and elaborately worked. It seemed to satisfy the woman.

'Have mercy, for the love of our Saviour,' she whispered. 'It is a hard life here. We have been flooded twice these last years and the swine drowned. Our son died of fever last Candlemas. My husband has not been the same since.'

The householder glowered at Dan and Dan knew he was weighing up his chances of snatching back his knife.

'The word at market is that the old King was killed by the Danes at Christmas or that he fled abroad to throw himself on the mercy of the pope.' The man paused before continuing slowly: 'There's talk that the young Aethelwold, son of the old King Aethelred, is ruling nowadays, with the support of the witan and with the might of all the Danes behind him. Makes no difference to me which King gives out gifts to the rich, there's none coming my way. Who's to say that you're not a Dane with the King's finger in your pouch as well as his ring?'

'I say and I am holding the knife,' Dan said, for no better reason than to shut the man up. He couldn't see why a king should be wandering the marshes alone, but it was not his business. 'Kneel to your King,' he added,

79

reasoning that a kneeling man was less likely to attack him.

'Now would be a good time for you to retrieve our weapons,' the King said mildly and the woman got to her feet and reluctantly fished them out of the wood store near the door. Dan suspected that his sword was worth a good deal more than a gold brooch. He had little doubt that if he had not woken up he would have been the householder's next target. He glanced at Aelfred and wondered if he had been injured somehow before Dan had rescued him; he was pale and sweating despite the chill within the house. Nonetheless he kept his voice steady.

'We will need food before we leave at dawn and the use of your boat. While we eat I will consider what is to be done with you.'

The woman nodded and Dan watched her carefully: he did not like accepting food off those he did not trust.

It was good to strap on his sword belt and to feel the comforting weight of Bright Killer at his hip. Aelfred too seemed relieved to have his own seax at his belt. The woman banked up the fire and fetched oats from a sack indoors and milk from a pail kept cool outside. There was nothing to sweeten the porridge and while Dan had grown used to sugarless food the last time he had been through the Veil, it tasted strange to someone who had readjusted to a twenty-first century diet. He ate nothing until the woman and her husband tasted their food and he noted that Aelfred did the same.

They ate in silence, the only sound coming from the flames and the scrape of bone spoons on wooden bowls.

Dan craved a cup of tea with two sugars, but had the strong feeling that it would be a while before he tasted that again.

By the time they had finished eating, the first feeble shafts of daylight could just be seen at the edge of the homestead's wooden door. Dan dressed again in his inadequate school uniform. He saw Aelfred staring at the crest of his school badge which was printed on to his blue sweatshirt. He stared at Dan's trainers equally curiously. They were not practical footwear for marshland – they still squelched slightly when he put his foot inside.

'Your boat?' Aelfred asked the householder pointedly.

'Sir, without that we'll struggle to keep body and soul together . . .'

'You may treat it as wergild for your attempt on my life. You are lucky not to pay a higher price.' Aelfred glanced at Dan's sword meaningfully. Dan thought he looked ill.

'You may return his weapon,' Aelfred instructed Dan, who gave the seax hilt first to the householder's wife: he did not trust the householder.

As Aelfred swept out of the small house with as much kingly splendour as one man in a shabby cloak could manage, Dan kept a wary eye on the woman and unsheathed his sword. 'You should know that if your husband tries anything I will kill him.'

She nodded as though what he told her was not news. 'Is he really the King?'

Dan shrugged. 'Maybe.'

She looked miserable. 'Then I hope he cannot find his way here again. Here.' She handed him an old much-mended cloak. 'We are not heathens and we have good reason not to trust strangers. There are people living hereabouts who've had to run for their lives. The Danes take what they want and there are other bandits newly come to the Levels who aren't any better. These are hard times. Perhaps you could tell your Lord that I meant no harm.'

Dan took the cloak gratefully. The draught through the open door told him that the morning air was damp and chill.

'I am new to his service,' he said carefully, 'but I will tell him of your kindness.' He did not know what else to say. He did not want Aelfred to be his Lord. He nodded a goodbye, not knowing quite what to think about the woman, then he ducked his head under the low doorway and followed King Aelfred outside. One way or another he'd had enough of kings.

~ Chapter Thirteen ~

When Ursula chose to look again through her own eyes, it was late afternoon and someone had taken away the food offering she had neglected to eat and replaced it with oatcakes drizzled with honey. Ursula found that her mouth began to water at the smell of such sweetness. She felt strangely light-headed – perhaps from hunger – and her body felt stiff and wooden when she finally decided to sit up. She was like some beginner puppeteer who hadn't quite worked out which string to pull. She lifted the wooden platter of cakes by the force of her will and set it beside her and then did the same with the gold chalice of milk. She was thirstier than she realised and almost spilled the milk down her chin. Her hands were shaking and her muscles felt weak, though the magic in her burned as strongly as ever.

The guards who were watching her – young men of around her own age – looked worried when she moved and one of them ran away. She guessed he had gone to take a message that she had woken again. She ate the cakes too quickly and felt slightly sick but a little less feeble. She made a mental note to remember to eat and drink. She was confident that the magic would keep her alive but the idea of being little more than an animated skeleton was not very appealing. She got awkwardly to her feet only to find that her legs were numb and she might have stumbled but that she kept herself upright with power. She floated a centimetre above the ground then gradually trusted her weight to her legs.

There was a distant commotion as the guard brought everyone from camp to see the Goddess eat. Ursula was tempted to escape mentally if not physically, but she did not. She needed to eat something else and she knew that should she ask these people would provide it.

The crowd clustered around her, keeping a respectful distance. Ursula made her blonde hair longer and thicker, made herself taller still and made her eyes flash with emerald fire. The crowd looked interested. The warrior who appeared to be their leader stepped forward and beckoned to one of the men who were bearing gifts – women's clothes and gold, roast venison and ale. At his leader's signal the gift-bearer stepped forward and Ursula got a closer look at his offering.

'Lady, Goddess, we have brought you more gifts and will be able to bring more still should you grant us your help in our campaign.'

The gift-bearer, a young blond man, laid out the clothes for her on the platform that had been her bed. There was a long fine linen shift and blue stockings, scarlet leather boots, which would be several sizes too small, a long violet overdress decorated with gold and silver braid, jewelled clasps and a thick fur-lined cloak. It would have been wonderful had she not been so tall. She made no move to take any of it. A second man made the food offerings, which she did take. She beckoned to him and noted the way his hands trembled when he gave them to her. She did nothing to put any of them at their ease – it did not occur to her. She tore at the venison with eager fingers and stuffed it into her mouth with no concern for appearances: the meat tasted wonderful. The crowd watched silently until she had devoured all that had been given for her and drunk the ale. She did not know if they had enough for themselves so she nodded her thanks. The crowd seemed pleased.

She then waved in the direction of the clothes so that one by one the garments were lifted in the air, displayed and then dropped back, discarded, on to the pallet. 'This women's stuff is fine enough but not big enough,' she said bluntly. 'I would have instead war gear and men's clothes more suited to my size.' She did not think a goddess would say please. The leader made a hand signal that sent a man scurrying back to camp.

'We have need of your wisdom,' the warrior said. Ursula nodded, unsurprised. She waited.

'We seek a man – an important man. He was once known as King here, before he was deposed. We need to know if he is alive and we need to know where he is.'

Another man emerged, dressed in elaborate robes. He did not speak the same language as the others, so that his servant had to translate. He was angry, frightened; dark

85

emotions swarmed round him like bees.

'I don't hold with witchcraft. The Lord will punish us if you carry on like this. We should not seek out Aelfred with witchcraft. We need not concern ourselves with him in any case. Our rightful King, Aethelwold, has all the support we need. He is, after all, the true heir. Our Lord God may punish us and take away that which we have fairly won if we consort with devils.'

The warrior's response was firm. 'Bishop Aethelred, your god has not seen fit to punish us yet. I am a simple warrior but it seems to me that if he exists at all he is weaker than our Odin and Thor.' There was a warning in his voice as he carried on. 'Guthrum wants Aelfred found and we will use whatever means we want to do that.'

He turned his attention back to Ursula. 'Lady, please help us find this man.'

'You think I am a common witch, some ordinary spae-wife?' The words came to her from the warrior's mind. That was what he hoped, she knew. A real goddess would be troublesome and distract his men from their real task. She also knew that he thought her power too great and her presence too imposing for his hope to be fulfilled.

'No, no, Lady . . .' he began earnestly, concerned that he had upset her. She wondered what he thought she might do. She could read his mind or squeeze his heart until it stopped beating, but she would not. The idea of herself as some kind of goddess was amusing. It was hard for Ursula to take the idea seriously. She laughed. Her laughter took the warrior by surprise.

'Bring me more food and clothing more suitable for a warrior and I will see . . .' she said. She liked the thought of having something to find in all this vastness of multiple impressions that was there for her taking. What did a king smell like? Look like? Was there something special about his thoughts that might draw her to him? It was a crazy idea that she could find one man she had never met just through the power of her magic, but the thought intrigued her.

She quickly became bored of waiting for the men to return and was on the point of leaving the tedious constraints of her body when the warrior leader, Gunnarr, said, 'We slew a Saxon giant not long ago.' His men produced a fine green tunic, a padded jacket, mail, a crested helmet with eye guards, leggings, large boots, a round shield, a spear and a sword. This was much more to Ursula's satisfaction – they looked like they would fit and, though the fabric was not so fine, she knew that it cost this war band much more to kit her out in warrior's gear than to give her women's clothes they had little use for. She might not be a real goddess but she had power and she was not to be palmed off with gaudy finery. She knew without being told that the sword was a gift of great value. More than one of the warriors still assembled round her gave it an envious look.

'And how will I know this sometime King that you want me to find?' Ursula asked as she helped herself to an assortment of roast birds.

'He stinks of sickness, so they say, and of herbs to cover the stench. I have not met him myself. He is not a big man, though handy enough in a fight. He serves the dead god on a tree with much devotion. The bishop claims that he did not serve him well enough. I do not know the details. The bishop thought it wise to negotiate with Guthrum and so raised the King's brother's son to the throne. This man, this former King, if he still lives, will be in hiding from Guthrum's men. If he is dead, then there will be plenty of his holy people all around.' Ursula could hear the contempt in his voice. 'They are always singing dull songs and praying. Guthrum, my kinsman, who is the power behind the throne of this Aethelwold, rules from the Great Hall at Cippenham and would pay well for news of Aelfred.' Gunnarr did not point out that Guthrum would look favourably on the man who would rid him of a potential rival for his easily influenced client king. Ursula understood that he hoped to gain favour with Guthrum any way he could. She had known men like him before somewhere else, and her attention was beginning to wander. The ale was making her feel sleepy and it was good to have a full belly again. She waved her arms and was immediately reclothed in the practical warrior's clothes that she favoured. They felt much like the clothes she had worn before – some other time. The speed of her transformation took those assembled by surprise and several of them cried out.

'Leave me now,' she said. She was not very interested by the story of Guthrum and the smelly, sick King. She removed her polished helm and lay down on the bed that had been made for her. She held the sword to discourage any of the warriors from taking back their gift. There was something comforting about holding a sword and something familiar about the male warrior dress. She gave herself up to the magic and let her awareness run free, and yet she could not quite forget the idea of the missing king and found herself seeking him out in all those places where people lived. She soon became entangled in the dreams of warriors, in the hopes of women spinning plans as they spun wool and in the worries of farmers frightened for their crops, fearful of the weather and the hungry hordes of foreigners who plundered and did not plough. Even Ursula, more interested in soaring with the eagles and running with wolves, could not help noticing that most of the people whose thoughts she glimpsed were afraid.

She found the King almost by accident while sharing the flight of a heron over the waterways and marshland of a drowned landscape. His thoughts were more full of fear than most and he projected a powerful sense of guilt and burning regret. It was the strength of his feeling that made Ursula notice him and drew her to investigate more closely. He was with another man, who pulsed a little of magic and who frightened her, reminding her of other people she'd known but couldn't remember – people of power if not of magic, people of will and focused passion. She was afraid of entering his consciousness. Something about him reminded her of shame. Both the one-time King and his companion made her feel confused and uncomfortable and she returned to her body in a kind of panic.

Gunnarr was keeping vigil by her body. When she opened her eyes, his steely gaze was the first thing she saw. 'The man you seek is to the west in the marsh, where the herons fly,' she said, and the warrior smiled.

~ Chapter Fourteen ~

The burly householder led Dan and King Aelfred across the small, dry patch of land on which he had built his homestead. The land was virtually an island, surrounded on three sides by reed beds and marsh and on the fourth by a sluggish, grey river swathed in a grey mist: everywhere was covered in mist – it seemed to be the island's natural condition.

The boat was more of a narrow raft with a pole for punting. It didn't look very robust.

'Is that it?' The King wasn't impressed. 'You may leave us,' Aelfred said, and their surly companion slunk off, still clutching his injured wrist. The look he gave Dan made him shiver; it would be as well if he never met him again.

The moment their reluctant host had gone, Aelfred fell to the ground clutching his stomach and was violently sick.

'Are you all right, Sire? Are you poisoned?'

Aelfred, spluttering, shook his head and wiped his mouth on some grasses.

'No, no. It is a sickness I have had for some time –

God's punishment for my failures and my sins.' Dan helped him to his feet. 'I need to get back to my family and my men. This trip was a pointless indulgence that could have got me killed but for your timely intervention. You have my thanks and perhaps one day, if I survive and can fight back against the invaders, the thanks of all of Wessex.' He brushed away Dan's supporting arm. 'Thank you. I am well.'

His face had a greenish look about it and he seemed anything but well. His breath smelled sour and he moved as though he carried a stomach wound. 'You will escort me back to my hearth troops?'

Dan nodded, though it was less of a question than a command. If Aelfred's claim to kingship was justified, he did not appear to be king of very much, but he spoke like a king and Dan felt helpless to refuse his request: perhaps one good turn might deserve another and this King might help him find Ursula.

Dan was very uncertain stepping on to the raft, which wobbled worryingly. Swimming was the one sport he'd been bad at in school and he knew just how cold and treacherous this water was. It took him a moment to get his balance right and then he helped the King aboard. Aelfred's grip was firm and, although he was not a big man, his arms had a sinewy strength. Sick though he was, Dan realised it would be a mistake to underestimate him.

'Steer into the sun as far as possible and you will come to my camp,' Aelfred said, sitting himself down carefully so as to counterbalance Dan's weight.

The mist muffled everything and the only sound came

from Dan's amateurish attempts to punt. It was harder than he imagined and he was lucky not to fall in when his pole got stuck in the mud. Dan's whole attention was taken with keeping them afloat and moving in broadly the right direction. The sky was the colour of cotton wool, uniformly clouded so that the sun appeared only as a pale golden haze. He headed towards the haze.

Aelfred did not speak for a while. The sickness appeared to have left him weakened and Dan did not much like the sound of his breathing, which was uneven; he suspected that the King was in a lot of pain and was only grateful that this time he did not share it. When Dan had served King Arturus, he had felt the pain of those around him as if it were his own: he never wanted to know that agony again. Even though he had lost that gift, or curse, of total empathy he was still sensitive to the moods of others and he could tell the King was very deeply troubled. He was about to ask him a little more about his situation when suddenly a distant jangle of metal made him stop punting.

Carefully, so as not to rock the raft, he crouched down low and clumsily got himself into a kneeling position. Aelfred seemed startled by Dan's action – he had been so lost in thought he did not appear to have heard the sound. Dan put his finger to his lips to signal silence and carefully adjusted his sword belt so that it didn't bang against the wood as he changed his weight. Somewhere a horse whickered and stomped. There were voices close by – male voices – and Dan's heart started to thunder in his chest.

As silently as possible he eased Bright Killer out of its scabbard, lifting its hilt up slightly; he was afraid that the damp conditions might make it stick. Aelfred pointed towards the shelter that lay under the low branches of a stumpy tree and the two of them hauled at the tree's low branches to pull themselves out of sight. Dan wrapped himself more tightly in the cloak the woman had given him; it was a faded red brown and effective camouflage for the vivid blue of his sweatshirt. The sunlight was finally beginning to burn away the mist and Dan could see that unless they were careful and lucky they would be all too visible. He hoped he never had to fight on a raft.

The mist did strange things to his concept of direction and even of distance. He was not at all sure of the exact location of the voices, though he strained to work it out. Dan could not at first understand what the men were talking about either. They were not speaking Aelfred's language – whatever that was – nor any of the other languages Dan knew. Remembering what had happened when he'd first met the King he forced himself to close his eyes and let his mind drift. It was very difficult to relax as the slightest shift in his weight threatened to overturn the raft. He forced himself to release the bunched muscles of his neck, to find his place of calm but not his place of madness. When he opened his eyes a moment later, he could see Aelfred staring at him curiously. He tried again. This time something seemed to click into place in his mind – like the moment of clarity when you finally grasped a difficult lesson in school. When the men spoke again, he understood.

There were two voices, one deeper than the other.

'Where do we look?'

'Gunnarr said he was in the western marshes, but you could hide a fleet in here. We need a boat, not a horse. The mounts will break a leg for sure if we ride through this midden.'

'What do we do?'

'Find a boat and come back.'

Dan hardly dared to breathe until he was certain that they had ridden out of earshot. It occurred to him that their departure might be a trick, so he waited longer still.

'You understood them?' Aelfred said accusingly.

Dan nodded.

'You are a Dane?'

Dan shook his head.

'Then whom do you serve? The sign on your breast – is it the crest and symbol of your Lord?' Aelfred sounded almost angry, affronted that Dan served some other unknown lord.

Dan tried to find the words to explain without actually explaining. He had been doing a lot of that lately.

'I have a . . .' He paused. 'I have a gift for languages, it is true, but I am not a Dane. I serve no lord here, or rather the Lords I have served are long dead.'

'You left your Lord to die?'

'No. Yes . . . I am not your enemy and I am not on the side of your enemies. I am a stranger here. I am looking for my companion and when I find her – him – I will leave. I am not involved in whatever is going on here.'

Aelfred did not appear satisfied, but turned to more

practical matters.

'They are looking for someone.'

'Yes.'

'Did they say who?'

'No, but surely if you are King they must be looking for you?'

'If?' Aelfred's voice took on the edge of steel and Dan found himself worrying again about fighting on the unstable raft. He should be able to beat the King should it come to a fight, but Dan did not want to land in the icy water. He was careful to sound conciliatory.

'I'm sorry, but I am a stranger here and . . .' He let his voice tail away. He did not want to get involved in the politics of kings; it was always dangerous. He wanted to find Ursula and get home. He changed tack. 'I do not doubt that you are a king, but it is strange that you're here without a retinue nor even an armed guard to protect you.'

Aelfred sighed. 'It was a foolish, prideful whim to want to be alone – away from my family and my advisors and even my priests.' He did not look at Dan. 'I wanted solitude, time to think . . . Men I trusted betrayed me and we were lucky to escape with our lives. Now my men are all so fearful.' He paused as if about to say more, but stopped. 'My responsibilities and my mistakes weigh too heavily on me. I need to be bold and yet . . .'

'So did it help to get away?' Dan thought that he should perhaps add some kind of honorific, but before he could think of the right one, Aelfred was already answering.

'Perhaps you have not heard, but Guthrum and his great heathen army attacked us as we celebrated Twelfth Night.' His face as he turned towards Dan was full of pain. He appeared surprised when Dan shook his head. 'You must truly be a stranger if you have not heard this bitter tale. My trusted ealdorman, Wulfhere of Wiltshire, and other ealdormen of Hampshire and Dorset, men who have benefited greatly from my gift-giving . . .' His voice shook and he took a moment to calm himself. 'These men conspired with my archbishop, Aethelred, who has accused me of much evil, to usurp my place upon the throne of Wessex and replace me with my brother's child – a pawn and client king who will lend Guthrum and his Danish heathens legitimacy while they ransack my kingdom, my people, and undo all that my grandfather and father have achieved.' His voice dropped to a whisper and he shook his head angrily. 'I was so foolish. I did not see it coming. I believed that all right-thinking men would choose Christian freedom over subordination to heathen pirates. But I was wrong. The Danes have wealth enough to buy the services of a puppet king. They have done it in Mercia and Northumbria. I had not thought the ealdormen who have served my family would let them do it here. For now I have no kingdom but this.'

He stretched out his hand to encompass the grey river, now bright with sunlight dappling the wind-rippled surface. The mist had gone as if it had never been and the sun shone from a clear sky; the windswept wilderness looked wild and eerily beautiful. Aelfred seemed to think so too because he added, 'And this is better than nothing, is it not?' He grinned and suddenly looked different: bolder and a good deal less ill. 'All I can say is that I'm not ready to give up. I may have been foolish, vain, ungodly and complacent, but with God's help I may not yet be defeated.'

Dan found himself grinning back. What he did not need was to get involved in a hopeless fight against the odds, against enemies not his own, for a king with no assets beyond a cheerful grin, but he could feel himself becoming more involved by the second. Aelfred's tale was bound to be more complicated than his simple summary, but Dan could sense the truth in what he said.

Without saying a word, he and Aelfred manoeuvred the raft away from the bank and Dan started punting the King back to his men.

~ Chapter Fifteen ~

The sunshine seemed to cheer Aelfred up and he started to talk, or rather to ask questions – about Dan's companion, about Dan's own origins. Dan was as cagey as possible and decided to refer to Ursula as if she were a man. He thought it would be simpler that way. He would describe her as his male companion, his comrade-in-arms, and if she had any magic in this world he knew that she would be able to play the part of a male warrior – she had done it so many times already. The difficulty was that he could not then ask Aelfred for his help in finding a tall blonde woman who may have shown signs of magical power.

'I do not understand how you separated,' Aelfred said. 'Surely you must have some idea as to where he went?' Dan shook his head. He did not want to embroider a lie. He wanted to say as little as possible and lapsed into a moody silence. She could be anywhere. Perhaps if she had magic she might be able to find him – if she wanted to. The thought that she might not want to ate away at him. She had not been herself when she ran through the Veil.

He had no idea what she might do, and with Ursula anything was possible.

After a while the river narrowed to nothing and Dan and Aelfred had to carry the raft between them and make their way over bogland. They had to stop often while the King dry-retched. He walked like a man in agony.

'Should I not go on ahead to fetch help?' Dan asked. His arms ached from the punting and the raft carrying. Although he was gym fit and strong he was not used to continuous hard physical work. Aelfred was breathing in shallow bursts and his face had turned grey with fatigue and pain. 'No. You will be killed. I must come with you or they may think you kidnapped me.'

'You didn't leave without telling anyone?' Dan asked, unable to keep the incredulity from his voice. In his experience kings were not inclined to wander hostile territory on their own. Aelfred bent double with some kind of stomach cramp.

'Yes. May God forgive me. I had not planned on being away so long. I lost my way.' His face creased as another wave of pain convulsed him.

'This is stupid,' Dan said. 'If you lie on the raft, I can perhaps pull you across the marsh.'

'No. I am all right. The pain will . . . pass . . . in a moment.' But Dan had already unstrapped his sword belt and the leather belt that held up his school trousers and was trying to come up with a way of securing both to the bindings of the raft. The King took off his own belt that held his seax. 'Keep your sword belt. We do not know that the Danes have gone and you may need your blade in a hurry. If I am lying on the raft, I need not sheathe my seax – I can hold it in readiness.' Dan did not argue.

The problem for Dan was not so much that the King was too heavy, but that getting a good enough grip on the belts to get the raft moving was very difficult. Dan tried walking backwards and pulling the raft, then he tried walking forwards, dragging the raft, and neither way worked well. He took off his sweatshirt and tied that to the belts to make them easier to hold, but the knots kept coming undone. He wasted quite a bit of energy cursing under his breath.

The King did not complain as Dan jolted and dragged him across the uneven terrain. A couple of times Aelfred almost fell off, but he gripped the wood of the raft with a long claw-like hand and smiled at the craziness of it.

'It is not exactly a king's progress,' Dan said through gritted teeth. His hair was plastered to his head with sweat and his muscles were trembling in revolt at the unnatural movement.

'But it is progress and for that we must thank God.' Aelfred responded.

Dan had little idea of how long he struggled with the raft but when the sun was quite high in the sky he had to stop.

'I'm sorry,' he said, 'I have to rest.' He slumped on the damp ground exhausted.

'That is fine. This is Athelney, my stronghold. My men are here now,' Aelfred said, and suddenly his seax was pointed Dan's way and three armed men emerged from behind low bushes all around him.

'What are you doing?' Dan asked, outraged.

'I'm sorry, I do not know your loyalties. You speak Danish. For all I know you could be a spy.'

'I saved your life. I've just dragged you for miles . . .'

Aelfred looked unhappy. 'It grieves me, it truly does, but there is more at stake here than my desire alone. We are on the brink of destruction. I cannot risk all on a stranger I happened upon in a swineherd's cottage.'

Dan could feel his anger growing. He reached for his sword and he batted Aelfred's seax away easily, knocking it from his grasp with the ringing sound of metal against metal. He did not put his sword to Aelfred's neck, though he was tempted. Instead he turned to face the armed men now running towards him.

'My Liege – stay back!' one of them called, and Dan was dimly aware of Aelfred hastening away on unsteady feet. Dan knew Aelfred had not recovered his knife and so dismissed him from his mind. He needed to focus on those who could do him harm – Aelfred was weak and unarmed.

The three men checked their pace when they saw the sword in Dan's hand. They carried spears and long knives but not swords. Dan had no shield but the raft and that was too cumbersome to wield. He pulled it up so that it was on end and dragged it backwards to stand by a small tree, the only thing of any size likely to offer his back some small protection from the spears.

There was a kind of joy in losing himself to his dark place of madness. He felt himself slipping away and did not resist . . . Madness was his only hope and he embraced it – he let himself fall into the place where he and his sword were one.

The first warrior was a lanky man of around twenty. He charged towards Dan and drove his spear over the top of Dan's makeshift defence. He had to come too close in order to get his spear over the top. Dan, cowering below the wall that the raft had made, sprang up and his powerful upward sword thrust found the unprotected area under the man's arm. He screamed in shock and pain and Dan pulled the spear from his unresisting hand and turned it on the second warrior, who had circled the raft to come upon him from the rear. Dan's speed startled the man who lost his footing on the uneven ground. That instant's loss of concentration as he tried to regain his balance cost him his life. Dan thrust the barbed point of the spear straight at the man's throat and pushed. The man toppled backwards. Dan placed his foot on the man's torso, to give him the necessary leverage, and pulled the spear free. Now that he only had one enemy to defeat, Dan abandoned his position and ran to do battle with the third man.

'Stop!' King Aelfred staggered from his safe place and screamed at Dan. There was a moment in which Dan might have killed him too, but he was not yet so far gone in his madness that he could not hear and understand. Dan lowered neither his sword nor his spear but he stopped running.

'There is no need to kill Eadric. They did not intend to kill you, only to take you prisoner.' He was paler than ever and appeared shocked by the swift turn of events.

Dan was breathing heavily and, now that his brain

began to clear, was beginning to wonder why he had allowed his madness the upper hand.

'Sire, you pointed your knife at me and set three armed men on me – what did you expect me to do? I am a warrior. I fight and I kill.'

'I can see that,' Aelfred said, 'and these deaths are also on my conscience. Will you drop your weapons?'

Dan dropped the gore-splattered spear on the ground. He did not much like spears. He wiped his stained sword on the grass, dried it carefully on his sweatshirt and sheathed it.

The remaining enemy let his spear and shield clatter to the ground and by the look on his face, pale beneath his helmet, was not sorry to let it end that way.

'I made a mistake in trying to take you prisoner,' Aelfred said quietly, 'and I have no doubt that my men thought you wished me harm.'

'I did not wish you harm, but attempting to have a man killed is not a good way of encouraging his respect or his loyalty – a true king should know that.'

Aelfred winced visibly: 'You are right. Please accept my apologies. I still do not have your name and title.'

Dan hesitated. The adrenalin that had sustained him in the fight left him and he felt weak, drained and full of remorse. He had not wanted to kill again. 'My name is Dan and I have no title,' he lied. In Macsen's world they had called him the Bear Sark, the berserker, but that was not a title he wished to deserve again.

'I will send men to bring these fallen warriors back for a Christian burial. Dan, let me introduce you to what remains of my court.'

Dan averted his eyes from the corpses that had been the price of his welcome and followed the sickly King across the marsh.

~ Chapter Sixteen ~

'I hope you have not arranged any other surprises,' Dan said. Bright Killer was in its scabbard, but as they progressed across open marshland he unsheathed it. Though he was in control of himself, he was angry at what Aelfred had tried to do and when he was angry his madness lay close by. The guard raised his spear and stepped between the King and Dan, but he looked frightened and Dan knew that the guard's fear would do half his job for him if it came to the fight. A small part of him was strangely content to be back in a world where his gift for brutality did not condemn him.

'There may be archers,' Aelfred said reluctantly. 'If you do not sheathe your sword, you will be killed for treachery.'

'If I sheathe this sword, a bowman or this spearman here may take a shot at me and I'll be dead anyway,' Dan said evenly, making no attempt to put away his sword. When he held it, all his doubts and uncertainties faded: he knew who he was. Already he had begun to distance himself from the death of the two hapless enemies. He could not afford to dwell on such things: keeping himself alive took up all his attention. 'I would like some guarantees that you will not have me killed once you are with your men. I have saved your life and could kill you now if I wanted to – surely that is proof enough that I am not your enemy. How many warriors do you have that you can afford to lose one like me?'

That at least seemed to get through to the King. He paused to speak – it seemed as if he could not walk and speak at once and was again struggling for breath.

'You're a warrior, I can see that, but you fight like a Dane – without mercy or conscience. I do not think I can trust you.'

Dan's sword arm moved almost of its own volition in the direction of the King's throat. The guardsman raised his spear. Dan ignored both it and him and met Aelfred's eyes.

'How can I prove to you that I am not a spy?'

Aelfred shook his head. 'You cannot. Not here. Not now. Unless I ask God to put you to the test.'

'What do you mean?'

'If you are truly innocent, and no spy, and we were to put you in the lake, yonder, God would accept your body into the depths. If you are guilty, he would reject you, allowing you to float.'

'So if I am innocent, I drown?'

'Of course not! We tie a rope around you and haul you up.'

Dan thought about it for a moment. It seemed ludicrous to him and of course it could be a trick, but

Aelfred's expression was earnest. Dan was still more sensitive to other people's feelings than he would have liked, so he knew that this was what Aelfred wanted him to do. He was good at sinking – his swimming teacher at school always accused him of having heavy bones. Dan's heart did some sinking of its own as he thought about what it might mean to allow himself to drop to the bottom of a lake, at the mercy of a man who might want him dead, trusting that he would bring him back to the surface. But without Aelfred's trust he would be dead soon anyway. He could not fight every man the King sent against him and there were too many ways of killing by stealth – a knife in the back, poison in the food; it was too risky. He tried to think of some other way to prove his innocence in Aelfred's eyes, but his mind remained unhelpfully blank.

'How can I trust that you will bring me to the surface when I am proved innocent?' Dan said, adding 'Sire' when he saw the look of outrage on the guardsman's face.

'I am the King of Wessex and my oath is binding.'

'I have your oath that if I do this thing, that if I prove my innocence, you will not let your men kill me?'

'You have my oath.'

'And will you help me find my comrade?'

King Aelfred smiled. 'You bargain with me?'

'I do not want to go into the lake. I already know that I'm not a spy.'

The King nodded. 'If God proves your innocence, I will do what I can to help you find your comrade, though you must know that my commitment to restoring my kingdom and atoning for my failings before God is my chief concern.'

'When do we do it?' Dan had to fight to keep his voice steady. He clutched his sword hilt tightly. He was shivering. He would rather face an army on his own than face his own fear of drowning.

'We are almost at the lake. My guardsman here carries a rope with him. The ground is so treacherous that parts of the land can bury a man in mud. We need a stout rope and a strong companion like we need our faith and God's saints.'

Aelfred did not lie and within a few more paces the thin grey line which Dan had taken to be the horizon proved itself to be a broad lake. The water looked grey and cold and as welcoming as a sea of spears. Dan's guts churned. He could see an island, a dark blob of rock and trees, and he wondered if he could perhaps swim for that until it occurred to him that the island was likely to be Aelfred's stronghold.

'He must drop his spear,' Dan said, indicating Aelfred's guard with a nod of his head. When the guardsman reluctantly complied, Dan sheathed his sword and gave the sword belt to Aelfred. 'I want it back.' He paused. 'Sire,' he said bluntly.

'It is too shallow here. We have to go out into the middle of the lake. You must be naked so that the weight of your clothes will not help you sink. It would be easier to do that now.'

Dan felt foolish. He was not shy about nudity but it was

not comfortable to be naked in front of clothed people, particularly clothed people who might want you dead. Reluctantly he removed his sweatshirt and trousers, his polo shirt, socks and trainers. He kept his boxers on even though the King looked at them curiously. When he had made a heap of his clothes, he wrapped himself in the cloak. He was cold and scared and his teeth had begun to chatter. He felt more than naked without the sword – he felt as though he had lost a limb.

Aelfred gave a loud and not very regal whistle and men emerged from the hidden places around the lake, and Dan scooped up his clothes and followed the King to a small boat moored out of sight by the lakeside. Aelfred's arrival caused a furore. It was clear to Dan that many of the men keeping watch on the lake had not expected to see their King again. With his men around him Aelfred immediately straightened his bowed back and began issuing orders. Dan watched to be certain that he did not give Bright Killer away.

The small boat had room only for Aelfred, the oarsman and an extra guard, in addition to the spearman Dan had considered killing. The spearman unwound a length of hemp rope from under his jerkin and tied it roughly around Dan's naked goose-pimpled chest, just under his arms. By the expression on the spearman's face he would have preferred to be tying it around Dan's neck.

Two of Aelfred's men pushed the boat, wading out into the lake until they were knee-deep in mud. The water when it splashed against Dan was icy. A storm was brewing; the bright sunlight of earlier in the day was gone and once they got into the lake a raw wind blew, turning ripples on the water into full-blown waves. The sky darkened and it began to rain. Dan hoped that Aelfred did not take all this as an omen of God's displeasure. Dan wanted to get the trial over with, before the bad weather hit.

'We will do it here,' Aelfred announced, taking the end of the rope and tying it round his own waist and that of the guardsman. Dan had grown a lot in the year or so he had spent since his first trip through the Veil. He might even have been as tall as Ursula – six foot one or so – and he knew that he was getting on for fifteen stone of hard-won muscle because he'd weighed himself in the gym the week before. That was a lot of weight to haul from the bottom of a lake in a storm, particularly if the King had anything to do with the hauling. Aelfred's skin looked green in the strange diffuse light and he didn't look capable of landing a small fish. Dan tried to control his trembling; he did not want to look like a guilty man.

Aelfred began to speak. 'In the absence of a priest I will lead the prayers and you men of my guard, my brothers in Christ, will be witness to what is done here today and no one who has seen what God is about to show us may doubt the truth of this judgement.' He fixed the two guardsmen with an intense glare which prompted them to mutter a hasty 'amen'.

He turned to Dan and spoke to him directly.

'May omnipotent God, who did order baptism to be made by water and did grant remission of sins to men through baptism, may He, through His mercy, decree a right judgement through that water. If, namely, thou art guilty in that matter, may the water which received Him in baptism not receive thee now; if, however, thou art innocent, may the water which received Him in baptism receive thee now. Through Christ our Lord.'

At the 'amen' strong hands pushed Dan into the choppy, white-crested waves. He had to fight a scream as the icy water engulfed him. Fortunately he remembered to keep his mouth closed. The water was so cold his body felt numb almost immediately. His instinct was to swim and in a moment of panic he almost did, but then he found his quiet place, the calm place that overrode panic and helped even his frozen brain to think. He tucked his knees up to his chest, let out an air-bubble stream and sank down through the dark water. The lake was deep – it had to be because it felt as though he were falling down for a long time. Surely the rope could not be much longer. How long could he hold his breath? His lungs hurt, he needed to breathe, he needed someone to pull him back to the surface, but still he remained in the water. At that moment, he knew it was a trick. Aelfred wanted him dead and did not want to lose more men in the process. Dan had been a fool to trust him and now he would never find Ursula, never let his sister Lizzie know how much he loved her, nor tell her that she should not take too much notice of Dad and his depressive moods and bad temper. It hurt to keep his eyes open when there was nothing to see, so he closed them, sealing himself into his own private world. He hoped Ursula would find her own way home – if home was what she wanted to find. He had expected, when he'd thought about it at all, that they would die together fighting somewhere. He would rather have died with Bright Killer in his hand, with Ursula and Braveheart beside him. Perhaps then he would have been less afraid. Maybe it wouldn't hurt too much? Perhaps the cold would let his brain shut down gently? He had always been afraid of water. He had never wanted to drown.

~ Chapter Seventeen ~

Dan must have lost consciousness or something because the next thing he knew he was coughing his guts out in the bottom of the wooden boat, while Aelfred covered him in his cloak.

Dan gulped air and vomited foul-smelling lake water where he lay. He could not stop shivering and his stomach heaved and twisted out of his control. He could not quite believe he had survived.

'God has spoken,' Aelfred said, patting Dan on his shoulder.

Dan still struggled to breathe between his racking coughs. Speaking was out of the question.

'It seems you are to be trusted,' Aelfred said and handed Dan his sword back. Dan nodded an acknowledgement and tried to clutch the sword hilt with what little strength he had, but his muscles refused to obey him and the sword clattered against the sides of the boat. Fortunately Aelfred caught it before it hit the bottom and landed in the bilge water. Perhaps he was supposed to thank Aelfred, but Dan was not feeling particularly grateful to the man who had all but drowned him. Aelfred, on the other hand, was elated. 'You have come to me for a reason, I know you have. You give me hope in these dark days.'

Dan's shivering did not abate, though Aelfred insisted that his guards loan him their cloaks in an effort to warm him up. Dan could not feel his hands or his feet and he did not think that was a good sign.

When they got to the shore, he had to be half carried, half dragged from the boat. He had only the vaguest impression of more marshy land lashed by the rain, of a huddle of people, many of them armoured men, and of the familiar sensation of being only partially tied to his body. He was brought back to himself by the sudden ambush of a monstrous beast. It came from nowhere, running at full pelt, and all but knocked over the men who were carrying Dan. Dan smelled his meaty breath. The animal's rough warm tongue was all over his face, licking his icy fingers, throwing himself at his chest and yelping with uncontrollable delight. It was Braveheart – Dan's war dog and the first good thing to have happened to Dan since he'd crossed the Veil. Dan suddenly found that he could not swallow; something caught in his throat. He struggled to move numb arms and to clasp the huge shaggy head of the dog to his face and breathe in the familiar scent of his wet fur.

If the King was bemused by the way the war dog greeted this apparent stranger, Dan did not notice. He allowed the guard to carry him to some kind of low-roofed, smoke-filled dwelling and to lay him on a straw-filled mattress close to the fire. The dog lay down beside him and his body heat slowly began to thaw Dan out. Dan drifted off to sleep, confident that Braveheart would not allow him to come to any harm.

When the great dog growled, he woke at once. Daylight shone through a vellum window, illuminating the room with a diffuse glow.

'I should have known that it would be you when they said the dog acted strangely.'

It took Dan a moment to realise that the woman speaking in the language of the Combrogi was talking to him. He opened his eyes and was quite unable to recognise the old crone he saw staring at him. One side of her face was horribly scarred, the skin raw and shiny as though she'd been burned. Her hair was hidden beneath a white coif. Only gradually did he realise who she was.

'Rhonwen?'

Her voice was older-sounding and huskier than it had been, but it still possessed a power, a kind of hidden fire that sent shivers down his spine.

'There is no need to talk just now. I hear you were tested by the King. The man is a fool if he tries to drown every new warrior that comes to his service – he's got few enough.' She touched Dan's face tenderly with soft, aged fingers. 'Still so young, so unchanged, and here am I so old – I have lost track of the number of summers I have seen. So many changes to my face – too many places in my memory.'

She patted his hand in a very maternal way and Braveheart licked her arm – not at all what Dan would have expected of Rhonwen. Seeing the look on his face, she cackled.

'The years have changed more than my face, sure enough. Our disagreements are so long in the past that they are scarcely a memory. I wish you no harm, though I fear it is coming your way whether I wish it or not.'

It was strange to hear the Combrogi language again. Stranger still to see Rhonwen, the fierce Combrogi princess who had also been a sorceress. It was hard to see much sign of either role in the woman leaning over him. All trace of her beauty and her regal pride had gone.

'Your body has got chilled through but your dog is giving the best medicine – body heat. I will get you a drink. You won't like it because it is strong-tasting and hot, but I am not trying to poison you – you can be sure of it. I am a herbalist, a healer here, and trusted to tend to the King himself.'

Given the King's evident poor health, Dan was not sure that was a recommendation, but he said nothing – not that he needed to: Rhonwen seemed to have a good idea of what he was thinking. She gave a wry smile. 'The King would be sicker yet without my care.' She disappeared from view, though Dan could hear her humming to herself as she made his drink. There was still a kind of magic in her voice because he found himself drifting off to sleep at its sound, lulled by the melody. Hearing the Combrogi language spoken again made him miss Ursula all the more. He had achieved little since he'd arrived through the Veil, beyond his own survival. He was no nearer to finding her than he had been that first moment when she'd launched herself into the Veil ahead of him.

Braveheart's restlessness alerted Dan to Rhonwen's return. He managed to sit up to accept the clay beaker of liquid.

'Rhonwen, do you still have magic here?'

'Drink this tonic and then I'll tell you.' For a strange and disturbing moment she reminded him of his long-dead mother. He did as he was told and held the steaming clay cup in both hands. The vapour cleared his head at once. The drink was strangely spicy, though not unpleasant compared with his last drink – lake water. He could feel the heat of it suffusing his whole body, starting at the neck and working downwards. Perhaps Rhonwen did still have magic, for he felt much better the moment he'd drunk her tonic.

'The answer is complicated,' she said. 'I can do little practical magic, though I am a good healer and often know what's wrong when others don't. I can see glimpses of the future – never comfortable and rarely helpful – and I can sense magic when it is used by others.' She looked at Dan very directly. 'You know you are still the Bear Sark and that you still have other small magics which may yet surprise you?'

He shrugged. 'Yes, I knew about the berserker thing. I'm hoping I can stay in control of it this time. I can also speak languages I never learned.'

Rhonwen nodded as if that came as no surprise. 'Aelfred is a Christian king, Dan. You must keep such skills secret from him. For him everything comes from God or from demons and he will not believe a berserker rage comes from God. This is a place where it is easy to make enemies. You know that he was betrayed – that his nephew has been elected to the throne and that a small core of former friends have sold out to the Danes? Aelfred is suspicious of everyone, with good cause: everyone who is now his friend may yet be his enemy. These are difficult times. Oh, nothing changes, Dan. Those we used to call the Aenglisc are as bad as the Combrogi for destroying themselves with dangerous allies.'

'These people are the Aenglisc?'

'Their descendants, mingled with old British blood, yes.'

'Is that why you are with Aelfred?'

Rhonwen looked thoughtful. 'I am with Aelfred because I think he is trying to do what Arturus tried to do, to keep civilisation alive in the face of chaos, and because the people who speak this Combrogi tongue had no ears for the wisdom I could offer them.' She pulled a face – something the younger Rhonwen never did. 'When faced with chaos or order, I have learned the hard way that it is better to choose order. These Danes, the ones who came a-Viking, have sacked monasteries and killed good men and women – holy men and women, some of them people that I knew and cared for. They have magic too, I fear: the dark kind. I want nothing more to do with that.'

Rhonwen had sought magical power as ruthlessly as anyone, so Dan was surprised to hear her condemn it. She seemed to lose the thread of her thoughts then, as if distracted by her own memories, but then continued, 'In this world I have chosen Aelfred, though these days my loyalty will give him little more than good herbs to settle his stomach and wise words should he choose to heed them. He hasn't yet.' She stroked Braveheart's head and gave him a morsel of meat, letting him lick her fingers of the fat.

Dan thought for a moment. 'If you can sense magic, you can sense Ursula. Where is she?'

Rhonwen looked serious. 'Yes, I can sense Ursula. She will be taken to Cippenham. She is in very grave danger and for once she may not be able to help herself.'

~ Chapter Eighteen ~

The arrival of Aelfred prevented Dan from demanding more information of Rhonwen. Braveheart barked once, but had forgotten none of his training; when Dan held out his hand to quiet him he stopped immediately and watched Dan adoringly for any further signals. That was as it should be.

Aelfred had changed into a more regal costume. His tunic was of good cloth and held in place with elaborate gold brooches; he was wearing a short green cloak and carrying a sword. He'd lost none of his pallor, and his clothes, though brushed, were still a little grubby. He was accompanied by two guards, a couple of servants and a monk. One of the servants was carrying a small casket.

'It would please me greatly if you would accept this gift of clothing and jewels. I am not yet in a position to be the gift-giver I would choose to be, but I trust you will accept these things from your King.' He turned to the monk. 'You see, Asser? He has the countenance of an angel and not a devil, and if I am not mistaken, he speaks your native tongue.'

Aelfred beamed at Dan, who tried to reorganise his own features into something less stricken; all he could think about was Ursula. He did not have time for social niceties.

'He has bewitched the war dog, Sire,' the monk said shortly in heavily accented Aenglisc.

'Might he not have the gifts of a saint, Asser? Are you not perhaps a little too quick to judge a man whose behaviour has been exemplary?'

Fortunately for Dan, Aelfred appeared to have forgotten the slaughter of two of his men. Asser's expression was cold and Dan found that he could not blame him for it. Dan had no desire to serve Aelfred and he supposed it might have shown.

'My Lord,' Dan began, 'I am most grateful for the honour you do me, but it is my wyrd to seek out my comrade-in-arms and until that is done I can think of nothing else.' Dan found that he was clenching his fist in an effort to wring appropriately courtly language out of his mouth. He wanted to scream, 'I've got to go!' but he had enough experience of kings to know that wouldn't work and could very well delay him – terminally.

'Ah yes, the lost comrade.' Aelfred looked uncomfortable. 'And does he fight with all your skill and passion?'

'And more, Sire.' Dan had a sudden vision of Ursula leading the charge at the Battle of Baddon Hill.

'You already have my word that I will aid you in finding this man in due course, but first I must have your oath and you must be baptised a Christian so I know that your oath will bind and that we are allies in Christ.'

Dan had known from the moment he had discovered Aelfred was King that this moment would come. He had given his oath to Macsen, pledged his sword to Arturus, now he must promise to serve yet another king. And this one seemed the least worthy – a sickly man who'd lost his kingdom and his way. Dan sighed inwardly. Of course, he had no choice.

'You may have my oath, but I have already been baptised a Christian.' He'd seen the pictures: his mother with a curly perm and eighties make-up proudly clutching a pale blob in white satin knickerbockers; his father smiling a smile so wide it all but split his face in two. Asser the monk might have argued, but Aelfred silenced him with a gesture and Dan knelt before Aelfred and bowed his head. He laid his hand on the cross of inlaid gold that formed the hilt of Aelfred's sword and acknowledged Aelfred as his King. He promised that his sword and life would be at Aelfred's service. The words made him shiver; he knew all too well that with this promise given he was bound to Aelfred by all the laws of this world, and even were he to find Ursula, they could not easily leave. He wished that he had never used Taliesin's crystal ball. He did not like where this was going.

Asser's rich, dramatic voice broke through his reverie; he was explaining what would happen if Dan broke his oath. 'If an oath-breaker be slain, let him lie uncompensated . . .' he began. It was clear that a long list of penalties for oath-breaking would follow, but Aelfred seemed to sympathise with Dan's evident impatience and halted the monk before he got into his stride.

'You understand what this oath means?' he asked gently.

Dan nodded. 'And what of my companion?' He tried not to sound too demanding, but Rhonwen's words had convinced him that he had no time to lose.

'There is much to do to regain my kingdom and I have need of a man with your skills . . . I intend to visit Cippenham to see for myself the forces of my enemy and I would have you as my companion and guard. Once that is done, then perhaps it might be possible to find your companion.'

Dan opened his mouth to protest and then closed it again. After all, Rhonwen had just said that Ursula was on her way to Cippenham. In serving the King's ends, he served his own. He ought to have known that once oath-bound to Aelfred his own needs would take second place.

Aelfred did not expect to hear any objections and Dan offered none. The King was already turning to go: 'We shall leave at once. I will explain the detail of my plan as we go. For now I will allow you to prepare for your journey.'

He nodded to one servant, who handed Dan a pile of clothes, and to the other, who gave Dan his sword belt and his precious sword. Dan took the latter a little too eagerly. Aelfred opened the casket and presented Dan with a pair of beautiful gold saucer-shaped brooches to secure his cloak.

'I will offer you better when my kingdom is restored. Then all shall be done well and in good order and my court will be a centre for fine craftsmanship, for all that is beautiful and made to the glory of God. One day our court will rival that of Charles the Bald and the glories of Rome; for now we shall make do.' He swept out, followed by the sour-looking monk, Asser, who snarled something under his breath and crossed himself as the hem of his long monk's robe touched Rhonwen.

'I would have you speak to the lady with more respect,' Dan said in the language of the Combrogi. He instinctively disliked the way Asser treated his former enemy.

'She is a pagan witch!' Asser responded fiercely. For some reason that angered Dan and he found his hand straying to his sword. Rhonwen's loose-fleshed hand was on his in a moment.

'Asser fears me because I am a woman and still beautiful. There is no need to worry.' She smiled and for an instant she was the beautiful dark-haired Princess he had first met. He blinked and she was a crone again.

Asser gasped and crossed himself once more. 'You shame the land of your birth with your sorcery,' he said and rushed from the room.

Rhonwen smiled. 'I should not tease him. He is a good enough man who will be important to Aelfred. But he is ill-suited to his monk's robes and, like Aelfred, has an eye for the ladies.'

Dan privately thought that quite unlikely.

'Tell me more about Ursula,' he said as he pulled on the warm, woven-wool clothes that Aelfred had gifted to him. They smelled a bit musty and damp and there was a memory of old sweat in the seams, but Dan was not in a position to be fussy about second-hand clothes and they were all in good condition and of fine cloth. He was particularly grateful for the boots, which were only slightly too small. He wrapped the short cloak round him and Rhonwen helped him to secure the brooches. 'You are sure that I will find Ursula at Cippenham?'

Rhonwen nodded. 'You are fortunate that your road is also the King's, but it is no coincidence. Aelfred's enemies have her and have taken her to their centre of power.'

'I don't understand. If Ursula has magic and all her strength, how could she not help herself? She can't be held against her will in captivity?' He tried to imagine Ursula, warrior and sorceress, held against her will, and struggled to picture it. She was too strong.

'Ursula is captive to the magic; she is in thrall to it,' Rhonwen said gravely. She reached out for Dan's hand and held it tightly. 'You must be prepared to face the worst. I don't know how much longer she can survive; the power that burns in her is overwhelming. I have never felt so much power. No one person could control it and, strong though she is, it is controlling her.'

Dan nodded, sickened. He could not lose Ursula. 'What do I have to do to save her?'

Rhonwen looked stricken. 'In truth I do not know. I have been trying to think of a way, but all I know is that you must save her. It is not just that she will die; I fear that if you cannot save her from the magic, Aelfred's kingdom will never be regained.'

Dan knew then that she had seen some vision of the future and he felt himself turn cold. 'Rhonwen, tell me. What have you seen?'

She shook her head. 'Fragments, frustrating fragments.

This country needs Aelfred as much as it needed Arturus. Somehow he must regain his kingdom. Ursula could stop him.'

'Will she fight with his enemies?'

Rhonwen shrugged. 'Her power may be used by his enemies but I don't know how. It is only one possible future. There are others where she dies.'

Dan licked his lips, which had suddenly gone dry. He refused to accept that those were the only options. 'Have you seen a future where I save her?'

Rhonwen shook her head. 'Not yet, but my talent is weak and unreliable. Either way I do not think you've got long and it's a good ride away. It took us four days to get here from Cippenham – those of us who got away. It is a sizeable place and the Danes will have it well defended. It is as good a base as any from which to control Wessex.'

Dan felt suddenly inadequate – how could he save Ursula if she could not save herself against the might of a Danish army? 'Do you have no herbs or spells that I could use to help her?'

'You've been taking too much notice of Asser. I'm not a witch and there's no potion on earth strong enough to match her magic. You could feed her deadly nightshade and she would live. All the magic on the earth is drawn to her as surely as water runs down a hill; she is the sea and the tides of magic that flow through her will kill her.' Rhonwen looked thoughtful. 'What I wouldn't give for a fraction of that power. I'd make myself young again and go home. For all my years of meddling I've little enough to show for my pains. Arturus's deeds are barely remembered here and . . .'

She shrugged. 'Ignore an old woman's meanderings. Go to your friend and may the blessings of your God be with you.' She patted Dan on his arm and Braveheart on the head and Dan got the strong feeling that she made little distinction between them.

~ Chapter Nineteen ~

The warrior, Gunnarr, came to Ursula many times after she answered his question. Each time he brought a small animal and slaughtered it. Sometimes he offered her the blood and one time, when she had been hunting with wolves, she came back to herself sufficiently to be able to drink it.

Sometimes she ate the offerings but mostly she ignored both the man and his questions. He wanted to know the future but when the present was so infinitely various, what did she care about the future? He talked too about the land he was going to be given by the war leader Guthrum, and how now that the fighting was done and Aelfred soon to be dead, he might give up the Viking life for the life of a landowner. Guthrum would give him land he was sure, and he knew quite a bit about farming. He had his eye on a local girl who was of high Aenglisc birth and had the body of a goddess, though, he added hastily, she was as a toothless old crone when compared to the loveliness of Ursula herself. Actually he called her 'Freya' but Ursula knew what he meant. She was only half aware of his low-voiced talk, though she found the soft rhythms of his voice soothing, almost like music, holding a part of her still connected to her own body, to her own ears and to that element within herself that still understood ambition and desire. She did not speak – the greater part of her mind was elsewhere – but the man's earnest confiding voice reminded her of something precious.

Time passed and the man went away and came back again. He was strong and single-handedly carried her to another cart. He would not let anyone else touch her. He alone arranged her robes around her and took care that the cart was well padded. In return she did not burn him or harm him in any way, but allowed his large calloused hands to handle her fevered flesh: she was on fire with magic. He rode at her side as she was conveyed somewhere else. He did not speak to her so much then but she knew he was her guard and her protector and that amused and comforted her, he got through to her even in her strange detachment. He was very like someone, but she could not remember who.

They travelled for a time and the warrior lifted her head and fed her the still warm blood of a deer they had slaughtered on the road. They ate the venison and this time Ursula allowed the warrior to feed her choice morsels while her mind still hunted with hawks and entangled herself in the roots of the sleeping forest. They were almost ready to wake, those roots. She could feel the power of future growth building within them. She amused herself by forcing some parts of the forest into an early growth, but it was cold and would do the plants no good, so she stopped.

They came at last to a sizeable town where the air was thick with pride and exultation, with the sense of conquest. There were women there too – captives chiefly, cowed and terrified. They feared more violence: the men had been drunk for weeks and they were running low on food. Ursula found it was difficult to engage with so many thoughts and emotions. It made her nervous and worried. There was death and there was birth and all around there was tension. She did not like it and let herself slip away to simpler, cleaner worlds of running and killing or flying and killing or hiding and killing, where all the killing made sense and where fear was easy to understand and untainted by the complexity of the thinking of men. She left even the warrior behind, though he still sat beside her in the middle of a garden in a small copse. They kept torches burning around her and a brazier to keep her warm, though she had need of neither the light nor the warmth, carrying her own flame of magic within her. The warrior stood guard and whispered to her still, but she could not stay to hear him and she only noticed that he was gone when music drew her back from her journeying.

'This is indeed a goddess. What does it mean that she is here?' It was a man's voice speaking when the music ended. She did not want to hear his thoughts, which were, in the main, ugly and confusing and full of desire.

'It means that good fortune will accompany you in all that you do. She is a being of great power and if she is with us, none can stand against us.' It was the voice of a woman and it chilled Ursula's overheated blood. It was a voice that knew how to call to the magic in her and she did not want that magic to be called. This was a person who knew about magic. She did not wield it – not as Ursula did – but she knew how it worked. Ursula wanted nothing to do with her. She turned her mind away from the woman and escaped.

It was the singing that brought her back, the high reedy voice of the woman chanting. Ursula's recumbent form developed goose pimples and shivered. The song was repetitive and tuneless, an unmusical refrain in a strange, unlovely soprano, but it called to the magic in Ursula and she found that she had to open her eyes. The woman was bending over her, stretching out her small hands over Ursula's body as though she was warming herself.

'Ah! The Goddess, she has come to us. She will speak to us, but you'd better be quick. She is little interested in the affairs of men.'

The woman was very small and childlike in appearance; perhaps, for all her authority, she was no more than a child. She was like a malnourished eleven-year-old with straggly, dirty blonde hair. It hung loosely in rat's tails about her thin shoulders. She smiled briefly at the leader, Guthrum. His emotions spilled out of him and into Ursula's awareness. Here was a man who liked killing for the sense of power it gave him, for the fine treasure in gold and silver it won him and for the sheer pleasure of seeing someone else suffer. Ursula saw that the girl, though frail, was enormously self-possessed. Guthrum was afraid of this snaggle-toothed girl and that gave her a great deal of power.

'What do I do?' Guthrum asked.

'Speak to her as you would to anyone else with power.' Ursula could feel the girl's quiet confidence like a small, cold hand on her heart. She thought she had the measure of Ursula as she had the measure of Guthrum. Ursula was aware of Guthrum nodding and gathering his thoughts. That did not take long; he did not have many that were worth gathering.

'Will I win?' he said, and without willing it Ursula had a vivid picture of the man drunkenly holding court in a gold-decked hall. He was sitting on a carved chair while men around him sat on benches. He was playing some game and betting wildly and luck was on his side. Ursula could feel the heat of the hearth fire in the centre of the hall. She could smell the ale and the stale smell of sweat and congealed grease and the musky odour of the dogs, one of which had been rolling in the rotting carcass of a rabbit. It was as if she were there. The raucous, triumphant sound of Guthrum's laughter rang in her ears. Her mouth was dry and it was difficult to get her voice to work again. It seemed to have been a long time since she'd spoken – she did not know how long; she had almost forgotten how to count the days.

'Yes,' she said throatily and then closed her eyes. She

had done what the woman had called her to do and she fled as far away as she could, letting the magic clear the memory of Guthrum's vileness from her and allowing the image of the girl's pale green, blind eyes to fade.

~ Chapter Twenty ~

Dan took Braveheart and made his way across the frozen rutted path that led towards the largest building on the small island – a hall built within the heart of an old fortress. This was Aelfred's stronghold, and Dan knew that he would find him there. He could not help noticing the poor state of the fort. The encircling timbers were rotten and the earth walls needed reinforcing, but to Dan's not inexperienced eyes it looked like a ramshackle but still defensible site. No one stopped him as he entered the hall, even though his sword was at his hip and his war dog was a killer. Aelfred definitely needed to tighten his control here.

Aelfred was in deep discussion with Asser and a plump woman with a mass of unruly dark hair.

'I need to see for myself,' he said shortly. 'This is not a subject that is open for discussion.' He looked up as Dan approached and smiled, his brow uncreasing. 'My companion in adventure! I have ordered a small pack to be made for our journey and then we should be off. First we must collect our horses and then we will go on to

Cippenham. Tell me, do you play an instrument of any kind? I was hoping to pose as a scop, a bard, and slip into the town that way. Don't worry if you can't play an instrument. There will be at least one musician in our party – we'll meet him on the way – but it would look better if you had some gift.'

'My Lord, would it not be better to send one of your loyal subjects to spy for you at Cippenham?'

'No! I cannot ask others to take risks while I do not. A king should not skulk in the marshes or hide in a hole in the corner of his kingdom and wait for events.'

'But who will supervise the rebuilding of the fortress and the recruitment of men if you are not here?' Dan said carefully.

Aelfred scowled. 'What is wrong with the fortress? No one knows we are here and the marsh itself protects us.'

Dan had no wish to start telling a king what to do, but he knew a little about defences and Aelfred's were not good enough.

'There are those who might betray you to your enemies,' Dan said, thinking of the householder whose boat they had taken. 'This place is easily reachable by boat and the fortress is rotting away. It would not take much to bring it up to a good standard, but it will take organisation. You are too easy to kill at the moment, Sire, and that is not a good quality in a king.' Dan was aware that both Asser and the woman were holding their breath, as if expecting Aelfred to order Dan's execution, but Dan had always told the truth as he saw it and the presence of Bright Killer at his hip and Braveheart at his side made him reckless. Aelfred raised a surprised eyebrow and cleared his throat.

'Well, of course, Aethelnoth, my dearest and most loyal friend, ealdorman of Somerset, will be left in charge of our defensive preparations. He is a good man and I can assure you that men do not need a king to oversee the chopping of wood or the organisation of a guard's roster or to plunder food from the farmers that were once under my protection . . .'

Aelfred's tone was bitter and Dan sensed that the King, shamed by the loss of his throne, was desperate for action, for some way to make himself feel better. He did not want to remain in the decayed fortress, being nagged by a monk and the woman Dan presumed was his wife. Dan was glad he was no longer truly empathic because he could imagine all too easily how Aelfred was feeling – trapped, just like Dan himself.

Asser was no fool either and he swallowed whatever he had intended to say next. His clear, shrewd eyes met Dan's. 'I was known as a tidy singer in my youth. I would travel with you if my presence was not an extra burden and if my Lady Ealswith could contrive to manage in my absence.' Asser added in his own language, 'If you are known to Rhonwen, I do not trust you. Be assured that if you cause harm to come to the King, God himself will strike you down. He is our earthly salvation, of that I'm sure.'

Dan nodded, amused by Aelfred's efforts to thank Asser for his concern and willingness to accept danger on his behalf, while disguising his horror at the very thought of

Asser pretending to be anything other than what he was. Asser's gleam of humour was not lost on Dan either; Asser understood Aelfred well enough.

It did not take long for Aelfred to be ready. Dan had expected some long and complicated arrangements, but there were none. He was relieved; he was desperate to get to Ursula before it was too late. Dan held on to Braveheart very tightly as their party crossed the now calm lake – not because he was afraid, but because he thought that the war dog must surely fear the water. Dan was wrong; the biggest difficulty was keeping Braveheart in the boat. Dan had not known it but Braveheart loved to swim and barked at the water as if it were an old friend. Dan, on the other hand was less enthusiastic. He found that his legs were shaking when he got off at the other side. The journey was not much helped by Aelfred's attempts to recall the songs from his youth. The King was better at hymns than at what Dan would properly call songs, and his grasp of a tune was tentative. Dan hoped that the bard Aelfred had mentioned was some kind of musical genius, or they would be killed as an act of mercy to all music lovers. He was not so tactless as to point it out, but the King was almost tone deaf.

There were five of them in the boat, all armed, and Dan hoped that the other three men would accompany them on their reconnaissance. Dan did not want to have sole responsibility for the King's protection, but Aelfred was not a man to think about other people's convenience, nor, it seemed, about his own safety.

After they had been walking a couple of hours the

ground became altogether firmer and more suitable for crops. The small party hid in a clump of trees to discuss their next move. Apparently they had left horses there in the care of the local farmer, but no one was sure of his loyalties. Dan was privately appalled that Aelfred knew so little about what was going on at his door.

'Do you have no spies working for you?' he asked in surprise.

'We fled Cippenham in some disarray. We have been living off the land and pillaging where necessary. I fear we are seen by some as outlaws. We have yet to organise our-selves – which is why it is important that we go back there to find out what we're up against. I have one spy sounding out the thegns nearest Cippenham. We will catch up with him on the road,' Aelfred said confidently.

Dan could not help thinking that it would make more sense to gain some local knowledge first; discovering whether their nearest neighbour was still loyal to this King struck him as an important place to start. It was on the tip of his tongue to say so, but he refrained.

'What now then?' Dan asked.

'Two of us should fetch the horses,' Aelfred said, get-ting ready to move.

'No, Sire. You should stay here. If there are Danes there, waiting for us, at least I speak the language,' Dan said a little wearily. Aelfred's enthusiasm for putting himself in danger to no purpose was likely to prove troublesome. There was a kind of desperation in him which worried Dan: desperate men were foolish more often than they were heroic.

One of the guard, a young man a little older than Dan with the easy balance of a fighter, caught Dan's eye and the two of them set off together across the open field. They kept low to the ground and made their way in a half-crouching run. Dan's neck and back prickled with an awareness of vulnerability. There was no cover and the farmer would have had plenty of time to ready himself if he wanted to take them on. Dan felt that churning in his stomach that was as much excitement as fear. There was a fight coming – he felt it in his bones. It was almost as if he could smell the threat of violence in the air. Something about his companion's stance suggested that he shared the same expectation. Part of Dan longed to fight, the part he always suppressed: his Bear Sark madness was only a heartbeat away.

'I am Aethelnoth, ealdorman of Somerset,' his comrade said in a low voice. 'I hear you are a fighter.'

Dan nodded. 'I am. My name is Dan, and if it comes to a fight, stay out of my way,' he replied in a tone that he hoped conveyed his seriousness. Dan sensed that Aethelnoth was about to make some light-hearted rejoinder, but he stopped when he glanced at Dan's face. Dan did not know what he saw there but his expression grew wary.

'You have the battle madness,' Aethelnoth said, and it was not a question. Dan gave him a terse nod. There wasn't time for more. Dan checked his sword and started to run in what was fast becoming a kind of a charge. There was no point in stealth. They had been seen, he was sure of it. There was no sign of movement at the farm and Dan was sure that there ought to be people about, working, doing whatever farmers did at this bleak time of year. The silence was ominous. Some enemy was waiting for them. Aethelnoth was sweating and it was not warm in the chill wind. Dan thought he caught the scent of death in the air, the taint of corruption.

He saw the bloodstains then and the twisted shape of a corpse.

He had time to shout out a warning to Aethelnoth and then suddenly the enemy was before him and the world slowed. Dan slipped the gear in his mind that set him free.

~ Chapter Twenty-one ~

Four men stepped out from the protection of the farm walls. They were big men, all of them – tall and muscular with the hard eyes and confident stance of men well used to violence. There was little in their dress to distinguish them from Aelfred's men – perhaps a different style of tunic – something too subtle for Dan to be able to isolate. Two were bare-headed and almost as tall as Dan, the other two wore helms – one of boiled leather and one of silver metal polished to a high shine. They were each armed with a spear and shield, while one also bore a war axe. The man with the metal helm looked a little older than the others. His dark blond beard was flecked with grey and he carried a heavy sword. Dan guessed that he was their leader. He alone wore a mail shirt. They were all warriors, veteran fighters, of that Dan had no doubt: they knew what they were doing.

So did Dan. At least he allowed that part of himself that was best equipped to deal with such a threat to take over, the Dan that waited in the calm core of his being, the Dan who had no conscience but was all swift action and focused concentration. It happened in the space of a breath, between one heartbeat and the next. Suddenly Bright Killer was in his hand – no, was part of his hand – not so much a tool as a manifestation of his will. Dan himself was nothing more than an instrument of death, his whole self focused only on killing, on fighting and winning. Nothing else mattered.

Braveheart was by his side, panting. His great shaggy body was taut with excitement, tense with the thrill of imminent battle. He was as alert as his master. He gave a low growl. They understood each other. Dan was aware of a moment of fierce joy as he charged towards his enemy, Braveheart beside him, his four powerful legs keeping pace with Dan's attack. It was Dan and his dog against the world. Then he was not aware of his own feelings at all; he became one with his task – a killer, killing.

He yelled an insult in Danish – who knew where it came from. He did not think about what it meant – it did not matter. What mattered was that hearing Dan shriek in their own language might be sufficient to confuse the enemy and gain him a slight advantage. Of such tiny, slight advantages, battles are won. In fact it gave him an unmeasurable extra moment to dodge the first of the spears, and that first spear was not wielded with its usual firmness or ferocity. The Dane feared they were attacking one of their own, that there was some mess-up and they were fighting a brother. He quickly changed his mind. While Dan's first adversary was focusing on sticking his spear in Dan's guts, Braveheart launched himself at the man's chest, under his spear arm. The war dog's weight and powerful forward impetus knocked the man off his feet. He overbalanced, fell backwards on to the packed mud of the farm's yard, and Braveheart tore out his throat.

Meanwhile Dan had moved on, each movement swift and precise. He trusted Braveheart to get on with his job and turned his own attention to the axeman, who had abandoned his shield to come to the aid of his comrade. He was breathing hard and Dan could see the fury in his eyes as he raised his axe to strike Dan dead. He was not quick enough. As he hefted his axe Dan's sword slashed across his exposed chest, severing muscle and veins, slicing through tunic, padding and flesh. Blood welled, staining the light green cloth. The man was a warrior and he did not drop his axe with the pain of his wound. He merely gave a blood-curdling yell and brought his axe crashing down on to Dan's head. Except that Dan was no longer there. Dan had gone and the injured axeman faced Braveheart's bared teeth, his throaty growl and the war dog's vicious jaws. By this time, Aethelnoth had his seax out and was engaging with the third enemy while the leader in the silver helm attempted to corner Dan. The presence of the dog and the speed of Dan's attack had unnerved him, that was clear, but he unsheathed his sword and abandoned his spear in favour of his heavy shield which, properly handled, became a weapon in itself. Dan had never bothered much with shields – in his berserker rage he had no fear and no need of a defence. He whistled to Braveheart, who was slavering over the body of the fallen axeman, and the pair of them ran at the swordsman.

He was not as tall a man as Dan, though considerably

broader. Braveheart leaped for the shield, fearless of the sword thrust in Dan's direction. The dog's attack meant that the Dane mistimed his lunge and Dan danced easily out of his reach and behind him. The man was unbalanced by his attempt to fend off the dog and in a moment Dan had the man's head in an armlock, forcing it backwards until a sliver of flesh was exposed between his mail shirt and the protection of his helmet – then Dan slit his throat. The man sagged against Dan's heaving chest. Dan let him fall. His tunic was stained with a broad stripe of the man's blood.

He looked around for someone else to kill. The first man he had fought was not quite dead and moaned a little – a horrible, pitiful sound. Dan finished him with a quick stab to his heart. There was only one other man left standing. He was bloodstained and staring at Dan with horror. Dan wiped his bloody sword on the tunic of his now dead enemy and strolled towards this last man. There was no need to hurry and it was only one against one. His opponent did not look ready to fight and was clearly unmanned by his fear. Dan found this surprising as he was well built and well armed. Dan moistened his lips and whistled for Braveheart to come to heel.

'Stop! Stop!' the man called, panic evident in his voice. 'It is me, Aethelnoth. We are allies!'

It took several seconds for the message to make sense to Dan, longer still for it to make him lower his sword arm. Braveheart turned to look at Dan, his muzzle stained with blood and gore, and Dan patted his head. 'Good boy,' he said.

'I've never seen anything like that before,' Aethelnoth said shakily. 'You are so fast – so ruthless.'

Dan shook his head. He did not want to think about what he'd just done.

'I'm sorry,' he said. 'I should have hung on a bit longer . . . I lost myself so quickly I . . .'

'Don't apologise. It was them or us. We were outnumbered and they were all veterans, I know.' He paused. 'I thought you were going to kill me too.'

Dan nodded. 'So did I for a moment.' He clapped Aethelnoth on the arm with a bloodied hand. 'But I didn't. You are unhurt?'

Aethelnoth nodded.

'Good. It is over then. We should go and find the horses.'

Dan's muscles still quivered with the aftermath of his exertion. He never noticed such things while he fought. He carefully avoided the bodies in the yard, which was a ridiculous kind of squeamishness given that he had killed them. He didn't like the smell or the ugly mess that all that ruined flesh made. It was shocking seeing men ripped open like that. He did not want to see it. He was as confused as he had ever been. Life through the Veil was so different it made him question everything. Who was he? Dan, a boy who wanted to do what was right, or Dan the psychopath, killing without fear or mercy?

He leaned for a moment against the wattle and daub of an outbuilding. His heart rate was high, but then fighting took a lot of energy. The quivering in his limbs had stopped. He was fit and he needed little recovery time.

His hands were steady and his breathing even – how could he be so little affected by what had happened? He watched Aethelnoth's hesitant progress – he seemed visibly shaken by his encounter with the Danes, his own brush with death. But Dan had not been afraid, not even for a moment.

It was not a good time for philosophical reflection: they did not know for sure that there were not more Danes in the farmhouse or in the outbuildings. Dan loosened his sword again – he needed to clean it properly as it was still sticky with body fluids – and followed Aethelnoth into the stable. He made Braveheart wait outside on guard. The horses were fine – in good condition, if upset by the unfamiliar sounds. They were skittish and nervy, but Dan could hear something else beside the sound of their hooves and anxious whinnying – a low moaning.

'Over here,' Aethelnoth said, and Dan found him crouched over the body of a small boy no more than six or seven, younger even than Bryn, Dan's former squire, had been when they'd first met. The boy had been sliced across the legs and chest, but although he was obviously in pain, Dan judged that he had not lost too much blood.

'It is all right now,' Dan said gently. 'We are not going to hurt you. Where does it hurt?'

The boy moved feebly to point to his injuries.

'What happened here? Can you tell us?'

'Vikings came yesterday. I hid here but one of them found me just now. I thought they were going to kill me.' He sobbed and Dan patted his thin shoulder.

'Hush – we'll take you somewhere safe. How many men

were there?' The boy held up his hand to show five fingers. 'And who was in the house? Do you know what happened to them?'

The boy shook his head and began to cry. 'You take him back to Aelfred,' Dan said, assuming control without thinking about it. 'We have only killed four.'

~ Chapter Twenty-two ~

What would he do if he were the fifth man holding the farmhouse? Dan knew that he would have joined his comrades in the fight, which made him deeply suspicious of the missing fifth man. He left the stable cautiously, indicating to Braveheart that he should stay. The war dog gave him a reproachful look and sank his great head down on to his front paws. Dan did not worry about danger coming from anywhere near the stable; Braveheart would take care of it.

He crossed the corpse-strewn yard. There were two bodies there for which he was not responsible – a middle-aged man and a woman. He presumed that they were the original owners of the farm. It looked from the position of the sprawled bodies as if the man had died trying to protect the woman. Dan averted his eyes, repelled by what he saw. He did not want another fight, but he drew his sword in readiness. He knew that he would have to kill again. He was afraid now not so much of what he might find in the house, but of what he might do if he unleashed his berserker self a second time. He wished Ursula were with him. She had always been able to help him.

The inside of the house was dark, so he waited a moment with his back against the light, listening and hoping that his eyes would get used to the gloom. There was a smell of decay that made his stomach tighten.

Dan stepped forward into the darkness, clutching Bright Killer as if it were a beacon. In truth the house was a simple one: a single room with two high sleeping platforms and few places to hide. The boots he had been lent were hobnailed – ideal for the mud and mush of Aelfred's camp, but far from silent on the wood board floor of the house. He winced at the noise he made. He almost skidded on their worn metal. He feared another ambush, but hung on to his self-control. He moved carefully, aware that he could too easily lose his footing. It helped to concentrate hard. He was Dan, a twenty-first century teenager. He was not a killer. He was kind and conscientious, a good person. He tried to think of his old life. He tried to think of Ursula – anything so that he would not turn into the berserker as a way of dealing with fear. What if some other child had survived the Viking attack?

He advanced cautiously through the house that was simply a larger and better version of the cottage he had come upon in the marshes. Flies buzzed around the remains of a chicken carcass that lay rotting on the floor; that accounted for the smell of decay, at least. He carefully inspected the remainder of the building: there was no one there. He paused just to be certain and held his breath.

Yes. He could hear something just below his feet. There must be a cellar below him. It was still difficult to see – even with the light from the open door. Dan opened the wooden shutters of the only window and looked around again. There were no signs of struggle, though he doubted that it was the family who had thrown the remnants of their meal upon the neatly swept floor. It took him a moment to find the trapdoor and the wooden steps that led into the cellar. The smell of human waste was very strong, as if someone had been using it as a toilet. There was someone down there, he was sure of it. A slight movement to his right had him ready for immediate action. Someone hurled themselves towards him, knife blade in hand. Without thinking Dan threw off his attacker, who, rather stupidly, had come at him from below, giving Dan the advantage. There was a loud thud and a muffled cry as Dan's attacker landed hard on the cellar floor. The cry was a mistake too, as it told Dan exactly where to aim his blow. He began to feel his conscious control slipping away. He preferred to leave the dirty work to his berserker self. He took two paces forward while his attacker struggled to his feet. He was small, slight and would be easily dispatched. NO. He was small and slight because he was no warrior but a child. Dan's sword was poised to strike; with an enormous effort of will he did not send the blade home. He lowered his sword arm, panting with the effort involved in taking such an unnatural action. It was hard for Dan to keep his arm relaxed, harder still to speak. His blood was up and the wild fury surging through him demanded the satisfaction of a kill. It was a second before he had sufficient command of himself to form coherent words in any language.

'What kind of man hides in the cellar while his comrades are killed?' Dan rasped, in Aelfred's tongue. 'Put down the seax and I won't kill you.'

'Killing me is not the worst that you people do,' his attacker replied. The voice was light and very youthful, definitely not a warrior's voice. Dan relaxed slightly: he had, after all, made the right call.

'I am not that kind of man,' Dan answered, hoping that it was true. 'Put down the knife.'

He was taken off guard when the owner of the young voice suddenly hurled himself forward, aiming low and knocking Dan over. There was a brief struggle before Dan knocked the seax from his opponent's hand and pressed it to his throat.

'Come with me,' he said and pushed his attacker roughly forward so that he nearly fell. Dan was angry with himself; there had to be a middle way between killing everything that moved and being a complete fool. If his attacker had been heavier and stronger, he would have been in trouble there.

As they emerged into the grey light of the ground floor it became clear that his attacker was in fact a frightened young girl. She looked about thirteen.

'Do you have a brother?'

She nodded. Dan said, 'I think he may still be alive, but the older people who lived here are dead. Were they your parents?'

She nodded but didn't cry. Dan thought she looked like someone who had no tears left.

'We heard the raiders coming. Da pushed me into the

cellar and told me not to come out until I'd heard no sound for a day. I didn't know how long a day was in the dark. Everyone knows what happens to girls when the Vikings come. Mother gave me the knife and told me to do whatever I had to do to live. Da put up a fight. I heard it, but when they didn't come for me I knew they were dead.' She supressed a sob and wiped her face with a grimy hand. 'Cealin gave the warning – he yelled from halfway over the field and Da yelled back for him to run and hide and find the . . .' She tailed away, uncertain as to how much information she ought to give.

'Your father told him to find the people who have sought sanctuary at Athelney?' Dan prompted.

'Yes. Da thought that with us looking after their horses they might be keeping an eye on us, keeping us safe, but they weren't.'

'I think that might change now,' Dan said. The girl did not look as if she believed him.

'I'm not going to hurt you,' he said, but by her expression she remained unconvinced. Dan glanced down and saw the dark stain of another man's lifeblood discolouring his tunic; she was right to fear him.

He could not protect her from the sight of her parents sprawled on the ground and he didn't try. She ran to them and Dan turned away to give her some privacy. His own mother's death had been bad enough, even though it had been expected and she'd died neatly and bloodlessly in a hospital bed. Dan stepped away to put distance between himself and the girl's keening. What was he becoming that he could not offer human comfort to a grieving child?

He made himself turn back to her.

'I will make sure that they are properly buried,' he said stiffly. He did not want to touch her for fear that she would misconstrue his intentions; instead he hung back, trying to suggest sympathy by his body language while keeping a wary eye out for the missing fifth man. There was no cover in the yard and he felt very exposed standing there next to the grieving girl while there could still be danger out there.

'I have come to take some of the horses – for the King, for King Aelfred,' he said at length. 'Once I have done that we can go and find your brother. I'm sure he'll be glad to see you.'

She took off her shawl and covered the faces of her parents with it.

'Do you think it was quick?' she asked.

'I'm sure it was,' Dan said, trying not to imagine what their last moments must have been like.

'It is a while since we have seen a priest . . .'

Her voice trailed off as she noticed the other corpses on the ground. Braveheart's enthusiasm had made it a rather messy scene. The girl flinched at the sight.

'I hope they suffered,' she said simply, and Dan did not know how to answer.

~ Chapter Twenty-three ~

Dan struggled to control his impatience. He wanted to be off and on the road to Cippenham, but the Aenglisc dead had to be given a Christian burial, which entailed someone going back to fetch Asser, and then the bodies of the Viking dead had to be stacked into a pyre for burning. It was grisly work. Dan forced himself to help. He'd made the mess so he had to clear it up, but, more than that, he had to see what his madness had done. It sickened him. It was also obvious that something had to be done to secure the farmhouse and to guard it from further attack.

Aelfred looked grave when Dan relayed the girl's criticisms. 'I have left undone those things I ought to have done. I have let these people down,' he said heavily.

Dan knew that it was not his place to advise this King he barely knew but old habits died hard. 'Perhaps it would be good, Sire, to let those supporters in the surrounding area know that you still command, that you can still be relied on. If it is thought that you will stand by and let your nearest neighbours be massacred, then all support will drain away and even those loyal to you will seek alliances with your enemy in order to protect themselves. You need to work secretly and carefully so that you have time to gather the fyrd, but no army will ever be gathered if you are seen as a spent force.' Dan clamped his mouth shut so that he didn't risk his life further by criticising the King. Aethelnoth said nothing, but something in his body language seemed to give his assent.

'And you, Aethelnoth, you agree with this upstart?'

Aethelnoth's face flushed. 'I do not like to think that we left these people undefended when we had men enough to watch over them,' he said carefully. 'And we could have lost our mounts.'

'What happened to the other farm workers? Did they run?' Aelfred asked.

Dan shrugged. 'The girl will know and her brother. Their local knowledge could be useful – and their contacts.'

Aelfred nodded. 'You are saying there is work to be done here, that my place is here, hidden away in a bog in Athelney?'

'I would not dare to advise a king, Sire,' Dan said with false humility, 'but it is my belief that if you are to be restored then you need to act like a king, to organise and dispatch others to work for you, to let people know that you are King still, even in exile. You have to fight the invaders, fight for your throne. It is true that you cannot do that with a few men in a bog in Athelney, but it is from this safe haven that you can begin to rebuild.'

'You do not think this is best done by disguising myself

and seeing for myself what needs to be done?'

'Why put yourself at risk to no purpose, my Lord? You need to gather support. You need people to believe that if they ally with you, you can protect them. A king wandering the country dressed as a scop – how will people feel such a man can help them? A king rebuilding a stronghold, sending out men to spy and to recruit, talking of the army being built and making it a reality – that is someone people might trust to help them.' Dan thought of Arturus and his endless planning and organising, his attention to detail. Dan had not liked him much, but he had admired his dedication.

There was a long pause. 'But I have to act. I have to *do* something,' Aelfred muttered. The King looked pale and sickly, though the smell of the pyre and of his own gore-stained garments made Dan feel sick too. Aelfred turned away from his men to stare at the bleak marshland which hid Athelney. Dan could not see his face but he could tell by the man's dejected stance that he had made an unwelcome decision. When he turned back to face them, he looked grim-faced and determined.

'My brother-in-law abandoned his kingdom for Rome and left Mercia to the Danes; my childhood friend Edmund of East Anglia wasted his life in a pointless, doomed attack. I do not want to fall into either trap. I have to build an army to win or my grandfather's heritage will be lost and all of this land will fall into the Danes' hands.'

He pulled at his thin beard distractedly. Dan felt for him. It was clear to Dan that Aelfred had been avoiding this moment for some time. When he spoke again, it was with all the confidence of a ruler: 'I have made my decision. It is my duty to defend the kingdom of Wessex, and, as God is my witness, that is what I will do. Aethelnoth, you will go on with Dan to Cippenham. You must try to catch up with our friend, the scop. You know his route through Wessex – follow it. Take horses and here, Aethelnoth, have my pack.' He eyed Braveheart doubtfully. 'Is it wise to take the beast?'

'I will sleep safer on the road knowing he is with us,' Aethelnoth answered firmly.

'May God be with you. There is no need for you to await Asser's return and the burial rite. It is best that you use what is left of the day.' Aelfred did not let any of his longing to leave with them leak into his voice and Dan admired him for that.

Dan was about to ask about the children of the farm but Aelfred got there first: 'The children's rights to their property will be respected, but for the moment I will put some of my own men to mount guard and tend to the horses and we will discuss a more permanent arrangement when they have recovered from the shock. The girl is of near marriageable age. It should not prove too difficult to arrange her a match and an appropriate bride price.'

Aelfred wished them well and explained in some detail what he wanted them to discover. It seemed that the reconnaissance party had shrunk to just the two of them, Dan and Aethelnoth, and the scop they would meet along the way. Dan had hoped for more backup. His plan was, after all, to rescue Ursula from under the nose of the

Danes and he was not sure that Aethelnoth was the man he most wished to have by his side. He seemed both wary and hostile, in spite of his earlier warmth, and Dan could not work it out. When they were out of earshot, Dan spoke.

'There is no reason to fear me. I am not likely to try to kill you.'

Aethelnoth shrugged. 'I had heard rumours of the Viking berserkers but had never seen one before.'

'You said yourself that it was them or us!'

'And now it is just you and me.'

Suddenly Dan understood. 'You think I am a Dane?'

'Why not? You speak their language and you fight like one. The King sets his store by trials and God's will, but I look to my own judgement, not God's. Your battle madness saved my skin and for that I'm grateful, but the more I have thought through what happened the less happy I am. You Danes do not seem to care for your own as we do. Guthrum slaughtered our hostages and did not spare a thought for his own people, whose lives were also forfeit. Perhaps you thought my trust was worth a few Danish lives.' He fingered his sword and Dan felt his own heartbeat begin to race. He might have to fight this man. He got ready, but Aethelnoth carried on talking. 'I have never seen a Christian man fight like a beast. I do not trust you and I am not afraid of you.' That wasn't true – Dan could see that in the way Aethelnoth cringed from him – but Aethelnoth would not acknowledge his fear. 'I will not let you betray the King. He is my oldest friend and the only one who has the right to contest the throne. He is the only man who can save Wessex.'

'I am not a Dane. Besides, I gave my oath to the King,' Dan said.

'So they say,' Aethelnoth replied, unconvinced. 'But you wouldn't be the first Viking to break an oath made to a God in whom you do not believe.'

Dan was at a loss as to how to respond. He had nothing further to say and simply followed Aethelnoth into the stables, with its familiar stench of dung and hay. He hadn't ridden for some time; it was not the kind of thing people like him did at home.

'You take that gelding. He is the least likely to be spooked by the hound,' Aethelnoth said.

Dan had to watch carefully as Aethelnoth gathered up saddles, harnesses and stirrups and tried to copy him as he strapped on the riding gear. It looked unnecessarily complicated to Dan, who had never before used stirrups and had rarely used a saddle. In any case, he'd always had a stable boy or Bryn to deal with the detail. He got on with it, reluctant to ask Aethelnoth for help. He did not know if ignorance of equestrian matters was likely to confirm Aethelnoth's suspicions that he was a Dane.

They led the horses outside to the yard. It had begun to rain and the day had turned as grey as the smoke that billowed from the charred bodies on the pyre. The horses were restless and unsettled. The rain plastered Dan's hair to his head and trickled down his neck; it soaked his borrowed clothes, reviving the smell of other men's sweat and the drying blood. He wished his cloak had been waterproofed against bad weather, but perhaps they did not do that in these days, as Aethelnoth was scarcely better dressed for the rain. It promised to be a miserable ride.

It was worse when he mounted up. He did not feel at all comfortable in the unfamiliar saddle and he couldn't see the point of the stirrups. He shifted his weight to find a better position at exactly the same moment as his mount became aware of the looming presence of Braveheart and freaked.

It had been a while since Dan had fallen quite so hard. Braveheart licked his face reassuringly, which did not help much when Dan remembered what else Braveheart had licked recently. The dog's breath stank.

'Not much of a warhorse,' he said, getting to his feet with as much dignity as he could manage.

'You hadn't tightened the girth strap properly. Maybe you'd be better on a boat.'

That decided it. Dan removed the saddle and left it on the damp ground. Free of the encumbrance of the saddle, he felt much more in control. He was relieved to find that he had not forgotten how to ride.

Aethelnoth looked disapproving. 'You'll do the horse no favours riding like that.'

'Let's just go,' Dan said, anxious to get away from the farmhouse and all that had happened there. Ursula needed him. He had to go to her; he had no time to waste on anything else.

~ Chapter Twenty-four ~

Ursula was beginning to get angry. The girl with blind green eyes kept summoning her from her explorations and she hated it. The magic that surged through her had a life of its own and the girl could call to that magic, could draw it like iron to a magnet, and where her power went, Ursula followed.

It took a while for her to discover that she was angry. She had lost so much of her sense of her own self that at first she had thought that the emotion came from the hares leaping across the hillside or from the wolf pack howling at the moon.

Every time the girl brought her back, it was to the sound of the thin, wailing voice chanting incantations. The noise made the skin on Ursula's real flesh-and-blood body shiver, as if it she'd heard chalk squeaking on a blackboard or a metal knife scraped across a china plate. There was always blood too when she awoke. The girl had killed some small animal and daubed herself and Ursula with gore. In the torchlight the faces of the Danes were fearful as the girl demanded that the Goddess speak.

The girl, who named herself Finna, was all focused will and strange magnetism. When Ursula tried to inhabit her mind, she found it hidden from her, as if the girl had lost herself in thick fog or the total darkness of a deep pit. There was no sense that the girl herself resisted Ursula's intrusion; she was simply not there. Ursula could have gathered her magic together and blown the girl apart; it was a possibility. Ursula knew that the magic would allow her to kill with ease. She resisted the temptation, not because she thought it wrong – she no longer thought at all in any normal way – but because somehow she knew it would not work, that the girl was hidden from her. When Finna called Ursula back from her travelling with her nasty high-pitched whining, the bonfire that burned out-doors to light the yard in front of the Great Hall blazed so fiercely that Guthrum feared it was out of control and set men with buckets of earth to dampen it. Ursula turned the gentle breeze that fanned the flames of the night torches into a wind fierce enough to snuff them out and set cloaks flapping like sails in a storm.

'The Goddess is growing angry,' the girl Finna said, and all present took a step back from Ursula's recumbent form and Ursula knew that the girl spoke the truth in that at least. Ursula was angry and growing angrier.

'What must we do to please her?' Guthrum asked anx-iously. Ursula knew that he gained much status from his men by having a goddess at his side. Already the word had spread throughout the country that Freya herself had declared that Guthrum would be victorious, and that had brought many Aenglisc allies who might otherwise have proved troublesome. Ursula knew that he thought that he had won already.

'Goddess!' At Finna's voice Ursula felt herself compelled to open her eyes, so that she saw the green-eyed girl's small smile of triumph. The fire blazed wildly again but Finna ignored it. She was a plain, undernourished thing and yet her confidence and authority lent her a kind of glamour; Guthrum was utterly in thrall to her.

'Are you hungry?' the girl asked. It took a while for Ursula to understand the question; she had shared many meals that night but none had given nourishment to her body. It was hard to think about her body, but when she tried she found that her mouth was dry and tasted bad and that her stomach ached a little. She thought that perhaps that was hunger. Ursula nodded slowly, remembering the taste of hot venison, the way it felt in her mouth, the way it made her body feel well.

'Then you shall be satisfied,' the girl said, and turning to the assembled warriors and the battered Aenglisc women who served them she declared: 'The Goddess hungers and she will be fed. We will prepare a sacrifice fit for her.'

Guthrum looked at Finna. 'How many will do it?'

'Twenty,' she replied firmly as if she spoke for Ursula, but Ursula did not know what she was talking about. She disliked being in the girl's presence. She disliked being close to Guthrum. There was much ugliness in the camp, too much fear and brutality and wild and dangerous drunkenness. Guthrum had made no effort to rein in the excesses of his troops and conditions in Cippenham were degenerating.

'I doubt that we have that many Aenglisc men still living and the women are too useful to lose.'

'Then find some men,' she answered. 'It is not wise to upset the Goddess.'

~ Chapter Twenty-five ~

The rain was unrelenting and Dan could do nothing but ride on and endure. He would have liked a raincoat or, better still, a car.

After the first shock of its encounter with Braveheart, his mount had calmed down. It was good to feel that unity of man and horse that he had known in Macsen's world. Without the saddle getting between them, he found Aelfred's horse responsive and easy to manage, though a little small for his frame. He felt sorry for the stoic mount, but he could not afford to set an easy pace with so much at stake. He was worried about Ursula and he was worried about the whereabouts of the fifth man – if there was a fifth man; it was always possible that the boy, Cealin, couldn't count.

Dan regretted his oath to Aelfred, which bound him to his cause, and to Dan it seemed like a lost cause. Not that Dan had been given much choice. It struck him that Taliesin had left Braveheart here for Dan and that Taliesin must therefore have known that the ridiculous crystal ball would not take him to Macsen's world but to this rain-sodden corner of Britain where the King, to whom he owed reluctant allegiance, had lost the plot. He was a sickly man ridden with guilt and, in Dan's opinion, he needed to get over himself and get organised. Dan cursed Taliesin silently. Why had he manipulated him into this mess? Why had Dan fallen for it?

After a couple of hours of misery they stopped and ate some bread and cheese from Aelfred's pack. Dan would have welcomed a fire but everything was too wet. There were blankets and cooking pots in the pack, a metal tinder box and some quantity of bread and cheese and smoked, dried fish, but it was not a great deal, and Dan was still a growing boy with a healthy appetite: Aelfred was not. Aethelnoth had Aelfred's harp strapped across his spare mount and Dan wondered if maybe Aelfred had expected them to sing for their supper – which would at least account for the meagre provisions. It was too much to hope that Aethelnoth knew what to do with the harp. They could have done with Taliesin's skill or, better still, with Bryn; if Dan's old squire had been with them they would have lived well on what his music would have brought them. As it was, Dan remained hungry and thought he was very likely to catch pneumonia.

The land was still flat and marshy, the sky the dull steel-grey of an uncherished sword. The rain had made the going heavy.

They rode on rough unmetalled tracks that were little more than bridle paths, overgrown and muddy, and Dan grew quite nostalgic for a Roman road. Aethelnoth took care to avoid anything that looked like a decent track and skirted around all the villages and hamlets that came into view. Dan did not understand why, for while both he and Aethelnoth looked half drowned and disreputable, he thought it likely that a lack of sartorial splendour would be acceptable in itinerant musicians. There was some coin in Aelfred's pack too, and Dan would have had no qualms about spending it for a waterproof cloak, some hot food and a change of tunic. Not that Dan made any suggestion at all – he had no wish to deepen Aethelnoth's mistrust because Aethelnoth knew the way to Cippenham and Dan did not.

Aethelnoth's silence was oppressive and irritating. There was little enough to do on a long ride and a bit of conversation would have been welcome. Eventually Dan broke.

'Can you play the harp then?' he asked, indicating Aelfred's instrument strapped to Aethelnoth's back.

'Well enough,' Aethelnoth answered and then, perhaps sharing Dan's need to pass the time more pleasantly, added, 'Can you?'

'No.' Dan's mum had tried to persuade him into piano lessons when he was small, but there was no way to explain that to Aethelnoth.

'Do you know any songs?'

Dan shook his head. 'Maybe you could teach me some? If we are going to pose as musicians, it might help.'

Although Aethelnoth expressed reluctance, the horses themselves were making enough noise to alert any enemy to their presence; there was nothing to lose by singing. It cheered Dan up and by the time the light began to fade, much of Aethelnoth's more obvious hostility had faded too.

They camped overnight in the tumbledown ruin of an ancient Roman villa. Little of the stone remained but there was enough left to offer some shelter and to allow them to build a fire.

'Should we not be rallying support for Aelfred's cause or, at the very least, seeing where loyalties lie?' Dan asked. This skulking around in the rain seemed to him a lost opportunity.

'That's not what Aelfred wants. He wants us to get to Cippenham by the shortest way and return with news. The man we are meeting should be a little way ahead. The King doesn't want us to put ourselves in danger.'

Dan did not argue but he thought the decision foolish. More than that, he had hoped for a warmer bed that night.

When the grey dawn light grew strong enough, they rode out again, through mist and dew-damp grass. They found some new cart tracks a little way from the villa and followed them for a time until the ground grew so rough that it was hard to tell whether the trail had deteriorated badly or they had lost it altogether.

'Do you know where you are going?' Dan asked.

By this time Aethelnoth was little more than a lumpy outline under a shroud of fog, and Dan was getting worried. It would be easy for his horse to lose its footing; it would be very easy to ride into a tree branch. He was not a fan of riding blind.

'Ye-es,' Aethelnoth answered without conviction.

'Maybe we should wait and see if the sun burns off the mist?'

'This is fog and it could be in for the day. I think we have to keep going.'

'If we're going in the right direction.'

The day had brightened to the extent that they moved through an all-pervading blanket of wet whiteness. The sun had risen but it was impossible to judge its position.

Dan's senses strained, but no bird sang, and then he heard a branch break with a sound as sharp as a shot, and a man's low voice spoke – in Danish. Somehow they had walked right into their enemy.

~ Chapter Twenty-six ~

D an signalled wildly for Aethelnoth to be silent, but he did not seem to notice.

'No. We're going the right way,' he said.

Dan held his breath and unsheathed Bright Killer inch by careful inch. Aethelnoth understood that gesture at least. Braveheart gave a warning growl from deep within his chest.

'You hear that?' the Danish voice spoke again, this time in a whisper that seemed to Dan's straining ears louder than a shout.

'Yeah. Sounds like mounted men. Unless they bother us keep going – it's the farm we want.'

Aethelnoth still looked puzzled and Dan wondered if there was something wrong with his hearing. Aethelnoth was about to speak again when Dan put his finger to his mouth and scowled at him so furiously that he closed his mouth with an almost audible snap. Dan waited. His horse stamped and whickered. He tensed, aware that he was already moving to the dark place where his mad self was king. He took control of himself with difficulty. Sweat beads formed on his brow. Braveheart was as tense as he was – every fibre taut, quivering, watching for Dan's hand signal. Dan waited still and no one came.

'What?' Aethelnoth said.

'Couldn't you hear them?'

'Who?'

'Danes. Over there.'

'I can't hear anything.'

'Shhh! If I can hear them, they may be able to hear us. I think they were looking for a farmhouse. Is there somewhere near here?'

Aethelnoth nodded. 'A dawn raid would be their style, but we are still a day from Cippenham. They must be running low on supplies to come so far out.' He paused as if to listen, then whispered, 'Are you sure you have not imagined it? I still can't hear a thing.'

Dan did not have time to argue about what he knew he'd heard. 'Is this Aenglisc land?'

He could not see Aethelnoth's expression but by the tone of his voice Dan could tell he found that a very odd question.

'It is all our land, or should be. We'll get it back too.' The last was as much a threat as a promise.

'We should go and protect the people at the farmhouse,' Dan said with a sinking heart. He was not sure he could prevent himself from turning into the Bear Sark. 'I think the two men I heard might have been scouts for some larger group.' Dan could not say why he thought that, but it was perhaps safer to assume that they would be fighting more than two men. His instincts were usually reliable. 'We must ride hard and get there in time to warn the people of the farmhouse. The two Danes I heard were on foot – with any luck the others won't be mounted either.'

Aethelnoth did not move.

'What are you waiting for?'

'I didn't hear anything. How do I know I can trust you?'

'Of course you can trust me. I could have killed you at any time if I'd a mind to. What is your problem?'

'The Dane who killed my wife was unusually tall – Gunnarr they called him. He wore a helm so I could not see the colour of his hair, but he fought with a sword. Not many Danes have swords, and he was handy with it too . . .'

Dan paused a moment to take this in. Aethelnoth was not more than twenty and might have been even younger, but men married young through the Veil.

'I'm sorry,' Dan said. 'I didn't know that you had lost your wife. All I can say is that it was not me who killed her . . .' He wanted to tell Aethelnoth that he came from far away and had arrived in Aethelnoth's world long after his wife was killed, but there was no way of explaining things so that they would have made any sense to the Aenglisc man. 'Please, Aethelnoth. Show me the way to the farm or other men's wives will die. We are their only hope.'

Aethelnoth's hesitation showed in his body language. Dan willed him to agree.

'There is a way through the forest. We ought to be able to find it now that the fog is lifting.'

Dan had barely registered the gradual dispersal of the fog. Suddenly he could see Aethelnoth's face clearly. He looked tired and careworn in the wintry light. His was a sad face and Dan had not noticed that before. There was no time for him to empathise with the older man. 'Let's go!' Dan said. 'Ride as quickly as you can.'

He manoeuvred his mount into position behind his companion and they set off at a brisk canter. Dan rode low keeping his head tucked over his mount's neck, to stay clear of low-hanging branches.

The farm lay in a hollow some way from the treeline. The remnants of the morning mist still veiled the buildings from view, but there didn't appear to be any defences. They were surrounded on all sides by fields which sloped gently downwards and a shallow stream ran nearby. Dan could hear it bubbling away. In other circumstances it might have been an idyllic spot; in these circumstances its geography was a problem. It was not easily defensible.

The farm comprised a long low hall and several smaller buildings nearby. Dan's sharp eyes spotted at least six people working in and around the yard.

'Is there no one close by who might come to help?' he asked Aethelnoth. He feared for the people in the yard, lost in their daily labours, unaware of the danger that stalked them.

Aethelnoth shook his head. 'The ealdorman is miles away – I thought he had sided with the Danes, which ought to have made his people safe from their marauding.' His tone was flat, resigned even. 'The nearest village is a good walk from here.'

'What if you were to ride – surely the nearest estate or village would have horses and you could bring men back with you?' Dan said urgently.

'I'm not leaving. Besides, you'll find that not many men have much stomach for fighting Danes these days.' He sounded bitter. 'Ealdorman Wulfhere of Wiltshire turned the witan against Aelfred and made a deal with Guthrum. They are on the same side and he will turn a blind eye to any small-scale pillaging of his land in return for his life and a chance of Viking gold. Our army has dispersed – there must be thousands of Vikings at Cippenham. The ealdorman will not raise a force against them.'

There wasn't time to do more than warn the people on the farm. Dan wondered if the few extra minutes he could buy them with his warning would be of any use at all. Perhaps it would be better to be slaughtered where they were than have time to fear. No. He told himself there might be time enough to hide the children at least.

'Come on!' Dan urged his horse forward and set off at a gallop across the field to the farm.

The first person he came to was a woman of about thirty or so. She ran from him, then tried to fend him off with a broom – the only weapon she had to hand.

'Hide the children! Arm yourselves! The Vikings are coming!' Dan shouted from behind a protective arm. She needed no further warning but screamed to the others and scooped up her children in a strong embrace and sprinted for the house as fast as her burden and long skirts permitted.

The others ran towards Dan, gathering up whatever

they could – farm implements, bill hooks and axes. Though they each wore a seax at their belt, those knives were too short to be much use except at very close quarters. A young boy of about fourteen – old enough to count himself a man – had a slingshot. By the time Dan saw Aethelnoth canter into view, he had a good idea of the force they had to work with.

Already they could hear the enemy approaching. The men were noisy, far noisier than an approaching army – more like a wild gang of thugs, pirates and hooligans. The sound of their war cries turned his blood to ice. He could not fight madmen when he himself was sane. Dan had guessed right; the men he'd heard talking earlier had been in the vanguard of a larger force. The Danes sounded drunk, out of control. Dan thought that perhaps a man had to be one or the other to attack unarmed farmers in their homes.

'What can we do?' The man who seemed to be the thegn sounded desperate and looked to Dan for leadership. There was so little time.

'We would stand more chance if we could cut off their attack from three directions so we could funnel them through one place. Have you anything you could burn? If you could make a wall of flame, they'd have to come at us through the way we choose.'

The thegn was off shouting orders to his workers. He, at least, had a sword and helm, which he grabbed as he ran. There wasn't really time to organise such a defence, but it was better to do something rather than wait for the source of the noise to emerge from out of the trees. Dan's heart sank when he saw the determined face of the boy, clutching his slingshot.

'Are you any good with that?' Dan asked, keeping his voice matter-of-fact.

The boy nodded, too frightened even for bravado.

'Grab stones and set yourself up on the roof. Once you've used all your stones, if we do not have victory, run – or better still ride.' Dan slid down from his horse and handed the boy the bridle. 'You must go and warn the next farm of what is coming.'

The boy nodded again, his face corpse-pale.

Dan patted his shoulder. 'Only you can do this. You must not let your family down. Do what you can with the sling, then do everything you have to stay alive. Take the horse and ride – do you understand?'

'You can rely on me, Sire,' the boy said in a voice that was not yet properly broken. When he was sane, Dan hated war.

He did not regret giving away his mount. There were many advantages to being on horseback against infantry, but though Bright Killer was a wonderful sword it was not a cavalry sword, and his horse was not up to the task of riding in close to armed men and cutting them down. He was better off relying on his own two legs and his madness. He knew, with a mixture of dread and excitement, that there was no possibility of doing this sane. He was not sure if it could be done at all.

Aethelnoth was about to dismount, to take his place beside Dan, but Dan stopped him. Aethelnoth was used to fighting with a spear and his horse seemed better suited to close-quarters fighting. He could perhaps make use of the power that came from a charging horse and a steady hand.

'You and I will try to take as many down as we can before they come into the yard,' Dan said to him. 'Do you think you can fight mounted?'

'I could wish for a shield wall to fight behind, but I will try to make do,' Aethelnoth answered. He looked slightly sick too. No one could be expected to survive this encounter.

Dan took a few seconds to speak to the farm workers. They were clearly wondering if it would be safer to run.

'Run if you want,' Dan said, 'but it may be better to die fighting. If I thought running would help, I'd be leading you.' That wasn't true, of course; his blood was already up and his conscious control was already slipping away. He called Braveheart to his side.

Nobody ran, but the woman blessed herself and gripped her husband's hand.

'You have to kill them,' she said. 'We have to keep them from the children.'

The thegn had fought before, that was clear in his stance, but the woman had only a hoe and a short seax. Dan knew by the look in her eyes that she was not going to let anyone near her children while she had breath in her. Unfortunately he did not think she'd have any breath for very long.

'Light the fires,' he shouted and one of the men ran to the house to grab a burning brand from the hearth and set fire to the dry hay and oil that they had strewn hastily around. Dan knew it would do little good. It took more than a few seconds' preparation to mount a defence. The farmer and his workers knew it was hopeless too. Dan could see it on their faces – the resignation and the fear. He looked up towards the trees and saw the enemy screaming, barking like a pack of wild dogs, charging towards them.

~ Chapter Twenty-seven ~

The first Vikings to emerge from the trees were both huge men, naked above the waist but for their badly cured wolfskin cloaks. The wolf's head each wore formed a kind of hood over their heads, so that they looked like pantomime creatures – or they might have done had not the men themselves been as wild and ferocious as beasts. The woman standing behind Dan let out a muted sob. Aethelnoth groaned.

'What is it?' Dan asked, hanging on to his sanity by a thread. His heart was pumping so hard and his whole body pulsed with such energy that he thought he might burst. His hand on Braveheart's head was shaking and it was not with nerves.

'They are berserkers – like you,' Aethelnoth said.

Something inside Dan thrilled at the prospect of meeting a worthy enemy. He hated himself for the thought. He had a farm to protect and were he to fail, people would die, and yet he relished the prospect of a good fight.

The two half-naked men were followed by five or six

other warriors kitted out in normal fighting clothes. To Dan's practised eye they looked to be professional soldiers, properly equipped. They hung well back from the two berserkers, who were slavering at the mouth and baying like wolves.

Dan thought that they looked completely insane with their long unkempt hair almost covering their faces. They were both unnaturally large men, almost as tall as Dan himself but bulky where he, in spite of his hours in the gym, still had the muscled slenderness of a youth. He did not know if he could keep the farmer and his family alive – not against madmen. He thought about Rhonwen's claim that he himself had magic that he had not yet discovered and hoped she was right. It was not looking good.

No one in the courtyard moved a muscle or made a sound; they seemed rooted to the spot by fear and horror. Dan roused himself and gave a loud cry. 'Get ready!' He turned to the boy on the roof and yelled, 'Hit them between the eyes!' He sounded as encouraging as he could, but he had seen that all but the berserkers wore helms and the boy's chance of doing any damage with a sling was minuscule. Still, every man needed hope and confidence before a battle and Dan did what he could to inspire it.

Braveheart was already snarling at his side, his growling slightly less bestial than the cries of the berserkers. Aethelnoth gripped his spear. He was breathing heavily in the rasping rapid rhythm of panic.

'It's fine,' Dan said, while he could still speak. 'They are only men.'

The pressure on him to run and kill was building. He wanted the fight very badly and it was getting harder to think of anything else. Almost without knowing what he was doing he ripped off his tunic to reveal his own naked torso – somewhat less impressive than that of his enemies – then squatted down on the ground to cover himself with mud. He took off his shoes too so that he could feel the ground beneath his feet, feel the power in the earth. Ursula had fed off the power of the land in Macsen's world – Dan hoped he could do the same in this one.

'Their blood will soak this earth!' he shrieked in what he trusted was a menacing way; it didn't come out very clearly. His tongue felt thick and overlarge in his mouth. He wished it was Ursula, not Aethelnoth, who was by his side. If he was going to die, he would have liked her near him, so that they could die as he'd always thought they might, shoulder to shoulder in the heat of battle. It was also true that with her strong arm and fearless heart on his side, death would have been a good deal less likely.

He tried to forget about her, about everything but what was to come. He wiped his muddy hand on his breeches and unsheathed his sword. Calling to Braveheart, he started to charge up to meet the enemy.

He was beginning to lose it as he ran to meet the two howling men. He was beginning to find that calm place within himself which was full of blood. He had to hope that whatever magic resided in him in this world would reveal itself, because he could not see that his own madness would be much use against theirs.

The shift happened; he was himself and then suddenly

he was a killer. There was no wild rage, only a curious calm and a strange joy. This was what he was born to do.

The first of the men hurled himself towards him, yowling and hissing like a thing possessed. Braveheart answered with a snarl and ran in to attack; the man batted him out of the way as if he were nothing. The giant dog, all muscle, sinew and vicious teeth, was flung through the air like a toy. He had done some damage first, tearing a chunk from the man's thigh. Blood seeped from the wound; the man did not appear to notice. He seemed impervious to pain. His eyes, under the stinking wolf's head, were bloodshot and crazed. Dan's sword stabbed at the man's naked chest but a great, brutish arm deflected the blade and two vast hands closed on Dan as if to strangle him or rend him limb from limb. Dan snarled.

It was not a noise that had ever issued from his throat before, but it felt right. The man was big but slow and Dan had plenty of time to bite down on the brawny arm as if he had jaws like Braveheart and the teeth of a predator. He felt the man's flesh tear, tasted hot blood and then headbutted the man out of his way. It was easy. Suddenly the man's strength no longer seemed so awesome; he was only a man. Dan did not know what he was – there was no time to evaluate, only to act – but with some part of his mind he did allow himself to wonder if he was still only a man, or even if he were a man at all.

Bright Killer lay on the ground a long arm's reach away, but he did not pick it up to finish off the berserker. He did not think it necessary. His own bare hands would be enough. Dan threw himself at the man, who still howled a war cry, thin and high and tinged with hysteria. Dan's body was a thing of enormous strength. He swiped at the man's naked chest with razor-sharp nails, raking it and making it bleed, as if his hands held knives as sharp and as steely as Bright Killer's blade. The man kept fighting back, though his torso was soaked in blood, though his resistance was weakening. Dan tired of the struggle and finished him quickly, snapping his neck with a violent twist of his massive paws.

The second man was approaching. Braveheart was whimpering somewhere out of his line of vision. Dan could smell death and fear. His balance was a bit off but he coped. He felt heavy and powerful. He dropped into something between a crouch and a crawl. The second berserker was screaming and foaming at the mouth. Dan pounced like some wild animal and killed this one with his teeth. It took a lot of self-control to make himself stop, even after the man was dead. The taste of blood and flesh was not repellent to him.

He got to his feet to take on the rest, the armed men – the men in helms and mail shirts – but they were running away, back towards the trees. Dan turned around to check on Braveheart, but the warhound was cowering from Dan, shivering and growling as though Dan himself had meta-morphosed into an enemy. 'Easy boy,' he said, but the words came out more like some kind of animal grumble: there was something wrong with his mouth. He did not let that worry him as there was still killing to be done. He smelled the enemy and heard them trampling in panic through the undergrowth; they would not escape.

Distantly he was aware that people were screaming. Had he missed an enemy? Someone was calling his name. He turned again to see a man he recognised standing by the warhound, stroking his head so that the dog's shivering was beginning to abate. Dan did not like other people comforting his dog and Braveheart was unquestionably his. He snarled reflexively and made to drive the man away, but the man raised a hand and suddenly Dan felt unbelievably sleepy, so sleepy that he had to lie down. Taliesin. The man's name was Taliesin. He was an enemy too, Dan thought, as sleep claimed him and he was lost to the world.

~ Chapter Twenty-eight ~

Dan woke to find Braveheart licking his face and a familiar voice patiently explaining why everything was fine.

'No, he is not a devil but one of God's own creatures. There is nothing to fear. Look, he is quite restored.'

Dan opened his eyes and closed them again rapidly. All he could see was Braveheart's open mouth and the grey sky heavy with imminent rain. He had a horrible taste in his own mouth and his limbs felt numb; he tried to clench his fist but it took too much effort. He took stock. He was alive and so was Braveheart. Taliesin lived, though Dan did not think that had been in doubt. It seemed that the thegn and his family still lived too. There had been a miracle of some sort and they had survived the onslaught of the Danes.

'Dan?' Taliesin must have seen the flicker of his eyelids. 'Dan, are you all right?'

Dan felt so strange that Taliesin's question proved difficult to answer. Taliesin's face appeared looking down at him – all creases, bags and tangled beard. His penetrating blue eyes were fearful.

'Yes. I feel strange. What happened? Have the Danes gone?'

A second figure, Aethelnoth, appeared and the two men helped Dan to his feet. He felt as unsteady as a toddler taking his first steps and had to clutch on to Taliesin's arm for support. It started to rain and he shivered with cold. For reasons that he now could not remember, he had removed most of his clothes. He was caked in quite a lot of dried blood. He was fairly sure that it was not his.

Taliesin led him to the farmhouse and Dan found it hard to avoid stumbling, as if his limbs were no longer his own, as if he'd been stretched on a rack. He ached all over. It struck him suddenly that Taliesin must be Aelfred's scop. When they got to the threshold, Taliesin called out a warning over the chatter of voices and helped him to the bench nearest the fire pit. The wife, whose life Dan thought he must have saved, crossed herself. That irritated him. That was the thing about being a killer: people depended on you doing what they hated and then they hated you for doing it.

The room seemed crowded – full of frightened children and the farmhands who had preceded him back to the house were now gathered round the hissing wood fire. The room reeked of smoke and sweat and the all-pervading scent of fear. He licked his lips. He was very thirsty, his throat sore as if he'd been shouting. Silence had fallen. Dan did not need to be an empath to know that he was very obviously not welcome.

'Fetch him a drink,' Taliesin demanded, and a boy

produced a clay beaker of water. All eyes were on Dan. Dan gulped the water swiftly, but it barely slaked his thirst. He nodded his thanks to the boy who'd given it to him, the boy who'd been ready to fight with the slingshot.

'How did you do it?' the boy asked boldly, swallowing down his terror. There was a communal intake of breath as all present listened for Dan's reply.

Dan realised that he'd probably killed a few Danes – if he hadn't done then these good people wouldn't all still be alive to stare at him as if he were some monster. Had he done something cruel or terrible to the enemy? He could not remember.

'How did I do what?' he answered evenly. He had better get the truth over with as soon as possible. Whatever it was he would have to live with it, add it to his already overburdened conscience.

The boy laughed nervously as though Dan had attempted to make a weak joke, which he might have done had he known what the boy was talking about. The boy explained: 'I mean how did you turn into a bear?'

There was a moment where Dan's mouth moved but no words came out. He remembered the taste of blood, the pliancy of flesh in his mouth, and ran from the house, stumbling on his unsteady legs. He knew it was true.

He was sick of course – who would not be? Then Taliesin was there beside him with more water and he rinsed his mouth out. It did not take away the taste, the metallic tang of blood. He could do little about his tears but wipe them roughly away. A warrior did not cry; a shape-shifter did not wail like a little child.

'Why?' Dan asked, more petulantly than he would have wanted, shamed to be showing so much weakness in front of Taliesin, who was not exactly his friend, who had tricked him into coming to this place.

'Need,' Taliesin said with a shrug. 'You called on the magic and you are the Bear Sark and a bear is what you became.'

'I killed with my teeth! I tasted flesh!' Taliesin's hand was on Dan's shoulder and he shrugged it away. 'Everyone is terrified of me now.'

'They think it is the work of the devil. If you were a Dane, it would be seen as Odin's work and a blessing, but not among the Aenglisc. If it is any help, I saw it all and I do not think you would have had any chance against them if you had fought as yourself – even lost in madness you would have been no match for those men. I am sorry this happened, Dan.'

'I don't believe you. You should not have brought me here,' Dan fired back, his anger growing. He felt it rise in him, a great tide of fury bubbling up and spilling out. Everything was Taliesin's fault. The very smell of him repulsed Dan. He could have torn him limb from limb. He wanted to tear him limb from limb. He could easily imagine how that would feel and he thought that it would feel very good. Taliesin was skinny, a tall man with little muscle to hold his bones in place. He seemed small to Dan, aware of his own muscular bulk, the huge force that lay under his skin. It would not take much strength to pull Taliesin apart like a doll, to crush his bones like dry sticks . . .

'Hush! Calm down – it is happening again.' Taliesin's voice was soothing, like a father to a child – and Dan was no child. Taliesin was always pushing him, manipulating him, getting him to act the way he wanted. Dan was fed up of it. He thrust away Taliesin's comforting arm with a hand grown heavy and immobile.

'Look at yourself!' Taliesin commanded with the power of enchantment in his voice. 'Look!'

Dan had no choice. Taliesin still had magic and under its compulsion Dan looked and saw his own forearm grown huge, knotted and bent out of shape. He saw his own deformed hand, as large as a man's head, rigid and darkened by fur, and with the claws of a bear. He screamed and his throat produced an inhuman sound which chilled even his own blood.

'You have to stop, Dan,' Taliesin said softly. 'My old friend Brother Frontalis would say that your soul is in danger and I fear that he would be right. You are losing your humanity. You have found a lust for blood that you never had before and the magic of this world is working on that, giving it physical form. You cannot lose control any more, Dan. Do you understand?'

Dan nodded; his head felt huge and fuzzy and it was hard to marshal his thoughts.

'You have to let me touch you. I can help, but you have to let me get close.'

Dan nodded again. He did not want to let the skinny human touch him though. He did not like his smell. Dan tried to make himself breathe slowly; he concentrated on that. His breath came out in bestial grunts, but he tried not to worry. He must not swipe at Taliesin with his great paw that could have knocked the man out with little more than a casual backhand slap. Dan managed to keep himself under control, he tried to remember his times tables, anything to override his instinct. He held himself rigid, growing hot with the effort of staying still. He allowed Taliesin to get close enough to touch his shoulder. Dan shuddered and something in him eased; the fury that he had held tight within him relaxed. It was magic, of course, and he mistrusted it, but he was not in a position to turn down help.

Taliesin stayed with his hand on Dan's shoulder for some time. Dan felt his anger die down, felt the exhaustion of the aftermath of strong emotion.

'Thank you,' he said at last in his own human voice that only sounded a little strange as he fought with his own complicated feelings and the tears he could not quite keep from shedding. 'What am I going to do? You said those people needed me to fight for them. I was trying to do the right thing. It isn't easy, you know, to run up to madmen knowing that they are going to hurt you. It isn't easy to fight when at any minute you know that it could be you with the sword in the belly, the spear through the spine. I have risked all that and now I am punished. I am a monster.'

Taliesin didn't say anything. A quick glance in his direction showed Dan that he was asleep – tired out from the effort of bringing Dan back to himself. Dan found himself smiling. It was typical of Taliesin to dodge the hard questions. He got to his feet. How ironic that he should end up being the bear when it was Ursula who was known as the Lady Ursa, the bear on the hillside, the brave spirit of Arturus's Britain. In all the madness of the previous few hours Dan had not forgotten what he was there for and he wasn't about to forget it now. He went to find his horse. He had kept the farm safe. The people there might not have liked the way he'd done it, but he had kept them safe and now he had Ursula to save.

~ Chapter Twenty-nine ~

Dan led his horse back to the yard to get Taliesin. Perhaps he ought to have realised earlier that Aelfred's scop, the man they had been trying to meet, would be Macsen's bard, Taliesin. It was obvious when he came to think about it and, on the plus side, Taliesin could play the harp better than anyone else Dan knew, so they were unlikely to be killed for their lack of musical prowess. It was always good to reduce the number of reasons your enemies might have for killing you.

Dan called out to Aethelnoth and to Braveheart to alert them that they should move on. He went alone to wash in the stream: cold but necessary ablutions. Things were not going the way he'd hoped. The magic of this world was not working on him in helpful ways. All he wanted was to find Ursula; it did not seem fair that such a simple desire was proving so difficult to satisfy. A sudden noise made him turn. He whipped round to face whatever the world should throw at him next.

'Please, don't hurt me!' It was the boy. He had put up his hand to defend himself and was trembling with fear –

his voice a frightened squeak. 'I picked up your sword and cleaned it and my mother asks you to take this cloak and shirt.'

The boy swallowed hard and Dan checked himself to make sure that he had not begun to transform again. His hands looked normal, if rather blue.

'We are grateful. You saved us. We know that – it was just . . .'

'Don't worry,' Dan said. 'I am frightened too. I don't want to be a bear.' That was true. This new gift was more frightening than anything that had gone before. It was worse than hearing other people's thoughts. Dan had to fight back tears and he did not want this boy to know of his weakness.

'I am a man and I am sorry that you had to see what I did – how I fought. I am ashamed of that. Battle is terrible and it turns men into beasts – inside.' He shrugged. 'I did not expect to be a beast on the outside too.'

'You were brave,' the boy said hesitantly.

'So were you,' Dan answered, with a smile which felt fake even though he meant it.

'I didn't have to do anything – they all ran away when . . . when you did what you did.'

Dan nodded. 'I am glad you did not have to do anything. It is a terrible thing to kill another person.'

'But sometimes it has to be done – doesn't it?' the boy said. Dan splashed icy water on his face.

'I don't know any more. I always thought I fought on the side of good, but all the killing . . . it has turned me into someone else, something else – a monster.'

'I am glad,' the boy said. 'If you hadn't been a bigger monster than them, I would be dead. They would have taken my mother and sister and killed us all.' He hooked the clean, dry garments on the branch of an overhanging tree along with a piece of rough cloth for Dan to dry himself.

'Thank you,' Dan said. 'You should probably know that King Aelfred is gathering an army to take back his lands from the Danes and to take back his throne from his nephew. There will be messengers, I'm sure . . . Think hard before you join him.'

The boy shook his head. 'I have to fight. I have to fight to keep the farm, to keep the others safe. There isn't anything to think about.'

He ran back the way he'd come and Dan was left wishing he could be as certain. He had lost count of the men he'd killed in his journeys through the Veil and that could not be a good thing. Perhaps each death had made him less a man and more a beast. Maybe he deserved to be a bear.

He took the new clothes gratefully, noticing their fine quality. The woman had given him the very best that she had. He didn't know if that made him feel better or worse.

By the time Dan returned from the stream, Aethelnoth had woken Taliesin and they were ready to leave. Only the boy waved them off. 'Think about what I said!' Dan called, by way of farewell, though he was certain his warning had fallen on deaf ears.

'So, still think I'm a Viking?' Dan asked Aethelnoth when they had left the farm behind.

Aethelnoth kept his horse well away from Dan's so that Dan had to shout back over his shoulder to be heard.

'I don't know what to think. I don't think such savagery can be godly.'

'Will you tell the King what happened?'

Aethelnoth's silence had an eloquence of its own. Dan doubted that in Aethelnoth's shoes he would want to tell a killer what he did not want to hear either.

They rode in silence again for a while. Braveheart was trotting by Dan's side. He at least seemed to have forgotten about Dan's unfortunate transformation into a wild beast; perhaps dogs were more forgiving. Dan's mount had for some reason decided that Braveheart was not a problem and was far better behaved than Dan had expected. It was a pity in a way, because at least a difficult mount would have given Dan something to think about besides the obvious. Perhaps that was why Taliesin chose to distract him with some questions of his own.

'Why did you say I was to blame – back when I first saw you?'

'Because you gave me that orb thing to raise the Veil and lied and told me that it would bring me back to Macsen.'

'Dan, I don't know what you are talking about. I haven't seen you since we crossed the Veil after we left the battlefield together at Camlann. I did as you said. I left you in the field before we got to the place of the huge land-ships. I took Braveheart, raised the Veil and found myself here. The presence of Rhonwen called to me, I suppose. I am bound to her after all, through thick and thin, through time and all the strangeness of the Veil.'

'Then I saw you in my past but your future,' Dan said with sudden certainty. 'Don't do it! When you get the chance, please don't give me the orb. I don't want to be here. I don't want Ursula to be here. None of it would have happened but for you.'

'I can't promise anything,' Taliesin said. 'If I brought you here, perhaps I have to bring you here – I am not fool enough to try to change what has to be.'

As Taliesin had been trying to change things since they first met, interfering and meddling in Dan's life, he felt a burst of hot rage at such a dishonest response. He forced himself to calm down. The bear was waiting for him on the other side of anger and he did not want to turn into that savage beast ever again.

'Whatever . . .' Dan said in English, which neither Taliesin nor Aethelnoth understood. He made himself breathe deeply and tried not to think of Taliesin as the interfering old man he undoubtedly was. If Taliesin knew anything of Dan's internal struggle, he didn't acknowledge it, but wittered on in a loud conversational voice, as if Dan cared at all about what he'd been doing.

'I have been out and about scouting for the King and he told me to meet Aethelnoth near here. I did not expect to see you again. I heard the Dane's charge and saw you transform. It was extraordinary. You were a magnificent beast – a giant even among béars. Amazing!'

'It did not feel amazing,' Dan said bleakly, but that was a lie. That was the worst thing. The bear had no conscience – men were meat and death was of no consequence, unless it was his own.

He had loved having that power, that strength, the weapons that were just there in his hands, in his mouth. He had not even needed Bright Killer. He was complete in himself. That was the worst thing of all. When he had been killing those men in such a violent and vicious way, it *had* felt amazing – he had been perfectly and completely happy. Taliesin shot him a quizzical look which Dan ignored and they rode on.

Dan realised that there were Danes ahead at about the same moment that Braveheart stopped, sniffed the air and growled. The scent of men was strong and Dan found himself licking his lips. 'There are Vikings ahead,' he said softly, 'and I want you, Taliesin, to put me to sleep. I will not fight as a monster.'

'But, Dan . . .'

'Do it!' Dan's sword was in his hand before he had finished the sentence. Taliesin looked mutinous. 'Do not trick me again, Taliesin. I am in this mess because of you and you are going to get me out of it. Put me to sleep.'

'They will kill us.'

'I am sure with all your spells and charms you can think of something,' Dan hissed. He knew that the transformation was coming. His body was heavier, denser, and he was growing; he could feel it. 'Make me sleep!'

Taliesin lifted his hands to do Dan's bidding. Dan heard the wild war cries of the charging enemy in the last instant before his eyelids closed.

~ Chapter Thirty ~

The girl who was her enemy called Ursula again. She did not like being brought back to her body any more. The pain that might have been hunger was stronger, nagging at her, and there was thirst too and other kinds of discomfort that even the power of magic did not entirely blunt.

They were all there when she opened her eyes. All staring at her hungrily, wanting things from her and giving nothing back. Guthrum, still drunk from the revelling of the previous night, sweaty and corpulent beneath his finery, stood at the front of the crowd of warriors and frightened, abused townswomen. She felt the women's pain as a great rolling tide of misery that repelled her. Her friend, Gunnarr, the one who had stood vigil by her side on the way to this awful place, stood nearby looking anxious. Things were not going quite as he had planned; Finna had taken the role of Guthrum's confidante that he had sought. Ursula felt Gunnarr's resentment and his disgust. The resentment she understood, but she did not at first recognise the source of his disgust. Her eye was inevitably drawn to the one who'd called her yet again, the one who'd dragged her to this place of misery. Ursula noted that the blind girl wore a huge brooch of precious stones, that her straggly unkempt hair had been washed and plaited and that the clothes that covered her thin body were of the richest colours, of the finest cloth and edged with the most intricate and costly silk braid. She was still the same underneath, though, still a curious absence; nothing more than a steely will hidden in mist. The magic in Ursula burned hot and dry and she was exhausted by it. The magic brought her back at Finna's calling and she did not like that. For the first time Ursula did not feel free, but chained by the power that held her in thrall to the whims of Finna.

'See what we have brought to feed you, Goddess,' Finna said.

It was then that Ursula saw them – the chained prisoners. Even then she did not guess at what was to come.

Dan woke to the tickle of Taliesin's beard against his ear and Taliesin's voice whispering urgently: 'Wake up now or you'll never wake.'

Maybe there was magic in that or maybe not – either way Dan did as he was told. It was dark and he was surrounded by shadows and the stink of human waste. Dan gagged. His sense of smell was all too acute, as if he retained the senses of a bear even after he had lost the form. It was some time since Talieisn had bathed and his clothes smelled like those of a tramp who'd lived rough for a couple of years.

'Where are Aethelnoth and Braveheart?' Dan whispered.

'Braveheart is muzzled and tied up, but he will be well cared for – the Vikings were impressed by his ferocity and he's been given as a gift to Guthrum. The news is not so good on Aethelnoth.' Dan felt the sudden chill of fear and guilt; if Aethelnoth had died because he had not been awake to fight for him there would be another death on his conscience. Taliesin seemed to guess at his concerns and patted Dan's arm reassuringly. 'He fought well enough and was captured as a warrior. He was barely injured . . .' Taliesin paused.

'So?'

'I'm sorry, Dan, but the Goddess has demanded the sacrifice of twenty warriors.'

'What goddess?' Dan asked, but he knew the answer even before he'd finished speaking. Ursula. 'What has happened to her?'

'She always did love magic,' Taliesin said softly. 'I fear it has consumed her and driven her mad.'

'Can you tell that, or is it just a guess?' Dan spoke more sharply than he had intended.

'I can feel her power, but I can't get near her,' Taliesin said. 'But why would she demand sacrifice if she was sane?'

Dan shook his head more to shake away the idea of Ursula turned mad than to disagree. 'I have to go to her!'

'Then your best bet is to get yourself recognised as a warrior and readied for sacrifice.'

It was not such a stupid idea, but Dan was not sure that

he could control the bear sufficiently to allow himself to be readied for sacrifice.

When Dan looked around him, he could see that he was corralled in a sheep pen with women, children and old men. He did not know what was to become of them, but he doubted that they would kill the women – not from chivalry, but because they could be put to good use. He was less confident about the children and the old men.

The pen was formed of nothing more secure than a loose fence, designed to contain sheep not men, but it was guarded by three well-armed warriors. When Dan touched his sword belt, he was surprised to find that Bright Killer was still there. Taliesin shrugged modestly. 'I have some power here. I made you look like an old man.'

'They might have killed me.'

'They would have killed you if they'd recognised you as the bear man. Some gratitude would not go amiss.'

Dan mumbled his thanks. 'What if I got all the able-bodied people left here to help me attack the guards?'

Taliesin raised an eyebrow. 'There are no able-bodied people here.'

But Dan wasn't listening; he'd spotted a young woman sitting alone. Something about her posture suggested that she still had some fight left in her. Dan moved stealthily to sidle alongside her.

'Do you want to help us get out?' he asked. She gave him a penetrating look. He did not know if Taleisin's glamour was still on him, but if it was she saw through it.

'What do you want me to do?'

'There are three guards – my friend and I might be able

to manage two. Could you take a third?'

She weighed up the possibility. 'I have this,' she said and, turning her back on Dan, fumbled under her over-dress to produce something that glinted dully in the moonlight.

Dan tested it with his thumb; it was sharp enough. 'Do you know what to do?'

He saw her teeth flash in the darkness. 'My father will help,' she said, indicating to an elderly man sitting nearby. 'He has killed men before.'

If her father had posed any danger, he would already be dead. Still, the Danes were drunk and not expecting trouble and if Taliesin were able to cast some spell, the old man might be some help. 'All right. Which one will you take?'

She pointed at the drunkest of them – a young lightly built man, barely out of his teens.

'When my friend starts to sing, start moving. When he stops – do what you can.'

He thought she smiled.

'Good luck,' he said and made his way back to Taliesin.

'I've got an idea, Taliesin. I don't know if it will work but I need to get to Ursula and I'm not going to do it here or tied up as a human sacrifice.' Dan could smell blood; the smell carried on the smoky air made him hungry and that made him angry. The bear was still there, scarcely under control.

'What do you want me to do?'

'Can you still use the magic of your voice – like you could when you were only a bard in Macsen's land?'

'I was never "only a bard", boy. My gifts were always exceptional.' Taliesin had slipped into the Combrogi tongue. Dan explained what he wanted Taliesin to do and eased Bright Killer from its scabbard.

Taliesin produced his harp from under his cloak. Dan could sense the magic as soon as Taliesin plucked his first note; his voice had not weakened or coarsened over time and a hush fell upon the captives. The beauty of the sound even calmed the irritation of the guards. No one moved and Dan's attempt to be inconspicuous, running with his body in a crouch position over bent knees, ought to have been very noticeable, but no one saw him.

The largest of the guardsmen was still a few inches shorter than Dan. He was a thickset man, leaning with his back against the fence, staring out towards the distant bonfire. He was lost in the spell of Taliesin's music. It was not difficult for Dan to slip under the fence and grab him from behind. It was more difficult for Dan to keep his aggression under control.

'You make a sound and I'll kill you,' Dan said and it was easy to make his words sound convincing because they were probably true. A part of him wanted to kill the guard. Taliesin was right: his soul was in danger. He had never felt that way before; he had never actually wanted to kill before. That shocked him. He let the man feel Bright Killer's blade against his neck. He had to be careful not to nick him with the edge. He was afraid that the smell of blood might arouse the bear.

The guard's companion, standing just a few feet away, gave no sign of having noticed anything untoward. He was gazing at the misty haze around the moon, beguiled by the voice of Taliesin.

'You and your companion here are going to escort me to the Goddess, and then you are going to leave me there, just as if you were on official business.' Dan did not succeed in keeping the pent-up aggression from his voice, but that might have been a good thing. The guard nodded his head rapidly, a tiny staccato movement; the blade was very close to his throat. Dan wrinkled his nose, as the man's personal hygiene was no better than Taliesin's and he stank of stale sweat.

There was a sound of struggle, a muffled shout and then silence. Dan hoped that the girl had subdued her man.

'Do not try anything clever with me,' Dan warned. 'My friend is gifted in magic. Should you disobey me, he will kill you when you sleep and it will not be the easy death of the sword. Let's go!' The guard believed him, Dan could tell. The man shook slightly as he beckoned to the other man.

'We have to take this one to the Goddess.'

'But we took all the ones she wanted already,' the second guard whined. Dan suspected that he wanted to stay and listen to the music. His eyes widened as he saw Dan's sword against his companion's neck. To do him credit he went for his own seax, but the man Dan held stopped him with a curse.

'Do as he says. What is an extra prisoner to us?'

Dan allowed himself to be flanked by the two guards. He cut the rope which tied the gate of the corral shut with one good blow of his strong blade. The Danes looked impressed and Dan realised that he had not yet seen a blade to rival Bright Killer in craftsmanship or edge. Dan waited for a moment to be certain that the rest of the plan would work. He nodded at Taliesin. The crowd parted to allow Taliesin through and when he got to the gate he changed his tune into something a little brighter, a joyous little dance. As he left the compound the Viking captives followed him in a daze, like rats enchanted by some Pied Piper. They were not far from the edge of Cippenham and in the darkness, with the town deserted, it might be possible for them to get some way along the road before their escape was noticed. Watching the hesitant way some of them walked, Dan was not certain they would get too far, but they would at least die free. The girl who had helped him blew him a kiss as she passed. She was little more than a kid. He nodded an acknowledgement.

Dan felt pleased. He didn't know what had happened to the third guard but he had achieved something without violence, without unleashing the wrath of the bear. He sheathed his sword, confident that the guards would not try to hurt him.

He had no idea what he would do next.

~ Chapter Thirty-one ~

The blind girl stepped forward to stand in the open space between Ursula, the prisoners and the crowd. Her voice was not loud and no one caught the first few words that she spoke, but then a hush descended as each person present strained to hear what she had to say. Ursula tried not to listen. She was not successful. Finna was saying something about the offerings for Freya ensuring victory for all those in Guthrum's army. The crowd cheered at the end of her brief speech and the prisoners looked bemused. They did not stay bemused for long. Within moments it was very clear what was about to happen.

First the men were stripped of their tunics, so that they were naked to the waist. Guthrum picked the strongest-looking man first. The prisoner's face was lost in the shadow, but Ursula saw the way he flinched slightly as Guthrum stepped towards him and unsheathed his seax. The blade looked wickedly sharp. Guthrum bowed to Ursula.

'May it please the Goddess,' he said in a bull's bellow,

and he began to carve the shape of an eagle into the man's naked back with bold, confident strokes. Somehow the man did not scream. Not that his outward stoicism made any difference to Ursula: Ursula heard the screaming in her own head. When he began to cut more deeply the man made a terrible little choked cry. Something about his agony reminded Ursula of who she was. More of Guthrum's men joined him in the ritual. The scene was loathsome and the ground around the captive's feet was spattered and darkened by blood and the men cutting him were splattered too. It was worse than battle, this cold deliberate infliction of pain. She remembered battles. The memory was hard to pin down but there was a time when she had fought and she remembered pain. What was happening was grotesque. The blind girl had her face turned towards the men, straining to hear what was going on. A small smile played around her lips. Ursula was truly repulsed. First she tried to run from the pain of it, but the girl Finna somehow, through the grim power of her will, kept Ursula there in the centre of the circle of bound and terror-stricken men. She could not escape; she had to watch and to share. The blazing bonfire bathed the rapt faces of the onlookers in demonic light. Ursula shut her eyes. She could do that. Finna could not stop her doing that, but it made no difference either; she could see what was going on through a hundred pairs of eyes; the horror was only magnified.

This was not the way things should be. This was not what she wanted. She had to stop this. She had grown unused to thinking like a person, she had trouble concentrating on one thing, but she could not let this carry on. She must set the prisoners free. That was easily done. She released the men from their bonds; with a little flick of her mind the hemp cords that held them slipped like coiled snakes to the floor. One punched his captor while another ran.

'Kill them!' Guthrum screamed when he realised what had happened and somehow the scene of sacrifice became a battle.

The prisoners were unarmed, so Ursula removed the knives of the Viking captors. They flew through the air like a hail of short spears and embedded themselves, blade first, in the earth around where she lay. That at least gave the captives a fighting chance, and fight they did. The air was filled with the grunts and thumps of men, with muffled war cries and the sound of impact and struggle. The captives were wrestling with their captors.

Soon armed men from the crowd joined in and blood began to flow. Ursula did not know what to do. For all her power she felt helpless. People were screaming and it was all confusion. She had to stop this madness. It was too complicated to disarm all those who now fought and she knew too well that a man's naked fist was sufficient to kill. In a moment of inspiration she called up a storm. Lightning crackled and it began to rain so fast and heavily that the ground became a mud bath in seconds, the bonfire went out and all was darkness. Finna's control did not falter; it made no difference to her whether the night was lit or not. She found her way to Ursula's side.

'That was not clever,' she said. 'You will damage your

reputation if you don't accept the gifts that are your due.'

Ursula refused to acknowledge her tormentor. It was difficult to narrow her awareness down to the scene before her, and when she managed to focus on the human beings involved it seemed clear that what she had done so far had resulted in more death not less. There was a wild animal loose among the struggling bodies and it was making things a good deal worse. She did not think that she was responsible for the presence of the beast but it was hard to be sure.

It took an enormous amount of energy to concentrate on the here and now. There were things that she ought to remember, things that had to do with the wild beast that was tearing its way through the tightly packed bodies of the men locked in such pointless combat. It was no good. She could not help. She could not keep track of what was happening and she could not think; she appeared to have forgotten how. She was trapped in this place that she did not want to be. Had she been just Ursula she might have cried tears of frustration, though she was not much given to such outbreaks of emotions; stuck in this one place with the body she had almost forgotten she owned, she let rip all her frustration and fury with herself, with Finna, with the stupid men who had gone on killing in spite of her best efforts. With one wild blast of power she reignited the sodden bonfire so it burned by her will alone. The flame towered above the desperate men fighting for their lives in the darkness. It reared up like some mythic creature made of flame, shaped like a bird; it flapped wings of fire and illuminated the whole horrible scene. It burned with unnatural heat, fuelled by Ursula's unnatural power, and she could not keep it bound in the shape she had chosen to cast it. The firebird's wings were huge and when they flapped stray sparks caught the timber frame of a nearby building and in seconds that too had begun to blaze. The women ran to save their former homes and Guthrum, fearing that he would lose his treasure as well as his temporary shelter, shrieked above the tumult, 'Cippenham is on fire! Save it!' Only then did the enemies pull apart.

Dan had arrived seconds before the rain came. He had known at once where Ursula lay. Each person had their own unique and distinctive smell; he had not always known that nor known that Ursula's was beautiful. That did not surprise him and he had no trouble recognising her scent, even though his nose had never been keen enough to perceive it before. She smelled like Ursula was. He stopped for a moment and sniffed the air, drinking her in. There had been moments when he'd doubted that he would ever find her again.

He began to run to her but there were people in his way and the scent of blood was maddening. The sounds of fighting excited him; he didn't like the way they made him feel. It was suddenly hard to concentrate. He felt that pulse of furious energy that signalled the beginning of change. The two men who were pretending to guard Dan took one look at the chaos before them and then at Dan's face. The bigger man let out a strangled cry and ran. His companion followed him an instant later. Perhaps he had forgotten Dan's promise to have him killed in his sleep; perhaps he did not care. Dan did not try to stop them; they were an irrelevance. He began to pick his way across the soft mud towards Ursula. He thought of her and that helped to keep the urge for violence at bay. His heart was beating very hard and he felt very powerful. He also felt uncomfortable; his boots were far too tight and he prised them off, using his left foot to remove his right and vice versa. It was good to feel the cold sludge-like earth between his toes and he was immediately better balanced.

He could smell Aethelnoth somewhere in that crowd of men battling to stay upright on treacherous ground, struggling to avoid a knife thrust, fighting blind in this mass insanity. Even Dan, on the brink of entering his own private madness, could see that what was going on lacked any reason. Loyalty to his comrade gave him the excuse he needed to turn his thoughts from Ursula for a moment. Loyalty allowed him to enter the fray: he had to help Aethelnoth.

The moon had all but disappeared beneath a thick veil of cloud. When it emerged briefly, its light offered Dan little useful information: a glint of metal, the paleness of flesh – nothing more. He had to rely on his hearing and his sense of smell. Fortunately they were both inhumanly sharp. Dan thought that he would be all right so long as he didn't get angry, so long as he didn't lose his temper, so long as he thought only about saving Aethelnoth. No one spoke; no one had the energy or the breath. The only sounds were grunts and curses, heavy frightened breath-ing, screams, cries of pain and the uncomfortable noises of impact – thuds, thumps, cracks and very occasionally the clash of metal or the sound of metal hitting flesh and bone. It was not noisy, not like some video game. Death came less dramatically, less neatly; it was all a horrible muddy mess and Dan threw himself into it with a kind of crazed joy, but he was still Dan. He gripped Bright Killer and began to slash his way through the packed melee to his former companion. Perhaps it was a mistake to believe he could retain control long enough to save Aethelnoth, perhaps it was foolish overconfidence, for the moment some poor unfortunate turned to retaliate for a glancing blow, Dan's fury blossomed into a wild anger that made his whole body sing with a kind of ecstasy of rage. He roared and ran the man through.

After that he lost it. He was aware of throwing men out of his way. He did not see how or where they landed and he ignored their screams and their palpable fear. Somehow he had the wit to sheathe his sword before his paws became too clumsy for such a delicate movement. He swiped at anything that got in his way. If it had been chaos before, the scene now became yet more hellish, as everyone tried to run from the monster he had turned into. Men trampled one another into the mud in their eagerness to get away.

The bear found Aethelnoth bleeding from an existing injury and struggling to defend himself. The bear charged towards his opponent, who dropped everything and backed away in obvious terror. The bear towered above the unfortunate Viking and raked him with his sharpened claws. The weight of his massive paw and the strength of his assault knocked the man down. The bear wanted to finish what he had started, but Dan remembered Aethelnoth. He clung to the memory like a drowning man might cling to a raft. He was there to save Aethelnoth.

The bear snarled, fighting the urge to tear up and destroy all the frail human bodies that still, in spite of their best efforts to run, pressed too close to him. With monumental effort Dan picked Aethelnoth up and carried him through the remaining combatants as they struggled to get out of his way. Not all of them managed to move quickly enough, but the bear dispatched them swiftly and without pleasure.

Suddenly the doused fire rekindled and the bear was forced to back away from the scorching heat of the blaze. The fire grew and spread until it took on the form of a great eagle flapping its wings. Ursula. The memory of Ursula's need helped Dan to get himself back under control. Somehow, he recognised the strange fiery manifestation of Ursula's power as a cry for help. She had turned herself into an eagle once and this bird of flame was just another manifestation of her magic. She needed him. He felt himself shrink to normal Dan proportions and he set Aethelnoth back down on his feet.

'Dan!' Aethelnoth gasped, gripping Dan's arm to steady himself. He was bleeding profusely but, as far as Dan could tell, not fatally. 'We have to get out of here.'

'Not yet.' Dan's words came out as a guttural grunt but at least they were comprehensible. 'We need to rescue Ursula.'

Ursula was lost. Finna had fled when the heat of the

flames had become too great. Guthrum, with unexpected chivalry, came and led her away. The scorching heat did not bother Ursula, who was unaware of its proximity to her body. She had fled the instant Finna let her go. She fled to other places where the night was cool, and the night birds and the nocturnal beasts went about their business of living and dying undisturbed by the madness of men.

Someone was calling to her. She heard a voice from far away, a man's voice calling a name that might have been hers. It was not 'Freya', nor 'Goddess', but something else – a name that brought with it pictures of a past that could have been hers, that was so far removed from her present that it was hard to be sure.

'Ursula.'

There was something about his voice that touched her, something that made her want to see him, to return to the hell from which she'd fled just to find out why his voice moved her. She forced herself back to the stink of smoke and the burning flames and opened her eyes. The heat was very intense and a man was lifting her over his shoulder. She was aware that her body was a dead weight but she seemed to have forgotten how to move it.

'Aethelnoth, give me a hand.'

The words were hard to hear because the man's voice sounded dry and he kept coughing. It was hard to breathe in the smoke. It was probably time to put out the fire; it was so hot and so close her hair was singed by it. Her fire creature had gone wild and it took some concentration to get it back under control. It had divided itself, multiplying until it was a flock of wild birds opening many wings to embrace everything in the world. It was beautiful and exhilarating and too much. She reached out her power and gently, regretfully, snuffed it out.

'That was close,' a man said. He was very frightened. He had been one of the prisoners. His torso was naked and bleeding from several cuts and contusions. One eye was swelling and shaded like a ripening plum where he must have been hit. He was coated in mud and soot. He was probably lucky to be alive.

'Dan! She's awake! Her eyes are open.'

If the man had sounded frightened before, he sounded terrified now. He was afraid of her. He saw her as the Goddess who had demanded his life as a sacrifice. She would have liked to explain that it was all a mistake, but no words came. The man carrying her, the man the prisoner called 'Dan', set her down on her feet so that she leaned against him.

'Can you walk?' he asked her.

She liked his voice. It reminded her of things just out of the reach of her memory. She struggled to focus on his question. She remembered about walking, of course she did, but she couldn't remember how to make her body obey her. She called to a horse in a field on the outskirts of the town so that it might carry her.

It was then that she saw him, this Dan. His face was blackened by soot but that only made his wild eyes seem brighter. He was tall – as tall as she was, and as strong as she had once been. His eyes scanned her face and suddenly he hugged her, kissing her face with a kind of desperation. She was like a rag doll in his arms, unable to respond, and then with a different kind of magic he was there in her mind, in that lonely lost place within her.

'*Ursula?*'

'*Dan?*'

'*Where have you been?*'

She could not answer, only let out a mental wail of anguish and relief. There was no word to describe where she'd been, but it had been very far away from Ursula.

She felt her body sag against him; her knees, which hadn't been doing a great job of bearing her weight, suddenly buckled as everything came flooding back. She started to cry. She could not help it. Great, ridiculous, childish sobs racked her.

'What's wrong?' the other man cried out in alarm, but Dan had his arms round her, holding her up. She let her head rest on his shoulder and allowed the tears to come.

'It's all right. She's come back to me,' Dan replied thickly. There was something not entirely right about him – Ursula knew that the moment his thoughts had touched hers – but for the present she was too grateful that he had found her to worry about what that might be. The horse she had called announced its arrival with a snort and a restless pawing of the ground. Ursula had given it orders and it had to obey.

'We should go. We are in danger here,' Dan said without moving. He was holding on to her as if she were his port in a storm and not the other way around. He kissed the top of her head and hugged her tighter. Ursula could not stop crying and was a long way off being capable of speech, but Dan understood her perfectly and that was all that mattered.

She felt the roughness of his tunic against her face. It was filthy, smeared with mud and blood and stinking of sweat, but she did not care. She tasted the salt of her own tears and breathed in the smell of Dan's hair. For the first time in a very long time she knew exactly where she was. She was Ursula and Dan had found her. She felt safe and she did not want to move.

'This is Ursula, my comrade-at-arms, the person I have been trying to find since before I came to Aelfred's court.'

'The Goddess?'

'She is not a goddess, she is my . . .' Dan hesitated. 'She is my heart.' That made Ursula want to smile. She was Dan's heart!

'We can't take her with us. The Danes will come back from fighting the fire and they will kill us if they think we've abducted the Goddess!'

The other man was so fearful he was beginning to get on Ursula's nerves. Did he not grasp that Dan had just saved her from a kind of strange living death? Did he not realise how much she had needed saving? Did he not know how Finna had used her? Finna might come! The thought flashed into her head. Worse, Finna might call her like she was some kind of dog. Ursula's response was instinctive. She had to get away from her, hide from her, so that Finna could not use her again. She was quite pleased with herself for recognising that she had been used; it was the nearest thing to reasoning she had done in a while. The need to get away from Finna forced her reluctantly from Dan's embrace.

Ursula still did not trust herself to speak and was glad that Dan seemed to see what needed to be done. He signalled for the other man to steady the horse and lifted her on to its back.

'I'm going back for Taliesin and Braveheart. Look after Ursula. She's not herself yet. Take her away from here. Head back to Athelney and I will find you on the road!'

The words did not mean much, and she had to focus very hard to keep herself within herself as Dan spoke to her again.

'Ursula. There are things I have to do. This is Aethelnoth, a comrade. He'll stay with you.' She sensed that Dan was as reluctant to leave her as she was to see him go. She still could not remember why they had become separated.

She did not enter Aethelnoth's thoughts or those of the horse. She did not even try to enter Dan's mind. She wanted to understand more of what had happened to her, but she did not want to use magic because Finna would know. She licked dry lips and touched the sword at her hip. She knew she was Ursula and that was a start.

'I'm OK,' she said and her voice came out all cracked and croaky.

Seeing Aethelnoth's blank look, she realised that she had used the wrong words. The right words were somewhere in her head. Aethelnoth did not speak the language of Gunnarr. She found the right words and made an effort to sound more like the Ursula she wanted to be.

'I can take care of myself. I don't need looking after. Just show me where to go.' The words came more easily. She cleared her throat and tried to smile. Her hand grasped the sword tightly and she remembered how to wield it. She straightened her posture. She knew who she was. She was Ursula, warrior and sorceress, and that was a good start.

She wanted to follow Dan, but knew that in her present state she would be little use. She had only just realised that she'd lost him and now he was gone again. She watched him walk into the heart of the town. He said that she was his heart. That made her feel so happy because . . . ? She pursued the question and suddenly she remembered the rest. She wasn't just a warrior and a sorceress; she was also Ursula Dorrington, who had screwed up badly. In a sudden flood of images she recalled what had happened in the library before she'd run away. She remembered hugging the tree and racing through the Veil, leaving Dan to follow behind. She hadn't behaved very well. She didn't like what she'd remembered, but Dan had forgiven her. She was his heart!

The magic she had craved so much had possessed and exhausted her and, sitting on her horse, leaving the scene of mayhem and murder, she felt like an old dried-out husk of a sometime person, worn out, weary and racked with sudden guilt. The buzz of magic in her blood no longer excited her; it felt as if it had eaten away at her until she was just this weak, enfeebled creature who had for too long forgotten even her name.

She had to pull herself together. The man, Aethelnoth,

who limped by her side, exuded resentment that he had been left to defend the very person for whom he was so nearly sacrificed. He was unarmed and in poor condition and the Danes would be after them soon.

It would have been easy to change her appearance, to heal her companion. Anything was possible with magic, but she dared not use it.

'We look like we are running away. You look like a prisoner and I, well . . .' Words failed her. 'We need to find you some clothes and I need a helm or something to cover my hair.'

'You have a plan?' Aethelnoth said mockingly. 'Why don't you just blast the Danes to hell, set fire to them? Why don't you use whatever demon power you have? I do not know where you and Dan came from but I think it would be better if Aelfred had nothing more to do with either of you. Your power does not come from God.'

Ursula was too tired to debate theology with her reluctant ally. Walking and talking took all her energy; thinking was still largely beyond her. She guided the horse to the edge of town and the bridge that led out of Cippenham. She did not know if that was the right way or not and Aethelnoth offered no guidance. As they approached they could see that there were guards on the gate. Ursula pulled the pony into the shelter of some trees.

She scraped her hair back from her head, plaiting it in the style favoured by some of the Danish warriors. Even such a simple task made her arms ache. 'You are my slave,' she said. 'Where can I claim to be going?'

Aehelnoth shrugged unhelpfully. 'You are the Viking goddess. You know more than I of their heathen ways.'

Ursula kept her temper with some difficulty. She did not know what would happen if she allowed herself to forget herself even for a second. The magic was still there. Every moment she had to fight the urge to use it. She wanted to turn herself into Boar Skull, her male alter ego, but she resisted. She was Ursula and that would have to be enough.

'Put your hands behind your back, bow your head and look beaten,' she hissed at Aethelnoth and rode confidently towards the bridge.

She greeted the guards in the bantering tones she had heard the warriors use among themselves. She kept her voice low and her body language masculine. It was a part she had played for so long in previous visits through the Veil that it came quite easily.

'I am taking this Aenglisc dog to a lady I know – a gift that may bring me her favour,' Ursula said by way of explanation. She winked broadly and their response were predictably obscene, then they waved her over the bridge.

'What did you say?' Aethelnoth asked when they were out of sight.

'Nothing worth repeating,' Ursula said. 'Barracks humour.'

'And what would you know of that?' Aethelnoth snorted.

'More than you might think,' she said wryly.

Her past was beginning to come back to her – her time as a Celtic warrior, disguised as a man, her time as a cavalry leader under the High King Arturus. She had neither the energy nor the inclination to explain anything to the sullen Aethelnoth. She unsheathed her sword and tested its edge and its balance: it was a well-made weapon.

The magic still burned her up, still built in her like water behind a dam but she would not release it; she would cope.

'You'd better ride,' she said to Aethelnoth. 'I need to walk.' Aethelnoth was about to argue, but she had already dismounted gracelessly and was clasping her hands to help him mount. She had to remember how to walk again, how to function as a person.

Aethelnoth obeyed her out of fear. She almost fell over as she took his weight and had to lean against the pony for balance. It helped a little, the rhythm of walking; it used energy and it kept her feet on the ground. The boots she had been given pinched her feet, but when she took them off the magic flowed through her body as if her bare feet on the wet earth completed some mystical circuit. Magic filled her up, flooded her with energy and strength so that she could barely contain it. 'I am Ursula Dorrington,' she muttered under her breath. 'I will not wield magic. I am Ursula and that is enough.'

~ Chapter Thirty-two ~

Dan was happy. He felt a lightness of spirit that he hadn't felt for months, that he hadn't felt since first discovering that Ursula was alive after they'd returned from Camlann. He had missed her, missed the connection between them, and now he had found both her and that precious connection! He felt guilty about his happiness, of course he did. It had been a night of slaughter, of burning and of fear, yet it didn't matter any more; he'd found Ursula. He didn't even worry about the fact that he hadn't been able to stop himself transforming again – that was a problem he was sure he could overcome now that Ursula was back beside him. He knew that she had experienced something very strange and disturbing in the days since they'd come through the Veil – that was obvious – and it was hard to see how she could be unchanged by it, but he would not worry. He'd help her get through it, as they'd helped each other before. They'd go back to Aelfred; Dan would explain to him that he was not someone Aelfred would want on his side – what with his tendency to turn into a wild beast at the first sign of trouble – and Aelfred would release him from his oath. Then all they had to do was get Taliesin to raise the Veil and they'd go home. Easy.

It was nearly dawn and he could see that Cippenham was not in great shape. The fire had destroyed the wooden buildings and a great pall of smoke still hung in the air, making his eyes stream. Men were emptying the smouldering houses of valuables, ordering terrified women to carry what could be rescued and to find somewhere dry to store it. The ground was muddy from the torrential rain and the Vikings were angry, injured and hungover. No one challenged Dan as he walked confidently through the quagmire searching for Taliesin, sniffing the air for the distinctive scent of his war dog.

There was a girl standing on her own, unmoving in the centre of the chaos.

She alone was still, her pale green eyes staring blindly, the eye of the storm. He stopped to look at her, transfixed. Her fine clothes, sodden with rain, clung to her malnourished frame; tendrils of hair were plastered to her pinched face. She did move when men approached her and they skirted round her as if she had some power to repel them. She knew Dan was there. She smiled and beckoned to him and began to sing. She was no singer, her voice as thin and unlovely as the rest of her, but as she sang he felt the bear within him grow.

'No!' Her singing made him shiver, made his body grow heavy and his thoughts dull. She would bring him meat, all the meat he could ever hunt and slaughter if he became her bear. He covered his ears with clumsy hands, then he heard Braveheart bark. His mind cleared. He could hear the dog, smell his scent in the air, but he could see no sign of him. He was disoriented, lost in the throng, hearing and smelling Braveheart and seeing only people and livestock. The girl's singing stopped as abruptly as it had begun and when he turned back towards her she was gone. The bear within him withdrew and he was still Dan.

He was shaken. Was the girl a sorceress? Taliesin would know. Dan sniffed the air, seeking his scent. Without his peculiarly enhanced sense of smell, Dan would have definitely walked past the one-time druid. Taliesin had disguised himself so that he appeared to be a very old man, a Dane, leading a scrawny pony that smelled like Braveheart. Dan was impressed. Taliesin's magic was worth something in this world. Dan fell in beside the old man and allowed Taliesin to lead him the short distance along the rutted cart track to the only bridge over the swollen river.

Cippenham was an important place by the standards of the time. It seemed small and inconsequential to Dan: no more than thirty or forty timber buildings, a long thatched hall, largely burned down, and a great deal of mud. But it was fortified, which indicated that it was significant. It was far from being a walled city, as Dan normally envisaged a fortified town, but it was surrounded by a high bank of earth surmounted by a wooden wall.

Dan did not relish another fight and hoped that in all the chaos of the night's events the gate might be unmanned. He hoped it was unmanned because Ursula and Aethelnoth had to cross it and he did not see how

Ursula would have been in any state to fight her way out, and Aethelnoth – well, he was injured.

As they approached the bridge Dan could see that his hopes of a peaceful departure were going to be dashed. Two men were watching the wooden bridge. Their faces had that grey pallor of people who had not slept and they were both liberally dusted with soot. They had their spears ready and both wore mail.

Dan felt his heart sink. His hand found Bright Killer. Taliesin gestured as if to prevent him from further action. so he did not unsheathe his sword. Neither of the men appeared to register their approach and Dan wondered if they were still drunk, or perhaps waiting for someone or something, because they did not even acknowledge their existence. Dan fought the urge to run, and forced himself to match Taliesin's slightly arthritic gait. Somehow Braveheart did not bark. The rather hopeless guards showed no sign of noticing them as they crossed the bridge, though the wooden boards trembled under their weight, giving a little as they were designed to do, and Dan could clearly hear the clattering of Braveheart's claws and his own hobnail boots.

He waited until they were out of earshot of the Danes before speaking.

'What did you do?'

The old man standing beside him suddenly looked a great deal like Taliesin, while the former pony leaped up and licked Dan affectionately and wetly all over his face. Braveheart's breath never smelled good and he'd been eating offal, though thankfully of a non-human variety.

Taliesin looked smug. 'I have a certain power here – more of a gift for deception and misdirection than for transformation, but still it works well enough. They never saw us.'

'Clever,' Dan said. 'How long can you hide us for?'

'Not long,' Taliesin admitted. 'If the guards were to look this way now they'd see us, so I suggest we keep moving.'

Dan needed no encouragement. He wanted to catch up with Ursula.

'What will happen when they find out Ursula is missing?'

'Don't worry. I have built an illusion to convince them that she is still there. It should last for a while at least. We should get a head start on them if they pursue us, or rather *when* they pursue us.'

Dan thought that any advantage that Taliesin's magic could bring was good news. 'Did the other captives get away?'

Taliesin shrugged. 'They won't last long without shelter and the Danes could capture them again easily enough if they wanted to.'

'They have other things on their mind for now.'

Taliesin sighed. 'As soon as they realise what has happened we will all be pursued. The Danes rule by fear. They will not allow any of us to get away.'

Dan absorbed that information. It was not what he wanted to hear. He wanted to get back to Aelfred and head for home. 'How many men do you think the Danes have?'

'Four to five thousand, well armed and well provisioned for now at least: that is considerably more than the King has.'

Dan nodded without giving Aelfred's problems any thought. There was no question in his mind that the King would release Dan from his oath and so it was no longer his concern.

'I don't know why you're so cheerful,' Taliesin grumbled. 'It's a long walk back to Athelney and . . .' He did not finish his sentence.

'And what?'

'Ursula is – '

'She's alive and she's not in bad shape. All she needs is a bit of time off school to get her strength back and she'll be fine.'

Taliesin looked uncomfortable. 'Dan, I am your friend and I'm telling you this as a friend: both you and Ursula are in real danger here. She has absorbed so much of the magic of this place I don't even know if she can leave, and you – the magic that has claimed you is . . .'

'Is what?' Dan asked more aggressively than he had intended.

Taliesin looked grave and turned to face Dan, so that his piercing eyes stared straight at him, boring into him. Taliesin hadn't always been a very good friend to him and Dan's attitude to the man was always lightly coloured by suspicion. This time when Dan looked into the other man's eyes he saw his earnestness. Taliesin was a powerful personality and it took all Dan's courage not to avert his eyes and look away. Taliesin smelled of truthfulness and fear.

'I am no expert,' Taliesin began, although he knew more about magic than anyone else Dan knew. 'Remember when, long ago, Ursula got stuck in the form of a bird?'

Dan nodded. It happened when they were in Macsen's land. She had taken on the form of a giant eagle to signal for their troops to advance. It had been a close-run thing, but Taliesin had brought her back with no harm done. Surely he had more magic in this world than he had back then? Dan was confident that Taliesin would be able to help again.

'Ursula chose to be an eagle because it suited her purposes, but you have not chosen to be a bear – it is your soul, your deepest self that longs to be a beast. If you cross worlds as a beast, it is as a beast that you may emerge.'

'You don't know that! You can't know about the state of my soul!' Dan felt his temper flare. The foolish old man knew nothing. Dan did not want to be a beast; he hated the violence of the bear.

There was no sense of change. Dan had no warning. He was shouting at Taliesin in his normal voice and then suddenly he lost the power of speech and was growling like the beast he did not want to be. He might have killed Taliesin then: the fury that surged through him was so powerful it blotted out thought. It was Braveheart that stopped him. He was a giant of a dog and though Dan could have killed him easily enough, he would not. Braveheart's loyalty had always been unambiguous. The hound leaped to Taliesin's defence, barking at Dan as if Dan were his enemy and not his master, his ally in too many battles. Dan would not turn on so faithful a companion; instead he grunted and turned away.

The Danes on watch who had failed to notice Taliesin and Dan slipping out of Cippenham could not help but notice the sudden appearance of a bear. Dan heard them yelling, calling for warriors. Their voices carried a long way in the still morning. Dan could hear the jingle of their mail and their running feet. Dan sniffed the air and smelled their excitement, their eagerness. He liked these men; he could understand them. They liked a good fight – what was wrong with that?

While Taliesin led Braveheart away, further along the cart road, Dan readied himself for the battle to come. He did not have to do much except tear away at the clothes that restricted him – especially the boots. He could not see the point of boots. The ground beneath his feet was a source of strength. He removed his sword belt, tearing at it and biting at it to get it free. The metal tasted bad and clunked against his teeth. He no longer liked the smell of man-made things. He dropped to all fours, glorying in the easy movement of powerful muscles, delighting in the way he could identify each man behind the stockade by scent alone. He could taste them in all their distinctness. He would know them again anywhere. The world of scents was extraordinary. He licked his lips and shut his eyes briefly. It was like seeing extra colours – the richness of it. He loved the sharp tang of human sweat in the air, the taint of ale and undigested meat, the smell of carrion. Dan shook himself and stretched, lumbering to his feet as three Viking warriors ran screaming to meet him. He wanted this. He needed the pleasure of the kill. This sharp sense of threat, the danger, the fight about to be won, filled him with joy.

This was what life was about – facing death, beating death, bringing death. Dan's mouth lacked the muscle to curl into a smile, but he did what he could and that was enough to make the men rushing towards him turn pale. The first man to reach him was small and quick, easily outrunning the others, which was probably a mistake on his part. He was young and a fuzzy down of golden hair covered his chin where his beard should have been. The youth was brave enough and tried to stick Dan with a well-sharpened spear, but Dan snapped it as easily as if it had been made of balsa wood and drove the shaft back into the belly of the enemy wielding it. The ash shaft snapped under the pressure before it pierced his mail, but it winded the boy so that he was unable to offer the bear much resistance. He did not have time to linger, so he snapped his neck and stepped over the limp corpse.

Two other men came for him then. They dragged a metal chain between them in what he guessed was an attempt to trip him, trap him and bind him. They must have thought him a dumb animal, which he was not. That made him angry, and anger did rather cloud his thinking. He wanted to rip the chain from their hands, but though he had the strength, his vast paws were clumsy and ill-suited to gripping. It was more difficult to deal with two men at once, but what he had lost in agility he had gained in power. He raked the first one with his claws, tearing at the mail with his teeth so that he could expose the frail flesh beneath. The man's companion attacked Dan from behind, trying to wrap the heavy chain round his throat, but Dan reared up and the man overbalanced, so that Dan's bulk could trample him and Dan's great paws rip at him until he was dead. The blood smell was strong. And Dan was ready for more. But there were no more warriors – unless he were to return across the bridge and find some. He dropped to all fours and began to run back the way he'd come, but someone was calling his name.

'Dan!'

Dan was a weakling. At the sound of that name he felt himself shrink down to the meagre proportions of a mere man. He was suddenly cold, standing half naked and barefoot outside the limits of Cippenham. He gathered up his torn clothes and his abandoned sword and stumbled across the rough ground towards the track where Taliesin waited.

~ Chapter Thirty-three ~

Taliesin did not speak as Dan struggled back into his clothes.

'Was that really necessary?' he said drily.

Dan did not trust himself to answer. His long-legged stride soon left Taliesin far behind. It did not matter what Taliesin thought – his good opinion was worthless: all that mattered was catching up with Ursula, seeing her again.

They were very fortunate not to have been followed and Dan knew it, and for a time their luck held. Dan found Aethelnoth and Ursula on the road without any trouble: they were barely half a mile ahead of him.

'Ursula!'

She turned her face to Dan at the sound of his voice and smiled, but her blue eyes had turned a green so dark that they looked black, the colour of the deepest ocean. She would not let him speak to her mind.

'Are you OK? You got past the guard all right?'

'She spoke to the guard in the devil's tongue. I do not know what she said.' Aethelnoth was riding Ursula's mount. He was shivering against the cold and obviously angry, though Dan didn't quite understand why.

Dan reached for Ursula's hand, which was hot and dry. It gave him a small shock, a thrill of static when he touched it, and she withdrew it swiftly. Her eyes had trouble focusing, seeing through and beyond him in a way he found chilling.

'It's the magic, Dan,' Ursula mumbled. 'I'm fighting it. Hard.'

She did not stay to talk but carried on walking barefoot through the mud like some zombie from a horror film. She would not ride. Dan struggled to keep up with her. He was losing her again. If she knew he walked beside her, she gave no real sign. She was battling demons but she shut him out. She should have let him help. Why did she not let him help? It all felt wrong. Ursula felt wrong and he felt wrong, as if he was in the wrong body. He was too small and too light, a shrunken, weakened creature: not himself at all.

Taliesin did not seem able to help Ursula either. She recognised him, or seemed to, mumbling something that sounded like his name. Dan asked Taliesin what was wrong with her, but he just looked grave and shook his head. It was not the response Dan wanted. Dan had hoped for better from the old bard, though at least he had found them food and borrowed clothes from those who were still loyal to Aelfred.

Aethelnoth led them on a circuitous route back to Athelney that kept them well away from friend and foe alike. He did not trust his companions and if he was grateful for Dan's rescue of him at Cippenham, he did not mention it.

When they rested on the second day of travelling, and Aethelnoth had gone in search of water, Dan took Taliesin to one side.

'I've been thinking,' he began.

'You surprise me, Daniel. I thought you might have forgotten how.' Taliesin spoke in the old tongue of the Combrogi, as a reminder of all that they'd shared. He clearly thought it safer to insult Dan that way. Dan felt a surge of annoyance, but kept it under control.

'I think that you should send us home now. I don't know why you wanted us here in the first place, but it doesn't matter. Ursula is in no state to help anyone. I want to get her home so she can be seen by a proper doctor.'

'Familiar with the ailments associated with magical power are they, your doctors?' Taliesin asked in a mocking tone of voice.

Dan stayed calm with difficulty. 'Taliesin, you brought me here under false pretences. You lied. You said that the crystal ball you gave me would bring us to Macsen's land. This wouldn't have happened to Ursula in Macsen's land. If she is strange now, it is your fault. You must raise the Veil and let us go home.'

'And what about your oath to Aelfred?'

'I will be helping him by going home. Do you think he'll want me on his side if I turn into a bear? You saw what happened at the farm. Even the people I saved thought I was some kind of devil. He won't want me and he won't want Ursula. He thought I was going to fetch a warrior. She's in no state to play a warrior's part.'

Taliesin stroked his white beard thoughtfully.

'I don't think it will work, Dan. Oaths bind and as I've said Ursula is too full of the magic of this world. My guess is that the magic will keep her here. It belongs here.'

'Don't guess,' Dan said coldly. His hand had sought the comfort of Bright Killer while Taliesin had been making his excuses. The man wanted them for his own purposes, to use them for some plan that Dan didn't yet understand. Dan wouldn't stand for it. He'd had enough of the old bard; he'd had enough of this world. He didn't like feeling ill at ease in his own human skin and he knew that the feeling was getting worse. He needed to go home, do his GCSEs, find a way to put all the violence behind him.

'What will you do if I say no, Dan? Will you rip my head off too?'

'There's no point in having a go at me about that either,' Dan said. He tried not to let his anger leak into his voice; he didn't want to sound like a petulant schoolboy. He probably didn't succeed. 'Look, none of this would have happened if you hadn't brought me here. It is your fault. There is something wrong with the world, with the way the magic works. I want you to get us home.'

Dan's hand was clenched into a fist and even he could see that there was something wrong with the way it looked: it was too large and beginning to thicken and stiffen into an animal's paw. He felt the increasingly familiar fury; as it built he could sense his outrage making him grow, making him heavy, making him strong and wild and free.

No. He forced himself to be calm. It was like starting to sprint and having to slam on the brakes. The effort left him feeling weak and breathless. He wanted to let go. He wanted to let the bear win, but he knew that this was not the time to turn. Now was the time for reason, the time to persuade Taliesin to let him go home. He knew that he was losing his unequal battle with the bear. Each time he lost his temper the bear took over more quickly. He retained enough of his sense of self to know that Taliesin was not wrong: he was becoming the beast. He had to go home before it took over entirely.

Taliesin didn't say anything but watched his struggle with a grave expression. Damn him. He could have helped. He had the magic, but as usual he did not have the will to be useful. That was typical of the man . . . Dan made himself take a deep breath. He tried to think of something calming. He thought of Ursula, but that didn't help. Ursula was lost because of Taliesin's interference. She would have been happy at home but for Taliesin's hospital visit. The man was nothing but trouble . . . No. Calm.

'Please, Taliesin . . . try.' Dan's voice was a little gruff but it was still human.

'Very well,' Taliesin sighed. 'Bring Ursula. I think I know a good spot near here. You'd better leave Braveheart. The stink of your world is not fit for dogs.'

Ursula did not look up as Dan approached. He was glad; he could not bear to look into her too-dark eyes. When he touched her on her shoulder and told her to go with him, she got up obediently. Ursula never did as she was told. It was as if she wasn't really there, as if she was just the husk of Ursula and the girl he loved was gone.

Dan held out his hand and this strange version of Ursula took it. It burned him, but he held on anyway. There was none of Ursula's strength in that hot hand and he felt a lump form in his throat. What was happening to her? He was too choked to be angry.

'Taliesin is going to get us home,' he said, trying not to speak to her as if she was a small, lost child.

Ursula nodded. 'Home,' she said. 'Ursula has a home. We are going to Ursula's home.' Had she lost her mind?

'Home is where your mother lives – remember? We go to school there? That's how we know each other – from school.'

When she looked at him with fathomless eyes, he could see no sign of the girl he knew in there.

'Ursula?' He could not keep that panic from his voice. What if she was gone for ever?

'Dan? My friend, Dan. Ursula. Dan.' She kept repeating the words like some mantra, muttering them under her breath, and he felt himself grow cold with fear for her.

'That's right. You're Ursula and I am Dan, your friend. I think it would be good if we both went home.'

Taliesin was already kneeling on the damp grass in the middle of a small clearing. Dan waited by the trees and watched him for a moment. He didn't entirely trust him. Taliesin took his seax and sliced his arm. The gash was about six centimetres long on the inside of his forearm, just missing the artery. Dan could smell the blood which welled up out of the wound and dripped on the ground. Taliesin was intoning something in a language unknown to Dan. It was a kind of prayer. Dan watched as yellow tendrils of mist, like smoke from a cigarette, began to coil around Taliesin's feet. He stepped back and the mist thickened into an eerie yellow smog. It smelled spicily of magic. Ursula let out a low moan.

'It's OK,' Dan said reassuringly in English and led her forward. She did not resist exactly, but Dan could sense her reluctance. She dragged her feet and he had to pull her towards the mist. Its pungent and unnatural scent bothered him; it caught in his throat and made it difficult to smell anything else.

Taliesin turned at the sound of his heavy tread.

'I have raised the Veil,' he said.

'I can see that,' Dan answered shortly. 'What do we do now?'

Ursula was pulling away from his hand, shaking her head. She was still muttering. Dan wanted to slap her. This was not the way Ursula behaved! Ursula was bold and brave. She didn't gibber like some idiot.

'What have you done to her?' Dan's voice had deepened into a growl. Whatever was going on it was Taliesin's fault – it had to be. Dan wanted his Ursula back, not this weird impostor beside him.

It was clear that she did not want to go through the Veil. He picked her up bodily. It was easier than it should have been. He had grown, so that they were near enough the same size, but it ought not to have been so easy to lift her. She was a muscular, well-built girl, strong as any man he'd met, but she felt light and insubstantial as he slung her across his shoulder. She cried out but she did not fight him. He wanted his feisty Ursula back. He lumbered purposefully towards the Veil. His sword belt pinched his flesh and got in the way, but he did not pause to loosen it. Taliesin stood in his path, telling him something that he did not hear; he did not care. All that mattered was getting back through the Veil.

He stepped forward and the mist retreated from him, withdrew itself as if it were a living thing. He took a second step forward and this time it was even more obvious. Where the mist touched his skin it dissolved and disappeared. He kept on walking, but there was no mist to enter.

'What is going on?' he shouted, but even to his own ears his response sounded thick and hard to understand. He put Ursula down gently on the ground. She was screaming as if she was in pain and it was hurting his sensitive ears.

'Stop!' Taliesin's voice must have had some magic resonance this time, some power of its own, because he did stop. 'If you walk into the Veil now, you will never see Ursula again. You will never be Dan again. Look at yourself!'

This time he had not even noticed the transition. He was a beast again and had not known it. He took a step forward and, without his burden, without Ursula, the Veil did not evaporate as it touched him. He could have gone on.

'Dan!' Ursula's voice had none of its usual raucous

power, but at least she sounded like herself, as if the shock of whatever had just happened had made her aware of him again. 'Please don't go. Don't leave me here!'

This last came out as a kind of wail of despair. Of course he couldn't leave her. He did not know what he had been thinking. Something bad was happening to her and he had been about to abandon her to its ravages. Dan pulled back away from the roiling mist. Taliesin dropped his hands and it whirled away into nothingness, like water down the plughole, until it was as if it had never been.

'Do you believe me now?' Taliesin asked. 'Ursula cannot leave and you should not leave until you have overcome your demons and fulfilled your oath. You leave this place as an oath-breaker and you will never be free of the beast inside you.'

The beast inside Dan had gone for the moment, leaving him feeling weak and strangely abandoned. He sat down next to Ursula and grabbed her hand. It still burned, but less fiercely.

'Are you OK?' he asked.

'Not really,' she said in a choked voice, but at least she sounded angry. 'You were about to abandon me.'

'No,' Dan said. 'But I was angry that you were being so . . .'

'Useless?'

'No. Well, yes.'

Ursula turned her head away from him, but she moved too slowly to prevent him from seeing her tears. 'You don't understand, Dan. The magic is filling me up, over-whelming me so that I can barely hold on to the threads of myself. I have to fight all the time not to use it, not to give into it. It's like trying to contain the sea in a thimble, Dan. I have to fight to remember who I am every second or I'll get swept away.' She wiped her face with the palm of her hand. 'I can't go home, can I? I'm so sorry I dragged you here.'

Dan was sorry too, but was not so thoughtless as to say so.

'What oath have you given this time?' she said. Her eyes were still the colour of the deepest ocean, but she was at least focusing on him and, though her speech was slow, as if she were drugged or drunk, she still sounded like Ursula.

'Did you learn about King Aelfred in junior school?'

She shrugged. 'Maybe. I don't remember much that I learned in junior school.'

'Well, he's here – or rather we're here with him, and he has to beat the Vikings – the ones who captured you – to take back his kingdom. He doesn't have an army and he doesn't have much of a clue and I promised to help him.'

She nodded without much interest, but Dan knew that she was trying her best to care.

'We'd better be going,' he said. He offered her his arm, but she refused it and staggered after him on bleeding feet with something like her usual determination. She was still Ursula.

~ Chapter Thirty-four ~

Dan pointed out that Ursula's feet were bleeding and that she should ride for a while. Her head cleared a little when her bare feet were no longer in contact with the ground. While walking kept her in touch with her own body, it also filled her with yet more power; she was bursting with it and every step had made it worse. Once mounted it was harder to stay rooted in her own perspective. She was not wielding the magic, but it brought with it images and experiences like debris dumped by the tide. It made holding on to the thread of her own history all the harder as she was assaulted by random experiences that were not hers. She watched the road and smelled incense. She saw a picture of a man at prayer, earnestly contemplating his sins. She felt the cold, damp earth make his knees cramp. He had been at his devotions for many hours. Her attention was caught by a tree just beginning to bud; the tree burned, then she smelled charring flesh, felt the heat of some great conflagration, and her ears rang to a woman's screams. It was a little like watching a TV with someone manically channel surfing, and she could not work out what the other channels were, let alone focus on what they were broadcasting. She needed help, but who could give it to her?

She might have turned to Dan, but she didn't have to be blessed with magic to know that he was halfway insane. She could see the bear in him every time she looked at him. It was fighting to get out and Dan was losing the battle to contain it. He needed help too and she was in no state to offer it. It was as well that over her time through the Veil she had become an accomplished rider, for she had no attention to spare on her physical surroundings. When she was next aware, they were riding through a marshy landscape and it was raining. Someone had wrapped her in a cloak, which was good because she had no desire to deal with rusty mail. Water trickled down her face and her hair dripped. She wanted the madness to end.

Two men leaped out of some unseen place to challenge them. Ursula had her sword out and would have fought if she could stay in the moment, but more images blew through her mind. She was lost in a crowd, then fighting in a shield wall, next weeping for a dead husband. By the time she had managed to regain her focus on the here and now, Aethelnoth and Taliesin had persuaded the guards that she and Dan were not enemies. She was not sure that was wise. Taliesin, at least, ought to have known better. She could see the nimbus of magic around him. He had power, enough to know what kind of a mess they were in, but not enough to prevent Dan running amok if Dan chose and nowhere near enough to be of any use to her. She had not thought Aethelnoth was a friend to her, but even he did not speak out against her.

Dan came to help her off the horse. She should not have needed help but her limbs felt heavy and only partially under her own control. She fell into his arms like some kind of hopeless, romantic heroine and she sensed Dan's irritation. He loved her for her strength, not her weakness. The bear peered out at her through Dan's brown eyes.

'Sorry,' she mumbled thickly, struggling with her unco-operative tongue, 'I'm struggling a bit. My legs don't seem to be working properly.' She must have spoken in English because no one but Dan gave any indication of having understood her. He didn't reply but hauled her over his shoulder. It wasn't very dignified but it was effective, and she'd long ago lost interest in anything so insignificant as dignity.

Dan carried her to a small boat and then her consciousness flicked to a conversation between some men drinking ale and arguing about the reliability of Danes. It wasn't like watching TV – that was a bad metaphor – it was as if she was in another place for a fragment of time. She could smell the smoke from their fire, the mutton in their meal and the milky odour of the woman who served them. She could sense the tension in the room and the caution of the man who was speaking: 'We still have a King,' he said.

Returning to herself was disorienting and she had to fight back nausea. Dan had set her back down on her feet and of course the power was surging through her again and she was leaning against him like some spineless stuffed toy. As for Dan, even his sweat smelled angry. He was in a bad way. She pulled away from him and balanced on her own two legs. The mail shirt she would once have worn so easily weighed her down. It took a moment for her eyes to focus and the light wasn't good within the hall, but then she saw the King, his thin, pale face and haunted eyes, and she recognised him: it was the man who had haunted her visions over the last few days, the King in the marshes she had sought under Finna's instruction, the sad, determined praying man. She had not made the connection until that moment but she had seen his thoughts and known his fears. It was strange to meet him finally and to know that he had no idea of their peculiar intimacy.

Their eyes met and she heard his stray thought as clearly as if he had spoken it aloud. *She is beautiful.* She glimpsed herself through his eyes, tall and gaunt, her eyes dark pits in an angular face, her blonde hair plastered to her head. She could not see the beauty in her face, only pain.

Dan bowed to the King and, because she had never learned to curtsey, Ursula did the same.

'My Liege, this is the friend of whom I spoke.'

'Your – comrade-in-arms?'

Ursula felt Dan's annoyance at the King's slightly mocking response. She hoped he did not let the bear emerge. She was not so lost to herself that she did not notice the armed men stationed around the hall, nor the boy with a nocked arrow trained at the newcomers, at Dan and herself. She would have liked to help calm him but she did not know how, not without magic anyway, and she would not wield it, not where Finna might find her.

'My Liege,' Taliesin began, 'the Lady Ursula has indeed been Dan's comrade-in-arms and fought beside him in many a battle.'

'A woman in battle – that I would like to see!' said Aelfred, with an uncharacteristic smirk.

The men and women who comprised Aelfred's court in exile tittered in the background and Dan's anger mounted.

It was up to Ursula to defuse the situation.

'Your Majesty,' she said, 'I have fought it is true and will do so again, but for now I am weakened and ill from my time as a Viking captive.' She produced the sword that Gunnarr had so reluctantly given her, which had been hanging forgotten at her hip. 'I lay my sword at your disposal.' She unsheathed it with a flourish as if for all her confusion her body retained muscle memory of her days of swordmanship.

There was a mass intake of breath, though whether at the sword or her boldness she could not say. Aelfred gave her a hard stare. She found his scrutiny discomforting.

'Both you and your sword are welcome,' he pronounced. A lean, horse-faced monk whispered in the King's ear. 'There are rumours that you have turned to sorcery. Is this true?' Aelfred asked. 'Though we are in exile this remains a Christian court and we have no truck with sorcery.'

Ursula's mind went blank, though at least she remained present at the scene – were she to have a fit of absence she was sure that would convince Aelfred she was some kind of sorceress weirdo. She waited for someone to come to her rescue. It was Taliesin.

'My Lord, the Lady Ursa was nearly burned alive in the conflagration that engulfed Cippenham. I respectfully request that she should be allowed to rest before you submit her to a full interrogation.'

Ursula saw Aelfred's eyes flick between the implacable face of the monk and the eager face of the former bard; Taliesin could be charm personified when he put his mind to it and Ursula knew he was putting everything, including a hint of magical manipulation, into getting Ursula off this particular hook. Ursula's own evident exhaustion probably tipped the balance in her favour. She swayed slightly under Aelfred's attention and had to grab Dan's arm for balance.

Aelfred signalled to one of the women in attendance. 'Take our guest to the healer. She has need of her ministrations.'

The monk snorted his derision and when Aelfred gave him a disapproving glare he tried to pretend that he had a cold.

Dan wanted to follow Ursula, she knew, to protect her and make sure that she was all right. He seemed to have no awareness that he was in worse shape than she was.

Once they had left the presence of the King behind, the woman who led her away gave her a look of disapproval so intense that Ursula felt it like a blow.

'I don't know what you're doing dressed like that, but we're all Christian women here and not given to dressing like boys – showing all our shape and putting even the King into a state. No good will come of it, I'm sure.' The woman crossed herself and led Ursula into another smoky dark hall, one that had a familiar feel. There was something about it that reminded her of . . .

'Boar Skull? Ursa?' The voice was different, older, yet it still conveyed its power.

Ursula sat down heavily on a low wooden platform of a bed. 'Rhonwen?' How could it be Rhonwen?

~ Chapter Thirty-five ~

Dan was glad that Ursula hadn't been made to fight to prove her manhood or her womanhood, or whatever it was that she had always been obliged to prove in order to get decent treatment from Kings. Macsen, Arturus, Aelfred – they were all the same. He could feel that fury fuelling him again and then Taliesin touched his arm, hard enough to pinch, and before he could slap him away he remembered: he couldn't afford to lose it in front of Aelfred. They could not get home. He and Ursula were stuck in this world that they did not know and didn't much care about. He needed to show that he was useful, that he was sane, or there would be no place for him in Aelfred's court. He did not know where else they could go.

Dan managed to keep very still and calm while Taliesin and Aethelnoth spoke of the military strength of the Danes and the attack on the farmhouse which could so easily have ended in a massacre. They were both diplomatically silent on how Dan managed to turn it into a rout of armed invaders rather than unarmed civilians and for that Dan was grateful.

Asser, however, smelled a rat. He had an instinct for untruth that was of itself almost magical.

'I find it extraordinary that Aethelnoth and Dan alone were able to defeat such a horde. Are you sure, Taliesin, that you did not call upon your arcane knowledge of the dark arts?'

'My Lord Bishop,' said the King, 'I do not think it appropriate for us to question our own people on their integrity. Taliesin has shown his dedication to our cause, Aethelnoth has ever been at our side, and Dan was tested by the Lord God Almighty and not found wanting. I have seen for myself that he has the strength and agility of ten. Is it so extraordinary that he should vanquish our enemies? He has God on his side. Is that not enough?'

Asser bowed his head in acceptance of the rebuke, but Dan knew that he was unconvinced. He was an astute man and he undoubtedly noticed that Dan held his breath at the question and that even Taliesin looked shifty.

The King was pleased to show Dan around the fort and Dan was impressed in spite of himself; they had achieved a lot in a short time. Much of the rotting timber had been replaced, guards were set around the perimeter and they looked awake, sober and well equipped, and in contrast to the situation a few days before, everything looked orderly and well run. When no one else was in earshot, Aelfred said to Dan, 'I am grateful to you for saving my life and for reminding me of my life's work. I had forgotten my duty to my people. I will not forget again.'

Dan was moved; Aelfred lacked Macsen's commanding

stature and Arturus's focused ruthlessness, but he had something special that might yet make him into a decent king. For a moment the anger burning in Dan was gone and he smiled like a free man.

'Thank you, My Liege. I am at a loss for words.'

Aelfred patted him on the arm and changed the subject. 'Your comrade-in-arms is beautiful. I did not intend to do her a discourtesy. Taliesin has explained that you are from a distant place where warrior women are not uncommon. You will, I hope, forgive me if I find the very idea . . . shocking.'

Dan nodded, wondering what on earth Taliesin had said, what version of almost truth he had come up with. Obviously he could not ask the King, but he would need to catch Taliesin later. Suddenly he felt unutterably weary and perhaps that showed because the King had him taken to a thatched hall, recently repaired, which acted as a kind of barracks for the thegns who'd followed Aelfred into exile. A couple of men were sleeping on straw pallets. Dan was comfortable with that and with a nod to those who rested there but were still awake he lay down on a bed, wrapped himself in a blanket and fell instantly asleep.

Asser was standing over him in the dimness when he woke up. Dan started and reached for Bright Killer.

'You won't need that, my boy,' the monk said calmly. 'Come and walk with me. We have a short while before Aelfred calls his Council of War. For reasons best known to himself he would not consider making serious plans without your presence.' Asser sniffed in such a way as to suggest that he thought little of Dan's likely contribution to such a council.

Dan got clumsily to his feet and followed Asser out of the low door; he was curious as to what Asser could want with him. Asser grabbed Dan's upper arm with his long fingers – his grip was much stronger than Dan would have expected. Dan's temper flared, but he did not pull his arm away and he did not lose control.

Asser guided him past the forge, steaming and sparking and overwhelming Dan's senses with the acrid smell of burning charcoal and hot metal and the copious sweat of the bearded smithy. They passed the carpenter shaving wood so that it fell in pale golden curls on the rush-strewn mud. Everywhere there were signs of a new energy and purpose.

Asser walked through the outer gate of the fortress to a small windowless hut made of rough timber. It stank of pigs, though an effort had been made to clean it out. Dan wrinkled his nose.

'I need solitude for my work and Aelfred generously allowed me to take this place for my own.'

Dan could not tell if Asser was being ironic or not, so he said nothing. Asser began working on the fire and with commendable speed, and nothing more elaborate than a small tinder box, soon had a reasonable fire going in the hearth. His face in the flames looked skeletal.

'I wanted to talk to you because Aelfred trusts you. I must say you have done well to get him to face up to his responsibilities. He is a new man since you came and, fond though I was of the old one, we need a stronger, more determined character to win back a kingdom.' He paused as if waiting for some response from Dan, but Dan merely warmed his hands on the fire and readjusted his weight on the uncomfortable stool: he could not think of anything to say.

'Dan, I am for all my faults a man of God and a man of prayer and what I see when I look in your eyes disturbs me more than I can say. Here in my private place I'm asking you to confess your sins to me in the full confidence that I will never tell any living person what you tell me as a man of God.'

Dan wondered if he dared. Asser's dark eyes burned with righteous fervour – could he trust him? What would Taliesin say? Taliesin would encourage him to lie. Taliesin's commitment to truth was erratic at best, but that was the thing he liked least about Taliesin. Dan was tired of having to keep the truth from people. Ever since he'd brought Ursula back half dead from Camlann, he knew that he'd felt lost and alone. He was still only sixteen, in spite of all the killing and all the weirdness. He wanted someone to tell him what to do, how to make things right. Dan found that his eyes were filling with tears. He was very afraid that he might break down and sob, like a much younger child. A bit of him just wanted to bawl that it wasn't fair, that everything he'd done he'd done from the best of motives, to keep people safe, to keep people alive – even the killing had been to keep people alive. He didn't say any of that, of course – he wasn't a fool – but he came very close to saying it.

'Dan,' Asser's voice was soft and earnest. He leaned forward so that Dan could not avoid his intense gaze. 'You need to remember that there is nothing that God cannot forgive. God has shown me that your soul is burdened. I would like to help you.' Asser's long talon-like fingers found Dan's hand. He had very big hands that were calloused and harder than Dan would have expected in a monk. 'Listen to me. You are a brother, you speak the true tongue. I will not betray you.'

Belatedly Dan realised that Asser had spoken in the old language of the Combrogi – one of the tribal languages that reminded him of Macsen and Kai and Ursula as she had been when she was a warrior. Dan wiped his eyes with the heel of his hand.

'I don't think I can explain what happened to me,' Dan began, haltingly. 'It is too strange.'

'However strange, Dan, it is not beyond the love of God.'

'What would you say if I told you I could turn into a bear?'

Asser made a clicking sound with his tongue. 'I would tell you that you had drunk too much of this strong Aenglisc ale, that you had spent too much time in the company of the heathen with all their tales of Odin and that you are a soul in torment.'

'You don't believe me?'

'I believe that you believe it, Dan. I know that you fight with all the ferocity of a bear. Is that what you mean?'

'It was like that to begin with. When I fight . . . I lose myself, I let my instincts take over and I don't think about what I'm doing. It is almost as if the part of me that is really Dan hides away and the other part, a colder person who knows how to kill, takes over.'

Asser tightened his grip on Dan's hand. Dan continued, 'But lately it has become more than that; it is as if I am possessed. I want to kill people.' He turned his head away from Asser's steady gaze. 'I like killing,' he said, dropping his voice to a whisper, 'and that has never happened to me before.'

'Can you show me?' Asser said.

Dan shook his head. 'I might kill you.'

'Let me worry about that, my boy. You might think me a foolish ageing monk, more used to ink on his fingers than blood on his hands, but there's not one of us alive now who has not had anger in his heart enough to kill. So many innocent, holy lives were lost in an orgy of killing when the Vikings came ashore and devastated our monasteries. There is such a thing as a just war and Aelfred is embarked upon it. He needs good men to fight in it. God has chosen you as one of his – in the test by water. It is not my job as a mere servant of God to argue with his decision, but it might be up to me to ensure that a good man does not turn bad.'

Dan was not at all sure that he had understood the monk. He spoke the tribal tongue with an unfamiliar accent and the language he used could not easily bear the sense he wanted to convey. Perhaps he was more like Dan's old friend, the monk Frontalis, than he had at first appeared.

'Come, Dan. We'll walk a little way from the fortress and you can show me what happens to you and I will ask for Our Lord's help in exorcising whatever demon possesses you.'

'What if the demon is me, Asser?'

'Well, that's the way with demons – men only welcome in the ones who are most like themselves. These things are mysteries and I do not claim to be an expert, though I have cast out demons before. I shall take a stout stick to fend you off should it all get a bit out of hand.'

Dan was powerless to explain how useless a stick might be against his own brand of wild madness. There was something about Asser that made Dan believe that if anyone could help him, Asser might have that power. He had something of the air of a fanatic, which made Dan uncomfortable, but who besides a fanatic would risk himself in this way? Who but a fanatic would even try to help a monster like Dan?

~ Chapter Thirty-six ~

Ursula stared in astonishment at her former enemy. 'What are you doing here? I thought we left you in Arturus's world.'

Rhonwen smiled. Ursula wasn't sure that she'd ever seen her smile before. The shadow of Rhonwen's youthful beauty transformed her face.

'Dan did not tell you I was here?'

Ursula shrugged. 'If he did, I didn't hear him.'

'Ah, my poor, brave, lost girl. You are not yourself.' She patted Ursula's cheek with her cool slack-skinned hand.

Ursula was bemused: since when had she been Rhonwen's 'girl'? They had been enemies for most of their association.

'I have travelled too many worlds since I left you at Camlann, telling the tale of Arturus and the battle for civilisation. I came here two or three years ago and Taliesin followed soon after.'

Ursula was confused by that. Rhonwen had fought for the Aenglisc, against Ursula and Taliesin and against Arturus, but then she had recanted at the last and changed sides. Here, both Rhonwen and Taliesin were siding with the Aenglisc: there was no logic to it.

'I don't understand,' Ursula said. She wasn't sure that she had understood anything since she came through the Veil.

'You are still so young, I wouldn't expect you to – but in the end I have come to see what is worth fighting for. I have come to believe that order and reason is better than chaos and madness. It isn't a hard choice. Aelfred represents the forces of order.'

Rhonwen looked at her hard, searching her face for something Ursula could not guess. 'It is so strange to see you still so childlike and beautiful after so long,' she said, wonder in her voice.

'I last saw you a few weeks ago,' Ursula said. Was that true? She was no longer sure of anything. Rhonwen clucked her tongue.

'You must find me much changed then.' Her expression was sad. 'I haven't much power in this world – no real gift of illusion. You see the woman I have become and I see that, for all your beauty, you are in a very poor state.' Rhonwen's hand felt strangely cooling as she tested the temperature of Ursula's head. 'The magic is still burning you up. How do you feel?'

'I don't know.'

'Ursula, I have not been your enemy for a long time – almost a lifetime. You can trust me.'

Ursula could feel Rhonwen's earnestness emanating from her with its own kind of heat. She could not doubt that Rhonwen spoke the truth.

'I don't feel good. I keep getting pictures – images of other people, thoughts – I can't shut them out. I am so full of power it is taking me over, diluting me, so that in all the magic in me there's barely any Ursula.' She gulped back tears. 'The Danes, they were going to sacrifice twenty men to me. I'm trying not to use the magic, but it won't let me go.'

'There, there.' Ursula had never expected to take comfort from Rhonwen. The old woman held Ursula against her thin body and patted her back as if she were a child. 'You are overwrought as well as overwhelmed. I have something that will help you sleep; you need to rest. To be restored. I believe your sleep will be dreamless. The tincture will not harm you, I promise you that.'

Ursula nodded wordlessly. She did not know when she had last slept. It was hard to tell. Night and day, dreaming and waking: it had all been one to her for too long. Nothing that had happened to her had seemed real.

'Do you think I can ever be free of it – the magic, I mean?'

Rhonwen sighed. 'I know what it is to be without it,' she said, pausing in the act of pouring out the tincture. 'Do you really want to be free of it?'

That was a question Ursula could not easily answer, but she knew that she did not want to feel that it controlled her. She took the tincture from Rhonwen's hands. It didn't smell harmful and she was sure that she would know if it were. 'I don't know what I want, but I think it would be good to sleep.'

She drank the drink down quickly: it tasted as foul as

the medicines her mother had given her when she was small. It seemed strange to link the sorceress Rhonwen with her mother's homely comfort, but this older Rhonwen, lacking her imperious loveliness, was more motherly than Ursula would have expected. Ursula lay down on the straw-filled pallet and let herself relax and let sleep come.

It was dark when she woke up. She was sitting at the fireside in Guthrum's hall, watching the Danes drink and relate their battle stories. Gunnarr was sitting a little apart, his handsome face clouded. It was clear to Ursula that he was being blamed for her disappearance and that it had gone badly for him since Finna had become so important. Finna! Ursula fled the scene before Finna could appear. She screamed and felt Rhonwen's hand on hers.

'It is all right, Ursula, come back to me.'

Ursula opened her eyes and saw Rhonwen as she had first seen her, before she had been horribly burned in the fire, before she'd become old. Ursula blinked and it was the old crone Rhonwen who stood over her, offering her clean water from a pottery beaker.

'How did you sleep?'

'Well to begin with, but then I saw Guthrum in his hall and I . . . I was afraid and came back here.'

'Why are you afraid of Guthrum? He has no power to hurt you, at least not while you are here and he is at Cippenham.'

Ursula only hesitated for an instant. She needed an ally and Dan was not up to much. She would not have chosen Rhonwen, but Taliesin had brought them to this world under false pretences and no one else understood about the magic. She took a sip of the clean water and cleared her throat.

'There was a girl with Guthrum. She has no power of her own but she called to mine.' Ursula could not stop her voice from shaking a little as she spoke of Finna. 'I dare not use magic or she will find me. It was she who made Guthrum make the sacrifice. She had strange power.' Ursula swallowed hard. 'She has influence now with the Vikings. She acted as my mouthpiece when I was lost to the magic. I could not resist her. She made me prophesy and I don't understand how she could compel me, but I had no choice but to do what she asked. What if she had asked me to do something really bad?'

Rhonwen sat down heavily on the stool beside Ursula. 'Ah. That is not good news, though it is also not so much of a surprise. I have seen this girl you call Finna in my own dreams and I believe Taliesin knows of her too.' She hesitated. 'He asked me if I knew anything about the gift of using the power of others. I thought he was being insulting because I called on his power, not my own, to draw him near.' She sighed. 'One day Taliesin will learn to be more direct. She may have tried to use him too. He has never said.

'I can sense magic, you see, even though I cannot wield it. Taliesin has some power here, enough for him to be useful to the King.'

'Do you miss using magic?' Ursula felt less over-whelmed in Rhonwen's cottage with a board floor and a bed between her flesh and the naked earth, but her nerves still felt raw and exposed, as if her skin was too thin, and even the gentle draught from under the door made her flinch as though from an assault. She knew that the magic was only dormant within her, quiet for a time.

Rhonwen's eyes searched Ursula's face. 'What do you think?'

'I hoped that maybe it mattered less . . .' She hesitated and Rhonwen cackled. 'You thought it might matter less now that I'm old and ugly?'

'No – I didn't mean that . . .' Ursula said hastily, but Rhonwen waved away her objections.

'Don't deny it. I do still miss it, but not as badly as I once did. It no longer drives me mad with longing. I can do small things – I see glimpses of the future, I can do a bit of healing, some magic detection, and I am gifted in the mixing of sleeping draughts. I have peace here – except when Asser chooses to cause trouble. He has an instinctive understanding of magic if only he'd admit it. He knows exactly when I have used a gift greater than potions.'

'He does not approve?'

'What does not come from God must come from the dark one.'

'Can it not come from God?' Ursula whispered, suddenly frightened. She had never thought that her magic was evil, not until she had come across Finna anyway.

'Your old friend at the court of Arturus, Brother Frontalis, thought so, but he was a rare man. Asser is a great believer in miracles, but very suspicious of any that come from women. It is not entirely his fault. He has been a monk all his life and has been taught to fear us. Still, he is a good man, though Aelfred takes too much notice of his counsel. He would do better to worry less about the state of his soul and look to the state of his kingdom.'

'Are things very bad?' Ursula said dully. She found it hard to care about the state of Aelfred's kingdom; the state of her own soul was worrying enough.

Rhonwen looked serious. 'If he does not rally his supporters soon, it will be too late. His nephew has been crowned in his stead and has the support of some of the ealdormen and the archbishop of course, but the real power lies with the Danes who pull the strings of a puppet King. The rest of the ealdormen will carry on as before, but their allegiance will be to the strongest leader and at the moment that is looking to be Guthrum.'

Ursula shivered at his name. 'He is not a good leader. He is vain and cruel and only interested in his own wealth, and I do not know what Finna wants exactly, only that she has power over him. She was not blamed for my escape.'

'I'm sure you're right. The Danes are susceptible to the influence of a good seith-wife, a powerful sorceress. Aelfred has to beat him – I have seen what happens otherwise. Order depends on Aelfred.' She looked grim-faced.

'Rhonwen, what am I going to do? What if Finna can find a way to use my power against us? Dan will never get home if he does not fulfil his oath and if he can't overcome the beast in him. Have you not seen it?' Rhonwen nodded. 'Somehow I have to help Dan and yet I cannot use magic or Finna will find me and if I can't get rid of my magic I will never get home either. All I wanted was magic and now . . . it is destroying me. What can I do?'

There was a long pause and Ursula wondered if Rhonwen had heard her. Then at last she spoke.

'You do not ask easy questions, but then you don't have easy problems. Let's think about Dan first. Let me ask you a question: do you love Dan?'

'Yes,' Ursula answered without hesitation.

'Does he love you?'

'Yes.' She knew it was true. She could not doubt it. He had accepted pain and risked death to save her at Camlann. He had opened the Veil for her after she'd nearly killed Lucy in the library. He had come to Cippenham to save her.

'Dan is soulsick and the magic of this place is making him worse. You may think this strange, but Asser is the expert on souls. He may be able to help Dan, and here, as everywhere, love has power that even Asser cannot think ungodly. I think we should talk to Asser.'

'Now?'

'We need Asser on your side and on Dan's side or he could make things difficult for you. He is already suspicious of you and he has so much influence over the King. He must not believe that you are evil. He does not have much truck with women, but he understands love.'

Ursula was confused – again. Was Asser an enemy or a friend? Could he actually help Dan or just keep the King from rejecting him? She caught the shawl that Rhonwen threw in her direction and wrapped it around herself for warmth. Rhonwen's presence had always had an effect on her: in this world it made Ursula feel safe and almost herself again. She did not know if it was due to the rest, the tincture or some gift of Rhonwen herself but her thoughts were less disrupted by the pulse of power. She followed Rhonwen's lead and walked out into the darkness.

~ Chapter Thirty-seven ~

'Now,' Asser said when they were almost by the water's edge, 'there is nowhere in this area which is not watched. I am glad to say that Aelfred has started to take more of an interest in keeping Athelney as a fortress should be kept. However, I believe that we are safe enough here and if I cannot truly fend you off, I am confident that God will come to my aid. Sometimes, however, it is good to make it easier for God to respond.' His smile was tight and it took Dan a moment to realise that he was making a joke.

Dan wondered if Asser was aware of just how many people were watching them. Dan could smell at least five guards and Braveheart waiting quietly by Taliesin's side, watching his master, ready to aid him should it become necessary.

'What do I have to do to make you turn into this bear?'

The sight of Asser in his long home-spun habit, clutching his stout stick and earnestly asking how to make Dan mad, amused Dan to the extent that he was further from madness than he had been for some time.

'Ah. Perhaps all I need do is speak of how your friend Ursula ought to repent of her immodest ways and wear a dress more becoming to her sex. I don't know what they do where you come from, but here no Christian woman or woman of breeding would think of exposing her limbs like a harlot in plain sight of the King himself, not to mention his men.'

Dan could feel his temper begin to rise, but how was a monk of this time going to understand about Ursula and female equality? He kept control, though he had to think about it. Dan did not want to hurt Asser and could not be sure that the guards peering in their direction were close enough to keep him safe should Dan begin to turn.

'Do not speak of her,' Dan said. 'If you knew her better, you would know how brave she is.'

'Is she not corrupted by the dark arts, just like Rhonwen? I have seen it in her face. I know that look. She is sick with sorcery and evil. They are all the same, the viper's brood ensnaring us with their wiles – tempting us as Eve tempted Adam.'

'No!' Dan shouted, dimly aware that shouting was more difficult than it should have been. 'She is a good person! She is . . .'

Words ceased to emerge from his constricted throat and the rest was meaningless babbling. He would crush the monk and all his lies between his paws. He would separate his head from his shoulders and shut up his filthy mouth for ever. The man smelled of pigs and milk, of incense and damp. He smelled of fear, but he did not run. There was suddenly no distance between them and the man had raised his feeble stick and was praying loudly. Dan reared up ready to tear him apart. The man was wild-eyed but still made no attempt to run. Other men were screaming. He could not understand the words – it was merely noise – and somewhere off to his right Braveheart barked and snarled. He did not respond – the dog's fury was as nothing compared to his own. The man did not scream but kept on intoning the same words over and over.

'Dan, stop it now!' The voice in his head was clear and cooling, like ice poured on his burning fury, soothing his wildness, driving away his madness.

'Back away!' Dan's vision blurred and he could do nothing other than obey. His limbs were shaking. He felt his rage shrink, like his body, to manageable, man-size proportions. He no longer towered above Asser; they stood eye to eye. Asser's were opened very wide. He was still praying.

'What happened?' Dan asked, dazed. Sweat glistened on Asser's bone-white face and his hands did not appear able to release the stick he still gripped.

Ursula was suddenly at Dan's side. He had not smelled her scent in the breeze. Her presence was a shock. She smelled of magic and of bitter herbs, of unwashed wool and of her own special scent. It was so familiar and so precious to him that he had to fight back tears.

'God's will has been done here today,' Asser said, when he had finished his thanksgiving prayer.

'And God has seen fit to bless your sister Ursula with the gifts necessary to keep the demons away. The Lord answered your prayers with her,' Rhonwen said, emerging from behind Ursula's broad back.

'She is a sinner, an immodest woman, a sorcerer,' Asser blustered, colouring, though whether with relief, embarrassment or anger it was hard for Dan to say.

'She is his friend and God has blessed her. Her love for him will keep him safe,' Rhonwen asserted confidently. Dan realised with surprise that they were both speaking in the old language of the Combrogi.

'It is my prayer that saved him,' Asser said.

'Where is your humility, Asser? Is it not enough that your prayer was answered? Dan's love for Ursula brought him back to himself.'

Asser looked as if he were about to argue, but he must have seen something in the way Dan looked at Ursula to change his mind. He studied Dan for what seemed like a long time and then spoke carefully.

'It grieves me, Dan, but I do not think the demon has left you. It may be a failure of mine, a faltering of my own faith, or perhaps a part of you still welcomes the demon, has made a den for him in your soul.' His tone was severe. 'I will pray for you. God will forgive, but you must truly repent: you must want to be free of this demon with all your heart.'

Dan nodded. The beast had kept him alive: without it he was only Dan. He did not know if he could truly renounce the demon that gave him strength. He needed the beast quite as much as he loathed him. Still, he was humbled by what Asser had tried to do. He had nothing but his stout stick and his faith and he had not backed down from the beast. As for Ursula, even in the middle of all her troubles she could still get to him, still reach him with her mind; she could still help him. He was overwhelmed with relief and with gratitude to both Ursula and the courageous, curmudgeonly, misogynistic monk who had been prepared to risk his life to rid Dan of his demon. He could not say anything – he was too full of emotion – but at least he now knew why he needed the beast: he did not have Asser's strength.

Dan looked up to see both Taliesin and Braveheart heading his way. Taliesin was grinning.

'I rather hoped that might happen. Ursula is much stronger than I am. She can keep the bear at bay,' he said.

Rhonwen snorted and Ursula looked at him in confusion.

'I had forgotten. You lied to me. Why did you bring me to this place?'

Ursula's eyes were cold and Dan felt suddenly afraid. 'Don't!' He grabbed her arm. He could not tell her that any sorcery might lose them whatever acceptance they had just won from Asser. Her flesh was hot to his touch, like she was burning up with a fever.

'Has Dan not explained? I haven't lied to you yet.' Dan saw Taliesin glance at Asser and he knew that he was reluctant to explain the anomalies of time travel in front of the monk, for which Dan could not blame him.

Asser still clutched his stout stick and Dan had no desire to see him use it. There was a mental toughness about the man that would make him a formidable enemy.

'This is no time for an open-air council. If our work is

done here, we should get back to the King. There is much to speak of and to decide. These private matters must be disputed some other time, though I urge you to examine your own conscience before you condemn any man for faults of which we are all too often guilty. We must pray now, together, and thank our Almighty Father for Dan's deliverance, however temporary, from the dark forces which almost overwhelmed him,' Asser said fervently. Dan sank to his knees, his gratitude genuine. 'Let us pray that his soul might be saved.'

Dan joined his voice with Asser's in a fervent 'Amen'.

~ Chapter Thirty-eight ~

Asser led the way back to the fortress. Ursula found Dan's hand when she was sure that Asser's back was turned.

'Thank you for following me through the Veil and for coming back for me.'

'Did you ever think I'd do anything else?' he said. She had thought that, of course she had. He had abandoned her in the hospital, barely spoken to her once they were back in school. She changed the subject.

'What's with the bear?'

'I turn berserker like I did in Macsen's land and then I really want to kill someone. It's not like before. It's changed me. When I'm the bear I want to kill.' He paused to get himself back under control. 'I hate it, Ursula. Asser's not wrong – it feels like a kind of possession, and yet I need it. Without the bear I would not have survived here. Does that make sense?'

She squeezed his hand and nodded. He was not as ignorant of his own condition as she'd feared. She could see the dark magic of the bear like a shadow over him.

Between them she and Asser had made the shadow a little less black, but the magic of this world had given his darkest self a physical form and she did not think Dan would ever be free of it while the magic endured.

'Don't leave me, Ursula.'

Even without her power his fear and his need would be easy to see; as it was she felt it as strongly as if it had been her own fear and her own need.

'I won't leave you. Not if I can help it, but I'm not free either.' The connection between them must have been working both ways, because he seemed to understand. He waited until the others were out of earshot before he asked, 'Are you going to tell me about it?'

She shut her eyes and with a little tiny impulse of power showed him what it had been like. It didn't take long. When she opened her eyes he was staring at her, an expression of horror on his face.

'And you think Finna can call you any time? Use you any time?'

Ursula was trembling at the thought. 'I don't know. I think she knows when I use magic, and Dan, I am magic; it flows through me like blood. Not using it is like trying not to think: by the time you've thought about it it's too late.'

'There must be something I can do?'

She shook her head.

'You have power, yeah, so why don't you put me in charge of it. Make me your keeper so that you can only use it when I say. I can't use it – at least I don't think I can. Wouldn't that work?'

275

It was an extraordinary idea, but she did not think Dan was capable of handling any more magic. 'Let me think about it. I don't know if it can be done. Maybe if Taliesin and Rhonwen helped, and Asser too?'

'You don't trust me?'

She looked away so that he could not read her expression.

'Of course I trust you. We'll talk about it later. We are expected at the Council of War.' She sighed. 'I am so tired of war. I wish that I'd had the strength to resist all this. To let us stay where we belonged.'

'Maybe we weren't ready, maybe we couldn't cope with civilisation.'

'It couldn't cope with us, you mean. All this has changed us so much, even if we could go home, could we really go back to just being kids doing our GCSEs? I never fitted in – not before we crossed the Veil nor after . . .'

Dan let go of her hand abruptly as Asser turned to check that they were still following him back to the fortress. Ursula couldn't help being a little hurt that he felt the need to drop her hand so quickly, as if their closeness was somehow shameful. Dan explained. 'He'll have us married off soon as look at us. He's so terrified of women – he thinks all you want to do is sin!'

Ursula laughed and the sound surprised even her. She didn't know that she still could.

Her laughter evaporated once inside the main hall of the fortress. Guardsmen took away their weapons. She could see Dan struggling to retain his self-control when he was forced to hand over Bright Killer. She didn't see that it made much difference – he was a killer with or without the sword.

Their presence was announced as if they were entering some great palace rather than an oversized barn. The inside of the hall was lit only by torches and by the central fire pit, but some effort had been made to make it seem fit for a king. Wall hangings had appeared from somewhere, and Aelfred's wooden chair was richly carved. He wore a gold and jewelled crown that was slightly bent and out of place; two of the jewels were missing. He was seated while his few remaining loyal ealdormen stood around him. He had done what he could to appear regal, but to Ursula's eyes he looked thin and ill and far from confident. Ursula and Rhonwen appeared to be the only women present. She wished that she'd had the sense to appear before the King as her male alter ego, Boar Skull – his form had served her well in Macsen's land. It would have made things easier, but it was too late now.

She smiled at Aethelnoth, the only other person she recognised, and he scowled back. She had done nothing to endear herself to him on their journey from Cippenham. Her appearance caused a ripple of consternation and Aelfred was not unaware of it. Taliesin whispered something in his ear. Aelfred shook his head in disbelief.

Ursula could not help accessing enough magic to hear them.

'I tell you, my Lord, it is Ursula who led Arturus's troops at Baddon Hill and at Camlann, and I was there.'

'The devil alone was both there and here, Taliesin.

Rhonwen has told me the same story and I do not believe it. I do not believe that you were there, nor could a woman ever fight as you suggest.'

Ursula felt that familiar churning in her guts. She needed no magical clairvoyance to know that at some point she would be asked to prove herself. She had fought at Camlann not much more than two months before, but she was not as fit as she had been. She had barely moved in her time through the Veil and muscle tone is quickly lost. She began to heal herself surreptitiously, using only the smallest quantity of magic needed to do the job. She felt sick and fearful as she directed magic again. It was hard to control. Taliesin, Rhonwen and even Asser looked at her curiously. The magic began to burn. She could not keep it under control. Dan grabbed her shoulders and started to shake her, but her skin was too hot and burned him. Taliesin raised his hand. She knew what he wanted to do and she tried to let him, but she could not and his small magic was no match for hers. All eyes were turning from the King towards her and she raced from the hall. Dan bowed his apologies to the King and followed her. She was seven foot tall and growing. She had muscles like something from the World's Strongest Man; hair sprouted along her forearms.

'Stop this, Ursula!'

She could not. She was nine foot tall and growing so that Dan was dwarfed. That was a mistake. She saw the bear in Dan appear in his eyes fractionally before his transformation. If Aelfred saw them like this, he would never accept them. Ursula still had her sword: she had cast a glamour over it without thinking, so that it could not be seen. The belt was so tight it threatened to cut off her circulation. The blade was tiny in her hand. The bear moved as quickly as Dan always had and batted it out of her hand. She looked into his eyes and could not find Dan there at all. She was not in danger; she could be thirty foot high if need be and no beast could triumph over a giant. But Dan. Dan was lost? That thought got through where nothing else had. What was she doing? She let the magic go. It was difficult, but she breathed it out and let herself shrink back to near normality.

'Dan?'

She found him with her mind and called to him as she had before. He shed the bear just as one of Aelfred's ealdormen emerged from the hall.

'What is the meaning of this? No one leaves the hall without the King's permission. He has had men imprisoned for less.'

Ursula did not reply that prison sounded a good alternative to her current enslavement to the magic she could not escape.

'We are sorry,' Dan said, his voice still coarsened by the growl of the bear. 'Ursula is unwell. She feared she might disgrace herself in front of the King.'

'She is a woman and too weak for the strong council of men. I do not understand why her presence is permitted among us.'

Ursula glanced anxiously at Dan – she knew such attitudes irritated him almost as much as they irritated her. He seemed to be keeping his temper; she was faring less well. She sighed and was well aware that her voice was as cold as she could make it: 'I am experienced in the arts of war and have been in combat many times. I imagine that is why my counsel is valued.'

The man actually shivered; it was possible that she had lowered the ambient temperature with her voice. He spat his disdain. 'You think we'll fall for that?'

She was not surprised. She had known that this was going to come from the moment she had walked into the hall and sensed the antagonism of Aelfred's men.

'You had best ask permission of the King to fight me in single combat, for I will not stand for that kind of abuse from you or anyone else. You lost your fight against Guthrum. I never lose.'

'I don't kill women,' he said disdainfully.

'I *have* killed men and I am prepared to do so again. Dan is my witness: I will have an apology for this,' Ursula indicated the spittle – a globule of bubbles white against the earth, 'or I will have satisfaction.' She answered firmly enough, though with a familiar sinking feeling in her guts.

The man nodded, a small self-satisfied smile playing around his lips. He did not seem to recognise that he was in danger. Ursula didn't understand it. Even without magical augmentation she stood several inches taller and heavier than the men of Aelfred's court. The man's confidence puzzled her.

She waited until her opponent turned on his heel to speak to the King and whispered to Dan, 'Can't they see that I'm dangerous?'

Dan looked at her thoughtfully. 'They do not believe

women can fight and that blinds them. Besides, you are beautiful, Ursula, and I don't think anyone can see beyond that.' He blushed and then changed the subject very rapidly: 'Do you want to use Bright Killer?'

The sword did not fit her hand well, having been moulded to fit Dan's in an earlier magical encounter, but it was a fine sword and, though ancient, she had not seen its match here. It was even better than the one given her by Gunnarr.

'That would be good. Oh Dan, I can't face this again,' she whispered. 'What if I let the magic get the better of me?'

'You can't allow that to happen, Ursula. You have to let me help. Let me into your head.'

She had not thought about it but she knew she had barricaded herself from Dan as well as from Finna of the pale green eyes. She swallowed hard. 'What if she finds me?'

'We have to work together – it's the only way we have ever managed to cope with all this weirdness. I can't fight the bear alone and you can't resist the magic. Let me help you.' His voice was earnest, compelling. She wanted him to persuade her. She did not want to be alone in this any more.

He took her hand again. His was still a little over-large, as if his transformation back from the bear was not quite complete. He squeezed her hand gently, as a kind of encouragement. She shut her eyes and forced herself to relax. Using magic had become so much a part of her that it was like breathing. She used magic with no more awareness than she used to make her heart beat; it was outside her conscious control. She did not know how to stop. She opened her eyes. Dan's were closed and she could sense the intensity of his concentration.

'Open the door to me, Ursula.'

That helped a little – to think of her mind as a room to be accessed. She closed her eyes again and with an enormous effort of will she allowed Dan in. She was dripping with sweat as if she had already fought her enemy.

'That's it!' She could feel Dan's steady presence inside her head. He did not seem any madder than usual. He was still Dan. His presence made her feel safe for no good reason. She relaxed a little further, but perhaps not enough.

'Ursula. Please trust me. I can help you. You have to let me.'

She opened her eyes to find that his were staring at her; he was holding on to her hand a little too tightly, as if he was trying to transfer his strength to her. As she had proved many times, she had enough strength of her own; it was his commitment to her weakness that she needed.

'We'd better go back in and face the King,' she said aloud.

'Don't be afraid.' He answered without words.

She felt horribly exposed, naked and uncertain walking back into the King's hall. She had come to depend on the mental barrier she had built against Finna. She was sure that without it it was only a matter of time before Finna too would hear her thoughts and call to her.

'I won't let her,' Dan said firmly. 'You've got that old look back in your eye. That guy should back down now.'

She smiled and squared her shoulders. She was still the Lady Ursa, Boar Skull, her courage battle-honed, her mettle tempered in the heat of combat. If men could not see that in her, it was because they did not know how to look.

She bowed to Aelfred. 'Your Majesty, please forgive my inopportune departure . . .' she began. She was about to say more but he halted her.

'You have challenged Ealdorman Redwald to single combat?'

'I have.'

He grinned broadly and she knew that he too had severely underestimated her. She was going to enjoy this.

The whole party left the hall en masse to find suitable ground on the levelled land outside. The ground was wet – it always seemed to be wet at Athelney – but at Aethelnoth's order someone began to lay straw over the mud. Ealdorman Redwald had no sword – he had lost it in the retreat from Cippenham. Instead he had a langseax and a shield. Ursula had never used a langseax before, but she could hardly fight a dual with a superior blade and so accepted Aethelnoth's offer of a similar blade. It was long and narrow with a broken-back shape and only a single edge. She tested it against her thumb – it was sharp enough and ended in a wicked point: a stabbing and hacking blade. That was OK. The blade itself was mottled and dull. She swung it a few times to get a feel for it: it was heavy and the long hilt suggested it was designed to be used with two hands. She tried it. Yes, it worked better that way, but if she were to use it as a two-handed blade she would have no hand free for the shield. That might not matter. She was not particularly used to fighting defensively anyway and her opponent, though wiry, was no more than five foot eight or ten; she would have the longer reach, and as neither of them wore mail, just light unpadded tunics, whoever hit first would almost certainly draw first blood.

Her biggest problem was not the sword or the shield but the magic. She could kill her opponent with a thought, stop his heart, empty him of breath. She could turn herself into a giant, a monster with eight arms, a wolf or a bear like Dan if that was what she wanted to do. She had not yet been tempted to do any such thing, but then she had not truly been under attack. It was important to her that she win this fight fairly – only she no longer knew where her own abilities ended and the magic began.

Dan was there in her head. She spoke to him. *'Do not let me use magic!'*

'Trust me, Ursula. It will be all right.'

Ursula's opponent had followed her lead and rejected the shield. There was something in his stance that suggested he knew what he was doing, a confidence that was more than arrogance. She resisted the urge to enter his mind and discover his plan of attack. She wanted to do this properly. She was scared. She wasn't sure if she was up to the task. She had used magic to restore her body that had been ravaged by magic, but she could not help thinking that a good meal and several nights of restorative sleep might have been more effective; magic was unpredictable, wild like fire, rarely under complete control.

The King was talking but she barely took in the words. There wasn't time for the more elaborate rituals of single combat – this would be a simple fight, man to man. Aelfred had got a laugh from that and amended it to man to woman. Even in the King's court that remark produced some crude jeering, which Ursula ignored. Her opponent was right-handed and looked to be generally stronger on the right side. He was laughing, a little embarrassed to be taking on a woman at all. Ursula cleared her mind of everything but the need to prove herself in this arena formed by the catcalling members of Aelfred's court.

She stepped into the centre of the ring. She was not quick and agile like Dan; she was strong and deliberate and calculating. If they had fought with shields, she would have been given a chance to hit her opponent first. She thought that bizarre and was quite relieved that this would be a free-for-all. Ursula licked her lips and tasted the salt of her sweat. She felt hot, but that might still be the magic burning away, eating at her from the inside.

'*Steady.*' It was Dan's voice in her head. '*He's right-handed.*'

What kind of idiot did Dan think she was? Of course he was right-handed.

Dan did not respond. Her opponent moved in quickly, charging at her. She met his blade with her own and there was a horrible clang of metal. Ursula realised too late that these weapons were not designed for swordplay but for butchery. The clash of seaxes had left both blades damaged. He was close to her now, murmuring insults about her body, about her sex. She could not afford to lose her temper or she would annihilate him, and that wasn't what this was about. She kicked him sharply in the kneecap and he went down on one knee. She thrust her blade towards his chest but he dodged and countered with a thrust of his own – Ursula was still standing and danced out of his way. He was beginning to take her more seriously, as were the crowd. Ursula waited until he had regained his feet.

'Have you had enough yet?' she asked sweetly. He spat a reply she didn't hear and immediately began to aim his blade at her abdomen. She could see why these men relied on their shields – she could not block his seax with hers without risking further damage to the blade. She was more used to fighting with a well-tempered sword. The obvious solution was to use her long legs to kick him away, and when he shifted his weight to move in for a close attack she stuck out a size eight foot to trip him up, so that he lay sprawled on the ground. His seax was flung from his hand and lay in a bed of mud-splattered straw. There was a hoot of laughter from the crowd, swiftly suppressed, and Ursula saw her opponent's face flush dark red with humiliation.

Once more she allowed him to get back on his feet. Rather than wait for him to retrieve his seax, she threw hers to Dan, who was standing at the edge of the crowd, watching her every move. He caught it deftly. Ursula's opponent seemed surprised. Perhaps he assumed she'd given away her advantage, but Ursula did not see how she could avoid killing the man if they continued fighting this way. Any hit would have to draw blood to count and she knew how easily a wound festered without the benefit of antibiotics. She did not want to kill this man just because he had had the temerity to assume she couldn't fight.

She had not done much unarmed combat beyond the odd fist fight in Macsen's world, but she knew she had a good punch on her. Of course you could kill a man with a bare-knuckle punch too; she'd just have to be careful.

'*What are you doing, Ursula?*' Dan's voice in her mind sounded confused. She ignored him. His job was to prevent her from turning to magic, not to advise her on her fight.

The man weighed her up properly, perhaps for the first time. Maybe her blonde hair had truly blinded him to the fact that she was six foot one and built like an athlete. She did not know. She would have liked briefly to see what he saw, just to understand how he'd misjudged her. Dan answered her request by sending her the briefest image of herself, crouching, ready to pounce. She was taken aback. Her eyes were hard and green as emeralds and they blazed with a cold fire. If she needed proof of how completely the magic possessed her, that would have been it: her eyes should have been blue.

She was distracted for a fraction of an instant – time enough for her opponent to go in low and rugby tackle her to the ground. She was winded by the force of the impact and angry with herself for getting sidetracked. It was her fault. She reached for the magic to blast him off her and Dan's voice in her head rebuked her. '*No! You can beat him. Fight back, Boar Skull!*' He was right. His arms were around her knees. She brought them up sharply, knocking him hard in the jaw, and then twisted out of his grip.

She launched herself at him as he began to find his feet, pinning him with her weight and grabbing him by the throat. She had big hands for a woman and her grip was relentless. He struggled under her but she winded him with her knee and he was at her mercy.

'That's enough now, Ursula,' Dan commanded as the man turned blue under the pressure of her hand. She looked to the King, who had paled visibly.

'Let him go!' he said imperiously. She thought he seemed shaken.

Ursula obeyed and her opponent gasped and panted for breath like a fish out of water. She stretched and clenched her hand repeatedly. The man turned his head away as if he did not want to see such weapons on a woman. Ursula wondered how long it would take for him to live it down.

The crowd was strangely sober. No one stamped or cheered and she found herself a little disappointed. She had not used magic, she had not killed him and she had won fair and square. She accepted that it had not been a very entertaining fight – it had been too quickly over and too decisive, but still she had expected more than this shocked, uncomfortable silence. She bowed her head to the King and picked up the abandoned seax to return it to its owner.

Her opponent was on his feet again now, unbowed and bristling with outrage. He almost shouted at the King, 'Sire, you cannot let this rest. She bewitched me with her green eyes. Did you not see how they flashed? She is nothing more than a Viking seith-wife. This is not justice.'

There was a murmur of agreement from the crowd. Ursula could feel herself getting hot and angry. '*Ursula, don't lose it now! They'll think you cheated in the fight. Stay calm.*' Dan's voice in her head was irritating, but he spoke the truth. She would quite like to thump him. She found even good advice hard to take. She swallowed down a blunt response and ground her teeth.

The King turned to Ursula gravely. 'And how do you answer this accusation?'

She almost said what she thought of people who could not lose gracefully but managed to bite that back too. She made herself speak calmly and with as much icy dignity as she could muster. 'Your Highness, I fought him fairly. When I brought him down I allowed him to regain his feet; when he dropped his seax I threw mine away. I tripped him, but I was not given any rules by which to fight this fight. And as for sorcery, ask your bishop, Asser. He will attest that I used no sorcery in this fight. He is a man of God and he always knows.'

Asser managed to look both pleased and embarrassed by her claim. All eyes turned to the dark-robed shadow standing like a gaunt crow at Aelfred's side. She wondered for a moment if she had made a mistake. She had believed Rhonwen when she claimed that Asser always knew when magic was used, but what if her silent mental conversation with Dan was a kind of a magic? Perhaps she had miscalculated.

Asser looked at her coolly for a full minute while she sweated under the hostile gaze of every man present, then he nodded, and she could release the breath she did not know she had been holding.

'She is telling the truth. I fear that Ealdorman Redwald was indeed bested by a woman and, if skill at unarmed combat be a qualification to your Council of War, she has every right to be present.' He sounded reluctant to make that admission, and, knowing his opinion of women in general and herself in particular, she was impressed by his honesty.

Ursula sensed Aelfred's surprise at his judgement. 'Then Ursula shall be deemed a worthy victor.'

Ursula beamed at Asser, whose face turned an unattractive shade of mottled purple. He gave her the curtest of curt nods and looked away. He had surprised himself too.

The man Ursula had bested would not meet her eye. He was lucky to be alive if he only knew it. But she had not made herself friends at court by proving herself a warrior. She did not understand it. She had led men before – many had been willing to follow her to their death – but here the mere fact that she was a woman was proving a serious sticking point. The King moved swiftly on, which was perhaps the wisest course. They all trooped back into the hall for the real business: Aelfred's Council of War.

~ Chapter Thirty-nine ~

Dan was not sorry to leave Ursula's mind. It had felt almost like being Ursula for a while, and being Ursula was not that much fun – not the way things were for her in this world. He understood that now and it frightened him. Sharing thoughts had always frightened him – the intimacy was disturbing, disorienting – but each time he had done it he had coped better, and so had she. This time, however, this time he knew how much trouble she was in and he was very afraid.

It was hard to concentrate on what Aelfred was saying. Dan's eye was drawn to Ursula's face. With his own more acute senses he thought that she even smelled of magic, a hint of something spicy, something strange under the distinctive and familiar smell of her sweat. He wanted to make it OK, to set her free, but he did not know how.

He wished her eyes were not so green, that she did not glow with magical heat. How long could a person live with all that power flowing through them? She was tough and strong, but how much could a body stand and how much mental strength would she need to resist its pull?

They might end up being part of this world for their whole lives. That thought made him angry and he couldn't risk being angry; seeing Ursula lost behind her green eyes made him angry too. He could not look at her any longer. Instead he turned all his attention to the King and to the assembled group. Somehow, during Dan's absence, the King had made contact with many more thegns and ealdormen, as well as with churchmen of every kind. Athelney had become a court in exile, and the Council of War an altogether more official body than Dan had envisaged; what finery still remained in Aenglisc hands was on display in the mail shirts and decorated helms of the aristocracy and the fine cloth and gold thread of the churchmen's copes. He was worried about the security of such a meeting. If word spread to Aelfred's enemies of his precise whereabouts, he might yet be attacked in Athelney, and though it was better run than previously, Dan did not think they had what it would take to withstand a siege. Aelfred, however, seemed relaxed and more regal than before.

'My grandfather, my father and my brother all laid down their lives for this land and while strength lies within me I will not let it pass from my hands. We will rebuild this kingdom so that it will rival the court of Charlamagne.' He got up from his chair, which Dan saw was a kind of carved wooden throne, and made eye contact with all those present. His pale eyes had a strange kind of power and for a sickly man Dan was surprised by his charisma.

Aelfred continued, 'We will regain our wealth and our

land and those who are loyal now will be amply repaid for their honourable service, their courage and their strength. We have all lived through dark days, days in which the heathen hordes have run amok among us, but now is the moment when the tide turns. We are sorry for all our failure, our faults and sins for which our God has punished us deservedly, but we have spent our days of repentance in the wilderness and now, by God's grace, we will emerge purified and consecrated to take back what is ours.'

The assembled nobles then stamped their feet in an unexpectedly passionate response. Aelfred was still without his kingdom, his army and his wealth. He still had little to give to those binding themselves to him with their renewed oaths of allegiance, but something had changed: he had started to believe he could win.

Dan did not grasp all that went on. There was detailed discussion of which ealdormen could be trusted, how many thegns would fight for them, of men killed in raids, horses and weapons lost, and food supplies running low. But in the last few days Aelfred had got a grip on more than the refurbishment of the fortress: he was getting a grip on the situation in his kingdom and on his own self. Gone was his indecision and uncertainty; instead Dan found himself faced with someone he could serve.

He had stopped paying close attention when the discussion moved on to specifics that he didn't understand, but then Aelfred mentioned him by name and he was drawn back.

'Your fighting prowess has been much talked of, Dan. We need to train our coerls and even some of our thegns in both armed and unarmed combat. It would help us greatly if you and your comrade-in-arms would assist us in that. We must all accept new ways of doing things if we are to overthrow the Danes, and expertise is to be valued from whomsoever it comes.'

Dan recognised that his somewhat reluctant compliment was aimed at Ursula. He wasn't sure that these men would take direction from her as so many other men had done. She caught his eye.

'*I will find a way, Dan. Don't make a fuss. I've done this before. How hard can it be?*'

The answer was, very hard indeed. Aelfred wished his army to be prepared by Whitsun, when the weather ought to be fine enough to move troops without too much trouble and when much of the early planting and labouring on the land would be done. Aelfred understood all too well that men did not fight well when they were worried about whether there would be food enough to eat at the end of the season.

'If I had more men I'd have two armies, so that there would always be men enough to tend the fields and our defences,' he confessed to Dan in one of their many private conversations, 'and I'd make sure that a good many of them could read. The job of gathering men would be so much easier if I could write to them in my own hand and be understood, rather than having to rely on messengers. How am I to be sure that they pass on my words and not some travesty of my intentions?' He fretted a lot about such things and about the spiritual welfare of his men. He was not at all what Dan had first believed him to be, but a thoughtful man who had lost everything and blamed himself.

'I was wild in my youth, Dan,' he confessed, 'and before my marriage I did not always conduct myself as befits a Christian man. When I settled gold on the Danes to stay away from Wessex, for five whole years I did not properly prepare for their return. There is so much that I ought to have done that I left undone. I sometimes feel that God is punishing me for my sins in particular.'

Dan did not know what to say.

'The important thing is that you are ready now, Sire,' he said; but he was not sure that they were ready. There were no more than a few hundred men at Athelney. As days passed a steady trickle of ceorls turned up when they could be spared from the land, but few were trained. Aelfred was confident that as word spread that the true King waited to reclaim his throne from those who bowed their knees to the heathen hordes, more men would come – that all the loyal men of Wessex would answer his call. Dan was less confident. How many men would Aelfred have to fight against the battle-hardened warriors of Guthrum?

Ursula battled on in her own private hell. She had not used her magic, but although she felt more herself when Dan or Rhonwen were near she was still struggling to contain the power that burned through her blood. She insulated herself from contact with the earth as much as possible, but there were no horses on Athelney and no need for them. Focusing on the moment was difficult and she felt weak with the effort and, worse, the longing to use the magic grew daily more powerful. Every second she fought the urge to do what came most naturally to her. The men did not help. They were reluctant to take heed of her, and as the rumours spread of her time in the Viking camp, they became more afraid and contemptuous of her; it was worse than school. In the past she had been buoyed up by the loyalty and love of the men she had fought with and the men she had led. She found this barely disguised hostility difficult to accept. It did not seem to matter that she could best any man there with any weapon they chose; they did not love her for it.

'I don't know what I'm doing wrong!' she complained to Dan after the first week. 'I don't think I'm being any different than I was with the cavalry before Baddon or Camlann, but I can't connect with these people.'

She felt disconnected from everything, as if in trying not to wield magic she had become a kind of a ghost, less than a person. Maybe the men knew that. In an unguarded moment Dan allowed her to see herself through his eyes and she did indeed resemble a ghost more than the living vital warrior she had been. She had grown thin as the magic burned her up from the inside. Her hair seemed bleached almost to whiteness and her face was pale and grey as the snow-laden clouds that threatened them with a return to winter. Her eyes looked like dark pits from which no warmth escaped.

'Ah,' she said, 'I understand how they might feel that Aelfred has given them over to a wraith.'

'But a warrior wraith,' Dan said in an effort to cheer

her up, but she could detect his concern for her in the tightness in his face and his forced good humour.

As if her days were not bad enough, her nights were worse. The visions that had plagued her continued. Mostly she could make little sense of them. She saw men whispering to each other of a great army building in the wild country of the marshes. She saw endless arguments and disputes about loyalty, fathers screaming at sons to stay and work the land, mothers entreating their children not to fight, and everywhere young men taking what weapons they had and slipping away from the fields to answer Aelfred's call. She saw a vast army of men on a high ridge, screaming to their gods. They banged their round shields with long knives and axes, shook their spears and gathered their courage, in a wild group battle madness. Against them, similarly dressed, she saw Aelfred's men tightly pressed shoulder to shoulder in a long wall of shields, yelling back their defiance. She knew that this was the future towards which they were all marching – and it filled her with fear.

Finna pursued her through her dreams, her pale blind eyes grown a darker shade of green, as if she had increased in power.

'Come, Freya, we call you back to your own people. We will bring you victory and much blood! You can bathe in the blood of our vanquished enemies. Come. We entreat you.'

Ursula felt herself being drawn towards the girl even in her sleep, but fought her and escaped. Unfortunately she could not escape from her dreams.

One night, some weeks after she had proved herself a warrior to Aelfred's court in exile, she dreamed of Gunnarr, her Viking friend and gentle champion, arguing with Guthrum. He objected to Finna's undue influence as he saw it and Guthrum released him from his oath of allegiance, sending him off to fight with the sons of Ragnarr up north. She thought that Guthrum might have killed him but they were kinsmen of a kind and that, perhaps, saved him. Gunnarr did not seem to feel that he was saved. She saw his stricken face as he rode out of Cippenham with all his hopes of advancement dashed. He did not set out north, however, but sought Ursula, calling to her in his dreams as Freya, his beloved. When she woke at dawn to the crowing of the rooster in the yard, she knew she had to help him.

For decency's sake Ursula did not sleep in the barracks with the men, so Dan could not help her fight her nightmares; instead she slept on a pallet beside her former enemy, Rhonwen. Rhonwen was herself a restless sleeper, much given to muttering in her sleep, and she was always awake before dawn – fussing with the fire, busy at her potions, her brewing and her baking.

'Well?' Rhonwen asked. 'The dreams were worse last night, I suppose?' She handed Ursula one of her pleasanter concoctions, a kind of herbal tea that tasted sweet: it calmed and settled Ursula's early morning jitters. It was not tea, but it offered her the same kind of comfort.

'How did you know?'

'You could say that your screams gave it away; but tell me, who is Gunnarr? Some Viking, I imagine?'

Ursula drained her beaker and considered telling Rhonwen all she knew. It was not much, but Rhonwen was an ally. Rhonwen filled up her beaker.

'He is a cousin of Guthrum who was kind to me when I was captive. He is looking for me. He and Guthrum have parted ways. I do not think he is loyal to him any longer, but they were close once. He knows things that might be useful. Do you think I should tell the King?'

'Is he coming this way?'

Ursula nodded. 'He was with Finna when she asked me to find Aelfred. The men that were sent to kill the King may never have found him, but Gunnarr is clever and we are not so difficult to find. Now that so many recruits have come here, the way is known.'

Rhonwen pulled a face and handed Ursula a piece of warm griddle cake from the bakestone over the fire.

'Yes, I think you should see the King. You should tell him of your visions, but I think you should talk to Asser first.'

'Asser?'

Rhonwen nodded grimly. 'If Asser takes you to the King, Aelfred will trust that your visions are of God.'

'But they are not evil, you know that, Rhonwen. They are just images of what is or is going to be.'

'Then you will have nothing to fear from Asser.'

'He doesn't like me.'

'He is full of nonsense about women. Take no notice. He wants what is best for Aelfred and Wessex. I will come with you if you like, but you would be better going alone.'

Ursula nodded. 'I will go alone.' She hesitated. 'Do you

think I should wear a dress?'

Rhonwen's throaty cackle made Ursula smile. 'We'll make a diplomat of you yet,' she said. 'I have clothes that might do, though I will have to lengthen them.' She patted Ursula's hand. 'Don't worry. Somehow it will work out all right.'

~ Chapter Forty ~

Rhonwen's cottage had no mirror of any kind, so Ursula had no idea how she looked in the sombre woollen garments she had been lent. Rhonwen had plaited her hair and arranged it in some fashion around her head so that she looked less wild. Rhonwen seemed happy with the finished effect.

'What of my sword?'

'You could wear it under your cloak if you insist. Why? Have you foreseen trouble?'

'Not exactly, but there is so much violence in the air – can't you feel it? I don't like to be weaponless.'

Rhonwen knew better than to mention Ursula's magic – a weapon like no other.

'Pinch your cheeks a bit to give yourself more colour,' she said, 'and don't be too bold when you speak to the bishop.' Ursula was about to argue, but Rhonwen hushed her. 'Charm is a weapon in its way and I learned of it too late. If you want to help Aelfred and save your friend Gunnarr, forget your wild foreign manners and act as Asser would expect of a virtuous, honourable woman –

that is, after all, what you are.'

Ursula was not so sure but said nothing. It was quite amusing to be told how to behave by a proud Combrogi princess who had always done exactly what she pleased without much thought of the consequences. Ursula took her advice in the spirit in which it was intended and walked carefully out of the cottage and out of the fortress to Asser's former sty. It was cold and the ground was crisp and iced with frost.

'Your Eminence,' she called into the blackness.

Asser was not asleep, but had just returned from prayer at the chapel. If he was startled to see Ursula in her modest robes and uncomfortable hairstyle, he gave no sign.

'My child, how can I help you?'

She told him, haltingly at first, about her visions of the battle to come and of Gunnarr's imminent arrival. He was a good listener and with a little careful prompting on his part she feared that she had told him more than she wanted, if less than the full truth. She dared not talk to him of magic.

He looked grave. 'My child, do you claim these visions are of God and not born of the evil witchcraft practised by my compatriot?'

'I do not think they are evil, Your Eminence, for I think they are true, and doesn't truth belong to God?'

Asser nodded. 'That is indeed so. We must inform the King. I think he will be glad to hear news of the battle to come, for by the sound of it we will have built an army fit to meet the Danes and that will give him heart.'

By this time the spring sun had begun to warm the air

and the frozen ground was once more reverting to mud.

Aelfred looked ashen and deep lines of illness and worry were inscribed on his face. Ursula took one look at him and recognised a fellow sufferer: someone else harried by dreams and nightmares. She smiled at him and was surprised to receive a warm answering smile that transformed his face.

'Lady Ursula, what drives you to seek an audience so early in the day?'

She repeated her story yet again. He was, as Asser had expected, heartened by her vision of a great Saxon army. He was less convinced that Gunnarr could be an ally.

'Lady Ursula, it grieves me to question your judgement but I have trusted these Danes to my cost in earlier years and have found them to hold the oaths that bind to be of little value; their loyalty is a slippery thing. I believe that Gunnarr might come here and offer his sword; what I find harder to accept is that we should trust him. When he has something that Guthrum wants, like the precise location of our fortress, he may well be welcomed back with open arms – a hero to his own people.'

Ursula had thought of that, but doubted Gunnarr was so fickle.

'I understand, Your Majesty, but I would ask that you speak to him before you condemn him. He was kind to me when I was captive there and I understand that he is a fine warrior and well respected by the men. If he were to fight for you, that may unsettle the Vikings. Guthrum is not much loved, though his record of victory earns its own respect.'

Aelfred scowled and played with his scrubby young man's beard.

'I will do this for you. I will send Dan, Aethelnoth and Taliesin to meet your Dane on the road. Between them they should come to a suitable conclusion.'

Ursula knew she had been dismissed and left the hall faintly dissatisfied and determined to accompany Dan and the others; she would be needed to find the way.

She dressed in her warrior's garb and met Dan a little later to cross the lake. He was fighting the bear valiantly, but at every small annoyance – the discomfort of the crossing, Aethelnoth's coolness towards her and Taliesin's inappropriate cheerfulness – she could see the bear peering out through his eyes. She held his hand surreptitiously, but though he smiled at her gratefully enough, the smile did not reach his eyes and she knew that her presence did not help. Mindful of her dreams of Finna she did not dare open her mind to him. She was too afraid.

Taliesin seemed to have cast himself in the role of court jester and would not stop talking, as if by his words alone he could glue their strange ill-suited party together. He didn't try magic, he wasn't stupid, but even so Ursula wished that he'd stop and leave them each to their own separate misery.

They had been travelling for about an hour, picking their way through the marsh, leading their mounts as often as they rode them because the ground was treacherous, when Ursula became sure that Gunnarr was close. Dan's animal senses picked up his scent a little later.

'He stinks like a Viking,' Dan grunted.

'I will go to him – it is me he wants,' Ursula said and was surprised when Dan responded with a growl.

'Why are you putting us all to this much trouble – the man's an enemy, isn't he?'

'He could be useful to Aelfred – he was close to Guthrum.'

'He is a spy more like and will betray us to his cousin as soon as he has drunk our ale and ravished our women; you know nothing of Danes.' That was the longest speech that Ursula had heard Aethelnoth give. His suspicion was obviously why Aelfred had insisted that he be one of their party.

'Danes, Saxons, Celts, Romans – there is good and bad in all . . .' Taliesin said, and looked taken aback when Ursula, Dan and Aelthelnoth all glared at him. Ursula mounted up and rode ahead without a backward glance. She wanted to speak to Gunnarr alone, out of range of Aethelnoth's sword and Dan's dangerous temper.

His sword was already drawn when she reached him.

'Freya?'

'My name is Ursula.'

'You are free? I feared that you had been taken and –'

'I can look after myself,' she answered shortly. 'I have come to tell you that I am with representatives of the true King of Wessex, Aelfred. He has a place for good warriors if you were to swear allegiance to him.' She found his expression hard to read. He was looking at her as if he had just had some kind of religious vision; it made her feel uncomfortable.

'You would have me betray my cousin?' he said at last.

Perhaps she had misunderstood what was going on. If Ursula was wrong about him and he was still loyal to Guthrum, her interference would cost him his life.

'I thought that you had argued with Guthrum, that Fin— the blind girl had become too influential.' It was impossible for Ursula to speak of Finna by name, for fear of alerting Finna to her presence on this undefended road. She swallowed hard.

'You are well informed, Goddess. I have parted company with Guthrum but I see no reason to fight on Aelfred's side. I could join any war band on this island!'

'Yes, but you are riding west across Wessex, while Mercia and Northumbria are north.'

'But you, my Lady, had gone west, or so it was rumoured. I had to find you, to be sure that you were unharmed.'

Ursula shrugged. 'I am unharmed. If you will not fight for Aelfred, you must ride north now as fast as you can because he knows you are coming and he will catch you if he can.'

'And why do you, a Viking goddess, serve this Aelfred who was dethroned by his own people? Why don't you come with me and together we will find a worthy leader: there is none here.'

Ursula was almost tempted for half a moment – she had missed the adoration that burned in his eyes; she had known little of it in Aelfred's world.

'My oath is already given,' she said. 'I serve King Aelfred.'

Gunnarr smiled. 'Then for your sake I will serve him too.'

It did not seem to Ursula to be the best way of deciding loyalties until she realised that it was exactly what she had done in choosing Aelfred. She chose Aelfred because Dan had chosen him.

'Good,' she said. There was no time to say more because at that moment Dan arrived, on foot in the guise of the bear.

~ Chapter Forty-one ~

Dan could not control the sudden surge of violent feeling he felt towards this 'kind' Gunnarr. He dismounted and removed his boots, his sword belt and most of his clothes without really being aware of what he was doing. By the time he had removed his second boot the transformation was complete.

'No, Dan!' Taliesin waved his arm in Dan's direction but he'd had enough of Taliesin's meddling and his power over Dan had ended. He unseated him with one swipe of his massive arm. If Aethelnoth had any plan to stop him, he kept it to himself and made sure that Dan could see both his hands in clear view. Dan didn't waste time worrying about either of his companions; he had to get to Ursula and rescue her from the charms of the Dane.

He saw that he'd startled her. She did not seem glad to see him. She gave him a very steely look, almost as if she were herself again.

The Dane had his sword drawn – a good sword, though no match for the bear's claws or teeth. Gunnarr was tall and, Dan supposed, good-looking if you admired long blond hair and chiselled features. He was muscular and strong too, but he was nothing compared to the bear.

Gunnarr dismounted with athletic ease and eyed the bear steadily. If he was terrified, he didn't show it. For some reason this made Dan even angrier and he began to salivate at the thought of removing Gunnarr's pretty blond head from his broad shoulders. Gunnarr attacked, but Dan blocked his sword easily and knocked it from his hand. Dan growled and moved in for the kill.

Suddenly the woman was there before him, protecting the Dane. Her eyes shone with dark fire and she held the sword as if she knew what to do with it. *'Stop it now, Dan.'*

The woman, Ursula, was in his head and he could not disobey her. He let his arm drop.

'Get a grip on yourself – Gunnarr has agreed to join us. Please don't kill Aelfred's allies – he needs everyone he can get.'

Something in Ursula's mental tone made him ashamed. He felt himself literally cut down to size, shrinking back to normal human proportions. He stood there in front of Gunnarr in his real form, that of a half-naked teenage boy. He could not help but feel puny beside the Viking warrior. He hung his head in shame and embarrassment.

'You are the Bear Sark. The one they talked about at Cippenham, one of Odin's blessed.' Gunnarr sounded awed, impressed, as if the fact that he had nearly been killed was unimportant.

Dan did not answer, mainly because he couldn't: Gunnarr was a warrior, and a brave one, and Dan had nearly killed him for no other reason than that Ursula admired him. He felt too mortified to answer. He hated what the magic of this world was doing to him. He was becoming more of a beast with every day he spent in Aelfred's world.

'Yes. This is my comrade-in-arms, Dan, and he is the Bear Sark, though I do not know if he is blessed or cursed,' Ursula said, and Dan knew that she was angry. He was becoming a liability, and without Ursula's presence he would have killed Gunnarr and perhaps Aethelnoth and Taliesin too. He hoped that he had not hurt Taliesin when he'd knocked him from the saddle. He was an old man.

Dan went to him at once to apologise as soon as he heard his approach. Taliesin looked pale and his left arm hung uselessly by his side.

'I'm so sorry. I did not know what I was doing.'

Taliesin looked sceptical.

'Yes, you did. You knew you were transforming – you took off your boots and your clothes. Aethelnoth put them with your horse.' He inclined his head to indicate a neat bundle that Aethelnoth had secured with the reins. 'Asser is right. You do not want to be rid of the beast. You are allowing it to take you over. I thought you were going to kill me. I know you have your reasons for being annoyed with me, but I have always been loyal to you in my way. I did not deserve this.'

Dan could feel his anger rising again even at this. Taliesin's loyalty was the kind he could well do without. He was so busy trying to stay in control of himself that he did not notice Aethelnoth's arrival. It was his scream of furious rage that got his attention. He turned in time to see the Aenglisc warrior hurl himself at the Dane.

Gunnarr was unarmed, his sword still lying where Dan had knocked it from his hand. Once more Ursula placed herself before the Dane and raised her own sword in defence.

Aethelnoth knew her reputation, had watched her fight, and yet he still did not believe he could be bested by a woman. Gunnarr stepped back out of reach of Ursula's sword arm and Aethelnoth screamed, 'Out of my way!'

He slashed at her and looked surprised as she parried his blow easily. As their blades locked she pushed him backwards. He had thought to drive her from his path to Gunnarr; he could not quite believe he had given ground. Dan saw Gunnarr grab his own sword and ready himself for an attack, but none was necessary. Ursula's face remained impassive but she would not let Aethelnoth pass. He was getting angry, his blows more frenzied. Dan knew that Ursula was fighting her magic as much as she was fighting Aethelnoth; he was a warrior of some reputation but he was not Ursula, and her steady, concentrated defence looked effortless. Dan had no worries about her swordsmanship; she would be fine as long as the magic did not distract her, as long as she could stay fixed in the moment. Having been inside her head, he knew that was not easy. Aethelnoth was not trying to hurt her, but as she frustrated his every attempt to disarm her so that he could get to the Dane, Dan saw his intention change: suddenly Aethelnoth saw her not as barrier to be surmounted but as an enemy to be killed. Dan saw the instant Aethlnoth's attitude shifted. He wanted to cry out to warn Ursula but did not dare distract her. He had to hope that she had noticed the change too. He ought to have had more faith. Aethelnoth stepped back, the better to lunge at her heart, and quicker than a snake Ursula's sword was at his throat. Dan had always admired her unflashy economy of movement.

'Stop now, Aethelnoth,' she said and for a moment she looked like the old Ursula. Her eyes were still their unnatural green, but less dark, and the look on her face was one Dan had seen many times before: triumph mixed with wonder.

'I am in awe,' Gunnarr said, sheathing his sword and smiling.

Dan had to fight down the bear when he saw Ursula's answering smile. She thought it was over. She turned away from Aethelnoth, withdrawing her blade, and in that moment Aethelnoth attacked. Dan's hands were still clumsy from his transformation but he launched himself at Ursula to knock her out of the way. Aethelnoth's sword was raised and it seemed certain that he would kill Gunnarr with a swift blow to the throat. Ursula cried out. Dan did not hear what she said but when he disentangled his limbs from hers, Aethelnoth stood frozen like a man turned to stone, his sword arm poised to strike. Although he could not move he could still speak. He let out a howl of anguish and frustration that chilled Dan's blood. But it was Ursula's angry voice in his mind that he heard first.

'Dan, you didn't stop me. I used magic. Finna will find me!'

It seemed to Dan as if he could do nothing right. He was about to make an angry response when he saw Ursula's face. She was staring at Aethelnoth. He was crying silently and glaring at Gunnarr, who seemed utterly unnerved. 'You killed her!' he said.

'What is going on?' Dan asked, as whatever it was seemed far from obvious.

Ursula answered him in such a way that he knew she thought he was being slow on the uptake. The bear seemed to have blunted his normal human sensitivity. 'Gunnarr killed Aethelnoth's wife in a raid a few months ago. It was not all he did.'

Dan let that sink in for a moment. He remembered that Aethelnoth had confused him with Gunnarr because of their height and skill with a sword.

'She was carrying our child,' Aethelnoth said in a voice so lost and full of despair that even Dan could understand the depth of his grief.

'I am sorry,' Gunnarr said, in halting Aenglisc. 'It is what happens in these times. Set him free, Goddess, and let him try to kill me. He has the right.'

Ursula shook her head. 'This is all madness. There needs to be an end to it. If you fight, you will both be injured, perhaps even die. What is the good in that?'

'I will give my life gladly to avenge my wife. Let me free.'

Taliesin spoke then for the first time and Dan suspected him of weaving magic into his tone. His voice sounded more beautiful than ever and subtly coaxing. Ursula looked surprised.

'Gunnarr, can you not pay wergild to Aethelnoth for his wife – wergild equivalent to the loss of a Viking warrior? In that way can you not satisfy honour and live,

Aethelnoth? Would you not agree to that, Gunnarr?' Taliesin asked.

'I don't know. I have no gold now, not enough anyway, but I will promise it. I will swear it on my own life.'

'Danish promises are worth nothing,' Aethelnoth, said and spat on the ground.

'I can make it bind,' Ursula said softly. 'It is a form of magic I will do – if it will save your lives. But, Aethelnoth, you must not tell Aelfred of this. I do not want him to see me as a sorceress.'

'Are you sure you want to do this, Ursula? What about Finna?' Dan asked, speaking without words.

'It is too late. She knows where I am – I can feel her pulling at me, like she has me on a tether. Help me not to give in!'

Dan did not have the slightest idea of how to do that but agreed readily. He would do whatever he could.

Ursula opened her fist, which until that moment she had been holding tightly clenched, and released what looked like a golden ribbon which writhed and twisted through the air like a water snake in a pond. As Dan watched, it lengthened and became a thin golden cord; one end wound its way around Gunnarr's chest, binding it tightly, while the other bound Aethelnoth's chest. The two men remained visibly tied together for a moment and then the cord seemed to change again, burrowing into the men's chests before apparently disappearing.

'That is what a binding oath looks like – a chain of gold that you cannot break.'

The men looked horrified; each stared at their chests in wonderment.

'I do not think you can kill each other now,' she said matter-of-factly. 'So I will release you, Aethelnoth, so that you may sheathe your sword. Aelfred will ask for your oath, Gunnarr, and you can be certain that too will bind you. Are you sure you want to make such a promise?'

Dan thought that Gunnarr coped remarkably well with so much strangeness. In response he nodded. 'I have wanted to serve a worthy leader and it seems that if this Aelfred is served by both a warrior goddess and the beloved of Odin, the Bear Sark, then he must be such a leader. I confess I did not think it obvious at Cippenham, but I have been wrong before. I will give you my oath now if that is what you wish.'

Taliesin intervened then and recited the form of words which Aelfred would accept and Gunnarr repeated them. Dan's attention wandered away. Ursula was about to faint. He rushed to her side and caught her as she fell.

'The Goddess – she is good?' Gunnarr asked in his awkward Aenglisc.

'I don't know,' Dan said, feeling suddenly coldly afraid. 'What do you know of the seith-wife who serves Guthrum? I am afraid this is Finna's work.'

~ Chapter Forty-two ~

It felt like she was drowning. Ursula could no longer hear the voices of her companions; she could no longer see Dan or Taliesin. She was in some dark place where she could no longer feel anything but fear and anger. She knew at once what had happened. Finna had called to the magic. If she had not succumbed to the magic, allowed it to flow through her again, whatever trap Finna had sprung could not have caught her. She had been a fool to wield the magic again – but what else could she have done? Allowed Dan to kill Gunnarr or Gunnarr to kill Aethelnoth? She didn't think that she could have stood by and let that happen. Neither anger nor fear was much help to her in her current situation. She needed to think, not to be overwhelmed. She needed to be brave.

Somewhere Finna was singing in her high reedy voice. It was the only sound that Ursula could hear and she rather wished she couldn't. Finna could not wield magic but she could call and bind it and at that moment that made her the one holding all the cards. Even the sound of her tuneless wailing made Ursula panic and that was not good. Ursula needed to remember that she was a warrior and a sorceress, and neither allowed themselves to panic. At least this time the magic had not overwhelmed her; at least this time she still knew who she was. This time Finna would have Ursula to contend with, not some goddess lost in a sea of myriad experiences. Ursula knew who she was. She knew that she was strong and that if only she could reach Dan he would help her, save her, allow her to break free.

She clung to that hope, and tried not to let fear overcome her. She was Ursula and not easily beaten.

It took Dan and Gunnarr's combined efforts to get Ursula on her horse. The beast refused to cooperate and it was some minutes before Dan was satisfied that she was safe and unlikely to slip and fall. They had to lay her across the back of the gelding – like a corpse in an old western, like a large rag doll; Dan hated seeing her that way.

Gunnarr knew little about Finna and less that helped. From what he had been able to find out from the women's gossip and the hazy recollections of the other warriors, Finna was the daughter of a warrior who had perished in one of the many Viking raids and had been born of a local woman, a slave who had died in the bearing of her. Finna was raised in a haphazard fashion by the slave's mistress – a noted seith-wife who had taught her all she knew. Gunnarr had been unable to find out more, as many of the slave women and the free Danish wives were frightened of her and regarded her as having the evil eye. The girl's mother had been taken from a convent and on finding herself pregnant had cursed the child she bore – which to some people made the curse more powerful as it was made more or less with her dying breath. Some people had said that Finna's mother, being a good Christian woman, was obliged to forgive her enemies and would never have been so wicked as to curse her only child, but either way the other slaves certainly believed that Finna was cursed, the more so when she was adopted by the heathen seith-wife. Saxon slave and Viking warrior alike agreed that she had bewitched Guthrum with her prophecies and promises of victory. Guthrum was putty in her thin, childish hands.

'What has she done to the Goddess?' Gunnarr asked.

'She's not a goddess. She is just Ursula, my comrade-in-arms, my friend,' Dan snapped back, keeping the bear under control with difficulty. 'Ursula has so much power. Unless this Finna is a very powerful sorceress I don't know what she can have done – do you, Taliesin?'

Taliesin touched Ursula's head gently and shut his eyes. Dan knew that he was using his own magic to try to seek Ursula out. When he opened his eyes, they were full of tears.

'I have been a fool,' he said. 'I have come across this Finna before – soon after I arrived here. It was before I had thrown in my lot with Aelfred, before I had found Rhonwen. She was a child and reputed to have great potential. I tried to find out but I could sense nothing. However, she visited me in my dreams for years after, promising to lock up my power and use it for herself. I took neither the rumours of her power nor the dreams seriously. I was wrong. I can't reach Ursula. This Finna has called to her somehow. She would not be in this state if she had a choice.'

'Tell us something we didn't know,' Dan said angrily.

'Dan, please, try to stay calm; you cannot let the bear out. You have to stay in control. If you change into a bear now, I cannot save you – we will all be lost without Ursula to help control the beast.'

'I have no friends besides Ursula – you are all just interested in what I can do. It is your fault for making her do magic and mine for not preventing it. I've let her down. I need to get her home!' It was hard for Dan to keep the bear at bay long enough to speak. He was angry with everyone, but reserved most of his fury for himself. He should have stopped her from using magic. He should have saved her.

Taliesin was explaining things to him carefully, like he was a little child, not a man. 'She cannot go home while the magic flows through her, Dan. You cannot take her through the Veil. You know that – we tried, remember?'

'Maybe you didn't try hard enough,' Dan snarled. What kind of idiot did Taliesin think he was? He could feel himself changing again. He had to fight it. Taliesin was right in one thing at least, that he dare not let the bear take over. That would not help Ursula. He had a new worry too: what if he became the bear and never changed back? Who would care about Ursula then? Taliesin was an interfering old man, but he was right. Asser was right. Dan had to fight the bear within. As his anger against Taliesin abated, he could feel the risk of transforming into the beast recede. Maybe that was the secret: to reason himself out of his temper. He tried to think of good things, things that wouldn't make him angry – beginning with Taliesin. Yes, he was an interfering old man, but he had helped them in the past. He had helped Dan get Ursula home after the Battle of Camlann. He had kept Braveheart safe. That was good; the bear-like feeling was beginning to go away. He had to keep thinking positively, fight the fury. He had to keep the bear away so that he could help Ursula.

He took a deep breath. No one here was his enemy: not Gunnarr, not Aethelnoth, not Taliesin. 'Let us get her back to Athelney. Perhaps Rhonwen can help her. What else can we do?' he said. No one argued.

They rode back following the route they had taken earlier. No one spoke – everyone seemed lost in their own thoughts: Dan was simply lost.

They had been travelling for about an hour when Dan became aware of an alien human scent – male – that he knew he had smelled before. Even so he was not as alert to danger as he might have been. He was so worried about Ursula. He should have stayed in her mind, protecting her.

The attack, when it came, took him by surprise. A man launched himself at Dan, screaming and wielding an axe, throwing himself at the horse, spitting venom. The man's fury had made him wild and careless. Dan's horse reared, and while he struggled to control his mount, both Aethelnoth and Gunnarr rode to his defence. The man's temper must have overridden his common sense for Aethelnoth disarmed him quickly with a swift blow of his sword. A second later Gunnarr dismounted and had his sword to the man's throat. Dan was angry that he had been caught unawares, but dared not give in to that emotion; he had to keep control.

The man was wild-eyed but silent. Gunnarr's blade was pressed hard against the thin flesh of his neck. The man was millimetres from death.

'Thank you,' Dan said. It was hard to get the words out. Even though, by some miracle, he had not become the bear, the bear's independence and reluctance to accept help made it difficult to thank anyone. 'You may let him speak. I know this man.' It was an overstatement, but he did finally recognise him. It was the householder he had first encountered – the one who had tried to kill the King.

Gunnarr moved the edge of his blade a little further from the man's throat so that he could speak.

'Why did you attack me?' Dan said.

'You know why,' the man answered. 'When you broke my wrist and took my boat, you took my livelihood. What am I to do now?'

'You could serve your King,' Aethelnoth said. 'I know who you are now and the King has told me of your treachery. I would sleep easier if you were dead. We have enough enemies among the Danes; we do not need native Wessex men against us. You should fall at Aelfred's feet and beg his forgiveness. As a Christian King he is always ready to allow a man to make penance and repent.'

The man made a noise at the back of his throat that

suggested he did not care much for kings. It was a risky response but one with which Dan had some sympathy.

'Give me one good reason why I should let you live,' Dan said, as Aethlnoth's threats seemed to be making little impact.

'I have something that you might want,' the man said sullenly. 'I will trade it for my life.'

'What is to stop me taking both it and your life?'

'I do not have it with me, but I will tell you where it is if you promise not to kill me.'

Gunnarr appeared to have grasped the essence of the man's little speech and said something obscene in Danish – his blade was perilously close to the man's jugular.

'You are in no position to negotiate,' Dan said. 'Where is this "thing" that you think I might want?'

The man clamped his mouth shut until Gunnarr's sword nicked his flesh and a small droplet of blood oozed from his neck. Aethlnoth began patting him down like a particularly officious guard at an airport. From a small pouch their resentful prisoner had tied around his waist he pulled the orb that Dan had lost in the bog when he had first emerged through the Veil.

Aethelnoth threw it towards Dan, who caught it easily. It felt warm to his touch, still heated with magic. Dan held it tightly. He looked over at the bard, who seemed oblivious to the significance of Aethelnoth's find. It was a way home that was not reliant upon Taliesin – it was a kind of freedom.

'What shall we do with him?' Gunnarr asked in Danish.

'Tie him up,' Dan said. 'His chief crime was against the

King; it is for him to decide his fate.'

He was proud of himself for that decision. He had not turned into the bear and he shown suitable mercy to an enemy; perhaps he was not entirely beyond hope.

Gunnarr tied the prisoner with some complex sailor's knot and attached his hands to a lead rein so that he could walk behind Gunnarr's horse.

Ursula did not stir. Dan held the orb close to her in case the magic within it might work to revive her, but it made no difference. Dan knew deep inside himself that it would take something far more powerful than a crystal ball to help her now.

~ Chapter Forty-three ~

Aelfred accepted Gunnarr's oath of allegiance – after he had agreed to convert to Christianity. Asser was given the task of preparing him for baptism and of learning whatever he could about Guthrum's strength. Asser spoke some Danish for reasons that he was reluctant to explain and when he needed further assistance he called on Dan's magically acquired linguistic gifts. The news was not good. Guthrum's forces did indeed number several thousand battle-hardened warriors, and in spite of the hard work of Aelfred's men recruiting troops from throughout Wessex, Aelfred could not currently field half so many and scarcely any had much in the way of weaponry or skill.

Athelney turned itself over to the production of spears and shields. They pilfered and borrowed what wood they could and used every scrap of metal they could find, even nails, to heat in the furnace and flatten and sharpen into spear heads. Athelney grew busier every day. Aelfred had sent out a call to craftsmen, promising them a king's commission and all the benefits that might come from serving the King of Wessex once he was restored to the throne.

Hope and confidence somehow began to grow and gambling men began to see the point in backing Aelfred. He was, after all, a Wessex man of good lineage and everyone knew that the Danes made unreliable friends.

Aelfred accepted their captive and did not condemn him to death. The man's father had been a blacksmith and though he had given up the craft after some undisclosed difference of opinion which saw him hiding out in the wilds of the levels. Aelfred was too practical to lose a potential smith, even one with an injured wrist, and put him to work as penance for his sins. Dan was pleased. He had a grudging admiration for the man's gritty kind of awkwardness. He was also relieved that he could still be heartened by a man's survival. It meant that he was not entirely lost to the bloodlust of the bear, that he could still find mercy and compassion somewhere in his soul.

Dan gave Ursula over to Rhonwen's care. She did not open her eyes or show any sign of awareness of her surroundings, almost as if she was in a coma. She looked like a fairytale princess waiting for Prince Charming to breathe life back into her. Dan found the idea disturbing – he'd never met anyone less in need of rescuing than Ursula, and yet here she was. He had to fight back the urge to kiss her, as if they really were in a fairy tale. He was not at all sure that he had any right to cast himself in the role of handsome prince – more like the beast in 'Beauty and the Beast'.

Dan did not hand her over easily. 'What can we do? Can I go and find this Finna or what?' the bear rumbled in Dan's voice.

'I don't know,' Rhonwen said tightly. 'I have tried all the charms I know and nothing is working. Asser is praying for Ursula night and day. Taliesin can seek her out, but I fear it will do no good. There are some particular herbs we can try that might help him, but then . . .'

It took Rhonwen some time to acquire the herbs she needed and it was not until the fourth night of Ursula's magical sleep that she was able to give Taliesin the sleeping draught she hoped would allow him to pursue Ursula.

'It is bitter, mind, and it might make you sick.'

Taliesin pulled a face as he downed her concoction in one, then lay down on the floor next to Ursula and held her limp hand. Rhonwen had to hold Dan back.

'For the love of all that is holy, Dan, do not hover over him like that. He will not hurt her. He needs to touch her in order to seek her. Watch yourself – we cannot have the bear in here.'

Dan made himself breathe deeply. He wanted to grab Ursula and shake some life into her, but even he could see that wouldn't help. The draught worked quickly. Taliesin's breathing slowed and his face became white and bloodless as a corpse.

'Are you sure that is supposed to happen?' Dan asked. Rhonwen's face was pale too, even in the warm light of the candles she had set about the room.

'Hush, Dan, you are not helping. This is risky. We know little more than you.' She got down awkwardly on to her knees, helping herself with the aid of a broom; she was too proud to use a stick. She put her ear to Taliesin's chest. 'His heart still beats so the draught has not killed him.'

Dan was silenced. It had not occurred to him that Rhonwen and Taliesin would risk so much. He helped Rhonwen to her feet.

'What do we do now?' he whispered.

'You can scream your head off now and he won't hear you. There is nothing to do but wait,' Rhonwen answered in an undertone.

It was not the first time Taliesin had sent his soul out of his body seeking what the earthbound human eye could not see, but Dan had never felt more concerned for his safe return. It was long after dawn that Taliesin finally awoke, wild-eyed and gasping for breath, as though he had been suffocated. Rhonwen rushed to get him water. He could not speak for several breaths. He had never looked more afraid.

'Finna!' he said. 'She has Ursula but I can't get to her. She almost had me.'

'Here, catch your breath. Have some water. Give yourself a minute to come to,' Rhonwen soothed him gently.

He gulped the liquid down and smoothed his wild hair with shaking hands.

'She has set a trap for magic. The minute I drank your cup I was there. I couldn't escape. Ursula is there but I had no power to talk to her or let her know that we are looking for her. I only got away because Finna was not looking for me. I doubt she even noticed me. She has all the power she can use in Ursula. We have to stop her. I cannot describe it but I know she could have made me do anything. I was not in control of myself.' Taliesin's voice trembled with shock and he suppressed a shudder.

Rhonwen thrust another of her tinctures into his hand. It smelled of honey.

Dan was on his feet and ready to leave. 'I'll find Finna and kill her!'

Taliesin shook his head. 'Dan, I believe Finna is at the heart of the Danish army. Even you cannot get to her there. You have to promise you will not try until you have Aelfred's forces behind you. When you become the bear, there will be no one to help you get back to being Dan. You may never get back to being yourself. Even you can see it would be madness.'

'I have kept control here.'

'You have done well. But you haven't had to fight an enemy. I don't believe you could keep control if sorely pressed.'

Dan would have liked to have claimed that he could keep control for Ursula's sake, but he knew it was not true: the bear was stronger than he was.

'What can we do then?'

'Wait and pray. Perhaps Ursula will find a way to break her bonds.'

Dan knew from the tone of Taliesin's voice that he did not believe it.

Ursula's breathing remained even and her colour good and Rhonwen said that she did not think she was about to die. The one-time sorceress found a way of getting Ursula to take some nourishment and Dan clung to her opinion. Ursula wasn't dead yet.

He did everything the King asked of him to keep his

mind off things, to fill the time. He helped to debrief Gunnarr. He helped to train troops, and listened to Aelfred and his ealdormen discussing strategy and logistics, adding a suggestion where his experience was of use. Long days passed. Aelfred finalised his plan. Dan did not feel able to judge whether the plan itself was good or bad, but he was relieved that they would finally see action. Waiting for battle overshadowed your days, formed a huge question mark in your life. Would this battle be the end? Would he die on some muddy field in some foreign version of an England he barely recognised? The bear did not much care, but Dan did.

Aelfred had sent out his messengers in force. The King's fyrd was to muster at Egbert's Stone, from which place they would move on to Iley Oak and make what preparations they could before marching to Cippenham to do battle with the treacherous former allies of Aelfred who had usurped him.

The King would have had Rhonwen and Ursula remain at Athelney along with his own wife and infants, but Taliesin and Aethelnoth backed Dan in his request to allow these two women to follow the army. As a result, Aelfred allowed Dan to commandeer a horse and cart from the farm he had defended so wildly. Ursula had to share it with provisions and with Rhonwen, but Dan was content with that. He was not sure he could have left her behind. He was grateful that his oath to Aelfred was not put to such a test.

In some ways it was good to be in an army again. Aelfred's trust in him gave him rank and many of the men he trained treated him as an ealdorman or as a war leader in spite of his youth. They were quick to recognise his skills and he had no trouble with the men, only with the bear that lurked constantly just below the surface of his mind, conjuring slights from thin air, making him jumpy and difficult where once he had been known as relaxed and easy-going. Still, it felt good to walk with men his own age and listen to their chatter, to feel part of something, even if that something was too brutal and violent to be valued in his own time. It was not exactly a march by the exacting standards of the Romans or even of the Romano-British – it was more a brisk if shambling walk through the country. It was warmer than it had been and the signs of spring were everywhere; the no-longer-naked trees and bushes offered much more shelter on the road. It seemed a better, brighter country than the one he had ridden with Aethelnoth and Taliesin in search of Ursula.

Few of the men who travelled the cross-country route to Egbert's Stone were properly armed or kitted out. Most only had their work clothes and perhaps a cap of boiled leather to protect their skull from spears and slingshot, the brunt of a blow from an axe, the blunt edge of a seax. Only a very few lucky wealthy men had proper metal helms – passed down from father to son through many generations. They were not much changed from the Roman helmets Dan had known in his other journeys through the Veil. Aelfred had brought all the new spears they had made and the shields, which were made from thick wooden planks and covered in stretched hide so as to make it more difficult for a spear point to bury itself in the wood. Dan knew from his training experience that trapping a spear did no man any good, rendering the shield useless and the spearman weaponless. Not many men carried swords and Dan's splendid ancient Celtic sword was a treasure and a wonder beyond price. Asser had gone so far as to suggest that it would be a worthy gift for a king, but Dan ignored him. Dan had pledged it to Aelfred's service and that was enough. He had given Bright Killer away once before and it was not something he intended to repeat. All the men carried seaxes: strong blades with one sharp edge for slicing, one blunt side for bludgeoning and a lethal point for stabbing – all attributes that would come in handy in the brutal close-quarters mayhem of the shield wall. Dan had always fought in Celtic fashion, as a free warrior among others – individualistic, wild to the point of insanity. He was fearful of standing shoulder to shoulder with other men; his madness was as likely to harm friend as foe. It was something he needed to talk to Aelfred about, though he had not yet found the courage.

Dan knew that he was not a coward in the usual sense. He had fought as a berserker, as an amnesiac, as an empath and as a bear, risking death and injury every time, and yet he was full of dread at the thought of joining the butcher's line of the shield war, the press of men, the tight ranks. He had listened to the talk of the veterans trying to prepare the unblooded men. One man, a thegn of almost thirty-five, had been most graphic.

'You have to look out for the men beside you, for none of you can shirk your duty or all will die. A broken line means you can be picked off, the enemy flooding in to take you, slaughtering the line from behind, killing you like beasts not men. When the line breaks, the men behind have to act quick and step on or over the fallen to take their place in the breach. It is their duty and the only proper act of a warrior. If the line is too tight packed, there is scarcely room to lift your arm above the shield and a man killed in the shield wall may not fall but stay propped between the living.'

It didn't take much imagination for Dan, familiar as he was with warfare, to imagine the press of men, the stink of fear, the screams of the dying and the terrible claustrophobia of the shield wall. Neither Dan nor the bear could fight that way and much as he did not want to be seen to be a coward, he knew that neither his strength nor his speed and agility would help him much when forced to fight hard up against his fellows, struggling to pull down opponents' shields and thrust his spear home. If he were to fight shoulder to shoulder with anyone, it ought to be Ursula. He thought of the recovered crystal orb he kept in a pouch under his tunic and mail. There had to be a way to free her, to get them both home.

~ Chapter Forty-four ~

As they approached Egbert's Stone a kind of hush settled on the marching men. They were far from silent – the thegns, the senior churchmen, the ealdormen and the King all rode, while men marching, even out of step, make a kind of thunder of their own, but all talk had ceased. How many would muster for the King?

No one knew. Dan sought out Taliesin who, in the guise of a travelling scop, had paved the way for some of the recruitment and reconnaissance on which all their hopes depended.

'Well, how many will come?'

Taliesin shook his head. 'I dare not use magic to find out, but I'm optimistic.'

'Surely we need at least five thousand men to stand a chance against Guthrum?' Dan said. He knew that to raise such a number the men would have to come from the thegns and ceorls of the loyal ealdormen and perhaps from some of the disloyal too. Even the veterans of such an army were not professional soldiers, while the Danish forces comprised fighting men well used to battle, to skirmish and to raid.

Taliesin tapped a tune with his harpist's fingers – a sure sign that he was nervous. 'Let us hope for one of Asser's miracles. I don't know. It is Aelfred's only chance. If he fails in this, he has no chance of regaining his throne. Wessex will be as Danish as Mercia.'

It was at that moment that Asser rode up to join them, his keen eyes scrutinising Dan's face for any sign of the madness of the bear and his ear ever alert to trouble for Aelfred. He responded robustly: 'Do not worry! God will not let this land fall to the heathen. He has punished us enough and in Aelfred we have a king who will fight to restore the study of the gospels and the restoration of all that the Church has lost to the marauding pagans. We cannot fail. You must have faith!'

Dan was impressed by the bishop's certainty until he saw that his fingernails were bitten down to the quick and his fingers torn and bloody from where he had worried them with his teeth. Asser noticed him looking and coloured.

'Faith will overcome doubt – even the saints have to experience doubt, face it and overcome it. Come along anyway; the King wishes to speak with you. There is much to organise while we wait for the muster to be complete.'

There was still no muster waiting for them when they finally reached the stone – just their small complement of a couple of hundred men.

Aelfred's face did not betray his own doubts for one moment. 'We will make camp here until the rest arrive. Aethelnoth will oversee the fair distribution of food, but it would help, Dan, if you could talk to the men and steady them. You have such a reputation that your presence can only help.'

Dan was all too aware that his reputation for heroics had only arisen because Aethelnoth and Taliesin had kept silent on the nature of his affliction and had led the King to believe that when they described him as fighting like a demon in human form they were using a metaphor, not speaking the simple truth. Keeping busy stopped him from dwelling on Ursula, still lying like some beautiful statue on Aelfred's cart under Rhonwen's watchful eye. They had no idea what Finna might make her do.

As the day wore on the tensions among the men grew and Dan knew, because they told him, that they were not prepared to go in alone against such a vastly greater force as Guthrum was known to field.

'The King would not ask it of you,' Dan said confidently. 'We have to win this battle to free Wessex and King Aelfred will not sacrifice men for a lost cause. When the others arrive, we will prevail.' He glanced at Taliesin and Asser, who were watching him with interest. Taliesin nodded his approval. Dan earnestly hoped that Taliesin knew something that he didn't, knew that men were on their way.

The tension in the royal party mounted as the spring daylight began to fade. Dan wandered away to find Rhonwen. All the emotion was making it harder for him to stay in control of his temper. He wanted to hit something and he knew that if he wasn't careful he *would* – and as the bear.

'Is there any change?' he asked Rhonwen.

'She is still breathing. That is all I can say.'

Taliesin joined them by the cart where Ursula lay. Somehow, her beauty in sleep had brought her more affection from the men than her courage and skill at fighting had. It was not something she would be pleased about if – no – when she woke.

They sat down together and Taliesin brought out his harp. 'It is time for a song, Rhonwen, to inspire the faint of heart.'

'I am too old to sing,' she said, but with a smile that suggested the contrary.

Taliesin struck up an ancient song, from the time before, from the time when he was a bard at the court of a Celtic king. Dan noted that it brought tears to Rhonwen's eyes.

'Not that, please,' she said. 'I cannot bear to think of home. I am too long gone from it and I know I will never go back.'

A kind of reverent hush had settled on the gathering, the kind of enchantment that always followed Taliesin's playing. Asser rushed over.

'It might be more fitting to hearten the men with Christian songs,' he said. 'Aelfred wants us to remember that we fight against the heathen, we fight for God.'

'Later, Asser. For now I am trying to find a song that Rhonwen knows, and sometimes the old ones are the best.'

'I did not know that you could sing,' Asser said to Rhonwen in some surprise, as if he'd heard that a horse could recite poetry.

'Once, Asser, my voice was regarded as a thing of beauty to vie with the perfection of my face,' she replied in that strange flirtatious way she used when speaking to him.

Asser made a disapproving noise, but he did not leave as Dan had expected. When Taliesin played again, it was Asser's voice, a surprisingly good baritone, that led the singing. Rhonwen joined him, and though her voice wobbled and creaked a little from long disuse, by the time they had finished that first song – an old Celtic melody – the lovely rich quality of her voice had begun to shine through.

'Not bad,' Asser said. 'Shall we try another?'

The music heartened the men and brought a genuine smile to the pinched and sickly face of the King. It calmed the beast within Dan and for a moment filled him with hope. In some wildly optimistic part of himself he had hoped that Ursula too might respond. Music had brought her back to him when once she'd been locked in the form of an eagle, but it was too much to hope that it would help her return to him this time.

At one point Taliesin switched tempo and sang songs that the Wessex men knew – sacred and secular all mixed up – and though some of the secular ones made Asser blush, he joined in with the parts he deemed suitable and did not stop Taliesin from singing the most ribald. Dan warmed to the bishop more and more.

'You should learn to sing, Dan,' Asser said, observing Dan's continued silence. Dan shook his head.

'I do not know these songs – and my heart is too full.'

He looked over at Ursula and Asser patted his shoulder.

'All will be well, Dan. We will get her back. Perhaps the time is not right yet. The Lord moves in mysterious ways and everything happens in its own good time.'

'Will the army come, do you think?'

Asser shrugged. 'The men we sent out to raise the muster were confident, but the men we are calling have no horses and will be walking to us. They may have finished their work on the land before leaving. They will come. Our cause is just. The men of Wessex will not let us down. Have faith!'

Dan spread out his cloak on a dryish patch of ground next to the wagon in which Ursula lay. Braveheart, who had been keeping guard over her, lay down next to him and with the familiar warmth of the war dog at his side he sat down with his back against the cartwheel to rest. Somehow the robust rhythm of the music, the raucous male voices following Taliesin's harp in simple harmony, lulled him. It would do no harm to let Taliesin's virtuoso performance take him to another place. Within moments he fell into a dreamless, restful sleep.

~ Chapter Forty-five ~

Ursula struggled to reach out with her magic, to break through whatever held her in this curious, sensory-deprived state. She had more power than Finna – how could Finna hold her captive? Once she thought she felt Taliesin seeking her, trying to rescue her, and that gave her hope. She banged against the invisible glass of her captivity, trying to reach him, to let him know that he was close, but he went away again and she wondered if it had perhaps been nothing more than her own desire feeding her imagination. She almost despaired then, because in the other times she had been lost, or locked in magic, she had needed Dan or Taliesin to guide her back. How could she find her way out if even Taliesin could not find her?

She still remembered Taliesin's song that had brought her back from near death after she had overreached herself and turned herself into an eagle. She did not remember the actual tune, but she remembered that it was beautiful and it occurred to her that if Finna could trap her with singing and chanting she might well be able to free herself by the same device. She had no awareness of her body, but that did not matter; she could sing in her head – recall somehow the music that meant something to her.

She remembered Bryn's Alleluia, the song he had sung to dispel Rhonwen's evil magic in the Battle of Baddon Hill. She remembered all the music her mother had played to her as a child and the music she herself played in the privacy of her own room. She wished she had a better memory for a tune, but even her rather impressionistic memory made her feel better and less alone. For a moment she thought she heard actual music: the unmistakable sound of Taliesin's harp, which held its own kind of magic, playing a strangely haunting air. She clung to that sound in the hope that it might bring her back from the nothingness of her strange captivity, but the harder she tried to grasp it, to connect with it, to allow it to catch in her mind and drag her free, the more elusive it became. Still, she felt she had found a small chink in her prison: Finna's trap was not entirely secure. Ursula had pushed against the invisible wall of nothing and allowed a tiny quantity of something to seep in.

She really needed to think hard about what the point of trapping her in this way might be: to prevent her power being used to the advantage of Aelfred? Or worse, to allow Finna to use her power to Guthrum's advantage. Memories of the horrible attempt at mass human sacrifice at Cippenham made Ursula recoil. She would not let that happen again. She was tired by her mental effort, ridiculous though that seemed. She let her mind drift into a dream-like state. She had to preserve her strength for the moment when she would need it. She had to be ready. Finna might not have recognised that warrior Ursula had reasserted herself, but she would find out soon enough.

Dan woke to the sound of raised voices, his heart racing. Something had changed: he could smell it. It was second nature to slide his sword from its scabbard and to get to his feet, his hand ready to wield Bright Killer, like some gunfighter ready for the quickest draw. He checked Ursula first. She seemed the same as before, though there was perhaps a little more colour in her cheeks. Rhonwen said it was his imagination, but that as far as she knew Ursula was no worse. Still, something had changed, he knew it. There was suddenly a lot of noise and movement in the camp – the smell of food cooking and a strangely festive air. He sought out Taliesin, who was sharing a cup of ale with the bishop – a somewhat unexpected sight.

'You see. All will be well. The men of Wessex are arriving in droves. We will take the fight to the Danes and restore Aelfred's throne!'

Events moved swiftly after that. Aelfred had picked an easy place to meet but was fearful of being caught in difficult territory. The men camped as best they could that night, sleeping rough around the campfires, sharing their rations and their hopes. Dan slept little, but patrolled the ragged lines of the campsite, Braveheart by his side. He was fearful as he had rarely been. He did not think he would die – the bear was a difficult creature to kill – but he was very afraid of ceasing to be Dan. Once battle began Dan knew he would not be able to hold on.

At daybreak the horde moved on. Aelfred had left men to guide any stragglers to the main group and a list of instructions for the preparation of latecomers which he wrote down, but which none of the men he left behind could read, while he led his growing army to the forest of Iley Oak. It was a huge area of dense woodland of the kind lost from the England of Dan's time. With the trees now in leaf it was a place big enough to hide an army ten times the size of Aelfred's forces. The smell of late spring was so powerful, it was almost maddening for Dan. He went foraging for food and he and Aethelnoth brought down several deer to go some way towards relieving the hunger of the horde. Nor were they the only ones to have luck in the hunt, and the smell of cooked meat and the sweet fragrance of woodsmoke lifted the spirits of the gathered army. No one now talked of defeat or of leaving Aelfred – all the talk was of victory and not of the grind of battle. Those with experience of the shield wall were suddenly 'close-mouthed as women reluctant to scare a young bride with talk of child bed', as Taliesin observed. Dan confessed that he wished they were more realistic about their chances. Though the numbers had evened out, battle was more than a numbers game and much would depend on the spirit of the men, their courage and their willingness to die for Aelfred and for the idea of Wessex. And still the army grew.

In fairness to Aelfred, he at least had not fallen prey to the overconfidence of the men. 'We need to train them. A shield wall stands or falls by the courage of the weakest man. We cannot afford to have weak men in the wall.

Every one of them has to be ready to die.'

Aelfred had a gift for delegation and he divided the men into units for the purposes of training, so that every man might get to know the men who stood beside him. Men from the same area had come together in any case, but Aelfred had also to build trust between strangers who had not laboured together on the same land, who had not intermarried and who had not served under the same thegn.

Dan begged to be excluded from leading the training. He had not fought in a shield war before, a fact that Aelfred refused to believe. Dan felt the bear growing ever stronger, feeding on the sharp musk of the men's excitement, the adrenalin and the testosterone which, to his animal senses, had a distinctive piquancy which flavoured the very air he breathed. Asser came to his rescue, persuading the King that Dan would be best used as part of a mobile force, the shock troops who must step into the breach when the wall looked set to crumble, who would need to reinforce the line and if necessary fight outside it should the line break and need to be reformed. Having no fixed place in the wall, Asser argued that Dan could continue to patrol the camp, and be in charge of the security of the army in training.

'Thank you,' Dan said when Aelfred had gone to take his place in the training of the men.

'Have faith. You have a part to play in this battle to come, of that I am sure, and it may be that God has a purpose even for that which we might abhor.'

Dan wished he could take comfort from that. He

checked the men on duty guarding the perimeter of the wood and then returned to Ursula's side.

He knew what magic could do. It didn't matter how well they had trained their troops if at the end they could all be drowned or burned if Finna should unleash Ursula's power against them. Rhonwen's face was pinched and tense. She had been busy dealing with training injuries and her own limited powers were stretched to the full keeping Ursula alive.

'You are sure that Finna will use her, aren't you?' Dan said.

'Pray to your God that she can't, Dan. More power runs through Ursula still than I ever have encountered before. I do not know anything about this Finna, but if Guthrum wins this fight through her, my guess is that she will rule Guthrum!'

Ursula's face was as white as marble, her lips bloodless and pale. Dan had to walk away. The sight of her like that while he could do nothing to help made him so angry he had to battle to keep the bear away.

They stayed in the wood for two days, but the longer the army was not engaged the more problems Aelfred would create. The land would need tending soon and it was no mean feat to keep four thousand hungry men fed and watered. If action was delayed too long the men would disappear as quickly as they came. Aelfred had to strike while he had numbers and passion on his side. If that was not a good enough reason to get moving, Taliesin had received word that Guthrum was mustering his own men. The good news was that usurper King Aethelwold was having trouble raising the fyrd: the men of Wessex were loyal to Aelfred. The bad news was that the Danes were not. Gunnarr was certain that the Danes who had remained would fight to defend their right to the wealth of Wessex. It was not long before they discovered that he was right. Guthrum was on the march.

~ Chapter Forty-six ~

Aelfred's scouts reported that Guthrum had left Cippenham and occupied the high ground near the village of Ethundun, an ancient fort. Guthrum began with the advantage of favourable terrain as well as superior numbers. Dan thought that it was not a good start.

The troops, untried farm boys and veterans, all clustered around the royal party. Dan could smell the fear in the air and the excitement. Too much ale had been drunk the night before and the stale stench of it, mingled with the pungent odour of the latrine trench, reminded Dan of other battles and did little to help his own nerves. Aelfred was dressed for war, while Asser wore uncharacteristic finery, a mantle of white worked with gold thread. To Dan's surprise he spoke first. He reminded them that it was Whitsun, the time when fifty days after the resurrection of our Lord the Holy Spirit had descended; now, fifty days after Aelfred had fled to Athelney, the Spirit would be with those who fought to restore the Christian kingdom of Wessex. Asser was a good orator and by the time he had finished and blessed the troops the army was already half won.

Dan had not expected Aelfred to have much charisma before a crowd. For all his wiry strength he looked frail. His beard was newly trimmed, which helped a little, and though his eyes were sunken they flashed with unexpected fervour and passion.

'We have one job to do today,' he said, projecting his voice across the silent crowd. The wind had dropped so that he could be heard by every man. Dan suspected a Taliesin trick because his voice rang so clearly it was almost as if it had been artificially amplified.

'We have to win. We have to break the ranks of the Danes with our strength, and break their spirit with our courage. We have to take back what is ours. I stand in the shadow of my grandfather and my father and I will not shame them by losing all that they had gained. We will fight and we will win!'

It was a very simple speech to Dan's relief and it was one which did the trick. The men roared their support and stank a little less of fear. The ealdormen, including Aethelnoth, organised them into fighting formation – one long shield wall moving slowly forward – and they began to climb the scarp slope of the ancient fort. Dan remained mounted along with the King, who would rally the troops and remain visible throughout. Dan's job was to tidy the line, to keep men firm and to fill any gaps that arose. He led a small party of grim-faced veterans. He called them to him, uncertain as to what he should say.

'You should know . . .' he began hesitantly. 'You should know that whatever happens I fight on the King's side and when it gets to battle – stay out of my way.'

'We know, Sire. Ealdorman Aethelnoth has told us what to expect. Don't you worry that we'll be panicked. We're all steady men. We will do what we have to do, whether you are able to lead us or not.'

Dan was relieved by that. He had done what he could to warn those he might hurt and now he had to concentrate on staying in control of himself and staying out of the line. A bear in a shield wall was a recipe for disaster.

The smell of fear was growing steadily more powerful, raising the hairs on his neck. The bear was waiting.

Ursula heard Finna's voice in her mind and recoiled.

'Goddess, battle is coming – are you ready?'

Suddenly, as if someone had switched on the radio, Ursula could hear. She could hear the roar of the wind and the sound of many men breathing, shuffling, talking – in Danish. It was disorienting and it took her a moment to realise what was going on. She could feel the warmth of the sun on her face and feel the breeze lift her hair. She was outdoors somewhere but could see nothing. She was somehow experiencing the world from Finna's perspective and Finna was blind.

'Show me what there is to see,' Finna's voice commanded and Ursula had no choice but to obey.

It was as if someone had turned on the light; it blinded her. For one fraction of an instant she saw the view from too many eyes at once, a dizzying, blinding confusion of images, of colours, textures and perspectives. She panicked. It made no sense. It was too much, a kind of sensory overload, and then she found a way to see from a single viewpoint at a time – it did not much matter whose. She was there at the battlefield and it was so much like her earlier vision of what was to come that, had it been possible, she would have gasped. It was everything she had thought it would be.

Finna was standing beside Guthrum, who was dressed in all his war gear – his mail and polished helm, his thick cloak and jewelled brooch, his stout axe, his sword and spear. His heavily muscled arms were adorned with arm rings. He narrowed his eyes against the wind, which caught his hair and made the raven banner flap. Ursula had rarely seen a man so confident of victory, so certain of his own strength. She balked a little when she saw the reason for his certainty. Before him lay all the might of the Danes. All were well-armed warriors, their spears sharpened on a whetstone to a fine point. They had the high ground – an ancient fort – but the ground underfoot was trampled and heavy, the churned grass swiftly return-ing to mud. The weather was fine and a bright spring sun glinted on the polished metal of their helms, on the steel of their blades and the glowing colours of their shields; it was a good day. Finna was excited. Ursula felt it, which meant that the exchange between them was not all one way. To see what Ursula saw, Finna had to weaken the barrier that divided them. It was not much, but it was a connection that Ursula could perceive and that perhaps she could use. Free to move vantage point if nothing else, Ursula sought out what she most wanted to see: Aelfred's troops and Dan.

Aelfred was mounted on a black horse. He wore no helm, so that his reddish hair and battered gold crown gleamed as he rode. The Wessex men were simply dressed and many who stood in the shield wall were bareheaded, and their hair blew around as they began the climb. They marched steadily but cautiously, for should anyone slip the whole line could fall. Ursula could feel no connection with her body, or indeed with Finna's, so she felt no tightening of her guts, no panicky beating of her heart, but she was afraid nonetheless. What could Finna make her do?

The thin line of men making their way towards her looked vulnerable. Ursula could see that some of the men seemed barely more than boys – beardless and slim built. How could they stand against the hard men of the Danes? And, if Aelfred fell, what would become of Dan? He had bound himself to Aelfred; his fate was somehow tied up with the King's. The odds did not seem to be stacked in Aelfred's favour.

Finna pulled her back so that she could see Guthrum's face as he turned to speak to her. The look he gave her was calculating, wary, respectful, but not loving. Ursula wondered if that was what Finna had expected to see. 'You are sure you can set their line on fire?'

'I am sure, My Lord. The power of the Goddess is great and you may be sure her power will answer my will.' Finna's thin voice was so full of certainty that Ursula believed her. But if she could see what she chose, surely she could flee. She tried to take herself back to where her body lay, but nothing happened. Her consciousness was like a balloon, free to follow the wind yet anchored firmly to Finna's controlling hand.

'Wait on my command.'

At least Ursula knew Finna's plan and that gave her some advantage, didn't it? She was not powerless; she had heard Taliesin sing even when locked in the world of nothingness. She was not so completely a prisoner as Finna believed.

Dan was afraid – afraid for the young boys in the front of the line, gripping their shields and their spears with white knuckles, fighting for calm. A couple were sick, which did not help as the ground was heavy and slippery without their adding to it. He felt sick himself. He saw Gunnarr in the line, flanked by two reliable veterans of Aethelnoth's group. Dan knew that Aethelnoth had given firm directions to kill him if he literally stepped out of line; Dan knew that Gunnarr knew this too. Dan had little doubt that the Dane would stand – he did not seem the type to dissemble. Gunnarr's face showed the total focus Dan had learned to recognise in fighters everywhere. It had hardened into a mask of concentration. Dan had every confidence that he would fight well.

Dan hung back a little – not out of fear, but because those had been his instructions. He kept his eyes on Aelfred's force, concentrating on them, checking that no one faltered. There was one very bad moment when one of the men in the wall lost his footing and almost slipped, but a push from behind righted him. At Aelfred's signal the men behind began to beat their shields with their long knives. It was louder than any drumbeat, a thrilling sound like the heartbeat of an army: rhythmic, powerful, stirring. It steadied them somehow, calmed them so that their hearts beat to that pulse rather than to the wilder beat of terror. The two armies were three steps from engagement – two – one. The first blow was struck and it began.

Ursula found herself drawn to the Wessex men's line. She could see the eyes of the Danes, blue eyes in weathered faces, squinting against the sun; hard eyes of men who had done this before, men who did not show fear, because the appearance of courage was itself a weapon. Their opponents were big men, tall and made stockier by their padded jerkins. They were so close she could smell their breath, see the texture of their skin, the whites of their eyes. Ursula had never fought in this claustrophobic formation. It was like being trapped in a crowd with nowhere to turn, like being pushed from behind into a forest of spikes, with nowhere to go but forward, no way to survive but to hold your ground, plant your feet and prod and poke and stab and push and try to stay standing.

There was a boy to her left, fair and freckled. Sweat poured down his face and his eyes were wide with terror. He was in danger of hyperventilating. He held his shield arm up and the man beside him, a grizzled veteran with blacksmith's arms, muttered, 'Steady, lad. I'm by you. They'll not bite if you hold steady.' The lad nodded and chewed his lip and then moved in with his spear stabbing through the gap in the shield wall, probing to find soft, vulnerable flesh unprotected by the leather-covered shields or by blade-repelling mail. On Ursula's right a man went down with a curse and a yell. The Vikings surged forward until the injured man was hauled back and another Wessex man took his place in a flurry of expletives.

Dan heard the Vikings yell and curse, heard Aelfred's men hurl insults and crude witticisms back, like a boozed-up football crowd in a brawl on some city street. The banter did not last long; it took too much breath and the men on both sides needed all they had to drag down the shields of the enemy. Each line used their spears, their war axes, their long knives and all their strength and ingenuity to pull down the enemies' shields, to open a crack in the defensive line, to turn the crack into a fissure and then into a full-scale collapse.

Once the shouting was over, it was a quiet battle, not so much the clash of metal as the steady thud and thump and punch of small confrontations. In the shield wall, each man had five immediate enemies – five men to kill or to be killed by. It was hard graft, gruelling and gritty work.

Dan saw the sweat glisten and fall, heard the men grunt as they thrust and yanked and clashed shield boss to shield boss when the lines got too close. There was no place here for brilliant swordsmen or for wild displays of courage. It was just the grind of line against line: a barrier forged of weary muscles used to the labour of the fields, of determination and the curious pack loyalty which made a man die for his mates.

Dan remained clear-headed, fully himself, until the line began to break on the right. A big heavy man had stumbled, had fallen backwards knocking back the man behind and the Danes had been swift to fill the hole and take full advantage, hacking at the Wessex line from behind as they poured into the breach. That end of the wall looked fit to fall, to break and to run. Dan dismounted and, yelling to the men of his company, threw himself into the gap. He pulled a young lad back, out of the reach of a Danish spear, and was rewarded by the grateful thanks of a familiar voice; it was the boy with the slingshot.

'Stay safe!' Dan called.

Dan lost it the second a spear jolted his shield. He discarded the shield with its embedded spear and removed the head of the Danish spearman who had left it there with his bare hands. There was quite a lot of blood which soaked the men around him. It was to their credit that Aethelnoth's men did not panic. 'Stay calm – he's one of ours: Aelfred's own berserker, blessed by all the saints. Hold steady.'

It was a kind of miracle that the line healed itself around the marauding bear who was unafraid of weapons of steel, who shrugged off the spears, batted away shields and had Guthrum's veteran warriors running back to the limited protection of the fortress. The Danish line was broken.

Dan was not, but he had lost control. He was a beast and he did not care what he killed. He was lost in the mayhem of blood and it was a pleasure. He fought his way through the line – though in truth little fighting was necessary. No Dane would stand and battle one of Odin's own.

Ursula was dragged from her view of the battle by Finna's demands. Finna had her look at the two armies locked together, two armoured snakes killing each other in the sunlight. The Viking snake was twisting away, giving ground, collapsing in on itself, and Aelfred's men were winning.

'Now, girl!' Guthrum shouted.

'Burn!' Finna said.

Ursula's magic that had lain unused ignited within her at Finna's word. Without fully knowing what she did or why, Ursula engaged with her magic. After such a long time of self-denial and deprivation, she possessed and commanded it once more. She allowed herself to bask in the glory of wielding it again. She had held back for so long the relief and the pleasure were dizzying. It felt so right to let the flame burst forth, fired by her will alone, to let the wind blow petals of flame blossom like wild flowers in the hedgerow: red and orange and yellow blooming along the shield wall. Then in the next instant she knew it was not by her will but by Finna's and they were not flowers blooming but men burning: Aelfred's men. She had less than a heartbeat of freedom, an instant when Finna allowed her delight to loosen her control. She followed the tiny thread that Finna had permitted to connect her with Ursula's vision. It emerged from the unknowable heart of Finna and it was more than a thread: it was a path to finding her, a cord to bind her. Ursula readied herself and then screamed out with all the power that she had.

'*Dan!*'

Suddenly Dan was distracted by an unnatural roar and a wall of heat – somehow the shields of Aelfred's army were aflame. Men dropped their shields, which burned with terrible ferocity, with a wild unearthly fire. Men screamed, struggling to disentangle themselves from the shield straps, stumbling over each other and falling on the churned ground – all discipline lost in their frantic efforts to flee the fire. The retreating, all but defeated Danes turned to press home their unexpected advantage. A fleeing army was a dead one.

'*Dan!*'

The thought cut through his confusion; that thought was a beacon of clarity in the dark muddle that was Dan's animal mind. Ursula needed him. He lumbered behind the enemy lines seeking out the source of that clarion call. There was a man – the leader, Guthrum – and his body-guard and standard-bearers. They all ran at Dan's approach. Dan thought of following, but got confused. There was another smaller creature. She had been standing next to the big one before he'd fled and there she remained, frozen for a moment. She was a thin, small female, Ursula's enemy, and she was held as if by a spell in his path. He had intended only to thrust her out of his way so that he could pursue Guthrum and somehow make him free Ursula, but this was the real enemy. He thought she would run, but she did not. She stayed as if rooted to the spot and he knocked her off her feet, and from the awkward way that she landed he knew that she was dead.

Ursula saw the bear that was Dan approach. Ursula used all her will, all the strength she could find, to take her opportunity. She found that small connection that Finna had opened between them and instead of sending Finna the gift of her vision she sent her another gift, a small spark of Ursula's will, and she willed her to stay still. She held her immobile, just for a moment, as Dan ran towards her. Guthrum should have dragged Finna to safety, but he feared Odin's wrath as much as the next man and had left his little sorceress to do what she could to defend herself. It wasn't enough. Perhaps Ursula could blame what came next as much on Guthrum as upon herself. He ought to have saved the girl.

Finna stood no chance. She had no time; in the instant she had wrestled control of herself back from Ursula it was too late. Finna fell, and Ursula, still linked to her by that small thread, heard Finna's neck snap and then the world went silent.

Ursula opened her eyes. Rhonwen was watching her, horror on her face.

'Thank God, you're free – now do something!' the former priestess screamed. 'Our wall is on fire! They are dying up there and there is no water!'

Ursula's mind was suddenly very clear. To be free, to wield the magic again, was a kind of ecstasy. First she did what she could to douse the flames. They were sustained by magic and the ground was damp; without the magic to make the fire live, the flames died down swiftly. She healed those she could – for many it was too late. The flames had taken their toll. Then Aelfred raised his sword and Aethelnoth and Gunnarr steadied the line and the Wessex men rallied.

It felt so good to let the magic fill her up. She could not think of anything else. How had she ever resisted it? She stood up in her own body and let the magic crackle like lightning from her fingertips. She wanted to cry out in joy. She stretched and let herself grow, expand to fill the room. She made roses bloom over the cart. She took Rhonwen's ageing hand in hers and with a little concentrated pulse of magic made her young again. She let herself feel the magic of the world surge through her, rebuilding muscles wasted in recent days, restoring herself to strength. She felt more alive than she ever had. On the invisible wings of power she saw the battlefield and Dan. He was the beast. He had not been able to find her and without her voice in his mind to remind himself of who he was, he was lost. She watched him feed on a corpse and did not look away.

She knew what had to be done. There was no other way. She had known for a long time. She had to save Dan. She had to keep him from remaining the monstrous bear for ever. There was only one way she could think of to do that properly, definitively. She had to make what was for her the ultimate sacrifice. She had to lock away the magic.

She did not actually know how to do it, but she

knew it could be done because someone had done it in her own world. Someone had found a way of pouring all that magical power into the core of the earth, locking it under tons of rock, safe from the meddling hands and whims of men and women who would use it for good or ill – who could always say which was which?

She restored herself to her usual size and walked a short distance to a grove of trees and knelt on the ground. Rhonwen followed her and Taliesin too, but she didn't take any notice. She wouldn't let them dissuade her. She took off her shoes and let the power of the earth surge through her, and then she laid her hands on the ground, closed her eyes and sent it home. She let her awareness travel to the deepest places of the earth at the burning core and she gave the earth its magic back. Ursula was soon drenched in sweat, swaying with the effort of it, but Rhonwen, who seemed to understand, held her in her arms and whispered to her as if she was a child in need of comfort.

'Go on, my sweet. This is the answer: lock it away – where no one can use it.'

She was surprised that Rhonwen supported her, in that one small part of her mind that was not totally focused on her task. Both she and Rhonwen were sobbing, trembling as Rhonwen lent her what help she could. Then Taliesin joined them, held Ursula steady when her whole body shuddered with the strain and the shock, as if she were a woman in childbirth, expelling her body's most precious gift.

He wiped her face and whispered, 'Go on, cariad! It is the only way to set him free!'

It hurt more than she could say. It felt like she was bleeding to death. It was as if someone was slicing through her bones and sucking out the marrow, tearing at her heart with talons of steel, leaching the very colour from her hair. It felt like she was burying almost all that made life worthwhile. The world shifted from technicolour to black and white. She grew small and ugly and ordinary. Her heartbeat felt sluggish, her blood without magic flowed like sludge through a body made of everyday stuff. She could not stop crying. It felt as if she was pouring everything that had made her someone worth knowing into the centre of the earth: her courage, her beauty, her strength. At the end she was just Ursula Dorrington again, no sorceress, no goddess, no warrior, just an ordinary sixteen-year-old girl. When she'd finished, she did not even know if she'd succeeded. She could not see Dan any more. She could not know if she'd saved him: even that gift had gone.

Rhonwen and Taliesin were both weeping too. They clung to each other, exhausted, drained. Rhonwen patted her cheek. 'It is as well. There was too much of it. That much power cannot help but corrupt.' She was the Rhonwen of old, before she was scarred – beautiful, imperious; her long dark hair hung round her face, a rich curtain of silk, but her eyes were no longer green but brown, devoid of magic.

'I'm sorry, Taliesin,' Ursula said. 'I grew to hate the magic. It filled me up, but I did not control it – it controlled me. I hope I didn't do wrong?'

'Asser will be very pleased,' he said, trying without much success not to sound bitter. Ursula knew that he too had enjoyed his power; it had never troubled his conscience. 'I am going to miss it but you were not wrong. The magic of this world is strange, perverse. You did right. It is just that I feel lost without it.'

Ursula did not feel so much lost as desolate, empty, a hollow girl in an alien world. Taliesin seemed to understand. He gave her a fatherly hug.

'You did it for the best of reasons. How else can we choose our way?'

Perhaps if she'd known how terrible she'd feel without the magic rushing through her, she might have hesitated. Perhaps she would not have done it at all – even for Dan. Ironically, now that she was free enough of magic to get back home, she had no magic to get her there and neither had Taliesin or Rhonwen. She was stuck for ever in this terrible world with no power, with nothing but her own ordinary self to work with.

'Can you see what is happening out there?' she said dully. 'Can you see Dan?'

Taliesin had obviously been using some of his magic to improve his vision, because he squinted at her shortsightedly. 'What do you think?'

Rhonwen shrugged. 'I don't know. You have done enough. We none of us can help. I will get us some of my tisane to steady us. I feel as if someone has been flaying my soul.'

Perhaps Ursula had been wrong. What if Dan had died

without the protection of the bear, without the bear's brute strength and thick fur-covered hide?

Dan's mind cleared almost immediately the magic disappeared. He felt himself shrink, felt the bear leave him, felt alone and small and vulnerable, separated from his own men and behind enemy lines.

By some miracle he had not discarded Bright Killer in his transformation into the beast and he was still wearing clothes, though he had avoided wearing mail because he knew the bear would not have been able to remove it. He picked up a discarded helmet and shield from the ground and thought about what to do. The Wessex line had been restored, though the air was still tainted by the terrible smell of burning flesh, leather and cloth. The raven banner lay on the ground where Guthrum and his standard-bearer had abandoned it. He picked that up too. Both shield walls had regrouped. Without the power of the bear, what could he do now?

He looked around for inspiration and spotted the horses that had been loosely tethered behind the Danish lines. There was still a measure of confusion. The appearance of the bear had created such panic that Guthrum and his bodyguard had retreated behind the line of horses. He approached the animals cautiously. They reared as if he still stank of the beast. Quickly he untied them and mounted the largest of them. He unsheathed his sword and raised the raven banner high. He thought he might die of fright, but he had to do something. Soon the enemy would realise who he was and if they thought that Odin had abandoned him, they would take the greatest pleasure in killing him. The capacity to find that calm, clear part of his mind that allowed him to focus utterly on the moment had not left him. Once he'd entered the Veil it had somehow become connected with and polluted by his berserker madness, but that was all gone now. He felt whole, clean, able to think. He took a deep breath. Ursula had called to him. Somehow she had set him free. Perhaps he would die, but at least he would die as Dan. He had a chance to make a difference, a chance to help Aelfred achieve victory without magic or madness, just by being himself, by concentrating and by taking the risk. He slapped the horses beside him hard with the flat of his sword, dug his heels into his horse's flanks and screamed 'For King Aelfred!', and raising the Dane's own banner he charged the rear of the Danish line.

To his surprise and relief the men's instinct was to press forward to avoid the trampling hooves of the wild and terrified horses. Some spearman ought to have turned and finished Dan off, but somehow no one thought of that, at least not in time. The line shrank from the horses and scattered, while Dan pressed on. The men at the front of the shield wall were being pushed from behind on to the spears of the Wessex men, who somehow heard Dan's cry and realised that the precious raven flag that had filled the Saxons with fear for so long was now wielded by one of their own. There was a moment when all hung in the balance, when Dan might have been cut down and when the Danes might have rallied, but perhaps word had spread of Guthrum's ignominious retreat from the bear, of the death of Finna at the hands of Odin, or perhaps the men just panicked when the horses charged. Either way the battle-hardened veterans of the Danish line decided that it was not their day to die. They broke the line and ran, and it was the men of Wessex, Aelfred's men, that had the day. They chased the Danes with wild cries, finding new energy in triumph, cutting down all the men they could. Dan left them to it. When he was sane and clear-headed, he had no stomach for slaughter. He rode back to their base camp and to Ursula.

~ Chapter Forty-seven ~

Ursula saw him riding into camp – whole and sane and without injury – and had to fight down a sob. She felt almost naked without her magic, strangely vulnerable. She was flanked by the two Combrogi whom she had known since that first time through the Veil. It seemed that their fates were still entwined. Taliesin rose to meet Dan and to Ursula's surprise Rhonwen found her hand and squeezed it.

'You saved him,' she said simply. 'And you saved the day for Aelfred too, though he'll never know what it cost you.'

Taliesin added, patting her shoulder, 'I now know why you had to come here. Without your action Finna would have used my power and the power of anyone with magic. You saved us. I will bring you here in my future if you tell me it was worth the pain.'

'I don't know. No. Now I can't get home,' Ursula said in a choked voice.

'Don't be so sure of that,' Taliesin said cryptically.

'Go to Dan,' Rhonwen whispered. 'Why do you hesitate?'

She couldn't explain about what had happened in their own world, the strange distance that had grown between them there and the peculiarity of their relationship in Aelfred's world. She had been half mad with magic and he had been half mad with the battle-lust of the bear. Who were they really? Had they ever known each other without magic in some way running through their veins and changing their reality?

'Get on with it, Ursula. You are not one for false shyness. You have saved him; the least you can do is give him a hug.' She pushed Ursula forward and then pointedly turned away to talk to Taliesin.

'You are safe!' Ursula said.

'I am not mad either,' Dan answered, strangely shy. 'How did you do it?'

'You saved me – by killing Finna. She had me trapped and then I locked away all the magic. You know how there is no magic in our world – I think that might have been down to me!'

'Is that why I feel so strange?'

'Probably.'

'I didn't mean to kill her. She was only a girl. Ursula, I've done so many bad things since we've been here. It has all been a nightmare.' Dan's face was contorted with grief. He dismounted and then sort of fell into her arms.

'I know, Dan,' she said, hugging him tightly. 'It's not your fault, it's mine. I should never have made you raise the Veil – it was wrong. I was wrong from the beginning. I wanted the magic too much – that's why I locked it away – but now we can't get home.'

Ursula could feel the dampness of Dan's tears against her cheek. She felt the sobs that wracked his body. 'I never want to hurt another human being again. I don't even know how many men I've killed.'

'Hush,' she said. 'It was the corrupting power of the magic, Dan. It changed us both. We've done wrong, but now we're free of it.'

He pulled away from her, wiping his eyes. 'I charged the line. I think it gave Aelfred the day – so that is one small thing I did. And you – you locked up the magic. That has to be a good thing, doesn't it?'

Ursula shrugged. 'I hope so. What can we do here now? We are no use to anyone as ourselves.'

'You are of use to me,' Dan said quietly. 'I'm sorry. I should have said so before, back at home, and I didn't dare – too proud, I think. I love you, Ursula.'

She smiled. 'I know,' she said, swallowing down a lump that had appeared unaccountably in her throat. 'I don't know why I ever doubted it. I love you too.'

They kissed briefly and clung to each other like sur-vivors from a shipwreck.

'Oh, Dan! I just want to go home!'

Dan remembered the orb that he had recovered from the disloyal householder. Amazingly it was still in the pouch he had tied round his waist. He had not forgotten the orb; he had kept it with him even in battle. It was a kind of miracle that he had not lost it in his Bear Sark madness; somehow it was still there, unbroken. The orb was heavy in his hand, but it still looked like a cheap prop in a bad play. It was hard to believe that it held any power.

'Will it still work?'

'Let's see.' He signalled to Taliesin to untie Braveheart, who had been whimpering his complaint at not being permitted to join the battle; war dogs were not best suited to the close press of the shield wall. The great dog bounded up to Dan, almost knocking him over in his enthusiasm, and licked Ursula's hand enthusiastically. He seemed as relieved as Ursula to find Dan restored – insofar as she could tell.

'This might work for you too,' Dan said, showing the orb. 'It brought us here.'

'Are you coming, Rhonwen?' Taliesin asked.

'Where?'

'Home, if we can get there – somewhere else if we can't.'

'What? You think that thing has the magic we do not? I'll give it a go but you're not still trying to marry me off to your old master, are you? Because I have to tell you I am a little past the age of heir-bearing.' Rhonwen took Taliesin's arm with that familiar flirtatious smile. Ursula wondered if in all the drama of the last few hours she even knew that her youthful beauty had been restored.

'I wouldn't be so sure of that,' Taliesin said. 'Let's see where we end up then, shall we?'

They walked for a while, back towards the great forest, each lost in their own thoughts, until Taliesin found a place they all agreed seemed likely, though it was hard to tell as there was no magic for any of them to use, only the orb, which seemed unchanged.

'I feel we should leave Aelfred a note or something – so

he knows that we did not break our oaths.'

'Were there no witnesses to your brave ride?'

'Yes.'

'Then he will know. You did not break your oaths. You fulfilled them better than anyone could have hoped.' Taliesin leaned in towards Ursula and whispered: 'Just tell me. Was it worth the pain?'

Ursula thought about the aching emptiness of the void the magic left, then she thought about what the magic had done to her and to Dan. She could live with the void if it meant she could have Dan.

'Yes,' she said quietly, and Taliesin smiled.

'Shall we try here?' he said more loudly, so that everyone could hear.

They all held hands and Dan cut his hand lightly with Bright Killer so that his blood, the necessary blood of sacrifice, began to fall. They clustered together as tightly as they could, heads bowed in private prayer. Taliesin rubbed the orb and to their immense relief tendrils of oily smoke curled around the ground, until the familiar dense yellow fog developed. As one, they stepped forward into the mist – home.

~ Chapter Forty-eight ~

'Aelfred ended up being one of Britain's most famous Kings. I feel we ought to have known that,' Ursula said as she turned the page of the only history book they'd been able to find in the library that told them anything useful about their one-time Liege Lord and King. 'I just wish we knew what happened to Asser and Gunnarr and Aethelnoth.'

'There will be other books, and we know that Asser at least must have lived long enough to write his history, which he hadn't even started when we knew him. I wonder if he got over Rhonwen?'

'He didn't fancy Rhonwen – you're kidding!'

They laughed together and then stopped. There hadn't been that much to laugh about since they got back.

They had arrived with impeccable timing, just after the police had been called to the incident in the library. They had run home to find more suitable clothes and to hide Bright Killer and then had to return to school to face the music. Ursula felt horribly guilty when she saw the damaged tree at the end of the school field. She had been mad then and that was a kind of proof.

In the end, Lucy did not press charges. Everyone in the library agreed that she had started the confrontation, even if Ursula had overreacted. Fortunately, as Lucy was unharmed, everyone felt that the whole unfortunate incident had something to do with whatever violent encounter Ursula had experienced that had left her nearly dead, and she was obliged to see a counsellor for a while. She had apologised endlessly but her brief period of popularity was over as everyone feared her as a dangerous freak. It did not matter. She had found Dan again. Dan went back to his sport and encouraged Ursula to join in. She was pleased to discover that the strength they both had gained in their encounters through the Veil was not lost – maybe the magic had caused a permanent change in their bodies. Ursula had somehow become an athlete.

'I wish we could be sure Taliesin and Rhonwen made it back and that they found somewhere for Braveheart,' Dan said for only the hundredth time since their return.

'We know Taliesin was OK because he persuaded us back into the Veil. If he was OK, I'm sure Rhonwen would be – she's tough as old boots.'

'Isn't it odd how she was our enemy for so long and now I worry about her?'

Ursula touched his hand reassuringly. 'That's why I told you to meet me here. I dreamed about her last night.'

'*Show me!*'

Ursula smiled. She could no longer wield magic – not here in her own time – but they could still speak to each other, and sometimes at night she dreamed of magic and sometimes she dreamed with magic and the previous night had been such a night.

She opened her mind to Dan and showed him the image she had of Rhonwen embracing a still handsome middle-aged Macsen. Braveheart was by her side.

'I think it's a true vision sent from Rhonwen herself.'

'That's great – if it's true and not just wishful thinking.'

'It's real.'

'As real as this?' Dan leaned forward and kissed Ursula, taking care that the librarian could not see him. She had not forgiven either Ursula or Dan for the chaos they'd caused in the library. It had taken her weeks to get it sorted out and some of the books had been torn, as she was fond of telling them.

Nothing is as real as that,' she said happily, mind to mind. She did not have to tell him, because he already knew that this was the happy ending she had always wanted. He did not have to tell her that it was what he had always wanted too.

~ Acknowledgements ~

I am, as always, grateful for the support of my editors at Bloomsbury, my agent, Mic Cheetham, and my family. I am very happy to have had the opportunity of completing the Warriors trilogy and rescuing Ursula from her unenviable state, hovering somewhere between life and death. She was in this rather unsatisfactory limbo for a number of years and, returning to her story after such a long break, it was very helpful to have the input of so many online and RL friends who read the early draft of *Warriors of Ethandun* for me. Special thanks therefore must go to: Paul and Owen Browne, Stephen Weddle, Michael R. Dolbear, Brian M. Scott, Elaine Thompson, Deborah Lane, Antti-Juhanii Kaijanaho, Jacey Bedford, Bill Swears and Catja Pafort. I found their help invaluable. I very much hope that all the readers who wrote to me wanting to know what happened to Ursula can now rest easy.